# DEATH
# AND
# DARK MONEY

## SEELEY JAMES

DEATH AND DARK MONEY is a work of fiction. All persons, places, things, characters and incidents are the product of the author's imagination or are used fictitiously. Any resemblance to real people, living or dead, or events or places, is purely coincidental—the author is simply not that smart. If you think some passages are about you, look in the mirror and keep telling yourself that for all I care. Who knows, maybe you'll end up talking to a Roman God too.

If you would like to use material from the book in any way, shape, or form, you must first obtain written permission. Send inquiries to: seeley@seeleyjames.com

Published by

Machined Media

12402 N 68th St

Scottsdale, AZ 85254

DEATH AND DARK MONEY Sabel Security #2 version 4.32

Original Publication, v4.21 March 8th, 2016

This version is v4.32, 12-April, 2019

Print ISBN: 978-0-9972306-1-1

Digital ISBN: 978-0-9972306-0-4

Distribution Print ISBN: 978-0-9972306-8-0

Formatting: BB eBooks

Cover Design: Jeroen ten berge

# ACKNOWLEDGMENTS

My heartfelt thanks to the beta readers and supporters who made this book the best book possible. Alphabetically: Rasana Atreya, Alison Cubitt, Krys Estabrooks, Court Kronk, Ell Meadow, R.W. Preston, Pam Safinuk (who keeps me honest and will never do this again until next time), and Chris York.

- Extraordinary Editor and Idea man: Lance Charnes, author of the highly acclaimed *Doha 12* and *SOUTH* and *FAKE* (coming soon). http://wombatgroup.com
- Medical Advisor: Louis Kirby, famed neurologist and author of *Shadow of Eden*. http://louiskirby.com
- Problem Solving Editor: Jane Turley, humorist, columnist, and author of *A Modern Life* and *The Changing Room*. http://janeturley.net
- Crucial Fixes Editor: Mary Maddox, horror and dark fantasy novelist, and author of the Daemon World Series http://marymaddox.com

A special thanks to my wife whose support has been above and beyond the call of duty. Last but not least, my children, Nicole, Amelia, and Christopher, ranging from age sixteen to forty-three, who have kept my imagination fresh and full of ideas.

ONCE YOU READ THIS BOOK, YOU'RE GOING TO WANT MORE!

JOIN THE VIP LIST:

SEELEYJAMES.COM/VIP

FOR MOTHER
1924-2074

# CHAPTER 1

BRENT ZOLA WAITED in a Washington DC diner on a frozen January evening, surrounded by the greasy smell of fries and the sharp clatter of dishes, unaware he was witnessing his best friend's last hour of life.

Through a crusty, frosted window, he watched David Gottleib skitter on the salted sidewalk into a cone of light across the intersection. His short, plump friend stepped into the crosswalk and landed on his butt in the middle of the street.

Zola snickered and sipped his coffee.

A stranger gave Gottleib a hand up and put him back on his feet. Gottleib dusted off his top coat, doubled his caution, and tiptoed the remaining distance to the diner door. Inside, he pulled off his leather gloves, slipped off his porkpie hat, and scanned the interior.

Zola waved him over.

Gottleib made his way through the packed space to the corner booth. He hung his coat on the hook, tossed his hat and laptop bag ahead of him, and slid across the vinyl opposite Zola.

Zola grinned and leaned back, spanning his arms over his side of the booth. "Ask me how it went."

Gottleib, looking pale and sickly, thumbed the menu to soups and grunted his reluctant interest.

"We were jamming with the Three Blondes." Zola waited for a certain amount of adoration that didn't come. "Like they were waiting for us, man."

"Who?"

"The Three Blondes. Reporters from *Hummingbird Online, FNC*, and the *New York Chronicle*. Between the three of them, they own political coverage." Zola leaned forward, incredulous. "*The Three Blondes*,

1

dude."

Gottleib looked up at the waitress as she twisted her way between patrons. "Chowder and a pilsner."

"Caesar with avocado, and another pilsner," Zola said.

She nodded without a word, grabbed the menus, stuck them between the napkin dispenser and the ketchup, and twisted back again.

"You're not impressed?" Zola asked.

"The last thing you want is press." Gottleib blew out a breath like a tired old man.

"They were there to intercept Koven. They're trippin' on the firm. They know we're changing the political process." Zola leaned across the table to play-punch Gottleib's shoulder. "It's like a sign, bro! They know we're ascending. They said Koven is the man of the year."

"They spoke to you?"

"Straight up." Zola leaned back again with an expansive grin. "They said Koven is the king of kingmakers."

"Duncan is the senior partner."

"Think about it," Zola said. "Duncan is old school, Koven is new gen. And the Three Blondes know he's going to the top. We're his guys, David. We're going with him. Remember that promise Koven made us? He took you, me, and Rip from the back alleys of Baghdad to the top floor of K Street—just like he said he would."

"What made them notice Koven? This town's loaded with lobbyists."

"We won two more accounts today—and we're going to move Sabel from Duncan to our side of the house."

"Moving Sabel is a bad idea."

"Oh, dude." Zola shook his head. "You're so negative. What's up with that? Alan Sabel RSVP'd to the symposium. He's practically in our hands."

Gottleib studied the laminated tabletop and swept some crumbs to the floor with the edge of his hand. "Alan Sabel doesn't own the company."

"What are you smokin' these days, crack or meth? C'mon, man. I said Alan Sabel will be chilling at the Future Crossroads Symposium. At the Château Malbrouck. In France. This week."

"Doesn't matter." Gottleib sank his head in his hands. "She'll never go along with this."

"She?" Zola laughed with his mouth wide open, tossing back his thick, sandy hair. "Do your homework, buddy. Alan Sabel, CEO of Sabel Industries, will hang with us. Plus, we already have the Omani contract—"

"Sabel Industries is a holding company. All shares are held by Sabel Trust 301." Gottleib pulled a folder out of his laptop bag and tossed it on the table. "Do *your* homework."

Zola frowned and picked up the folder. He flipped through a few pages and stopped on one with a sticky flag attached. After reading and re-reading it, he whistled. "When will she turn twenty-six?"

"Three weeks ago."

"Holy shit. Why didn't you text me?"

"I just came from the trust attorney's office." Gottleib locked eyes with Zola. "Brent, we are *so* screwed. If she figures out why—"

"Relax, bro. Everything we do is legal. Citizens United is the law of the land."

"Should it be?"

"We're just doing what the court approved." Zola adjusted the ketchup rack and smoothed his tie.

Gottleib clenched his fists and leaned forward. "The Supreme Court did *not* approve what we're doing and you damn well know it."

"They approved it. Maybe not intentionally, but same difference." Zola calmed himself, then spread his hands wide across the table, palms up. "OK. Chill. We've hashed this out too many times. I know that's how you see it, but…"

Sleet pelted the window, drawing their attention for a moment. The waitress slapped their dishes on the table and dropped bent steel utensils wrapped in thin paper napkins. She turned and walked away.

"That's how anyone who follows the money will see it," Gottleib said. "And believe me, when she finds the $20 million, she *will* follow the money."

"C'mon." Zola took a bite of salad and spoke with his mouth half full. "She's just an athlete and—according to you—a multi-billionaire. How would she even notice a hundred million contract, much less $20 million in icing?"

"She doesn't need our deal." Gottleib pushed his chowder away and tossed his napkin on the table. For a moment, he watched the sleet pepper the glass. "So what did the 'Three Blondes' tell you?" He made air quotes with his fingers. "Or did they just pump you for information?"

Zola's grin reappeared. "It was unreal. Like a dream. There they were, in the flesh, wearing party dresses and drinking Manhattans." He laughed. "It's like they bugged our meetings, dude. They're clairvoyant or something. They knew we landed the new deals before the ink was dry. Awesome."

"You're celebrity-drunk."

"They called him, 'King of Kingmakers'." Zola closed his eyes, remembering the moment, then looked at Gottleib. "They knew we'd been promoted to junior partners. And they said my son would be running the firm someday. Can you imagine? Duncan, Hyde, and Zola?"

Gottleib scowled. "He's fifteen and lives with his mother in California. You haven't seen him in a year."

"Ouch." Zola crunched more of his salad.

Gottleib exhaled. "What else did they tell you?"

"That's it. We danced with them on the Ritz's fogged-up dance floor. When we came back with more drinks—poof—they ghosted on us."

"Did you make any deals with them?"

Zola's face pinched. "Of course not. We're not going to do anything crazy just to get on TV."

Gottleib stared at Zola with his mouth drawn tight.

"Calm down," Zola said. "They can't make us commit felonies."

"We already have."

"You've got them all wrong." Zola's eyes opened wide. "They're sucking up to Koven because he has $100 million set aside for Super PACs. And Super PACs control the elections."

"Do they know about the sources, Brent?" Gottleib balled up his fists. "Remember why we joined the Marines? Why we went to law school? We wanted to make a difference."

"Take it easy, David." Zola struggled for words. "We don't make the rules, we use them."

4

Gottleib frowned.

"If we don't control the candidates, someone else will." Zola spread his hands wide again. "You and I can keep tabs on these guys. We can drive this country."

"Not me." Gottleib sighed. "I texted in my resignation. I'm done."

Zola's mouth fell open. "We're partners. We've been through some serious shit."

"Not anymore."

"That's crazy. Do you even have a job lined up?" Zola watched his friend gravely shake his head. "Then, what're you going to do?"

"Remember Jacob Stearne?"

"Everyone in the 3/2 remembers that whacko. Is he still alive? What's he doing now?"

"Works for Sabel Security. He can save us."

Zola grabbed his wrist. "You're not going to do anything stupid, are you?"

Gottleib gripped his beer so hard his knuckles turned white.

Zola let go.

After a long moment, Gottleib pushed the beer away. He put his hat on and started to say something, then bit back his words. He scooted out of the booth, pulled his heavy coat off the hook, grabbed his laptop case, gave Zola a curt nod, and wound his way through the tangle of diners to the exit.

# CHAPTER 2

SIXTEEN MINUTES BEFORE David Gottleib died, I was alarmed that a nearly-naked black man leaned against my refrigerator with a casual grin. It wasn't because he was tall with supernaturally chiseled muscles. Nor was it the lone fig leaf he sported over his substantial manhood. It wasn't the leather sandals or the bronze helmet with small bronze wings either. What alarmed me was that I could see him at all.

No one can see a god.

At least, no one with a shred of sanity left.

The baking sheet in my hand fell to the stove top.

I closed my eyes and wished he would go away.

Behind me, Bianca kept talking. "So, I appreciate that you invited me over for dinner, Jacob. I'm flattered, actually. Um. But there's something I think we should discuss before you open that bottle of wine. You know what I mean? Like. We should have a clear understanding of ... expectations. You know? Right? Jacob?"

I couldn't take my eyes off him. He looked like Will Smith from his Fresh Prince days. My brain dialed up an instant replay of my last session with my psychiatrist. He told me, "Remember, you're only in trouble if you hear more than two voices talking at the same time or if you see someone who's not there. Either of those things happens, restart your medication and call me right away."

"Jacob?" Bianca's voice drifted to my ears from a million miles away even though she was sitting at my in-kitchen table. "Are you OK?"

Mercury said, *Bro, if you're planning on hitting that tonight, you should talk to her. Never ignore a woman. Besides, she's got something important to tell you.*

I said, *You're black.*

7

Mercury said, *Duh.*

Bianca said, "Jacob? Are you spacing out on me?"

I craned over my shoulder to look at her. Bianca Dominguez defined gorgeous. Like most women at Sabel Security, she took her fashion tips from the boss in the form of a burgundy pullover with a Vinyasa scarf artfully draped around her neck. Washington's most beautiful Latina was the focus of my renewed search for a soul mate and life partner. Her long, black hair curled around her perfect face, swooped down her strong shoulders, and rested on her small, perfect boobs. Her athletic legs were minimally obscured by her multi-colored yoga pants but remained eternally visible in my imagination.

I said, "Uh, yeah. I'm trying to remember the recipe."

"Don't you just put them in the oven?" she asked.

"Sometimes." I looked at the baking sheet with four homemade brioche buns on it. "Um. I meant the main course."

I brushed imaginary crumbs from my Henley and opened the preheated oven. I placed the buns on the rack and closed the door and stole one more look at Mercury, the winged messenger of the Roman gods.

Mercury said, *What's the matter, bru-THA? You worried about something?*

I said, *Mercury was Roman, not African.*

Mercury said, *Oh, that is so racist. With a capital R, dude. I can't believe that a man, even a man of your limited intellect, would stoop so low. Well get this, homie: the Creator made man in His image. And the first human beings evolved in what part of the world? That's right, the Rift Valley. On what continent do we find the Rift Valley? That's right, A-F-R-I-C-A. Which means, Adam and Eve were what? That's right—*

I said, *But the paintings and statues—*

Mercury said, *Were made by Romans, dawg. Guess what kind of revisionist crap they threw down. But, I don't mind 'cause I'm bigger than that. Oh, but you should hear Jesus going on about his portraits. Is there even one painting of a short Jew, plump with curly black hair and a bald spot? Not.*

Bianca said, "Were you smoking dope before I came over?"

Facing her, I smiled. "Sorry, babe. You were saying?"

She crossed her arms and leaned back in the chair. "Now that we work together, I thought we should have a clear understanding of, uh." She forced a smile.

"Sure, sure, babe. Working and dating can be awkward if not handled by mature adults, but I think we're both qualified to handle it. Whatever it might be."

She squirmed in her chair and leaned her forearms on the table. Her necklace swung free, reflecting golden sparkles on her soft brown cheeks.

Adorable.

"Well, that's the question, isn't it?" she asked. "Whatever it might be might not be what you expect it to be."

I opened the refrigerator door in the face of my ancient deity and retrieved the salads for our first course. A dressing of extra-virgin olive oil, lemon juice, and Maldon salt sprinkled over hand-trimmed snap peas mixed with a pinch of mint on a bed of delicate arugula. Placing the dishes on the table, I grabbed my lighter and lit all five candles in one fluid motion.

Her hands fell in her lap, her back straightened.

"Wow," she said. "You put a lot of effort into this."

"Oh, not really. Hand trimming peas and cleaning hothouse lettuce only takes an hour." I sat, pulled my napkin from the ring, and put it in my lap. "Most of my day went into the main course."

Impressing the ladies played a big role in my decision to attend the Culinary Institute after leaving the Army. My dream of becoming a world-class chef had gone on hold while I sorted out Ms. Sabel's security, but I could still whip up a dish or two for a special occasion.

"You shouldn't have gone to all this trouble." She picked up the wrong fork and speared a pea pod.

I watched her lips close around her first bite. Her eyelids dropped, she inhaled, and her face froze mid-chew.

Why do I love to cook? That perfect moment when you know the meal won her over.

Bianca Dominguez was mine. I could see her in a bridal gown, flowing up the aisle to me. The deal would be sealed in a few moments, when I brought out the lobster tacos. I'd spent all afternoon mincing fresh lobster with parsley, tarragon, chervil, and hand-picked black peppercorns which I then stuffed into the most delicate handmade taco shells. She would experience multiple culinary orgasms.

"Mmm." She finished her bite. "But, still, we need to discuss—"

Mercury said, *Are your ears are open, dude? Do you hear what's going down at the back of your crib?*

Through battle after battle, Mercury had warned me about my future. He told me who was coming for me and where to aim, even in the dark. He told me when I could rest my war-torn soul. He made my ammo last longer than everyone else's. He guided me along the paths where others fell to their deaths. He calmed me when the absurdity of war and the certainty of death closed in around me and shut out the light of day. He saved my life, time after time.

But I never pictured him naked—or black.

Not that I had anything against black gods, they just didn't dominate my religious experience.

Huh. I guess that says something.

Mercury said, *Are you listening to me?*

I said, *Could you put some clothes on?*

Mercury flapped his fig leaf in my face. *What's the matter, homeboy? Feelin' some homo-tingles? Can't think about Bianca when you have a god to worship?*

I said, *Knock it off.*

Mercury said, *Oh, don't worry, homophobe. I'm not Greek. Bacchus is always surprised by whom he finds in his bed, but the rest of us are pretty sure about our sexuality.*

I said, *I do not want to hear about your sex life. What did you say about something going down out back?*

A strange scratching sound came from the back bedroom. It sounded like glass cracking.

My puppy Anoshni barked up a storm. I tossed him a treat and hushed him.

"Jacob?" Bianca snapped her fingers. "Did you hear me?"

"Sorry, I thought I heard something in the other room." I pushed back from the table and rose.

"But you get that, right?" she asked.

It was the quiver in her voice that stopped me in my tracks.

I dropped my napkin on the table and cocked my ear to the back room. "Sure. Um. Get what?"

"I'm so glad to hear you say that. You're cool with it, then? We're good? No hard feelings?"

I looked down at her. "No hard feelings … what?"

"Jesus, did you hear anything I said at all?"

My mind raced through the possible directions the conversation might have gone while I dealt with my derelict god and his disturbing sense of humor. "You don't want anyone at work to know we're dating. I'm cool with that."

"Sit down and look at me."

Torn between investigating the noise and my future bride, I retook my seat. She reached her hands across the table. I took them in mine. I looked into her eyes. She was beyond gorgeous. She was the one. I'd never been so sure of anything before in my life.

"We had sex once, but that doesn't mean…" She stopped talking.

So that's where this was going. "No problem, I understand. You want to take it slow—"

She pulled her hands away and threw her napkin on the table. "Damn it, Jacob. What part of *lesbian* don't you understand?"

Another noise came from the back room. I glanced at the hallway where Mercury stood in a short, white toga with only one shoulder exposed. Male strippers would blush. It was a modest improvement to be sure, but I appreciated the gesture anyway. He shrugged.

Bianca's words pulled my attention back to her. "Lesbian? No way! We had sex."

Suddenly, serving lobster tacos seemed like a bad joke.

"Yeah," she said, "that was wrong of me. I'm not proud of that."

"But. You had a great time—I thought. Oh no. Did you fake it? That's so wrong."

She blushed. "The only thing I faked was the intensity. You were OK as long as I thought about someone else. But you heard me, you know why I did it. Do you forgive me?"

Mercury laughed like a maniac. *Well, lover boy? Did you hear? I don't think you did.*

I said, *Help me out here. What did she say?*

Mercury said, *She only slept with you to get to Pia Sabel. She thought all female athletes were gay. Her plan almost worked except for that one little problem—Pia isn't gay. And now that Bianca's working for Sabel Security, she doesn't want her new boss to get creeped out. She wants you to be her beard. And that means the "Stearne-Dominguez" wedding just went out the window—unless she marries your sister.*

Mercury howled.

My heart broke in half and fell over. I was crushed and speechless. She used me. Despicable.

I have never used someone in that way.

Probably.

The distinct sound of breaking wood came from the back room.

I bolted down the hall and threw open the door to my home office. I flipped on the lights. One drawer in my wall-sized gun cabinet stood open, the lock pried out with a crowbar. My rare 1972 Walther PP Ultra was missing along with a magazine and a box of the equally rare 9x18mm Ultra bullets. A framed set of replica guns was missing from the wall as well.

Anoshni followed me in and started barking. I leaned down and scratched his ear. He cocked his head and watched me.

An icy breeze came from the window. The glass was missing.

Mercury said, *Get out front, you've got company coming in.*

I said, *Who took my Walther?*

Mercury said, *Get out front, something important is going down.*

I pushed past Bianca and ran down the hallway.

A car's headlights swung into my driveway. The engine cut off. The car door opened at the same time I opened my front door.

BANG.

A silhouette near the driver's door grabbed his chest and dropped to his knees.

The distinct pop of a Walther PP Ultra reverberated in my tight Maryland suburb. I dropped to the ground and rolled behind an elm tree, reaching for a weapon I'd left inside.

Behind me, Bianca switched off the lights and took cover in my living room. She peered around the jamb with my puppy under her arm, breathing hard.

"Where is he?" she asked, referring to the shooter.

"Left, in the street, I think," I whisper-shouted. "Grab my pistol on the kitchen counter."

She scrambled around inside the house, came back, and whistled. I crouch-ran to the front door, grabbed it from her, and pointed it in every direction. I found nothing. I stepped closer to the street, aiming at anything that moved.

Nothing moved.

Bianca called 9-1-1.

Mercury said, *Now's the time for gallantry, bro. Step out there and see if he takes a shot at you.*

Even though it was a dangerous and stupid idea, I stepped into the street, tracking down the narrow, tree lined lane. My heart beat zoomed up to top speed, filled with adrenaline and ready for battle like a race car on nitro. A shadow flickered between trees, eight houses down, running away. Beyond my field of vision, a car door slammed, an engine started up, headlights snapped on aiming away from me. The killer pulled out and drove away.

I stuck my weapon in my belt and ran up my driveway.

A body lay crumpled against the front tire of a new Audi, breathing in wet, ragged gasps.

Kneeling in front of him, I grabbed his wrist and felt a weak pulse. I knocked his porkpie hat off and felt his clammy forehead. His life spilled out of a two-inch chest wound and flowed down his top coat. He had ten minutes to live, tops. "Hey, buddy, you're going to be OK. Hang in there, ambulance is on the way."

Bianca slid to her knees next to me. "Who is he?"

"No idea." I whipped off my shirt and held it to his chest. The winter air stung my skin and sleet strafed my back.

Anoshni crept up and sniffed at the blood. I stared him down. "Don't you dare."

The pup gave me an innocent head-tilt.

The dying man grabbed my neck and tugged me in close. "Jacob?"

"Save your strength, pal. We're going to get you to the hospital."

"Remember me? David Gottlieb, 3rd Battalion, 2nd Marines, the 3/2, Glory Platoon." He coughed up a chunk of blood and spat it. "Nasiriyah. You saved us."

"Sorry, friend, you've confused me with someone else. I was a Ranger, not a Marine."

He fumbled for something in his pocket. Under the heavy coat, he wore an expensive suit with a starched shirt and sleek tie. After a few seconds, he pulled out a bloody .50 BMG cartridge, a bullet from an M2 machine gun, and pushed it in my face.

"You gave us these." He gasped. "To remember you."

Something rang familiar about handing out bullets. The Battle of Nasiriyah was a hazy memory over a decade old and shrouded in fear and confusion. But the bullet dragged fragments out of my past into the present. I was nineteen and fresh out of Ranger School. I'd been awake for three days and lived through four nasty firefights. My Humvee took an RPG that killed my sergeant. Dazed, I ran through narrow lanes trying to find a friendly face who could point me back to my company.

Instead I ran into a squad of Saddam's Republican Guard on a cigarette break. They were as shocked as I. We stared at each other, eight of them and one of me, for an eternity lasting two whole seconds. Before they could level a rifle, I took off through alleys and backyards faster than I'd ever run before. I stumbled into a Marine platoon. I thought I was saved—but they had it worse, pinned down on all sides and taking casualties.

"I modified it for you," Gottlieb said and pushed the bloody bullet against my cheek. He coughed with less strength. Bloody bubbles formed on his lips.

"Take it. Keep it." He tried to breathe but couldn't get much air. "Important."

I knew what the bloody bubbles meant: his lungs were filling with blood. Internal bleeding or a collapsed lung or something else beyond my limited medical knowledge. I revised my estimate of Mr. Gottleib's lifespan to a few seconds.

"You saved the Glory Platoon. Now you have to save…" His eyes opened wide, he gripped my shoulder.

His first death throe.

I'd seen too many of those.

"Just relax, they'll be here any minute."

"No. Listen." He wheezed more blood, breathing shallow and short. "You have to stop them. Save the country. You…"

He spasmed again, the pain wracking his body like an electric shock. His fingers dug into my shoulder, then relaxed.

David Gottleib slumped and exhaled his last.

# CHAPTER 3

AS GOTTLEIB DIED at Jacob's house, Pia Sabel stood in the homeless shelter's unpainted supply room, her forearms extended level in front of her, while the supply lady stood on her tiptoes to add a third stack of bedding. The shorter woman couldn't reach.

Pia bent her knees, glad she'd worn her yoga pants, and lowered herself six inches. She smiled over the stack. The woman smiled back and placed the extra sheets on top.

Fully loaded, Pia locked the bedding under her chin and made her way down the hall to the second door on the right.

As drab as the place was, it felt more like home than the palace her father built. This was a place where families rekindled hope after crashing to the economic sea floor. In a tangential way, Pia knew the feeling.

For twenty years, soccer had kept her on top of the world. Cheering fans wore her jersey and begged for selfies and sent adoring tweets. Coaches counted on her to do the impossible when everything else failed. And she did the impossible. She volleyed goals, sent assists, stole passes. It was a high unlike any other. A world where she instinctively understood the physics and knew where each split-second decision would lead. Keeping focused on the game left no time to remember her parents' murders or the man she killed. Leaving all the focused training and game time left her feeling as if she had crashed to the sea floor.

She didn't feel homeless or sad. She felt lost.

All she wanted in life was what she felt at the shelter. Hope.

Halfway between rooms five and six, she opened the closet where the setup crew left the mattresses. Back in Room 2, she laid a mattress on the frame and snapped a sheet over it. After tucking it in, she added the top, and the blanket. She stood up, pulled out her scrunchie, shook her dirty-blonde mane, tossed her head down and back and slipped the scrunchie back in tight.

Pia repeated her bed-making routine and was bringing in the third mattress when Jonelle Jackson, president of Sabel Security, known to employees as "the Major", entered. Agent Marty limped a step behind her, leaning on his cane.

Agent Carlos Valdez, the new guy, stayed by the door, the snake tattoo on his neck twisting as he glanced around the room. Short and thick, like a welterweight boxer, he took in the water-stained ceiling tiles and the peeling wallpaper and the pine floor that had long since lost its varnish. He backed against the wall and stood at a close approximation to attention that someone who had never served in the military might think was about right.

The Major and Marty gave him a brief, disdainful glance.

"I'm sorry for dragging you to this part of town so late at night," Pia said, "but I wanted to settle this right away."

She laid out the bottom sheet and tucked it in.

"We've already deployed our people," the Major said.

"Don't worry, I'm not going to cancel the Omani deal. It was detailed and well-planned. We need to discuss the payment."

The Major turned to Marty, who shrugged.

"They've already paid us in full," Marty said. "Including the contingencies."

Pia flapped out the last top sheet and settled it. She tucked it in and smoothed it out. Then shook out the blanket. "Tell me about the contingencies."

Marty took a breath before explaining the complex contract for oilfield security services. "The new oilfield is close to Yemen and they are concerned the civil war might spill across the border. They proposed a contingency plan for extracting our people should anything get out of control."

"The Sultan of Oman is in ill health and has not named a viable successor." Pia tugged a corner of the blanket to smooth a wrinkle. "Prince Taimur, who awarded us the contract, is seventh in line for succession."

"Yes."

"And we're putting eight hundred American veterans on his southern border." Pia checked her work. "He insisted on veterans who've seen action."

"He didn't want mall cops and was willing to pay extra."

"Does the contract allow him to call our people to the capitol?" Pia fluffed a pillow at the head of a bed.

"Only for their own safety," Marty said. "It's part of the emergency extraction plan."

"Who decides when their safety is in jeopardy?"

"The prince. He has the intelligence reports for the border area."

"In a worst-case scenario, could our people fight their way out of Oman?" Pia asked.

"No question."

"Under the terms of the contract," Pia asked, "could Prince Taimur call our people to the capitol—for their 'safety'—and put them in the situation where they had to fight their way out? And could that fight cause them to wipe out specific elements of the Omani Army loyal to someone other than Prince Taimur?"

"You mean drag us into a civil war?" Marty asked. "He's not that kind of man."

"Have you studied the history of monarchies in transition, Marty?"

"Maybe three hundred years ago brothers killed each other for the throne."

"Sultan Qaboos came to power by overthrowing his father." Pia paused. "Could eight hundred heavily armed, well-trained American veterans tip the balance of power in a small country today?"

The Major watched Marty flounder for a second, then said, "I will personally monitor the situation to ensure nothing like that happens. I will arrange ships to extract our people before it comes to that."

Pia turned from her bed making duties to face her employees. "Oman overpaid by $20 million dollars. Why?"

"The money came from their representatives," the Major said. "The lobbying firm of Duncan, Hyde and Koven, DHK. We think there was a miscommunication. We inquired about that two days ago."

"DHK didn't respond right away?" Pia asked. "We're talking about enough money to fund two hundred college educations."

The Major and Marty exchanged glances.

"They said instructions would follow."

"Return the money, immediately," Pia said.

"That would be premature," Marty said. "DHK represents over fifty major overseas companies. They've always worked with Velox Deployment in the past. The Omani deal changes that. This is our first shot at impressing them."

"We do not impress clients. We save them."

"But we landed a hundred-million-dollar deal," Marty said.

"And it's a good deal," Pia said. "But the extra $20 million is *too good.* When someone gives you something you didn't earn, they'll want something in return." Pia waited a beat. "Under no circumstances are you to overcharge, or allow a client to overpay, without specific details."

Marty gripped his cane. His mouth tightened.

The Major looked him over, then faced Pia. "In this case, waiting for the instructions could be prudent. Your father has worked with Tom Duncan for years, and he—"

Pia held up a hand, cutting her off.

A long silence stretched between them. Marty shifted his weight.

The Major cracked first. "As you wish, Pia. We'll wire the money back in the morning."

Agent Marty pursed his lips and turned on his cane. The Major followed him out. Carlos turned to follow them.

"A minute, Carlos," Pia said.

Surprised, the muscular man stopped and turned. They stood for an awkward moment as he searched for the right posture.

"The first day is always rough." Pia smiled and patted his shoulder. "You aced boot camp, so you can relax. Act as if you are talking to a new business associate."

"Sorry, *chica* … uh, ma'am." He blushed. "But where I'm from, I kept a gun in my hand when I talked to a new business associate."

"Leave it holstered, thank you." She laughed. "Tell me what you thought of that exchange."

Carlos's eyebrows went up and his eyes bulged for a second before he pulled himself together. "You want to know what *I* think?"

"You survived for a long time in a tough business before joining us. You must have some insights."

The tension in his shoulders lessened, he bit his lip and looked at the floor. "You're good. You knew where you were going before you began, you listened to them first, you laid out your plan, then laid down your law. When they tried to change your mind, you listened to the guy, not the lady, and you never repeated yourself. That's *El Camino del Jefe.*"

Pia squinted. "The way of the boss?"

"More or less," Carlos said.

"I like that."

"They're not afraid to argue with you. That means you respect them."

"Marty took a bullet trying to save me. That's how he ended up with a cane. The Major was the first person in the company to believe in me, so I made her run the place. I trust them." She thought a moment. "What was that about 'not the lady'?"

"You cut her off when she brought up your old man." He shrugged. "You got some daddy-issues?"

"Different strategies." She watched his eyes as they struggled to meet hers.

"He did good in a tough business, too," Carlos said. "Maybe you should listen to him."

She picked up one of two overstuffed trash bags in the corner and started for the door. "Have you met your *jefes* yet?"

"*Si.*" He picked up the other trash bag. "Jacob doesn't like me but he'll work with me because you say so. That Tania lady, though…"

"She has her reasons," Pia said. "But she's a professional, she'll get over it." Pia stopped in the doorway and caught his eye. "Working for people like them, respecting them, that must be tough for you. I understand that. But you can do it, Carlos."

"It's only for a little while." His eyes rose to meet hers. "Tell me something. You got maids all over Sabel Gardens. Cooks, guards, drivers, you got everything. Why you come down here and work like the *peón?*"

"What does every human strive for?" Pia strolled down the hall.

"Money and power."

"Everyone wants to be important." Pia stopped. "Whether a guy's building a huge tower to put his name at the top, or tying his daughter's shoelaces and sending her off to school, everyone wants someone to think they're important. The banker, the drug dealer, the schoolteacher, the president, everyone. It drives people to commit crimes or achieve greatness."

She faced him. "You want your son to know how important you are. In a good way."

"True that."

She continued down the hall. They walked a couple yards before Carlos had to ask. "What's so important here?"

"After dinner, a young, single dad is going to take his two daughters to that room back there and they'll get into those beds. It will be the first time they've slept outside of his car in weeks. That's important."

As they neared the community room, she smiled over her shoulder. "By the way, as long as your intent is respectful, I prefer *chica* to ma'am."

Carlos's phone buzzed. He checked it. "Uh, ma'am ... *chica*, do you have your phone?"

"I prefer to stay focused on the task when I'm working in the shelter. Why?"

"Jacob's been arrested."

# CHAPTER 4

DARYL KOVEN TRIED to speak to his wife across the first-class aisle on the Air France flight to Paris before realizing he would have to take his feet off the footrest to pull back the curtain. He sat up, reached the drape, and twisted around it to face her. When he caught her gaze, she smiled and reached out a hand. He took it in his and crossed the aisle to sit on her footrest.

He forgot what he wanted to say. And he knew why.

Koven was a man of average height and average looks and average fitness whose hair went gray after thirty. Nothing anyone said about George Clooney made him feel better. Where nature failed him, he compensated with a singular focus on his agenda. His intensity won him many deals and promotions over the years. Only Marthe could derail his thoughts.

"I'm proud of you, Daryl," Marthe said. "They were right; you *are* destined to be the king of kingmakers. You're running the partnership now."

His career had stalled before he met her. He began to rely on her as his other half almost immediately after they met. She shared his ambition and helped him make decisions.

After seven years of marriage, he still saw her as his stylish and pretty bride. She had jet-black hair and a figure that drove him mad. Especially in her designer fashions, always black. This evening's choice was a black crepe de chine dress, flared with a spread collar. She looked fabulous.

Koven laughed gently at her mistake. "Rip Blackson is managing partner. I'll have to leapfrog him before I'm anything more than Duncan's second lapdog."

"But he's a junior partner."

"Our line of succession's as arcane as a Scottish monarchy. It's a partnership, we work like three small businesses sharing resources. We have separate client lists and staff. Rip Blackson works with Duncan's clients while David and Brent work on mine. Sorry, David *used* to work on my client list. Anyway, Duncan set it up so Rip gets the clout and I get my name on the door. It's his way of making us compete for everything. In other words, Duncan still has all the power."

"You get that power when Duncan retires?"

"The shares are his until he dies. He'll never retire."

A flight attendant approached and offered more champagne. They accepted refills.

"I have to be honest," Koven said, "I would kill for Duncan's client list."

"Not a bad idea." She squeezed his hand.

He tried not to look as startled as he felt.

She sipped her bubbly and pointed at his seat.

"Sit," she said. "I want to run some ideas through your ear."

He craned over his shoulder to glance at his reclining seat, then returned to it.

She followed and dropped in his lap. She pressed a button and the blue shade buzzed down with machined precision. She dimmed the light and drew circles around his ear with her finger. "The reporters told you what to do, Daryl."

"I don't know what you mean, my love." He laughed and ran his hand up her skirt to stroke her thigh. "Tell me what you're thinking."

"If only I were a war hero like you, with your strength and courage. As it is, I have the resolve and you're just an innocent flower in the garden." Moving close, her lips brushed his. "You have to transform yourself. It's time to become the snake."

Koven leaned back and searched her eyes. "What on earth are you talking about?"

"The Three Blondes will help you every step of the way. They need headlines and you can bring them. But don't think they'll wait for you. Thousands of people are pouring money into campaigns, they could move on to someone else tomorrow. And what has Duncan even done with the Sabel fortune? Nothing. It's going to waste. We need to act now. My cousin heads the Gendarmes and will handle the investigation; your reporters will handle the spin."

They were silent for a moment. The puzzled look on Koven's face turned sour.

"My dear Marthe," he whispered, "I don't want to say what you're thinking, but the second name on the door is Hyde. If anything happens to Tom Duncan, I'll become a senior partner, but his entire network will move to Senator Hyde."

"In rehab?" she scoffed. "Everyone knows about his little monthly binge-vacations. What was it last week, his ninth trip? You've already moved most of his clients to your operation while he was away. Would Duncan's clients trust him with the kind work you do? Think, Daryl, think."

Her face was too close to see.

She drew back, sat up straight. "Why did the Three Blondes talk to you and not Duncan? Why you and not Blackson?"

He shrugged.

"Duncan plays with Super PACs like a child with toys. He has no stomach for the work. Blackson is a boy scout, sticking to the outdated rules for lobbyists. Everyone knows you bring in the new ideas, the fresh players, the big opportunities. It's your destiny to be the king of kingmakers. The nation needs you."

She smiled, her dark hair falling over one eye.

"You're giving me the creeps." Daryl Koven squeezed her arms and pushed her back.

Turning his scowl to the window, he raised the shade. Outside, a setting sun spilled pale hues of lavender across the cloud tops. She was right and he knew it. With Duncan's client list in his hands, a hundred million was nothing. If he could move Sabel, there would be no limits. He could have all of Congress eating out of his trough. They would come to him asking how to vote on any given bill. All Duncan did with those clients was listen to them whine and bicker over ideology as if any of it mattered. All that really mattered in life was having power.

She squirmed back into his lap, one hand soothing his chest, the other stroking his face. "If you want something, you have to step up and take it. You need a mean streak, Daryl, one that gives you the authority to act when action is required."

"I've arrived at my position by taking action. Honest action." Koven squinted at her. "You've been aware of my decisions."

"You've left me to clarify your decisions too many times." She wrapped her arms around his neck. "I've taken liberties with your most loyal people and it always worked out. This Duncan business is over my head. I don't know how to do what needs to be done, but I know it needs to be done now."

"What do you mean 'taken liberties'?"

"Why do you think Alan Sabel is coming to your symposium?"

"Because Duncan invited him."

"Wrong," she cooed. "He's coming because I invited his daughter."

Koven laughed. "You?"

"I found a girls' football team who're fans of hers and arranged for her to address them while her father attends the seminar."

"Brilliant." He smiled and stroked her face. "When I first met you, I knew you were a force to be reckoned with. You know, for those three days while you thought it over, I was worried sick you weren't going to marry me."

A sly grin stretched one side of her mouth. "I love that story."


AFTER A GOOD night's sleep and fresh breakfast, they landed at DeGaulle and caught the TGV to Metz near the German border. They settled in their first-class seats and read newspapers.

Brent Zola ran up the aisle. "Sorry to bother you, sir. Is your phone off?"

Koven pulled it from his pocket and glanced at it. "Damn, I forgot to charge it. Why?"

"Duncan's been trying to catch you. He wants to crash the symposium. He's a few hours behind us."

Koven's scowl pushed Zola back.

"I thought you'd be stoked," Zola said.

"He is stoked," Marthe said, leaning across her husband. "Thank you for bringing such great news. It will be great to see Mr. Duncan again. I'm sorry to hear about your friend. I wish we could've stayed in Washington for the funeral. Were you close?"

"Since boot camp, ma'am." Zola swallowed hard.

She gave him a moment to compose himself. "Did they catch his killer?"

"I heard they took Jacob Stearne into custody." Koven leaned forward.

"They changed their minds after the Sabel attorney showed up."

"Why the hell did Gottleib go to that nut-job's house anyway?"

"He was tripping about something, sir." Zola met his boss's gaze and held it for a minute, then shrugged. "I don't know what it was."

"Stearne cracked under the stress of combat years ago," Koven said, his voice deepening. "They should've discharged him after Nasiriyah. The man was the very definition of 'mentally unfit for duty' way back then. I knew it was only a matter of time before he went on a rampage."

Marthe leaned over Koven and touched Zola's hand. "You've done great work for Daryl. Is there a seat left in this section you could upgrade to?"

Koven saw Zola's eyes light up and tried to give his wife a subtle wave-off that was noticed.

"No, I'm fine," Zola said. "Thank you anyway. European trains are much nicer than Amtrak."

"We insist," Marthe said, squeezing her husband's hand. "This row is full, but find an open seat and Daryl will handle the porter."

Zola checked around and grabbed a seat four rows back.

Marthe pulled her husband's chin until he met her gaze. "This is it, Daryl. Duncan won't leave Château de Malbrouck alive."

"You gave my man an upgrade."

"Get with the program and don't give yourself away." Her snarl turned softer. "Be generous and happy. Greet people like long-lost friends. Tonight will set the path for our future." She squeezed his knee. "Aren't you excited?"

He was excited.

He'd always imagined it would take decades to take over the firm.

Could the future really be that close at hand? She was right, this was the perfect moment. Marthe's extended French family had all the right connections and the Three Blondes were ready to believe anything he told them. It was as if the stars had finally aligned for him.

Marthe crossed her arms and then her leg. Koven glanced at her and patted her knee.

She brushed him away.

"Go talk to your boy about Gottleib," she said. "He lost his friend and you didn't say anything, much less give him time to mourn."

"Stop telling me what to do," Koven hissed.

He folded his newspaper, tucked it into the seat back in front of him, and sighed.

He rose, stretched, and walked back to Zola. The younger man brought his eyes, red and shiny with tears, back from the window. He looked much older than the happy-go-lucky surfer who fled California's beaches for the Marines just to pay child support.

"Hey," Koven said. "It's a shame we had the symposium lined up this week, otherwise I'd have stayed for the funeral. You?"

Zola didn't answer.

"Sorry, dumb question." Koven pointed at the adjoining empty seat and Zola nodded. Slipping in, he patted his friend's arm. "We'll grieve when we get back. We'll make time, take a few days off, sit Shiva with his mother."

"Thank you, sir."

Koven regarded him. The younger man looked lost, confused, pale, and unsteady.

"It's a shame the Jews move so quickly to bury their dead. If they'd just wait a few days…" Koven trailed off when he felt Zola's open-mouthed stare. He cleared his throat. "We'll wrap up Sabel Industries this week. That should lift morale."

"Alan Sabel is the CEO of all the Sabel companies, right?"

"Of course." Koven gave him a curious look.

"I've heard his chief advisor is—"

"His daughter, Pia," Koven said. "Why do you think I invited her to the symposium?"

"I heard she was apolitical." Zola leaned back. "Did she accept?"

Koven smirked. "I've made arrangements for her to address a women's football club nearby."

"Awesome." Zola admired his boss for a minute. "She's the one we should focus on."

"Why do you say that?" Koven asked.

"She's an unknown in political circles and has the potential to smoke our biggest spenders. Duncan's worked with Alan for years, so we should focus on Pia for the win." He paused and tried to grin. "Besides, it's our only play."

They sat in silence for a mile or more, then Koven said, "Have you given any thought to what the Three Blondes told us?"

"Tons. You deserve the attention, sir. They know you're the rising star."

"And what they said about your son?"

"I called him last night." Zola sighed. "First time in way too long. He's set on Berkeley, but I don't know if he has the grades for it."

"He's a fine boy, I'm sure. Maybe he could intern this summer. Get his feet wet and spend some time with you."

"Really? You mean it?" Zola smiled. "We've never had a high school intern. That would be great. Maybe those crazy women were right."

# CHAPTER 5

I DROVE UP Georgia Avenue to Olney, Maryland on a dark, overcast afternoon past cars that managed to smash into each other on only half an inch of snow. I hadn't seen Mercury all morning, which was good and bad. Good because I could imagine, however briefly, I wasn't nuts. Bad because I'd come to rely on him, even if it was just a matter of time before he talked me into killing an innocent bystander.

The Judean Memorial Garden and its iconic modern chapel were easy to find. The sign reading "David Gottleib Funeral" confirmed I'd found the right place. I parked and walked into a remarkable space with wooden pews and walls of maple. Above me the ceiling soared thirty feet. Directly below the highest point was the pulpit. Next to it rested a closed casket of unfinished pine. The people milling about were not dressed up, making me feel better about my turtleneck sweater over jeans. It was the only black sweater I owned.

A bearded man said something to me in Hebrew. In his outstretched hand was a folded program for the service. He checked my confused expression and swapped the paper in his hand for one on the table behind him. I took what he offered and checked it: the memorial service in English and printed left to right. I gave the guy an appreciative nod that he returned. He pointed to a pile of kippahs. I grabbed one and topped my buzz cut. The front rows were filling with family and friends talking in hushed whispers. I left a couple empty pews for mourners who knew the deceased better than I and studied the guide for non-Jews. This wasn't my first Jewish funeral, but combat chaplains don't always get it right.

Three guys dropped into the pew in front of me, moving in unison, shoulder to shoulder. Two wore black armbands, but the third had a purposefully torn shirt. I recalled there was a ritual rending of clothes for close friends and family dating back to the book of Genesis. After a moment of meditation, they huddled to talk. Their suits were threadbare and outdated by ten years, probably the same suits they wore to their prom.

The guy on the right eyed me as he leaned in to his pals. He did a double take and twisted around to face me. He asked, "Are you Jacob Stearne?"

I nodded.

His pals craned around, examined me, then looked at each other, then back at me.

The first guy leaned over the pew and whispered, "You know who killed David?"

I shrugged and shook my head with heartfelt regret. "Were you friends of his?"

"From high school." His pals nodded solemnly. "We joined the Marines together, the 3/2. Band of brothers."

"Not like those other guys," the chubby one said.

"Who?" I shrugged.

He glanced around the room as if we were spies in hostile territory. Mourners trudged past us with lead feet and sullen voices and filled in the pews. "After Iraq, he changed. He went to college with Zola and Blackson. They joined that lobbying firm."

The first guy said, "But you're going to find the guy, right?"

Mercury slid next to me. Whoa, brotha! Did you become a homicide detective while I was away?

My eyes snapped to my discarded god. His toga was soaking wet.

I said, *What the hell happened to you?*

Mercury said, *I took a ritual bath. Didn't you?*

I said, *Jews don't take a ritual bath before a funeral.*

Mercury said, *No? Maybe I was thinking of the Hindus.*

I said, *Hindus don't take a ritual bath either.*

Mercury said, *Oh really, Mr. Smarty-pants? Then why are they always flinging themselves in the Ganges? Oh wait. You're right. My bad. Hey, don't look at me like that, it could happen to anybody.*

And Rome trusted their vital messages to this god. No wonder the Visigoths took them down.

When I turned back to the three guys, their eyes had been looking off in the direction of Mercury. In unison, their eyes tracked back to me. Then slowly, still in unison, they tracked the other direction. Satisfied our conversation remained confidential, they came back to me with expectation in their faces.

I said, "Montgomery County has their top homicide detectives on the case. They've taken my statement and they're looking for the killer as we speak."

"I heard they arrested you for it."

"That simple mistake was cleared up when my attorney arrived. They've asked me to be available for further questions."

"The cops only look for the most convenient suspect," the chubby one said.

"You're going to find out who hired the triggerman, right?" the first guy asked.

"No."

"You saved us once," the chubby one whispered. "You gotta do it again."

"Saved you?"

Music blasted over the speaker system for a few beats before someone turned it down a hundred decibels.

The service commenced and proceeded in Hebrew. After missing a few cues, I gave up trying to follow along with the English version and just said *Amen* with everyone else. Lucky for me, the homily was in English.

Afterwards, the congregation filed out quietly, and we made our way graveside through trees whose bare branches stretched for the sky, ready for a horror movie. Gentle snowflakes fell as the dim light faded into a sunset obscured by clouds.

I stayed well back, uncertain of why I came.

Mercury stood on his tiptoes to see over the crowd. *Where's the river? Aren't they going to set him on fire and toss his ashes in the river?*

I said, *You've got Hindu-on-the-brain. You need some cultural diversity.*

Mercury said, *What's with the attitude, bro? I see enough of those Hindus at the gods' convention every year, waving all their freakin' arms around. Gives me the willies.*

The band-of-brothers guys broke off from the main group and huddled around me.

"We need your help," the chubby one whispered and looked around at the clouds and trees.

"David was onto something big," the first guy said.

The guy with the torn shirt had yet to speak a word. I stared at him. "'Something big' is pretty vague. Care to explain?"

Mr. Silent didn't speak or flinch, not even his eyelashes moved.

"It's the company he worked for," the chubby one said. "Duncan and Hyde. They're into some heavy stuff, like mafia or something. I don't know."

A man in front of us scowled over his shoulder.

My new friends quieted and shuffled from foot to foot while examining the slush we were standing in. Closer to the grave, more prayers were offered and the crowd murmured *Amen.*

"Remember Lieutenant Koven?" the first guy asked. "The officer you were about to kill?"

A dim memory of threatening an officer in Nasiriyah bubbled up from the depths of my nightmares. But it could've been the power of suggestion. While the Army is made up of an overwhelming number of outstanding officers, there are a few no one would miss. Still, it's a court-martial offense that can carry the death penalty. It's reasonable to assume I would try to forget an incident like that. If these guys had witnessed that kind of crime and didn't report me to their chain of command, they must've been on the verge of killing this Koven guy themselves.

Snowflakes coated our shoulders in pearlescent white.

"Nasiriyah was a long time ago," I said. "What does this lieutenant have to do with Gottleib?"

All three of them stared at me as if I'd armed a grenade.

I waited them out.

Finally, the silent guy with the torn shirt spoke with a thick Hebrew accent. "Koven is *harah*."

And then he spat on the ground.

I'd never heard the word before, but I didn't need to look it up in my Hebrew dictionary.

I said, "Have you told the police this guy is a … whatever you said?"

"We went to see them," the first guy said. "They weren't interested. Called us conspiracy theorists. No one cares after they've convinced themselves the lie is the truth."

"But you care," the chubby one patted my shoulder. "David thought so."

Mercury said, *Oh look, the huddled masses turn to you in despair, isn't that sweet? Doesn't look like they were terribly prosperous after their brief stints as jarheads, so there's no point in taking on their cause just to get me new worshippers. Let's go get a warm cup of soup somewhere—like the Ritz Carlton. Now that's where you should be evangelizing. We can get a better class of followers in that part of town. Ya feel me, dawg?*

"Do you have any idea what David was worked up about?" I asked.

Two of them shook their heads. The quiet guy stared me down.

"Check out the company he worked for," the chubby one said. "David wasn't the first guy they killed."

"You think Koven killed him?"

"Koven doesn't have the stomach for murder," the first guy said. "Someone did it for him. It was a contract killing."

"Do you have any reason to believe that?"

"Koven is *harah*," the quiet one said.

"You've mentioned that." I stepped forward and turned to face all three of them. "Look guys, if you have anything, or can find anything, tell the cops."

The quiet guy poked me with a finger. "I help you."

"I don't need help for something I'm not going to do."

The chubby one stuck a card in my coat pocket. "Call that guy. David and I bought him some drinks one night and he started to tell us stuff, but they showed up out of nowhere and carted him off before we could make sense of what he was telling us."

I glanced at the card. Senator William Hyde, of the firm Duncan, Hyde and Koven. It meant nothing to me. "Then go back and buy him more drinks. Why is this my problem?"

The three of them looked away in different directions.

The first guy's gaze came back to me. "David got us together last week. He wouldn't tell us what it was—wanted to keep us out of it—but he had a problem and wanted our help figuring out who could help. We thought of all kinds of people, cops, reporters, FBI, but he said any one of them could be part of the problem. We had to think outside the system. Then we remembered you."

The chubby guy reached in his pocket and pulled out a clenched hand. He turned it over and opened it like a flower. In his palm lay a .50 caliber BMG cartridge which he presented like a sacred talisman.

The second presentation in twenty-four hours.

I looked at it. I looked at him. And back and forth three more times.

He didn't explain.

The mourners said an *Amen* with a finality that indicated the burial was wrapping up. After the family tossed dirt in the grave, we formed into two lines with an aisle between. The bereaved mother tottered up the row, leaning her sad weight on a teenage boy. She spoke to people and they said kind words in soft tones, often in Hebrew.

Mercury said, *When she gets near, you should say the right prayer,* Ha-Makom yenahem etkhem b'tokh sha ar aveilei Tzion vYerushalayim. *May the Omnipresent comfort you among all the mourners of Zion and Jerusalem.*

I said, *This isn't one of your pranks, is it? Does that really mean what you said?*

Mercury looked offended. *Would I do a thing like that? I still feel bad about sacking their temple, homie.*

Mrs. Gottleib made her way to where I stood. She stopped in front of me when she saw me and opened her mouth to say something. My Hebrew was nonexistent, but I concentrated really hard and did my best to get the prayer right. Before my first syllable came out, I realized she was not actually speaking to me.

She was screaming at me.

"How dare you! You, you … murderer! You're the man who killed my David!"

# CHAPTER 6

PIA SABEL STARED aimlessly at the London skyline from her eighth-floor suite in the Four Seasons Park Lane Hotel, and decided it was one of those things in life that one must do: listen to Dad's life lessons. If only she could go one day without one. Whether the lesson was relevant was irrelevant. Alan Sabel's rumbling baritone ran on, something about allies and enemies. It was her own fault though; she should never have asked him why the Omanis refused her $20 million refund.

She couldn't deny her adopted father understood the path to success. He'd gone from penniless grad student to billionaire before the police gave up on solving her parents' murders. But his latest effort to download everything he knew grated on her nerves like steel wool on a skinned shin.

The last glow of daylight contrasted Parliament against heavy clouds as Pia shrugged her shearling coat over double layers. Alan kept talking about business relationships and trust. Then he paused to take a call.

Pia turned to the mirror and fixed her lipstick. Ready, she nodded to Tania. Her agents led the way to the elevator and waited while Alan finished the call. Agent Carlos joined her inside the lift and flattened himself against the wall. When Alan clicked off, he filled the remaining space with his large frame. Agent Tania glanced at the tiny, crowded box, gave Carlos a lingering glare, and indicated she would take the stairs. The doors closed and they whirred downward.

Alan Sabel looked down his nose from his six-foot, five-inch height at the new agent. "How is anger management going?"

"Hard, sir." Carlos returned Alan's icy stare. "My gut still tightens when someone tries to dis me by reminding me of where I came from—but then I think of where I'm going and I chill."

"There's only one opinion that matters around here." Pia patted his shoulder. "You're doing fine."

When the elevator opened on the ground floor, Tania was waiting for them.

Carlos scanned the lobby before taking the lead, his head swiveling imperceptibly left and right.

When they reached the road, Alan called out and waved to a well-dressed man emerging from a limo at the InterContinental Hotel across Hamilton Place. The man returned the wave and shouted a warm greeting. They changed direction, crossing the lane, and met the man and a woman draped in fur and diamonds.

"Paul, you remember my daughter, Pia." Alan spread his arms wide enough for a group hug. "Pia, this is Paul Benning, CEO of Esson Oil, and his wife, uh…"

With a glint in his eye, Paul took Pia's hand. "You've grown to be quite a beauty."

Before he could kiss the back of her hand, Pia pulled his hand to a more conventional position and shook.

"Alan, you not remembering?" The woman in fur spoke with a heavy Russian accent. She turned to Pia, extending her hand as if Pia would kiss the back of it. "Olga Benning, so nice."

Pia took her hand and shook it. She turned to Paul. "What brings you to London?"

Paul glanced at Alan. "I'm going to the Future Crossroads Symposium this week and thought we'd swing through Harrods first."

Pia grabbed her father's elbow. "Good to see you again, Paul, but we're running late. Olga, it was 'so nice'."

She wheeled her father around and quickstepped to the sidewalk. Darkness dropped like a shadow over the city. Street lights flickered on, store windows lit up.

"That was rude," Alan said. "You could chat a little, be social."

Pia picked up the pace. "What's he really doing in London, Dad?"

"Same thing we are—clandestine meetings with politicians before going to Duncan's symposium."

"Tom Duncan isn't involved," she said. "It's his younger partner,

Daryl Koven."

Alan stopped walking for a beat, scratched his chin, then doubled his steps to catch up. "So you've researched the symposium? That's good. It shows initiative. But I've spoken to Duncan. He's going to be there, and that's what matters."

"I'd like to meet him. Schedule it."

Alan fired off a text. "Done. But next time, I'd appreciate being asked nicely."

She considered his request as they walked. Why she was short-tempered with him eluded her no matter how often she reminded herself of his kindness.

He tapped her shoulder as if he'd just thought of something. "How did a junior partner like Koven get all these top CEOs to attend? I've never heard of him."

"Timing," she said. "It's on the way to Davos."

He snapped his fingers. "Spend three days at a symposium on the French-German border before going to the World Economic Forum." Alan paused a moment. "Got to hand it to him, this Koven is clever."

Carlos stopped at the corner in front of a traffic circle. Keeping his vigil, Pia and Alan slowed while Tania made her way past them and took the lead on the next street. In a carefully synchronized movement, Carlos fell in behind.

The Four Seasons is situated on a narrow triangular block with a dining garden for outdoor serving in the summer at the thinnest point. They walked up one side of the triangle and turned back around the thin point, allowing her a clear view of the well-dressed, thin man following them on the far side of the ice-crusted garden. Their tail had no choice but to pretend his destination was elsewhere up the street.

Pia's group continued down Old Park Lane, passed the *Rose and Crown*, and around the corner. They crossed into Green Park, swimming upstream against a river of tired tourists returning from Buckingham Palace as an icy drizzle wet their faces. Tania pulled on a knit cap over her mass of wild, black hair.

Deep in the Park, they came to the Canada Memorial. A red granite fountain turned off for the winter, it usually featured a gentle flow of water across its angled surface.

It was a dark, untraveled corner of the park. A hundred yards south of them through a stand of trees, Buckingham Palace lit up the fog and rain with floodlights. Three hundred yards north, the Picadilly hummed with traffic.

Pia puffed white breath-clouds and shuffled her feet to stay warm.

Carlos took up a position twenty yards away, his back against a tree. Tania inspected the area, then returned to Pia and her father.

"Pia, this guy is a big mistake." Tania nosed at Carlos. "He's been through training and still can't do anything right."

"We're not going there." Pia turned away.

"You know how this hurts me. My sister's rotting in jail because of guys—"

"Enough." Pia gave her a withering glance.

Tania stomped away to a position across the memorial from Carlos, covering the Sabels from the widest angle. She gave a cough and spoke in a soft voice over the comm link. "Is that your guy?"

Pia and Alan looked behind them as an older gentleman approached, his coat flapping open as he walked.

Alan said, "Only a senator from Minnesota would stroll through this cold with his coat unbuttoned."

Twenty yards away, Senator Jeff Smith waved off his bodyguard. Nearing them, he extended his right hand to Alan while encircling Pia with his left. "Oh, it is so good to see you both. We live in the same town yet we never see each other anymore."

Alan reciprocated pleasantries, draining Pia's patience.

The senator turned to Pia. "Young lady, you're amazing. You've accomplished so much—"

"I was born with every advantage," she said. "Claressa 'T-Rex' Shields is 'accomplished'."

He searched for words.

She crossed her arms. "Why the cloak-and-dagger, Jeff?"

He pulled his hat off, exposing his thin gray hair to the frozen drizzle. "No need to rush into things just yet. Let's catch up on—"

"I can tell by the tension in Dad's posture that this isn't going to be

good. You have bad news; I want to hear it."

"Pia," Alan said, a father's sharpness in his voice, "this is not the plan we discussed."

Pia held Smith's gaze.

"All right," Smith said. "You want to be direct, I can appreciate that. Here it is: a bipartisan group is working on legislation to ban the use of American military expertise by foreign entities. They're calling it the Mercenary Restrictions Act, MRA."

"Why?"

"The American taxpayers paid for training and expertise of these veterans to defend the USA, not Lithuania or Uruguay or Oman."

"Defense contractors and airplane manufacturers have been doing it for ages."

"We have strict controls on the technology those companies sell to any given regime," Senator Smith said. "But when the best fighting force in the world becomes a militia for hire, well, that's a different story."

"Militia for hire?" Pia snapped. "Is that what you think of my people?"

"It's not me. The group behind the bill."

"So they intend to block Sabel Security from winning foreign business?"

"The people pushing this legislation are concerned that another country, let's say Botswana, could start a war with Zimbabwe using US citizens trained in US military tactics to advance their agenda. They say it interferes with the affairs of state."

"Is President Hunter behind this?" Pia asked.

"She's free-trade," Smith said. "She's taken a position against it at this time."

Pia turned and paced. Her father and Smith followed her a few feet behind.

"Only two companies would be affected," Pia said, "Sabel and Velox Deployment. What do they—"

"Velox Deployment was specifically exempted due to national security concerns," Smith said. "At least, they are in this draft."

"So the only company affected by this legislation is mine?"

"I am merely the messenger."

Alan Sabel leaned back against the high end of the Canadian Memorial and folded his arms. Pia turned and regarded him.

"You knew about this?" she asked.

"I've heard rumors," her father said.

Carlos caught her eye from his position by the tree and nosed in the direction of Buckingham Palace. She mouthed, *I know*. He nodded and checked the opposite direction, then back toward the palace.

"Who sponsored the bill?" she asked Smith.

"Several upstart freshman representatives from both parties got it rolling."

"Why are you the messenger, Jeff?" Pia looked him up and down. "What's your position on the legislation?"

"I've always been there for you, Pia." He held his hands out wide. "When you had problems in Puerto Rico, I was on the tarmac, greeting the children you so bravely saved."

"A few months later, your campaign portrayed you as the liberator."

"Your office approved those." Smith looked to Alan.

Pia's eyes narrowed as she shifted her gaze to her father. So many of his lectures were about the "requirement for integrity in all communications" and yet every day she learned about something else he'd neglected to communicate. She doubted he was covering up anything, it was more likely that he didn't trust her to understand his decisions. Which was annoying, to say the least. Or, was he was afraid she would overrule him? She tapped her chin.

She faced Smith again. "How do I stop this legislation?"

"If you'd like me to make inquiries, I can do that quietly. First we'll have to find a position that resonates with the voters, and then take the pulse of both parties. We'll find a couple fringe players, one on the left and another on the right, and let them shout from the balcony, see how it plays out."

"Fine," Pia said.

She felt her face flush with anger and turned away. These politicians thought they could take advantage of her because she was young and hot headed. She'd love to teach them not to underestimate her.

"Once we get the right message," the senator continued, "we'll set up a Super PAC to make voters aware of how important this issue is and where each politician stands."

"What's a Super PAC?"

"Political Action Committee with unlimited funding, but don't worry about that part."

"And how much will that cost?" she asked.

"Your father and I have worked together for many years. We've shepherded lots of deals beneficial to—"

"You may leave."

"Excuse me?" Smith said.

"I'm terribly sorry about Pia's behavior, Jeff." Alan wrapped a big arm around the senator and began walking him away. "Something's gotten into her lately. It must be her insomnia catching up with her after all these years."

Their voices softened in the distance.

Pia stared at the headlights flying by on Picadilly, her head ready to explode. She counted to ten, then counted to ten again. It didn't do any good. She heard her father's footsteps approaching. He stopped several yards short of her.

Pia said, "Why did this legislation come up now?"

"Welcome to the big leagues," he said. "You've just been shaken down by the American political system. They put up legislation that will shut you down until you put up campaign contributions. Then everyone settles down. It's the price of success."

"You told him I've taken control of my shares, that I effectively own Sabel Industries."

"No," Alan said. "But the news appears to have spread like wildfire in the last forty-eight hours."

"This is extortion. Legislative extortion and it must be illegal."

"Nothing illegal about Congress passing laws. This is how the system works."

"No way," she said, her voice rising hard. "I'll find out who's pushing this bill and throw money at anyone willing to run against them."

"That will take years. By then the legislation will be in place and

Sabel Industries, not just Sabel Security, will be running on fumes. You stand to lose half a billion dollars the instant President Hunter signs the bill. Another billion when they turn off federal contracts with Sabel Technologies. One by one, they'll take down our companies, Sabel Satellite, Communications, Capital, and the rest. They'll keep coming after us until we play their game."

"I refuse to play. I'll fight it. I don't care about money."

Alan stepped in front of her and grabbed her arms. "It's not about you, Pia. Look over there at Carlos. Now look at Tania. You have to lay one of them off if you fight this. You've grown the security division to five thousand employees. Veterans, ATF, Secret Service, FBI are lining up to work for you. But more than half of those people are deployed on foreign soil. This legislation will end those jobs overnight."

He loosened his grip.

"Those are hardworking veterans," he said. "Your employees count on their paycheck for food and rent. You can't abandon them just because you don't like the game."

Alan pushed off and headed back to the hotel alone.

She watched him recede into the dark, hating that he was right. She did have to play the game, wretched as it was.

Tania moved in with caution. "What the hell was that all about?"

Pia faced her. "Catch up with Dad, and stick with him. I'm going to run an errand. Back in twenty."

Carlos closed in, watching the south and west.

Tania's eyes widened. "Oh no, Pia. Tell me it ain't true. You're not gonna... Hey, none of my business, but he's such bad news in so many ways, you can *not* be—"

"I'm not asking, Tania. Stay with Dad."

Tania's eyes bulged and her mouth drew tight. She turned on her heel and strode into the dark.

Pia turned to Carlos. "Let's go this way, shall we?"

They walked thirty yards toward Buckingham Palace, heading for a silhouette in the trees. Carlos turned left and quickened his pace, setting himself at an angle to the profile, and zeroed in. Still twenty yards away, their target spooked and started running toward Hyde Park.

Pia, the world-class sprinter and Olympic soccer star, ran the man down in twenty strides.

She hooked her arm around his neck and a toe around his ankle. He flew through the air, landing on his belly and outstretched hands in the icy grass with Pia on top. A plastic dish with a microphone in the center rolled to a stop three yards away.

With one knee in his back, she pulled her arm tight around his neck and yanked his chin off the ground. "Normally I shoot stalkers, but I've never seen one as well-dressed as you. Who are you?"

The man grunted, unable to speak because of the headlock. She checked him out: tall and lean, African-American heritage, a designer suit, and expensive shoes.

Carlos caught up and held a Glock 19 at the man's head. "Answer the lady."

The man's eyes blew open at the sight of the pistol.

"Don't worry," she told him. "Handguns are illegal in England. He's holding a Sabel Dart gun. It fires a needle filled with concentrate of Inland Taipan snake venom backed with a dose of a powerful sleeping medication. The venom causes instant flaccid paralysis lasting long enough for the sleep medication to take effect."

"Actually, *chica*," Carlos said, "Jacob told me not to bother with darts. He said to bring hollow points."

"What? Damn it." Pia bent her captive's neck further when she looked at her agent. "We'll discuss it later."

She lowered the stalker's head. "You've been following me for half an hour without a formal introduction. I don't like that. I'm only going to ask you one more time then he pulls the trigger. Who are you?"

She loosened her grip.

He gasped for air. "Rip Blackson. Duncan, Hyde and Koven."

# CHAPTER 7

DARYL KOVEN CONTEMPLATED the power of ancient monarchies from the southern battlement of Château de Malbrouck overlooking the village of Manderen. If the president was king, then his secretaries were cardinals, and senators were dukes. Before democracy, cardinals made pompous noises and gave speeches, but the dukes fought the wars and therefore held the power.

The castle Marthe rented for the symposium was named for John Churchill, 1$^{st}$ Duke of Marlborough. He made it his headquarters for two weeks in 1705, during the War of Spanish Succession. Even though the Château had been built three hundred years before the Duke arrived, it still carried his name three hundred years later. Such was the power of a duke.

Koven smiled. He funneled hundreds of millions to senatorial campaigns. Who is the duke now, the senator—or the man who handed him the office?

Brent Zola strolled from the *Tour de la Sorcière*—Tower of the Witch—and joined him on the curtain wall high above the ground.

The two of them leaned their forearms on the parapet overlooking the valley below and admired the cold afternoon. Tucked in the northeastern corner of rural France, a mile from the German border and four miles south of Luxembourg, the château was a pile of rubble before the locals restored it and made a summer attraction out of it. A stone rectangle, the château would cover two football fields. Big enough to impress the guests, remote enough for privacy.

Below them, a foot of snow contrasted the bare trees and covered barren farmland as far as they could see. Light gray clouds, darker and foreboding to the west, hung over them while a wintry breeze stung their cheeks.

Koven broke their contemplation. "Our primary goal is to move Alan Sabel from Duncan's camp to ours."

"I still say Pia is the key, sir."

"You know something." Koven eyed his man. "What is it?"

Zola bit his lip then faced his boss. "David discovered she owns an epic interest in Sabel Industries. More than anyone realized."

"And you didn't think to tell me that right away?" Koven's voice echoed in the courtyard below them. He took a deep breath and leaned back, looking his man over, head to toe. "Did he tell you anything else?"

Zola folded his arms and tightened his eyes and said nothing.

"What a terrible loss." Koven returned to the view. "I heard the police let Stearne walk."

"Jacob didn't kill him."

"Do you work for him or me?" Koven's voice rang the stones around them.

Zola backed up, his hands up. "You, sir. I'm sorry, it's just that—"

A limousine twisted its way up the hill toward them.

"That must be Duncan," Koven said. "The early guests don't arrive for a few hours, and the rest will come in the morning."

They jogged down the tower's narrow stone staircase and onto the icy cobblestones. Marthe was ahead of them, struggling with the fifteen-foot iron gates wearing a heavy coat over her sheath dress. Her outfit couldn't keep her warm, yet she worked the bolt without a word of complaint.

Koven pitched in and yanked the heavy latch clear. Together, they swung the gate open as the limo pulled up on the other side of the bridge fifty yards away.

Marthe smiled only when etiquette dictated, but otherwise remained intent on her immediate goals. He liked that about her most of the time, but now he wanted her graciousness to appear. He gave her a smile. She read his mind and beamed her warmest greeting across the bridge to the senior partner.

Tom Duncan emerged, followed by two security guards. He waved and smiled, stopping to admire the view. His handsome, rugged face gave him the look of an archetypal statesman who surveyed the frontier before conquering the land. Only a few streaks of gray hair remained on his head. He turned and called out before crossing the moat. "Marthe, you've made a spectacular choice. This is magnificent!"

His driver struggled with luggage on a cart designed for sidewalks while Duncan met his hosts.

"If I were you, Marthe," Duncan said when they embraced, "I would've told an interloper like me there is no room at the inn." His laugh warmed the group. "And yet here you are as gracious a hostess as I've ever seen."

"Thank you," Marthe said. "You're most kind. The firm is paying for it, so technically everything here is yours. If it weren't, I'd give it to you for making Daryl a partner. That was the most generous gift."

Duncan turned to Zola and put a hand on his shoulder. "France agrees with you, Brent. This castle has such a pleasant view; it seems to sweeten your mood in this heartbreaking time."

Zola shook his hand. "The birds like it here so much, they forgot to wing it south for the winter."

Koven eyed his protégé, then turned to Duncan. "Thank you for having the confidence in me to pull off the symposium, Tom. I assure you good things will come of it." He gestured the way to the Great Room.

Duncan took Marthe's hand and strolled across the courtyard. "How on earth did you get this castle?"

"I was born here. My grandmother still lives down the hill in Manderen. I came here every summer as a child."

"France is the luckiest country in the world, then." To Koven, he said, "How many guests are already engaged with the firm?"

"Exactly half are our biggest boosters," Koven answered. "We will pair them up with the new prospects."

"Genius, Daryl, pure genius." He laughed and slapped Koven on the back. Then leaned in for a confidential word. "I appreciate the work you did on the Oman deal. We had reasons to keep Velox involved in that one. But what's done is done, right?" He paused and lowered his voice. "Just leave the Sabels to me from now on."

Without looking at her, Koven felt Marthe's glare as she leaned around Duncan.

CLOAKED IN THE dark night, the château's Great Hall echoed with clinking silver on china and hummed with the genteel conversations of the symposium's early arrivals. Marthe chatted up an oil company CEO while Zola was spellbound by the founder of Jenkins Pharmaceuticals. Koven remained unengaged, his dinner untouched.

Without warning, the consequences of his ambitious plans erupted in his stomach, leaving him nauseous and dizzy.

He excused himself.

The Great Hall, being true to the architecture of the time, left no room for modern caterers. The chef had two tents, one for cooking, the other for serving and clearing. Koven stepped into the empty serving tent, mopping his forehead on his sleeve.

His thoughts turned to his wife's dark suggestion. In her naiveté, she believed they would simply kill Duncan and that would be the end of it. If only life were that simple. The very idea of killing him was a betrayal of every oath Koven had ever taken: the Boy Scouts, the Marines, and the Bar. Compounding matters was Duncan's kindness; the man exuded good manners. He'd never said an unkind word about his partners. Even Senator Hyde, who embodied sloth and the most disgusting habits, never heard censure from Duncan. One of the few lobbyists loved on the Hill by both parties and the press, the public outcry for justice would unmask Duncan's killers in a matter of hours. So why even entertain the idea of murder?

Marthe pulled back the heavy plastic curtain. "Daryl, what are you doing? It's freezing out here and Duncan is waiting to toast us."

He wrapped his arms around her. She pressed into him, her arms circling his waist, and laid her head on his chest.

"I came out here to think," he said. "I've decided not to go through with it. We've won enough victories for now. I'm a partner, the symposium is on the verge of success, I'm grateful for what we've achieved." He felt her tense against him. "And you were there, making everything work. You are the reason for my success."

She leaned away from his body, remaining in his arms while probing his eyes with hers. "Two glasses of champagne are all it takes to get you drunk?"

"What are you talking about?"

"On the flight over, we discussed this. When you went to bed, you were my hero. Did you wake up a trembling coward like your men in Nasiriyah? Is this how you want me to think of you from now on? You, my brave lieutenant, suddenly afraid to act?"

"Marthe, that's not the case. I simply—"

"You know you deserve this. The Three Blondes know it too. They're waiting for you to become the man I know you are."

"Later, darling, later. This is all wrong. Gottleib was murdered two days ago. We are Duncan's hosts—we'll be the first suspects."

"What kind of man are you?" She glared at him. "We're entitled to the same respect as these sound-bite-singing robots you toss into office like a mailman delivering letters. These CEOs should be begging to come to my table, pleading for a few minutes with you, the king of kingmakers. But if Duncan keeps the Sabels to himself, you're nothing."

He pulled his hands back and stepped away. "But Marthe, he's the senior—"

"Duncan flies on private jets. The Sabels fly on private jets. The Bennings fly on private jets. Why do I fly Air France?" She fisted her hips, pushed her chin out. "You promised me success when we married. Where is it?"

Koven felt his guts constrict in pangs as if she had tightened a belt around them with several sharp tugs. He checked around them to make sure they were still alone. He lowered his voice to a tense whisper. "Murder is not that easy. It takes something away from you. It makes you less human, not more."

"How did you survive the war then? You killed men, didn't you?"

"That was different. The government sanctioned it. Besides, my men did the killing."

"You and I sanctioned this. Be strong enough to live up to your side of the bargain for once."

"But think about the risks—"

"If you find the courage you claim in your war stories, there is no risk." She pushed her face up to his. "I have every step of this planned. Do you trust me?"

KOVEN OPENED THE tower door and found the battlement covered in a dusting of snow, a pale glow in the waning moonlight. A lone figure stood halfway across, barely visible. "Who's there?"

The figure gestured and said something softly, then turned. "Sorry sir, I can't get a signal in my room so I came out here to call Flip."

"Zola, you startled me." Koven crossed to him.

Zola stuffed the phone in his pocket. "Big ass time difference from home, so after midnight here is good."

They faced each other then turned to the view. Zola said, "The Three Blondes are hanging in the village tonight. Is that a good thing?"

"Until we met them, you hardly mentioned your son."

"His mother and I were teenagers. Things got gnarly and I ran off to join the Marines. Different paths, right? But they gave me a reason to rethink my relationship with him. I'm hoping to chill with him again."

Koven nodded.

"Oh, I almost forgot. Mr. Duncan was looking for your wife a while ago. He heard she went to the village so he went to bed, but he told me to give you this." Zola extended a hand with a Tiffany blue box. "It's a token of how awesome Mrs. Koven is."

Koven eyed him carefully and took the box. When he opened it, sparkles of moonlight popped out. A pendant with a diamond the size of a pencil eraser reflected the lunar glow.

He looked up at Zola. "It's a shame we weren't able to entertain him better."

They forced a laugh.

Koven breathed in the cold air and relaxed just a little.

"Let's set a meeting when this is over and map out our futures." He pointed a fatherly finger at Zola. "You've been a good ally, Brent. I've made good on my promise. Stick by me when the time comes and they'll make statues in our honor."

"As long as we don't get smoked busting campaign rules, I'll always have your six, sir."

Koven patted Zola's shoulder and made his way toward the far tower. Zola went the opposite direction.

Marthe stood just inside the door. "They're passed out."

"Who?" Koven whispered.

"The Velox guards."

"How did you do that so quickly?"

"A little feminine charm—and two bottles of recapped beer stuffed with roofies." She held out a Ruger with a sound suppressor attached.

"What is this? Where did you—"

"Don't forget these." She held out two devices the size of a key fob, each with a thick rubber ball on one end.

He took the gear and walked quietly down the spiral stairs.

Inside Duncan's suite, two guards were sprawled out, one in a chair, the other on the floor. The man in the chair had a holster with a pistol in it. The other guard's was empty. Koven's mind swam with fears and doubts that would quickly turn to panic if he let it. Pushing one man aside, he opened the chamber door and paced quickly to the head of the bed.

In the gray moonlight, Duncan's eyes fluttered open. The two men stared at each other for a moment. Koven's heart pounded hard enough to burst through his rib cage, his panic went wild. Kill the man who started him in business or explain his presence, those were his options. His breathing came fast and shallow. Duncan squinted, about to ask the question.

It was now or never. Koven pulled the trigger three times.

Bits of blood and brains and skull spattered the headboard and Koven's shirt.

The blast reverberated in the small stone space. Koven held his hands over his ears, gasped, and ran out.

The two Velox guards hadn't flinched. The suppressor twisted off easily. He dropped the gun by the guard with the empty holster and ran upstairs.

Marthe stopped him at the landing.

Koven grabbed her. "Did you hear it?"

"Nothing more than a distant door slam."

"God, I have blood on me." Koven gasped as if he were drowning. "I stood too close. His brains splattered…"

"Pull yourself together." She grabbed his hands and pulled him to the window where moonlight spilled in. "You'll give us away talking like that."

"There was so much blood."

She slapped him. "Now there's as much blood on me. We're in this together. Man up."

"The noise. It was deafening."

"The walls are twelve feet thick and the doors were closed. All the noise bounced around inside. Nothing escaped." She looked at his bulging pockets. "Did you put those remotes where I told you?"

He pulled them out of his pocket and stared at them. "I can't go back. I can't even think about … this. I can't stand to look at him again."

"You coward." She ripped the devices from his hand and disappeared down the steps, only to return seconds later.

Marthe grabbed her husband's hand. "Quick, let's shower."

"No, we'll stain the stall." His face bunched up like a man about to cry. "What have we done?"

She stroked his cheek. "You stepped up, the way true leaders do in difficult times. You did what needed to be done, without hesitation. You didn't let synthetic morals hold you back. I'm proud of you, Daryl." She wrapped her arms around his bloody chest. "Let's wash everything down the drain."

# CHAPTER 8

I STARED AT the detective and the detective stared at me and I counted to three because that's what my attorney, the fat guy on my left, told me to do before answering each question. He wanted time to shout an objection or advise me on an answer. We sat across from the detective, a cheap laminate table between us in a cinderblock room painted in a hundred layers of godawful-green enamel paint. The fluorescent tubes overhead cast a dull yellow light that sucked the will from your bones and buzzed loud enough to make you contemplate suicide.

My attorney leaned forward and rapped his knuckle on the table. He said, "Asked and answered."

"I want to hear it again," the detective said.

"Rewind your tape."

"OK, let's try it this way." The detective leaned back. "Mr. Stearne, have you ever spoken to Mr. Gottleib, at all, about anything before he died in your driveway?"

I counted to three. "As I've said several times, if I ever met the man he didn't leave an impression."

"Is it possible that you served with the Marines and forgot?"

I stood up, pulled my belt from my waist, checked my boxers, then looked up. "They're still there, so—no."

"Not funny." The detective tugged his sleeve over the *Semper Fidelis* tattoo on his wrist.

"Neither was your question, detective," my attorney said. "Do you have anything serious to ask my client? This is your third interrogation and I'm not hearing anything new here. Mr. Stearne is cooperating as any good citizen would, but you're pushing our patience."

"Take it easy, counselor." The detective leaned forward, pulled up his notepad, and flipped another page. The overhead light buzzed while he took a look at his notes. "Mr. Stearne, do you own a pair of rubber gloves?"

"No."

"Are you sure?"

"Asked and answered," the attorney said. "Detective, if you can't pay attention—"

"Allow me to clarify," the detective said after scowling at my man. "If we found a pair of rubber gloves near the crime scene, with GSR on them, would we find your DNA inside them?"

"Only if you put it there."

Silence stretched, the fluorescents buzzed, and the detective scribbled some notes without looking at me. "And the serial number of the missing pistol?"

"I don't have it memorized." I pulled my phone out and fiddled with my cloud app until I found it. "I do have my insurance inventory with the serial numbers of all my weapons. I'll forward it to you, what's your email address?"

He gave me his email address and insisted the spelling of Czajkowski was a simple matter of phonetics.

His better half, Senior Detective Lovett, kicked at the door until it separated from where it was stuck to the jamb at the bottom. Freed up, it smacked my attorney's chair, which earned a searing glare from him as Lovett tried to enter the cramped space. The equally obese detective glared back and squeezed between the wall and the table, then around the end, trying to reach his chair on the other side of Czajkowski. The younger fit and trim detective rose, scooted his chair in, and made himself as thin as possible. Lovett pushed between the wall and his fellow officer without any lubrication, which became a predictably painful exercise for both men.

After turning beet red, Czajkowski picked up his notepad and exchanged it for Lovett's stack of papers. "I'll just sit over here, Larry."

My eyes floated to the ceiling where Mercury lay upside down, as if the ceiling were a floor, in his toga, eating an apple.

I gagged.

Mercury said, *I like the lawyer. Good thing Pia-Caesar-Sabel thinks you're worth a thousand an hour. But watch out for Lovett. He's a hater, bro.*

I closed my eyes and pretended my freeloading god wasn't there.

Lovett settled in with exaggerated movements before he spoke. "So you're sticking with your story that an unknown party broke into your house, left the rifles, the Glock, the Astra, and the rest of your arsenal in plain sight, crowbarred open a locked drawer, stole a rare gun plus the ammo, a few replicas, then ran back outside and shot Mr. Gottlieb?"

"I did not state," I said, "because I do not know who shot Mr. Gottlieb."

"Nice try, detective." My attorney gave me an atta-boy grin.

Lovett reached up and smacked the fluorescent fixture. The buzzing stopped. He picked up his papers and butted them on the table, then shuffled a couple items until he found the folder he'd brought in with him. "Your service record is missing a few critical pieces, Mr. Stearne. Where are the four psychiatric evaluations?"

"Classified."

The buzzing started up again. Lovett and Czajkowski looked at the fixture in unison, then back at me.

Lovett said, "It's personal, I get that. But sometimes it feels good to get things off your chest, isn't that right?" When I didn't answer, he plowed on. "Did you have any outbursts of violence during your tours of duty?"

"I had extremely violent outbursts on all my tours, detective. I was a soldier in a war zone."

Czajkowski stifled a smirk.

"Fair enough. Did you have any violent outbursts off the battlefield, when you were home or off duty?"

"One time, on leave, I discovered a guy raping a woman at the Iowa State Fair. That turned violent."

"Were the police involved?"

"They arrived after I broke the guy's right femur and crushed—"

My attorney pushed his forearm across my chest. "I think what the detective means is, did you initiate any violent outbursts without provocation. Is that correct, gentlemen?"

Lovett pursed his lips. "No. I want to know about the psychiatric evaluations. Why are they classified?"

"Because I was a Ranger and some big general somewhere doesn't want people like you to know what Rangers do. I'm not allowed to discuss my missions until 2058."

"That's not what I mean." He hesitated and drew a breath. "Why four? Why so close together? What happened?"

My attorney said, "Until you get a letter from the Secretary of Defense or the President authorizing my client to breach—"

"Yeah, yeah, yeah." Lovett waved off the rest of the objection.

He took a deep breath and looked at me with a heartfelt sadness in his eyes. "Mr. Stearne, I know what therapy's like. I've been through some tough times on the force. My therapists always helped me through those times by encouraging me to talk about what bothered me. Even the little things, like how my wife leaves the toothpaste on the counter and how the neighbor's dog always craps under my boxwoods. Talking things through helps. Maybe it will help you. Let's try it: does it bother you that Mr. Gottleib is dead?"

I counted to three. "Yes and no. Someone murdered him in cold blood, that bothers me. He died while I tried to stop the bleeding, that bothers me. He was desperately trying to tell me something that came out as babble, and that bothers me. But, Mr. Lovett, I didn't know the guy. Other than the proximity to his death, I don't feel any better or worse about it than you."

Lovett was no poker player. His face turned red, both his chins and all his jowls began trembling. "Listen up, Stearne. When some guy gets four psych evals in two weeks, I know damn well there's something wrong with him. And when that guy comes to me with a story about killer-shadows running in the trees, I'm thinking I have someone who's about to lose it and go on a rampage. And I worry because that guy has a gun cabinet filled with weapons, mostly AR15s made by arms makers I've never heard of. Hell, you have enough firepower to start a fucking revolution. And you're nuts. I can see it in your eyes. I'm not going to turn you loose so you can mow down the citizens of Montgomery

County, Maryland."

"We've heard enough of this ridiculous crap," my attorney said. "You've ignored the eyewitness statement who said she was having dinner—"

"Girls never lie to protect their murdering boyfriends." Lovett was about to have a stroke. "And the Easter Bunny is real."

Lightning bolts of tension sizzled between the two.

Lovett sat with his fists clenched on the table, making up his mind about something. Then he said, "Screw it. I'm going to keep Montgomery County safe. You're under arrest for the murder—"

A kick opened the door and the crewcut head of a square-jawed older guy pushed in. "Lovett, CJ, out here now."

The head disappeared and a split second later, so did Lovett and Czajkowski. My attorney and I shrugged at each other.

Mercury said, *Jupiter is pulling some strings for you, dude. He'd appreciate an honorable mention. You feel me?*

I said, *Not happening.*

Mercury said, *Homie! We're busting you out of here. You could show a little gratitude. Some people give thanks and praise when a god saves them from a rush to judgement, you know what I'm saying? Bro, ya feel me? Hey, look at me. Oh, you're gonna ignore me. Well. Two can play that game. Whatever.*

Voices in the hall rose in volume and filtered through the door. One voice said, "Because you don't have a shred of evidence that ties him to the murder weapon, nor do you have a murder weapon. And the only witness—"

Their voices dropped a notch below eavesdropping range. The distinct tone of resignation followed and we heard dejected feet shuffling away.

The gray crewcut stuck his head in the door and glanced around before stepping in. He'd once been fit and proud but his athleticism was diminishing with every passing year, evidenced by two center buttons on his shirt stretched enough to expose the white t-shirt underneath. He was on the backside of middle age and the chances for promotion were waning. He wanted a big arrest, but he was a professional who wanted it clean.

"I'm Captain Cates," he said. "You're free to go."

Mercury said, *Still don't believe me, scumbag?*

My attorney glanced at me with a whaddaya-know shrug. He pushed his chair back and struggled to his feet. I waited until he cleared the area.

"If you don't mind, counselor," Cates said, "I'd like to have an informal word with your client, veteran to veteran."

"I don't mind at all," my attorney said. "As long as you don't mind my remaining here to ensure you don't stick a gun in his hand and claim you found his fingerprints on the murder weapon."

Cates's fists tightened and his square jaw flexed until he worked through his reaction. He responded through clenched teeth. "Understood."

Cates faced me and pulled something out of his pocket but kept it in his closed fist. "I never had the opportunity to thank you for Nasiriyah, Stearne. What you did was nothing short of miraculous. If I had been a decent officer back then, I would have commended you for a Silver Star, but that was the day CENTCOM decided to make a beeline for Baghdad and we were flying as fast as the Humvees could carry us." He extended his hand. "I know this means a lot to you as a reminder of that day, so I'm returning it to you."

He opened his palm as if he were giving me the Cullinan Diamond. It held a .50 BMG cartridge, clean and shiny.

I stared at it then peered at Cates. "What's this?"

"It's the one Gottleib gave you."

"The one he gave me wasn't polished."

My attorney nearly leaped on Cates. I put a hand out to hold him back.

"Sorry, I, uh." Cates closed his hand and rubbed the back of his neck. "To tell the truth, I can't let the other one out of evidence. But, as a soldier, I know these little totems have deep meaning and I thought you'd like to have one just like it. Go ahead, take it."

"Sorry, Captain Cates, but it means nothing to me. The only thing I remember about Nasiriyah is being scared to death." I grabbed my coat. "Good luck with your totem."

He squeezed his fist around the bullet and closed his eyes. I stepped around him and nodded my attorney toward the hall.

My attorney said, "Hey Cates, I don't know why Lovett has a hard-on for Jacob, but he's ignoring enough evidence and testimony to make it look like he's being paid to frame my decorated veteran here. I'm putting my investigators on your team for some deep research. If any of these guys has one problem with chain of custody, erased interview tapes, or any funny business with evidence in the last ten years, I'm reopening all your cases and working for the incarcerated victims pro bono."

"Go for it, counselor." Cates twisted an ear in our direction. "They're not my team. Their captain is on vacation and the chief called me in a few minutes ago to make sure we don't piss off Alan Sabel."

There was something strangely competitive in his reply. I guessed the vacationing captain was younger and looser around the rule book. The kind of guy clean players hate but the brass promotes.

"Tell the regular guy, no funny business on this one. Mr. Stearne is a decorated veteran and—"

I tugged his arm.

Cates didn't look up and didn't speak.

We shrugged into our heavy coats as we walked out.

My attorney's big Mercedes sank three inches when he got in. I tried not to watch him struggle with his seatbelt. He cranked up the heat and drove three blocks before saying anything. "What the fuck was with the bullet?"

"I have no idea," I said. "Hey, where're you heading? I live in Bethesda."

"He was trying to trick you into saying something."

"Ya think? Where are we going?"

"What's the deal on the robbery? How many people know enough about your collection to know where you keep the rare guns?"

"Tons. I show it off at parties."

A lie. Only my buddy Miguel and a few select others had ever set foot in that room. Although anyone who knows a veteran with too many tours behind him, knows he owns a cabinet like mine—just in case.

But there was one time, when we had to negotiate a split contract with our competitor, Velox Deployment, we used my house for neutral ground. One of their guys took a long bathroom break—I found him in my office, admiring my collection.

I gave my attorney a look. "Where. Are. We. Going?"

"Your shrink. We're getting the insanity crap off the table right now. I don't want to get blindsided if they pry those files open."

"Et tu, Brute?" I said.

There was no end to people worrying about my mental health. I have no idea why.

Mercury said, *Now do you believe, dude? Cates was in the 3/2. He was Daryl Koven's commanding officer. I told you Jupiter was pulling some strings.*

I said, *What the hell are you talking about? Why would I care about Cates? And who is Koven?*

Mercury said, *You don't remember that day? It was the day we met, dawg. You were bawling for Jesus like a little girl. You were visibly disappointed when I showed up—but I let that shit slide. Nasiriyah was our first big win, brutha! Remember? What? Nothing? Man, you suck. I gotta find a better mortal to evangelize on our behalf cuz you just ain't pulling your weight.*

I craned over my shoulder to glare at the world's most obnoxious god, in his paper-thin toga, sprawled across the back seat like he owned it. I shook my head.

"Is someone following us?" My attorney tried to look over his shoulder.

"Thought I knew a guy back there."

The attorney dropped me at Dr. Harrison's office.

My shrink's goatee was gray, his spectacles round, his cashmere sweater a shade of muted-blah. I sat on the far end of a long couch, he sat in a wingback. A glass coffee table separated us. We exchanged tense pleasantries until he figured I wasn't warming up.

"Look, Jacob," Dr. Harrison said with a clenched jaw, "you don't want to be here, I don't want you to be here, but your attorney wants to put this whole god-business to rest."

"You told him?"

"No, of course not. You and I know about your imaginary friend, but I would never—"

I jumped to my feet. "He is *not* imaginary."

My voice was so loud it shook his lace curtains.

"Take it easy." Harrison pushed down the air in front of him with his palms. "My bad, as they say. I meant that everything you say in here is private. It never leaves this room. You can rest assured I would never betray your trust."

Mercury said, *That slimy rat bastard already betrayed us, and will again anytime someone sticks a knife in his face. Hey, dawg, you're recording this session, right?*

I said, *Recording it?*

Mercury said, *On your earbud-phone thingy. Trust me on this one.*

Why not?

The link to record blinked and I dropped my earbud in my shirt pocket as if I were turning everything off to give him my full attention. Dr. Harrison smiled his thanks. I retook the couch and Mercury stood behind the wingback, pretending to give Harrison a scalp massage. The doctor and I let the tension fade before attempting more.

"What's the career path for a psychiatrist?" I asked.

He shrugged. "Doing good is my reward. Maybe a published book about an extraordinary patient would cap off a career nicely."

"How about a patient who talks to a god? Would that help you write a book?"

"That would be perfect!" He laughed. "Now, I'm going to run through a series of simple questions to see if your voice is internal or supernatural."

Mercury said, *WTF? Internal? Like talking to yourself? Who does this guy think he is? How dare he test me! Does he have a planet named after him? I don't think so. Not even a comet. Best he could hope for is one of those Kuiper Belt rocks, out in the cheap seats with those idiot Greeks, Uranus and Pluto.*

Harrison kept talking. "I've reviewed your scholastic record and have a good idea of your lesser subjects. For example, I see you never excelled at mathematics. So let's start there. Can you tell me any three-digit prime number?"

Mercury said, *Oh easy, 101, 103, 107, 109…*

I repeated Mercury's words until we reached 997, all 143 prime numbers in the range.

Harrison's mouth hung open. He looked at his pad. "You missed 864."

"Not a prime number."

"Very good." He nodded like a bobble-head.

Repeating Mercury's words again, I said, "Do you want the Centered Squared Primes? Or the maybe the Harmonic Prime?"

"That's fine. Let's move on to history. Who was the Emperor of Rome before Severus Alexander?"

Again I parroted Mercury's answer. "Marcus Aurelius Antoninus Augustus, but you probably know him as Elagabalus, the name they gave him after he died. He was so depraved his grandmother had the Praetorian Guard murder him at the ripe old age of 18. Did you know he married three women and two men?"

Harrison stared at me like I'd pulled a dragon out of my ear.

I texted Agent Miguel, my old Army buddy and best friend, to pick me up.

"My word." My psychiatrist's face paled with wonder. "It's real, isn't it? I mean, you couldn't have known all that. You really do talk to God."

"Look, doc, I get it. You're not sure where to go with this." I rose and grabbed my coat. "Trust me, neither do I because he's not the kind of god you bring home to Mom. You know what I'm saying? So. We're done here."

"Wait," Harrison said. "Tell me my future."

"What?"

"Say something you couldn't have learned from a book."

"You're a whack job—I didn't learn that in a book."

Harrison got up and stepped into my path. He put his hands on my arms as if his aging, overweight body could stop me from leaving. He looked up into my eyes as if I were Jesus returned.

I gave him my soldier stare: let-go-or-die.

He didn't budge. He said, "Tell me something about my future."

Mercury said, *He's going to smack his shin on the coffee table.*

I told the doc his fortune.

The man spun around to look at the coffee table and smacked his shin on it. He grabbed his knee and fell to the floor, laughing and yelling at the same time. "Ow. It's true! Oh my god! Ow. It's true."

"Excuse me, Doc. I have to catch a killer 'cause the cops can't be bothered with getting the right guy."

I stepped over him and went downstairs and out the front door and waited on the sidewalk for Miguel. The freezing air stung my cheeks as much as it burned my nostrils.

Mercury stood a few feet away in his mini-skirt toga. *I can't believe it. You finally got a convert.*

# CHAPTER 9

AT 3:04 AM, Pia woke up in her suite at the Four Seasons hotel struggling for air and fighting a pillow held firmly against her face. She kicked and bucked and threw her assailant to the floor. She leaped from the bed, landed on her feet, her fists raised and ready for a fight.

She blinked into the empty room. Like every night, the dream had been more real than life. This time her tormentor screamed about saving her country from foreign campaign contributions and something else about innocent men dying in France. With her heart hammering hard enough to burst from her chest, she closed her eyes and took a deep breath. She hoped for one full night of sleep just once in her life.

Tania swept into the room, leading with her pistol. "You okay? I heard the scream."

Pia shook her head. "Fine."

She put on her running gear and left. She told Tania to let her run alone reasoning that good guys can't keep up, and bad guys don't get up that early.

Two hours later, Pia led her group from the helicopter through wet snow across the executive apron at London's Luton airport. They sprinted up the airstair and boarded her jet.

Pia, in a double set of heathered pullovers, took her favorite chair at the front, her father the seat opposite.

Tania pointed down the aisle. "Anywhere is fine, Mr. Blackson. Pia will call you when she's ready to talk."

Rip Blackson took off his hat, nodded at Pia and her dad, and made his way to the sofa in back. Carlos chose a row behind Pia, folded his arms, tilted against the window, and closed his eyes.

Tania remained in the aisle, staring at her boss with arms crossed.

"It's not a discussion," Pia said. "Carlos stays and you deal with it."

Tania harrumphed and took a seat farther down the aisle.

"Before you lecture me about the need for lobbyists," Pia said to her father, "tell me about your relationship with Duncan, and why Rip Blackson was following me with a parabolic microphone."

Alan Sabel sighed. "The biggest advantage in business is knowledge. My guess? Duncan sent him to find out if you're going to retain his firm. The obvious question is, will you?"

"Who wants to know, you or Duncan?"

"Everyone. What you do in the coming months impacts thousands of lives. Not just lobbyists, but the contractors who launch Sabel satellites, the customers who hire Sabel Technologies to fix their networks, the captain of our yacht, the people who clean your bedroom—they're all stressed about their future."

Pia considered her responsibilities while the roar of engines drowned out further discussion. It was part of the stress that gnawed on her nerves, everyone waited for her to make decisions when she didn't even know there were decisions to be made.

They rolled down the runway and into the darkness, launching upward at a steep angle.

"Nothing has changed," Pia said. "You still run Sabel Industries. But you haven't answered my question. What is your relationship with Duncan?"

"They're worried because you're young, and young people are idealistic." Alan leaned his elbows on the table. "I was idealistic when I was your age. But once you take on the responsibility of keeping people employed, when you realize the gravity of your decisions, when you see former employees bagging groceries, you begin to guard your company like Gollum protecting his ring."

Pia put a hand out: *stop*. "What does Duncan do?"

"Duncan represents our interests in political circles. Politicians can help or hurt you. But, as you've learned, they sure as hell won't leave you alone." He tugged at his cuffs and glanced around. When he met her gaze, he shrugged. "Tom Duncan looks for political winners. For example, three years ago, he told me to back a certain Maryland State's

Attorney. The guy won. And a few days ago, after I texted him, that same attorney released Jacob Stearne."

"We bought the state prosecutor?" Pia's eyebrows rose.

"Certainly not. We supported him, we're his constituents, and when detectives pursued the most convenient suspect, we asked him to review the relevant facts. Because we supported him, he extended the courtesy of acting on my request. And Jacob was released. But if Jacob did commit the murder, campaign contributions will not get him off."

"What else has Duncan done for us?"

"We backed the governor in Wisconsin and a congressman in Idaho and—"

"Do we have operations in Wisconsin?" Pia asked.

"We considered building an aerospace engineering office for Sabel Satellite out there." Alan leaned back and brushed his slacks with the edge of his hand. "The governor had other backers who used our designated tax incentives for private prisons instead."

"We backed a governor who chose blue-collar jobs over highly paid aerospace engineers?" Pia huffed. "Is Duncan the guy who told you to back Veronica Hunter for President?"

"As it turns out," Alan said, "Duncan is old school. He thought $20 million would give me access to the president, but that was before Citizens United opened the floodgates. $20 million won't get you coffee with her Chief of Staff anymore."

"Citizen's what?"

"It's a Supreme Court decision. They ruled that corporations and unions can raise money on behalf of political candidates and issues as long as they don't coordinate with the candidate and they disclose their donors."

"How do we know if they break the rules?"

Alan shook his head. "We don't."

"We're Jeff Smith's biggest donors. Why is he shaking me down for more donations?"

"He isn't driving this," Alan said. "When representatives are new and insecure, they look for any excuse to get in the news. They found a cause that gets voters talking."

Pia thought about her growing profile in political circles, an area where she'd prefer more anonymity. Politicians controlled more than regulations, they could bring down armies on your head, as she knew all too well. The thought of tangling with them made her head swim. Plato was right, politicians should be set aside in a special class that could own nothing, all their needs given to them from the public trust to keep them above corruption.

"Wake my stalker for me." Pia nodded at Blackson, who'd fallen asleep on the sofa.

Alan woke the lobbyist and coaxed him to the front. Blackson took the seat opposite her, his shirt rumpled, his eyes bloodshot.

He tried to brave it out with a forced smile. "When you offered me a ride, I didn't realize you meant five in the morning. So the rumors are true, you're an insomniac?"

Pia let his question sit for an uncomfortable minute.

"When I was four," she said, "I watched a man strangle my mother to death. I stabbed the guy but it was too late. Alan Sabel adopted me and sent me to the best therapists in the world, but you can't erase that kind of trauma. Ever since then, I've slept for no more than three hours."

She watched Blackson think through a hundred apologies that he wisely chose not to voice. The silence stretched to the breaking point.

"Why the microphone?" she asked.

"It was a present from a friend. Looked kinda cool, so I thought I'd test it out in a crowded…"

She knew the power her piercing gray-green eyes could bring to bear and saw it working on Blackson. His head sank and he placed both palms on the table.

"Why did you miss your coworker's funeral to eavesdrop on me, Mr. Blackson?"

His head snapped up, his eyes fixed on her, but he had no answer.

"Were you close to David Gottleib?"

Blackson drew back and inhaled. "Since Camp Lejeune."

"Do you think Jacob Stearne killed your friend?"

"No, ma'am."

"How do you know?"

Blackson squinted as if she'd asked if the sun would rise in the morning. "He's the kind of guy who saves people. I called David's mom and tried to explain it to her, but she and those detectives—"

"What did Mr. Gottleib want with Jacob?"

Blackson rubbed his palms together and thought. He kept thinking for a long time.

Pia put a hand on his wrist, forcing him to look up. "If I can't trust you to answer difficult questions, why would I keep your firm?"

Blackson bit his lip and closed his eyes. She let go of his wrist.

After a few moments, he looked up. "David was a proud Jew, the kind who kept kosher even at business meetings. It was hard for him to work with Arabs. For the last several weeks, David was getting upset about money pouring into the firm. Not just Arab money, but Russian and German and Indian. When his team worked on a Saudi deal, he turned bitter. He was going to tell me about it—but someone killed him first."

"What do you know about the Oman deal?" she asked.

"Nothing. I work on Duncan's side of the firm. David and Brent work for Daryl Koven. Our business has many sensitive issues, so each partner is treated like a separate silo."

Pia leaned back and waited.

"I was there because I thought you'd clear Jacob by finding David's killer. I was hoping to find out who did it."

A moment later, the pilot announced their landing approach to Metz-Nancy-Lorraine airport.


WIND WHIPPED THE coats of Pia and her group as they stood in the predawn dark before the square-lattice ironwork of Château de Malbrouck. Tania reached around Carlos and shook the castle gate again.

He gave her a scowl over his shoulder. "You think I do that wrong too?"

Tania turned up her nose.

Rip Blackson dialed his phone and spoke to someone. When he clicked off, he reported to the group. "He was asleep."

A blast of icy air howled across the courtyard and through the gate.

A few minutes later, a man with an electric lantern staggered from the nearest tower. Lightly dressed and disheveled clothes, he stopped three yards from the entry tunnel and squinted at Pia's party of five. He approached as if they were wild animals until his light cast a brighter light on their faces.

Looking at Tania, the man slurred his words. "Well, well, well. Ain't you the, the, hottie?" He balanced the lamp on his head and rested his hands in the iron grate. He pressed his face in for a better look. "You gotta be. Be really anxious—visiting this time of night."

Ugly scars ran across either side of his face where he once had ears.

His eyes stopped rolling and focused. His mouth dropped open.

"I'll be damned." Tania grabbed one of his hands. "Kasey Earl. You're still alive? And someone gave you the keys to the gate?"

Kasey tried to pull away. "Hey now, you got no call—"

Carlos reached through the ironwork to grab the lantern as it fell.

"Open the gate, Kasey," Blackson said. He turned to Tania. "He works for us. Security."

"It's a wonder you're still alive," Tania said.

Kasey dropped the keys. Weaving in place, he bent to pick them up and missed on the first pass. His hands dangled above the ground while he inhaled and began a second attempt that sounded, judging from his breathing, as if he were bench-pressing three hundred pounds.

Blackson said, "Have you been drinking?"

"Hey, I ain't on duty." Kasey glanced up and pointed vaguely at Tania. "It's. It's. Fuck. She cut my ears off."

"Wrong," Tania said. "Jacob took one of them off before I had the chance."

Blackson watched her while Kasey fumbled the key into the lock and managed to turn it, then yanked it open.

Kasey reached for the lantern. Carlos waved him off and kept it.

"You know the trouble with partying all night?" Kasey asked Blackson as they followed him in.

"You get fired in the morning?"

"Nah, that's not it. Trouble. Trouble is. Liquor's a liar. He makes you think you're golden but when the hot chicks get here, you don't have a chance."

"As if." Tania shoved his shoulder, spinning him around.

Pia stepped between them. Kasey Earl looked up at her and squinted.

She said, "We have an appointment to see Tom Duncan."

# CHAPTER 10

MARTHE KOVEN STOOD in the dark, a full step back from the second-floor window watching her wind-whipped visitors. When she heard the word "appointment", she turned to her husband and whispered. "Go. Now."

Daryl Koven disappeared down the dark hall stairs, emerging beneath her a moment later wearing his heavy trench coat. His boots crunched through the snow on the paving stones as he greeted his guests.

Rip Blackson set the pace alongside the security guard, Kasey.

A handsome, barrel-chested man with broad shoulders in a shimmering suit was flanked by a tall, athletic girl wearing an open duster. She walked with the silky, confident gait of a tiger stalking her prey.

A shiver ran down Marthe's spine.

She knew those two without any introduction.

In front of them, an exotic, multiracial woman with a mane of dark curly hair flowing over her shoulders examined every nook and cranny in the courtyard. At the back, a Mexican who looked out of place in the entourage.

Marthe bit her fingernail.

"Welcome." She heard her husband's words filtered through the window. "Welcome to the Château de Malbrouck and the Future Crossroads Symposium. You must be cold and tired. Please, come with me. The Great Hall is right this way."

He gestured toward a door, the wind snapping his clothes. The group started in. He held out a hand. "Not you, Kasey."

"I'll get Duncan then."

"You're finished for the night," Daryl said.

Kasey waved dismissively and stumbled away in the dark.

Without warning, Pia Sabel stared directly into Marthe's window. As if the girl had the instincts of a supernatural predator and could sense Marthe's presence.

Marthe stepped back.

As Pia walked around her husband, Marthe heard him speak. "Ms. Sabel, so good of you to come. If I'd known you were meeting Tom, I'd have woken him so he could greet you himself."

Marthe inched closer to the window.

Pia Sabel stared at her husband.

She had seen the Sabel girl on TV. A small athlete on a large field of grass. In person, she was different. Even from her high angle, she could tell the girl was a couple of inches taller than Daryl. Her gaze pierced the man as if she could look inside him and read his soul.

The girl went inside without speaking or breaking stride.

Marthe pulled her robe tighter and hugged herself.

"I'll wake Mr. Duncan," Blackson said. "You have plenty of work ahead of you."

"What I do is more joy than work," Daryl said. "But, thank you, I'll see to the guests. He's in the adjoining tower."

Blackson tilted into the wind.

Daryl checked the courtyard then disappeared from her view. When she heard the door close, Marthe ran down the steps and down the dark, cramped connecting hall. She stopped before the edge of light in the well-lit Great Room and found a sleepy servant. Tugging the girl's arm, she ordered her to make coffee.

She pressed her cheek to the stone and peered around the corner, assessing her guests from the shadow. She took a deep breath to fill herself with resolve. She would need to establish herself as the hostess and find a way to keep the Sabel girl in her place.

The object of her concern stood in the center of the space, admiring the hand-hewn beams that arched to the ceiling.

Her husband crossed to the girl and looked up. "The place was a ruin a hundred years ago. The restoration started in 1991 and lasted until '98. They were faithful to the architecture of late fifteenth century—"

"Were you close to David Gottleib, Mr. Koven?" Pia asked, her gaze still on the woodwork above.

Marthe tensed. Daryl was hardly the master of debate when pitted against a woman's carefully constructed interrogation.

"He worked for me," Daryl said. "I'd known him for almost a decade."

"Was he a valuable employee?"

"Of course. One of our best."

Pia faced him. "Why didn't you postpone your symposium for his funeral?"

Daryl opened his mouth. And closed it. Marthe could almost see his words winging back to his brain for reevaluation. After considering his response, he said, "The people attending later today are very important people. You don't reschedule on the rich and powerful."

"What makes us rich and powerful is the quality of our friends. Don't they deserve a day of mourning?"

Marthe cursed herself for not postponing two weeks. She'd been too eager for Daryl's moment to come.

Daryl studied his questioner. "Well, I guess you could—"

Shouts rang from the courtyard. The door flew open.

Blackson staggered in. "Call 9-1-1, I mean, 1-1-2. Duncan's been murdered! Oh god. Shot in the face. The blood. It's awful."

The Sabel agents moved into defensive positions on either side of the Sabels, facing opposite directions, their weapons drawn and ready. Marthe both feared and admired their instant efficiency.

"What?" Daryl screamed. "My god, man, don't joke about a thing like that."

"He's dead. It was horrible, horrible. I can't describe it. Where's Brent?"

"I don't understand. Duncan was fine when he turned in."

"Go see for yourself." Blackson dialed his phone. As it connected, he shouted to the servant. "Find Brent Zola."

Daryl ran outside. Pia guided Blackson to a table and pulled a chair for him. He dropped into it.

Marthe realized Pia was taking on the role of hostess due to her absence. She glanced down at her nightgown and robe. It would have to do. With her black hair flowing behind her, she ran straight to Blackson.

"What happened? Why are you shouting?" Marthe asked.

Blackson looked up, the phone still pressed to his ear. Holding a finger to her, he spoke to the emergency operator. "I must report a murder at the Château de Malbrouck."

Brent Zola joined them, out of breath from running. He asked, "Who?"

"Duncan." Blackson returned to the phone.

"At our symposium?" Marthe fell into the chair next to him and slumped, her gaze swept the floor.

She turned to Pia. "Who are you?"

Pia introduced herself and her father. "If there's anything we can do to help."

"Haven't you done enough?" Marthe asked. "Wasn't it one of your people who killed David Gottleib?"

"No," Blackson and Zola said in unison.

"If you need anything at all." Pia backed away a respectful distance.

Several shots, muffled by the stone walls, rang out. First one, then a second. After short moment, two more followed by another pause and two more.

Marthe observed each person in the room as they recognized the noise. There would be no hiding it. Where Duncan's murder had been late at night and inside a chamber within a chamber, these shots came from the outer room and Daryl, in his haste, left all the doors open.

Instantly, the multiracial woman ran to the door.

"Guard them," Pia told her other agent, pointing to Marthe and the others, then followed her bodyguard.

The Mexican surveyed his charges.

Marthe rose. "I'm going with them."

The Mexican said, "It might not be safe out—"

"It's my event, my responsibility." She left, closing the door behind her as quietly as she could to avoid alerting the Sabel girl.

Across the courtyard, she found the tower door standing open. She slipped inside, took off her wet shoes, and tiptoed up the cold stone stairs. The spiral led her to a position where she could observe the girl and her bodyguard. One crouched low, the other stood tall, ready to burst in on Daryl.

Marthe thought hard. There were so many ways things could go wrong but at some point, she had to trust her husband.

Operating on some sort of telepathy, the two women burst into the outer chamber of Duncan's room. The multiracial girl rolled in low to the right, while the Sabel girl swung in left. Their guns swept the room.

"PUT YOUR WEAPON ON THE FLOOR NOW!" The guard yelled in a commanding voice.

Marthe flinched.

"I don't know if they're still dangerous." Daryl's voice sounded strained.

"PUT YOUR WEAPON ON THE FLOOR! DO IT NOW!" the agent repeated.

"It's OK," Daryl said. "I've got them."

Marthe tiptoed to the doorframe and stood behind the half-open door. She peered through the gap between the door and jamb. Daryl was bent at the waist. He rose slowly, his hands above him.

The Sabel agent kicked his gun out of reach. "What were you picking up when I came in?"

"I was checking their pulses," Daryl said. "I think they're dead."

The agent relaxed her stance but pressed her muzzle to Daryl's chest, aimed at his heart, and studied the room.

The Sabel girl loosened the weapons from the dead men's grip, leaving them near the bodies but out of reach in case the men weren't dead. She pressed her fingers to their necks.

She looked up at Marthe's hiding place, her gaze drilling through her, but said nothing.

Daryl headed for the door. "Are the police—"

"Don't move," the agent said. "Until the police arrive, you stay right here."

"What?" Daryl asked. "Why? There won't be any questions. They tried to kill me to cover up their crime. Surely you can see that."

"Tell me what happened."

Marthe closed her eyes and prayed he would keep his mouth shut.

"Can I sit for a moment and collect my wits?" Daryl asked.

"No."

The Sabel girl crossed to the door, looking through the jamb's narrow slot. "You don't have to stay back there, Ms. Koven, but you don't want to see this."

"Is my husband hurt?"

"As you might expect in a shooting of this type—he's unscathed."

The Sabel girl's eyes could penetrate steel. She felt the girl's stare reach inside her and read her part in the conspiracy as if it were written in a book.

Marthe shivered again.

She stepped out from behind the door and kept her head down, averting her gaze from the dead men.

"Oh, no, Marthe," Daryl said. "This is no place for you."

"I want to see," she said. "I made the arrangements for this castle, I'm liable for what happens here."

"What's that on your wrist?" Pia asked.

Marthe tugged her sleeve down. "Moisturizer, I just woke up."

She pulled up her chin and walked in.

The Sabel girl stepped back, allowing Marthe to see the room. The gore was appalling. Two bodies were sprawled on the floor, one flat, the rug beneath him soaked in blood. The other man was sprawled between the chair and floor. Blood soaked the chair's seat cushion.

Daryl watched her take it all in. "My dear, you should wait with the others. The police will be here shortly."

"No. I want to be here." She reached out and grabbed his hand.

She turned to the Sabel agent. "I'm sorry, we haven't been properly introduced. I'm Marthe Koven."

"Tania Cooper." The agent glanced her way then spoke to Daryl. "How did this go down?"

"I rushed in," Daryl said. "I didn't notice them in the outer chamber, but I think they were in these chairs, sleeping. I don't remember. Anyway, I ran to Tom's bedside. You can see the blood and bone. Oh god. It's as if a shining light has gone out. I can't believe they would kill him."

The Sabel girl edged around the bodies and went into the bedroom. Marthe wanted to stop her but could think of no good reason. While they weren't official detectives, security was their business.

"Who are these guys?" Tania pointed at the bodies.

"Velox Deployment guards. I don't know their names."

"You rushed in, saw the body, then what?"

"I appreciate your experience," Marthe said, "but I'd rather wait for the gendarmes."

"I was an Army MP. I've investigated more murders than the local cops by a long shot. Let me help you out."

"That's thoughtful of you," Daryl said. "We'll wait."

"You're in France," Tania said. "You get thirty minutes with a lawyer for every twenty-four hours they hold you for interrogation. They can hold you up to ninety-six hours before determining if they want to press charges. You can remain silent during questioning, but in this country, that works against you."

Daryl nodded and squeezed Marthe's hand. "There was Duncan, just lying there, covered in blood, murdered, his head blown open..." Daryl took a moment. "I was shocked, sickened, furious, all at once. I lost it. I stormed back in here and demanded to know what happened. I shook one of them until he woke up." Koven gestured and turned away. "When they realized they'd been caught, they turned aggressive and threatened me."

"How did it escalate to gunfire?"

"It happened so fast." Daryl looked at his hands, turning them over as if he'd never seen them before. "They were yelling and the guns came out. One of them shot and missed me. I guess I shot him."

"Was he standing, or lying down?"

"That's enough," Marthe said. "He doesn't have to explain anything to you."

The Sabel girl returned from the bedroom. Her gaze rose above and behind Marthe's head.

Marthe turned to see what held her interest but saw only a chip in the stone wall. When she looked back, the Sabel girl was snapping pictures of the artwork, the walls, and the bodies.

"Stop that," Marthe said. "You have no right to take pictures."

The girl shrugged and pushed her phone into her jacket pocket.

Daryl glared at Tania. "I'm not going to say anything more. Get out."

The Sabel girl tugged Tania's sleeve and the two women left down the stairwell.

# CHAPTER 11

TRAFFIC HONKED DOWN K Street and wipers smacked the midday sleet from their windshields as I slammed the guy against the trash bin in the alley. I pressed the back of my knife to his throat. My victim was a short, thin fellow with thick brow ridges accented by a v-shaped scar in the middle. His eyebrows arched to the top of his head but his heart rate remained calm.

"Why do you find me so interesting, Skippy?" I asked.

"Money's in my pocket, sir. Please don't hurt me."

There was a sneer in his voice.

A guy who didn't quiver when attacked was not the kind of guy I expected to follow me through the Metro and around a four-block circle. I had him pegged for a Fed. If you pull a knife on a Fed, he pulls some ID and starts throwing his weight around, because it's going to be career limiting when his boss finds out. The guy I held by the hair was mocking me, feigning fear as he calculated how to reach the pistol in his coat pocket.

I shoved a knee between his legs, unsportsmanlike conduct meant to surprise even the most jaded mafia goon. The pain was evident in his repressed flinch.

He jabbed a hand in his pocket only to find mine already wrapped around the grip of his handgun, finger on the trigger.

"What story will you tell your boss when he picks you up at the hospital?" I asked.

Fear crossed his face in a short-lived flash. "Hospital?"

"After I blow your toe off—with your gun—it would be smart to have a professional stitch up the stump."

He didn't answer.

Using his thigh as a friction stop, I ejected the chambered round and the magazine while he fought for the weapon. The poor bastard managed to catch that soft piece of flesh between the thumb and index finger in the gun's slide. My new friend's heart rate rose fast.

I like to see fear in my adversaries. It helps establish my alpha status and improves my negotiating position. I turned my blade around, letting the sharp edge shave a small piece of his neck.

Pulling the weapon out of his pocket, I held it up for scrutiny. A Springfield Armory 1911 TRP. A century of proven American pistol technology in a .45 caliber. It was a beautiful piece with rails for lights or lasers. The weapon of choice for the FBI.

But this guy was hardly FBI material.

He tried to squirm out of my grip.

My kick landed just below the back of his knee. If you hit the spot hard enough you can deliver a compound fracture to the tibia, popping it out the front of your adversary's leg and shredding his ligaments. I didn't have the room for that violent a blow, but mine was effective enough to send him sprawling knees-first across the alley's filthy asphalt.

I sat on his back and went through his pockets. He attempted a wrestling move or two that caused him to utter painful groans, which I attributed to his dysfunctional knee.

Jago Seyton of Duncan, Hyde and Koven had a nice white business card with no title next to his name. Interesting. Tailed by an employee of the very lobbying firm I was assigned to visit. The lobbying business was tougher than I thought.

Mercury said, *Oh dude, this is going to be so awkward. You totally overreacted. I said he was following you, not trying to kill your mama.*

I said, *Your exact words were, 'shoot him in the head.'*

Mercury picked at his toga. *That was before I knew who he was.*

Rising, I kicked Jago. He craned over his shoulder with a look I'd only seen in the *other* hemisphere.

When you defeat an enemy without killing him, he's either a) submissive; b) resentful but compliant; or c) driven to a new state of hateful revenge—like a jihadist. This guy was in the hateful revenge camp.

"Why the cloak-and-dagger crap, Skippy?" I tried to help him up.

He refused my hand. "Name's Jago. On my way to work. You assaulted me."

"You passed your office—twice."

His knee refused to cooperate so I yanked his coat collar and brought him upright. I offered him a piece of chewing gum which he refused, so I chomped on it. "Talk to me, Skippy. Make up a good one."

"It's Jago." He turned to hobble away.

I spun him back around. "Who wants to know where I go and what I do?"

He pulled back and said nothing.

"Tell you what," I said. "You introduce me to Senator Hyde and I won't say anything about your abject failure at tailing me today."

Another fleeting look of fear crossed his face. Nothing scares a clandestine type more than telling his boss his target beat him. He twisted out of my grip and limped to the street. I followed a step behind and stuck my wad of gum deep into the barrel of his pistol.

We wove our way through pedestrians to his building and up the elevator. Our carriage doors opened into a marble-and-oak reception lobby resembling the Senate floor. A stunning young lady behind a huge desk smeared her makeup with a tissue.

"Wants to see the Senator." Jago thumbed over his shoulder at me. He walked away.

The girl sniffled into a fresh tissue and held up a finger to put me on hold.

Another supermodel secretary rounded the corner. The two women looked at each other and burst into tears.

I took off my topcoat, folded it over my arm, and double-checked my suit. If Jago left his blood on it, I was going to be pissed. I only own one and it cost more than my first car. I was too cheap to spring for the shirt and tie and everything else the salesman wanted to nickel-and-dime me with, so I had on a t-shirt that read, WANT TO MEET ALLAH? PISS OFF AN ARMY RANGER. When you wear a shirt like that, you find out how many of your friends are Muslims. I wore it once and got an earful from everyone, but I skipped laundry day last week, so.

A third secretary came in, wearing a hijab. I pulled my jacket tight and buttoned it.

The crying was punctuated by statements of grief: he was so young; what will the firm do without him; he was the best boss ever.

Tom Duncan's existence was as much of a shock to me as his death was to them, but Ms. Sabel texted a cryptic instruction and I was learning about the firm on my way. The guys from the Gottleib funeral would be pleased.

"Excuse me." I leaned over the reception desk. "It's been a while. He's still in the corner office on the right?"

One of them nodded and pointed. I moved quickly through pale beige halls filled with mutually consoling co-workers until I saw Mercury leaning against a massive oak door.

Mercury said, *You don't have an appointment, bro. Maybe you should pull the fire alarm.*

I said, *I got this.*

Mercury said, *This place gives me the creeps. I'll chill with the ladies at the front desk. Someone needs to help them with their grieving, give them a shoulder to cry on. You need me, just holla.*

The door behind him swung open and a stately woman wearing an Akris business suit stalked out. I only knew the brand because Ms. Sabel bought one for her grandmother's birthday and sent me to pick it up. The thing cost as much as a college education.

As we passed in the hall, the lady squinted at me as if I were mud on her shoe. She had a helmet of auburn hair without a trace of the gray one expects in a woman of her age. Some women are just lucky, I guess. I tried to place her familiar face. She'd been on the news. Maybe she was a prime minister or a queen somewhere. I leaned toward queen. She looked like the kind who would have your head chopped off with a wave of her hand.

I averted my eyes.

When I reached the door she'd exited, I cranked the knob and threw it open. An old guy with a beet-red, swollen nose looked up from a memo. A ring of white hair circled his head just above his ears. A smudge of lipstick stood out on his white collar, just below his ear. He was on the bottom end of his career, a candidate for retirement in any other company, his job safe only because his name was on the door.

"Senator Hyde, Alan Sabel sent me on behalf of Sabel Industries to offer a toast in Tom's memory."

He blinked his red, puffy eyes at me.

I stood at attention. "Jacob Stearne, at your service, sir."

Hyde dropped his memo and leaned back, regarding me. "Bullshit."

"I would never bullshit a senator, sir." I reached in my coat pocket, pulled a sterling silver flask bearing Alan Sabel's initials, and filled from his personal bar at Sabel Gardens. I set it on the desk. From my side pocket, I produced two shot glasses with sterling silver inlays of the big guy's initials and set them next to the flask.

He smiled and let out a wet, congested laugh. He waggled two fingers at the flask.

I handed it to him.

He popped the cap and sniffed, raising one eyebrow. He recapped the flask and handed it back to me. "Alan Sabel sent me to fucking rehab. He did *not* send you to toast my partner's murder."

"Oh, sorry, sir." I coughed. "I didn't know. The tequila was my idea. I'm not good with Washington etiquette, so I relied on my upbringing. No offense intended."

"Where you from, boy?"

"Iowa. We toast on the news of someone's passing, sir."

Behind him, Mercury walked on the credenza and stopped at the crystal decanter. He picked it up, pulled the top, and turned the empty vessel upside down.

I said, *I thought you were helping the ladies.*

Mercury said, *Bunch of goddamn atheists.*

Hyde nodded and stuck out his bottom lip as he thought. "Just out of curiosity, what kind of tequila is it?"

"Trono Imperialista, Añejo, 1987."

"As I recall, we had the same tradition in South Dakota." He nodded at the flask. Then at the glasses. He sniffed and licked his lips and leaned forward.

I poured out a shot each, held one, and offered the other. He took it, downed the shot like a pro, and held up the glass for a refill.

Mercury said, *You've done some sleazy shit in your day, Dawg, but this one ranks up there with sleeping with your best friend's wife.*

I said, *Hey! She told me he left her. How was I supposed to know he only 'left her' for a weekend in the reserves? But yeah, this feels as bad as that turned out.*

I poured Hyde another.

"What's your toast then?" he asked. He held the glass under his nose and inhaled.

I stood up straight. "Tom Duncan lives in the hearts he left behind and therefore will never die."

We clinked glasses. I sipped and Hyde gulped.

His eyes watered, he smacked his lips as he exhaled. "Sweet *and* aged, a worthy combination. Thank god it was better than your toast."

He held up his glass. I poured.

Hyde turned to the ceiling and offered a toast of his own. "Until we meet again Tom Duncan, may God hold you in the palm of his hand."

An instant later, he motioned for a refill.

He laughed his second toast. "Here's to being single, drinking doubles, and seeing triple."

My first shot was still half-full when he held up his glass for his fifth. The flask was light, but I poured with a flourish and saw his face fall when I shook out the last drop. He held his drink close to his chest as if someone might try to wrench it out of his hands.

"What do you know about these Velox fellows?" he asked.

"They're competitors, Senator."

He pointed to the chair behind me. "Sabel's full of veterans, Velox is full of veterans. I'm sure you know some of them. I can't believe they'd murder Tom for sport."

"I know a few." I took the offered seat. "One was charged with rape but got off on a technicality. Another one did two years for spilling classified intel. Those are the only guys I know."

He sighed, patted his tie, and turned to the window. When my eyes followed his gaze, he downed his last drink.

"What kind of argument did you have with Gottleib, anyway?" he asked.

"Someone else had an argument with Gottleib."

"Shame about that young man. He had a future. Not like some of these other guys."

"He worked for you?"

"Tom pulled the staff out from under me after my last accident."

Yet another supermodel with ruined makeup leaned in the door. "I'm sorry to interrupt. What should I tell people about a funeral?"

His watery eyes swam up and down her figure. "Take names and email addresses, tell them we'll inform them when we know."

"Who is going to make arrangements?" she asked.

"How the hell would I know?" Hyde said with a quick glare. He turned away. "Marthe Koven, I suppose. She'll know what to do."

With a scornful look at me, she pulled the door closed behind her.

"What did Gottleib tell you?" Hyde asked.

"He said I saved the 3/2 and now I had to save something else, but he died before he explained."

Hyde nodded and looked at his empty glass. "You know what I hate?"

"No, sir."

"Women in tears." He stood, shrugged into his suit jacket, stuck his winter coat under his arm. "You're a good listener and I need lunch."

He gestured to the door. We hurried past the worker bees as if we were making a prison break and grabbed an elevator.

Powdered snow, light enough to float on the breeze instead of falling to the ground, swirled around us as we made our way up K Street. Traffic filled streets narrowed by slush.

"You got me thinking," I said. "I don't see the Velox guys shooting your partner in the face."

"You don't think they're killers?"

"They're killers all right, but they'd shoot him in the back."

He laughed.

I was serious.

"Who was that woman who left your office before I came in?" Our feet crunched on the snow covered sidewalk and slipped on the ice underneath. "She looked familiar."

"Katy Hellman, the former heiress to Fuchs News." He laughed. "She'd kill to scoop headlines."

"Former?"

"Her father, being an old-school sexist, recently announced he's leaving the news empire to his lazy son instead of Katy. She's not amused, to say the least."

A man stepped into our path, opening the door to DC Coast, one of the finest eateries in the area. "Senator, it's been too long. Your usual table?"

Hyde gave the man a polite nod. We followed him to a booth in back.

I ordered the goat cheese chili relleno and the catfish tacos because the chef inside of me wanted to steal the recipes. He ordered a shot of tequila and a piece of bread. The instant our waiter left, the bartender appeared and flourished a cocktail napkin on the table and set a shot glass on it. They exchanged appreciative nods.

"It's not polite to stare at a man while he's drinking." He took half a sip of the gold liquid. "I'm grieving. I've lost a partner and my firm."

I closed my mouth and felt bad for a second.

"Who do you think killed David Gottleib?" I asked.

He adjusted the napkin under his shot glass. "Who killed Tom Duncan?"

"Word is the crime scene contradicts statements made." My chili relleno arrived, steaming. "What kind of thing was Gottleib into that someone would kill for?"

Hyde smiled and waved at someone across the room.

I dug into the relleno and nearly burned my tongue. Melted cheese can be deceptively hot.

"Do you know the founder of Velox, Shane Diabulus?" He downed the rest of his drink and waved his empty at the bartender.

"I shot him once, does that count?" I forked open the relleno to cool it. Wild mushrooms and corn relish topped with a mild salsa. "Unfortunately, he lived."

Hyde kept his attention on the bartender until he was acknowledged.

I said, "What kind of lobbying do you do that calls for Shane's type of protection?"

Mercury slid into the booth too close for comfort. *Dude, so uncool. Not only are you feeding alcohol to an addict, you're letting him pump you for information? Get your sorry act together.*

I said, *I can handle this if you just let me concentrate.*

Mercury said, *I know how hard that is for you. Just pay attention this time. He's a high functioning binge drinker.*

Hyde said, "Daryl Koven pushed the Oman deal to your firm but Pia Sabel hasn't had the decency to send a thank-you note much less schedule a meeting. A hundred-million-dollar contract and she's not even asking about special instructions. What an ill-mannered diva. I heard Alan's out and she's in, taking over everything. Is she dumping her father's business partners?"

I chopped up the big pepper and blew on it. "What did you guys expect her to do with the extra $20 million?"

"I asked you a question," he said.

"No change in the executive offices." I dug into my food.

He stared at me long enough to make me uncomfortable. I dropped my fork and stared back.

"The cops accused me of murder," I said. "Why aren't you afraid of me?"

"Alan Sabel didn't send you." He cackled his way into a hacking cough. "He would've sent a polished exec who appreciates subtlety."

He watched me eat as if the sight of solid food revolted him.

Between bites, I turned a wistful gaze toward the ceiling and let a finger wave to the beat of my words. "You know that thing the Midwestern moms do, where Mary brings Cathy lettuce from her garden one day and Cathy returns with tomatoes for Mary the next? That's the part of *back home* I miss. Neighborly exchanges like that." I turned my gaze to him. "Wouldn't it be neighborly to answer one of my questions since I've been nice enough to answer yours?"

Hyde downed his shot, exhaled, and rolled the empty glass between his palms. "That was subtle."

I ate while he thought. "I'm not afraid of you because you didn't kill David."

"How do you know?"

He sighed and looked three different directions before reluctantly meeting my gaze. "Blackson vouched for you. Said they knew you from some battle the jarheads are always bragging about."

"What is Ms. Sabel supposed to do with the $20 mil?"

"I couldn't tell you the details." He paused to shoot a mean glare at the bartender, who was busy hitting on a woman at the bar. "Koven took over some of the contract negotiations while I was away. But when a contract reaches those proportions, there are special circumstances that executives at the highest level need to discuss in person. Not in writing. Not in email. Not over the phone. She should meet with Koven and work it out."

I polished off the last bite and pushed the plate to the side.

The waiter brought Hyde another shot of tequila and dropped off my tacos. Avacado crèma and pineapple salsa would be laughed out of Mexico, but smelled fine to me.

"How did you meet Shane Diabulus?" I asked.

We eyeballed each other while I chewed.

"He was recommended by staffers on the Senate Intelligence Committee." He nursed his drink. "Apparently, the CIA has them do all kinds of special work. We found him some investors to grow his business, and he assigns men to keep us covered."

We skipped commenting on the irony with a thoughtful—and awkward—glance at each other.

"Why weren't you at the Gottleib funeral?"

"Does that bother you?" He grinned and sipped his tequila slowly, never taking his bloodshot eyes off me. "Those boys were Koven's, followed him all over the world. I never knew them that well. Besides, I was in the hospital. Anemia."

I polished off the first taco and resisted licking my fingers. "What do you think of Daryl Koven?"

He leaned back and let his smile light up his face. "Ah. Now we get to why she sent you. She thinks Koven did it."

"She'll let the gendarmes point fingers. Do you feel the need to watch your back?"

"Usurpers lurk behind every curtain, don't they? I have people who watch my back for me." He hacked up another laugh. "Maybe you should watch yours."

I finished the last bite while he sipped his drink. I wiped my mouth, dropped my napkin on the plate, and pushed out of the booth.

"I'm not as smart as you, Senator, but I have some valuable advice." Standing in front of him, I pulled Jago's empty 1911, weighed it in my hand, then tossed it on the table. "Don't let amateurs watch your back."

# CHAPTER 12

FROM THE WALKWAY above the courtyard, Pia watched a hawk screeching to scare pigeons from their roosts in the château's towers. The bird formed a black silhouette sailing against a ceiling of dark clouds.

Sometimes she felt like the hawk. Circling around others, never in the conversation, too tall or too rich or too accomplished for people at ground level to warm up to. Sometimes that distance worked to her advantage, and other times kept her out of the fun. People saw her as intimidating, almost scary when she simply stood still. In college she'd see a circle of girls talking about a party, they'd look up at her with furtive glances and scatter like field mice from the hawk.

Owning a company made her more distant than ever. They were afraid of her in a strange new way. They thought her capable of firing them for the slightest gaffe even though the Major handled all personnel matters. Jacob was different. She would fire him from time to time just for fun. And there was Tania. The first time they met, Tania called her a "rich bitch". She found the honesty refreshing. Those were her two strongest relationships in many years. The only two who didn't see her as a hawk, circling before diving in for the kill.

She wanted justice for Duncan and the unfortunate Velox guards but couldn't think of how to employ her intimidating nature to her advantage. Koven spun his story and everyone believed him. If the police were as naïve, she'd have to do that one terrible thing she never wanted to do: ask her father for advice.

Below her, at ground level, the castle walls echoed with the subdued voices of policemen trying to calm her impatient father. Outside the walls, the rattle of reporters and gawkers echoed through the woods as they pried information from the officers who'd held a tight perimeter since dawn.

She drew in the sterile, frozen air and went back inside. Carlos fell in behind her, quiet as a château mouse.

Rip Blackson stood with Brent Zola at the far end of the Great Hall, the chairs and tables having been pushed to one side. A circle of French police held the center space. Kasey Earl, the last Velox agent onsite, leaned against an oak beam, his eyes barely open.

Pia and her agents stood near a stone hallway that led to a cramped kitchen.

Deeper in the dark passageway, Daryl and Marthe held each other in a tight embrace like teenagers.

Pia studied Carlos. The man's eyes never stopped moving. They sized up each policeman in turn, then the Kovens, followed by the windows and doors and gloomier nooks. He repeated his visual rounds, always suspicious, always vigilant, as if he'd spent his life expecting death at any moment from any corner.

She knew that feeling. She also grew up under a constant threat, but she had an advantage Carlos could never have afforded: Sabel Security. Alan created it to make her feel safe after her parents' murders.

Two new men came in the main door. They stamped their feet, shook off their coats, and surveyed the room. The cadre of police in the center of the room straightened up and faced them. Marthe Koven nearly ran to the thin one. She spoke a flurry of French that escaped Pia's limited knowledge. The man nodded gravely without speaking, then looked over her head at the other officials. Marthe took him by the hand and led him there, bouncing on her toes. Then she waved her husband out of the dark shoals.

Pia watched Koven, a shadowy form in the murky corridor. He patted the pockets of his overcoat, pulled a fistful of something out, and dropped whatever it was on a serving table. Moving into the light, he met his wife and reached for her hand.

She introduced him to the Capitaine of the Gendarmerie in Metz.

The thin man nodded and turned away. With an abrupt statement and a wave of his hand, everyone scattered. The Capitaine crossed to Rip Blackson, pulled up a chair, and spoke to both Blackson and Zola in

English.

Pia slipped back a few steps and wandered with a bored gait toward the serving table. On it she saw three devices. One was a keychain with three buttons and a red light. The other two were rubber cylinders the diameter of her little finger.

Using only the tip of her fingernail, she tapped one of the keychain buttons. Its red light blinked and a corresponding light on one of the cylinders blinked. The cylinder swelled to the size of a golf ball, then deflated. She knew right away what they were for and how they'd been used. She pressed the buttons again and took a video of the resulting actions.

"What the hell do you think you're doing?" Marthe Koven asked.

Pia turned to her. "I found the most curious device. I think your husband used—"

"You have no right to take pictures here! For god's sake, this is not some reality TV show for spoiled rich girls. There's been a murder. I demand you delete all those pictures this minute."

Without looking at her phone, Pia clicked an app.

She closed the short distance between them, using her height to intimidate her hostess. "Why delete them? The Capitaine might find them interesting."

Marthe stomped a foot and spun away. She strode straight to the Capitaine and spoke to him.

He held up a finger to stop her, excused Blackson and Zola, and sent them to have their statements taken by separate detectives. He waved over Daryl and allowed Marthe to speak.

Marthe's voice was too low to hear, but her finger pointed at Pia. The Capitaine's disdainful gaze fell on her. He motioned for her to join them.

Pia took her time.

The Capitaine said, "Our investigation is not for you to interfere. You have taken photographs. Now you are to delete them."

Pia showed him her camera roll, selected the offending pictures, and deleted them. "Satisfied?"

Marthe rose to her full height and crossed her arms.

Pia paused a moment, looking at the Capitaine's aquiline nose and chin. She studied the same features on Marthe. "Such a strong resemblance. Are you related?"

"Enough of your impudence," Marthe said.

"Daughter of my cousin," Capitaine said at the same time.

Pia bowed and returned to her agents, where she remained in an unblinking staring contest with Marthe the whole time the Kovens spoke to the Capitaine.

When he handed them off to detectives for formal statements, he summoned Pia and Tania.

After a few pleasantries and general questions in fair English, he asked, "You heard gunfire and yet you enter the room?"

"Four years in the military police," Tania said. "I'm fully qualified to handle active shooter situations."

He nodded. "Mssr. Koven is not qualified, yet he subdued his attackers without your help."

"Wait, you believe his crap?" Tania nearly shouted.

"His story is consistent with the evidence. Do you have reasons to contradict his version of events?"

Tania bolted forward in her chair.

Pia grabbed her shoulder and pressed her back.

"Capitaine," Pia said, "I don't have your ballistics expertise. Could you tell me, if you are standing, and your adversary is standing, and you shoot him in the head, where would you expect to find the blood splatter?"

"If you are near a wall, on the wall. In the center of a round room, it may not spray far. There are involved many variables."

"Would you expect to find the blood on a chair, directly beneath the victim?"

"The victim is Tom Duncan."

"Would the bullet continue through the skull, more or less on its original trajectory?"

He raised an eyebrow. "Do you mind if I ask the questions?"

He finished his interrogation and sent them to the detectives for formal statements.

While giving hers, Pia noticed three attractive blondes, one in front of a video camera, interviewing Daryl Koven under an explosion of bright light. Marthe sat next to him, holding his hand. She heard him say, "They were deranged on drugs, shooting at me."

Near the door, Blackson and Zola bowed their heads together in a conspiratorial shadow.

When Pia finished giving her statement, she approached the duo.

They broke their conversation mid-syllable.

"Mr. Blackson," she said, "I'm leaving shortly. Do you need a ride back to London?"

The two men glanced at each other. Blackson shook his head. "I should stay and help here. We've cancelled the symposium and have to make arrangements for the guests."

"Please extend my condolences to your boss." She nodded at the interview. "He seems to be occupied with the most important aspects of Mr. Duncan's murder."

They watched Koven under the lights for a moment with what she surmised was either bewilderment or regret. Reading people in grief is difficult under any circumstance and she left her opinion of them open for the time being.

A glance at her buzzing phone told her Jacob was calling. She excused herself and took the call.

"Whooee, Hyde can drink," Jacob said. "A guy that drunk couldn't have made the Gottleib shot. That one was through the heart in the dark, tough to make in daylight if you're sober."

He reported on his day at DHK. "He might not be drunk all the time though. I think Hellman and Hyde were having a quickie in his office if the lipstick is any indicator."

"At their age?" Pia asked. "Never mind, love is ageless."

Pia updated him on what she'd seen and they clicked off.

As soon as the police released them, Pia led her group to the parking lot and climbed in the limousine. Tania rode with the driver, Carlos sat on the jump seat facing Alan and Pia.

They drove in silence into the sunless cold.

The limo swayed down the hill and through the village of Manderen before Alan spoke. "I can't believe Tom's gone."

"How rough is the lobbying business?" Pia asked.

"Heated debates and vicious emails, but until now it remained non-violent." He rubbed his chin. "Who would do such a thing?"

"Marthe Koven," Pia said.

Alan gave her a sharp look of disapproval. "Why would *she* do it at her husband's symposium? This was his moment to shine."

"I don't have that part figured out. But I know what happened in that tower."

"I heard your disagreement with the police. I'm sure you have theories." He held up a hand to stop her outburst before she began. "But think this through. There is no statute of limitations on murder. Take your time to check your facts. Let the killer weave his web of lies before you reveal the truth."

"What's my next step, then?"

"Learn more about their motivation." Alan thought for a moment. "Koven brought me three deals a while back. One of them was the Oman deal. One was a Saudi and the other was in Dresden, Lars Müller. Maybe he could shed some light on the firm's inner workings."

And there it was, advice from Dad—and it hadn't even hurt to ask. Maybe the big guy did know a few things. She allowed herself a smile.

Carlos looked at his phone. "A reporter for the *Post* is trying to reach you on Skype."

Pia nodded, reached out, and took his phone.

On the small screen, Emily Lunger's face was red. "How could you do this to me? I thought we were friends?"

"Of course we're friends—"

"The Three Blondes are breaking a murder story—and you don't call me?" Emily huffed. "*Hummingbird Online, FNC*, and the *Chronicle* are live-streaming from a castle in France. Are you telling me you don't know anything about a murder? 'Cause they're implying you did it."

Pia took a deep breath and brought up *Fuchs News Channel's* streaming site on her phone. A former Miss America, her forty-something face plastered with enough makeup to hide the smallest of wrinkles, prattled on about the bucolic region. A headline scroll at the bottom read, "...no suspects in custody. Two Velox Deployment

Services employees dead, a Washington attorney murdered at a French château..."

Holding a phone in each hand, Pia turned up the volume on the news. The reporter said, "Repeating the headline story, Daryl Koven, partner in the venerable Washington law firm, Duncan, Hyde and Koven, shot and killed two drug-crazed security guards after they killed his senior partner, Tom Duncan. A spokesman for the Gendarmes lauded Mr. Koven's courage in this horrific incident as 'beyond exceptional'. Sabel Security owner, Pia Sabel, a competitor to the dead security men, arrived on the scene shortly before the discovery of Mr. Duncan's murder. She fled abruptly after a heated argument with local police. She refused to make a statement. Our exclusive interview with the brave Daryl Koven will begin right after these important messages."

Pia closed the link and watched the branches of trees clawing at the low hanging clouds outside her window.

Emily tapped her screen. "Hello. Earth to Pia. If you have breaking news, I can fix it."

She looked at the reporter and blinked.

"Well?" Emily said. "Did you kill him?"

# CHAPTER 13

KOVEN INHALED THE clear, frozen country air and admired the blue skies opening above the château's curtain wall. The late afternoon sun delivered weak rays to his upturned face. It was all coming together. The Three Blondes had come through as promised; Tweets and Facebook memes hailed his heroism. A morning talk show scheduled an interview. The police inquiry had concluded for the day. His destiny lay within his grasp. He smiled, descended the steps, crossed the courtyard, and entered the Great Hall.

Marthe's voice floated in from the kitchen, instructing the staff on some detail or another.

Blackson and Zola huddled at a table. Their pale faces hung on slumped shoulders. A tired, defeated posture sure to introduce depression to his triumph.

Zola glanced up at him for a split second. What was in that look, disrespect? Did Zola know something? The boy had been talking to Pia Sabel before she left. Had she planted some ridiculous ideas in his impressionable mind? And was he now relaying those doubts to Blackson? He would have to keep them busy, off balance.

"Have all the arrangements been made?" His voice boomed across the room. "Are all the guests satisfied with their schedules? Do they understand the symposium will reconvene in two weeks?"

The young men muttered a response.

"What's that?" Koven asked as he strode toward them, stopping a few yards away. "Speak up."

"Sorry sir," Zola said. "Mr. Benning's wife is wigging out. His corporate jet went on to Dubai and won't return for two days. Warren Buffer wanted—"

"Did you call FlexJets or XOJets to get the Bennings home?"

Blackson and Zola stared at each other.

"Well?" Koven demanded.

Blackson rose and smoothed his rumpled suit. "To be honest, sir, we were taking a moment to reflect on Mr. Duncan's life and career."

Koven studied their red eyes and haggard faces. Neither man would look at him. "Seven billion people in this world and only a handful ever heard the man's name. The rest of them expect their lights to go on when they flip the switch. They don't expect us to sit on our butts, crying about the dead when there's work to be done. Your careers won't be marked by how you grieved over the loss of some old man long past his prime. You'll be judged by how hard you worked under the most difficult of circumstances. Now is not the time to wring your hands. Now is the time to prove our clients can rely on us."

Blackson turned his wide eyes to Zola. They said nothing.

Koven came closer. "I don't understand. What happened to those swaggering young men who blew through Tulane, drinking and carousing every night? Where are the boisterous boys who bragged and pushed each other from Basrah to Baghdad?"

Zola rubbed his face. "With all due respect, sir, one of those swaggering young men was shredded two days ago. Instead of hanging with his family we were here, working. And now Duncan. The strain is … we're trashed. I don't expect—"

"That reminds me," Koven stepped toe-to-toe with Blackson. "What were you doing in London?"

Blackson looked away. "Following up on some business between Mr. Sabel and Mr. Duncan, sir."

"What," Koven paused, "business was it?"

"A few details about their meetings."

"I'll be handling those meetings going forward. Fill me in."

"Um." Blackson flushed. "Mr. Duncan thought the Sabels, being in the security business, might know who killed David or why."

"And did they?"

"Ms. Sabel is not easy to work with."

"Did you fail to find out what they know?" Koven asked.

"They were preoccupied by some legislation that could hurt Sabel Security, sir."

"Who told them about the Mercenary Restrictions Act?"

"Jefferson Smith."

"That fucking loudmouth. I'll teach him who butters his bread." Koven turned to Zola. "Did you know about this?"

"No sir," Zola said. "I've been by your side since we met with the Three—"

"True enough." Koven paced to the middle of the room and back, biting his knuckle.

Blackson looked at Zola and patted his thighs.

"What is it?" Koven asked. "Am I tiring you? Go catch up with Paul Benning and charter a jet for him. Make sure he leaves town happy, damn it."

Blackson dipped his head, grabbed his overcoat, and strode out the door.

The moment the door closed behind him, Koven spun to face Zola. "What were you thinking? You haven't told him we talked to the Three Blondes, have you? You couldn't be that stupid."

Zola turned away.

"My god." Koven sat in the chair facing his junior partner. He took a deep breath as Zola raised his eyes.

"First Gottleib, now Duncan," Zola said. "Doesn't it hurt?"

Koven planted his feet, his hands on his knees. "What hurts me was seeing you flirting with the reporters like a schoolboy."

"Wha—?"

"Don't deny it. As soon as the camera went off, you jumped in there to reintroduce yourself. I saw you."

"Sir! I would never—"

"It's my own fault. I've treated you like an equal too often. It's natural for you to envy their interest in me." Koven rose. "Discipline in the ranks—the Marines taught me that. I've slipped. I never should have trusted you with so much. You weren't ready."

"Sir, I've followed you everywhere." Zola leaped to his feet, his hands spread wide. "I've done nothing disloyal. I only spoke to the news crew to make sure they knew how to get back. You know I still cover you the way I did in Nasiriyah."

"Times like these will test that loyalty, Brent." Koven stared hard. "Sometimes there are things that need to be done. Difficult things. Things that will keep the unit together."

"I understand that, sir."

"With Duncan gone, every firm in the city will go after our clients. If there is one whiff of impropriety or scandal, we're finished. We lose one client—we lose them all. And if we lose clients, we lose our livelihoods. You understand that."

Zola straightened. "Yes, sir."

"You've reconnected with your son, Philip, and you need—"

"Flip."

"What's that?" Koven asked.

"We call him, Flip, sir."

"Whatever. You need to put him through college soon. That takes big resources. Especially if you believe what the Three Blondes said about his future. That means we have to protect the firm."

"I will do that sir."

"What is the biggest threat to the firm at this moment, Brent?"

Zola thought for a moment before shaking his head.

"Rip Blackson," Koven said.

Zola stepped back. "Sir, he's no threat to—"

"Why was he in London?"

Zola shrugged. "Because Duncan sent him, like he said."

"Tom told me he gave Rip a couple days for David's funeral."

Zola gulped.

"That's right," Koven said. "Your good friend lied to you."

"I'll speak to him. I'll get this straightened—"

"Don't speak to him." Koven moved in and poked Zola with two fingers. "You already know he lied to you." Poke. "You can't trust him." Poke. "Look at his phone, read his emails, find out what he knows. If he's planning to take the Sabels to some other firm or start his own, we need to know that before he brings down holy hell on our heads."

Zola paled more. "He wouldn't do that."

"We have $20 million sitting on the Sabel books right now. If Sabel goes to another firm, what will any accountant ask about that $20 million?"

Zola shook his head. "He'd want to know how to categorize it."

"Where will that lead?" Koven watched his reaction closely. "Get your ass on Benning's jet and get back to Washington before Rip. Break into his house, read his emails, find his texts, get his backups. We need to know everything he knows about the Sabels."

"But I wouldn't do—"

"You have to. Your choice is between putting Philip through college—and Blackson. Where do your loyalties lie?"

"Yeah. Guess so." Zola tightened his face and nodded. He clenched his fists and hunched his shoulders. "OK, I'll see what I can do."

"Don't see what you can do. Make it happen."

Zola snapped a salute, turned away, and stuck one arm into his coat sleeve.

"Brent," Koven said, "you were the last one to speak to David before he died. What was on his mind?"

Zola stood still for a long time, his gaze glued to the far wall, his body turned partially away from his boss, his coat halfway on.

Koven remained as still as a statue as the seconds turned into a minute.

Zola finished putting on his coat. "One of his crazy conspiracy theories. I've heard so many of them I get lost."

"Our server logs everything the employees do. Gottleib downloaded five gigabytes that night."

"He worked too much." Zola pulled gloves from his pocket and put them on.

"They weren't client files. And he resigned."

Zola pursed his lips and threw up his hands. "He was talking about gibberish one of our Saudi clients funding Daesh. Maybe he thought he found a smoking gun. But why would we have it on our servers? I didn't believe—"

"Don't lie to me, Brent." Koven clenched his jaw.

"I swear. I didn't pay attention to his ramblings." Zola shoved his fists in his pockets. "Did you?"

For another minute, they stared at each other.

Koven broke the tension. "Turn off your phone. You don't want any interruptions. Then find out everything. As soon as the police finish their inquiry, maybe a couple days, I'll join you in Washington and we'll sit with Mrs. Gottleib, if it's not too late."

Zola nodded. Tears formed in his eyes. He turned quickly and left.

Marthe came in carrying a tray. She set it on the table and laid out two plates of sandwiches and two bowls of soup. She swept her hand over the arrangement, beckoning her husband to join her. "An early supper for a hard-working man."

"You're too good to me." He took his seat.

She clasped his hand as he smelled his steaming bowl of vegetable soup. "I eavesdropped. You don't mind, do you? You were wonderful. You handled those boys like the leader of the pack, the true senior partner."

He loved her praises, they salved the tension of the day and made him feel calm. He gave her a smile.

They ate in silence, looking into each other's eyes, the stone walls echoing every spoon clatter. When they finished, Marthe swept up the table setting.

She stopped as she was about to walk away. "That Sabel girl. She makes my skin crawl. I feel like she can see everything in my past, from Duncan's blood on my hands, all the way back to … my early days."

"There is nothing she can say that would tear me away from you."

Marthe glanced over her shoulder, winked, and returned to the kitchen.

Rip Blackson opened the front door. A swirl of snow followed his feet inside.

"The skies were clear and sunny just a few minutes ago," Koven said.

"It didn't last."

"Sit." Koven patted the chair in front of him. "We have important matters to discuss."

Blackson approached, looking for a trap. Tossing his overcoat on the table, he unbuttoned his jacket. "Brent's not answering his phone."

"We'll get to that. But first, we have to discuss the firm."

Blackson took a seat, his hands on his knees.

"William Hyde and I are the named partners, but you know how much we can rely on our good senator." Koven leaned forward. "Rip, this company means a lot to me. I'm not going to let it fall apart. I can't afford to."

"I'm sure you will do a fine—"

"The company supports a lot of people, good people, who count on us to do what needs to be done. And it's not just our co-workers and employees, Rip. Their husbands and wives, sons and daughters, all count on that paycheck to keep their lives intact." Koven smiled. "Is your wife working?"

"On her masters at Georgetown."

"And your daughter will start at Washington Episcopal in the fall?"

"I get your point."

"We can't let these tragic events threaten our firm," Koven said. "Now that you're a junior partner, you understand our precarious position. We have to guard the organization, not just from other lobbying firms poaching our clients, but from anyone planning to hurt our reputation."

"Sure, I understand how—"

"Our responsibilities dictate that we hold loyalty to the firm above relationships with friends and family. You and I must stick together, support each other, and be open and honest if we expect the firm to survive."

Rip Blackson met Koven's gaze.

Koven said, "Zola and Gottleib copied five gigabytes of files from our server the night David died. What were they planning?"

"That's not possible," Blackson said. "Brent would've told me if—"

Koven jumped to his feet. "You're working with them?"

"No, I meant that David and Brent are just as loyal to the firm as—"

"If he was so loyal, why did David resign?"

"Brent and I were shocked." Blackson stood. "Brent said he left without explaining anything, then he was killed."

"Wait, who told you about his resignation?" Koven asked.

"Brent."

"Were they together when they told you?"

"We met for dinner, but David walked out before I arrived."

Koven paced away, rubbing his chin. "So, it was just the two of them."

"Sir, I swear Brent Zola has no intention of—"

"Are you willing to bet your daughter's education? Are you willing to gamble with your wife's masters that Brent is not going to ruin the firm?"

Blackson looked at the floor and shook his head.

"You're no summer soldier," Koven said quietly. "You know what needs to be done in trying times."

"I'm not sure I follow you." Blackson met his gaze and squinted.

"The firm has clients, but one of them stands out as having both the biggest potential and the greatest liability, Sabel Industries. We need the Sabels. They are critical to our future." Koven squeezed Blackson's shoulder. "Brent admitted that he and David discovered Pia Sabel is now in control of the company."

Blackson shook his head, confused.

"They've been doing some deep research on their own. Without you. They were planning to stab our firm in the back, Rip. Planning to steal our clients."

"Why would they do that?"

"What would any lobbying firm give Zola if he could bring in Sabel Industries?"

Blackson reeled back on his heels.

"He could finish us," Koven said. "And he doesn't answer his phone. Why is that?"

# CHAPTER 14

FROM RIP BLACKSON'S darkened bedroom in McLean, Virginia, I drew back an inch of curtain and watched a lone driver get out of the car in the driveway. Breaking and entering was bad enough; getting caught in the act while the police were about to book me for murder would ratchet up the awkward factor a few notches. The figure in the driveway went to the mailbox.

Not good. Definitely not good.

Mercury stood by the book case with his hands open wide, looking incredulous. *What'd I tell you, dude? Did I say run for it?*

I said, *You told me to shoot out his headlights. That would've escalated things.*

Mercury said, *But you could've slipped out while he was ducking for cover.*

I said, *And evade the Fairfax County SWAT team and their two choppers? This is modern American suburbia, we're not dodging Hannibal's elephants in some Etruscan village.*

Mercury said, *Could've worked. Probably.*

I tiptoed down the carpeted stairs. My ninja outfit gave me a small advantage in the dark. My Glock was filled with hollow points which would be loud and lethal if fired. That kind of noise in this placid corner of Virginia would have ten neighbors calling 9-1-1 after the first shot. I checked my pouches for some nice, quiet, barely-effective Sabel Darts. The one time they might've been useful, I didn't have any. I rounded the hallway as the kitchen lit up like daylight.

With my back to the hall wall, half a step from the archway into the kitchen, I raised my weapon and waited.

The slap of letters landing on a granite counter top was followed by the whoosh of an opened refrigerator. The gatecrasher clinked bottles around and hesitated. I risked a peek around the corner and saw an averaged sized white man in a heavy coat with sandy hair, reading the label on a bottle of Rolling Rock. He tossed it in his hand while he thought, then put it back on the shelf. The refrigerator whooshed closed.

I snapped back from the archway.

There were more sounds of milling around. Then his footsteps approached my position in the hall. I slipped around a grandfather clock that was too skinny to hide my whole body. He walked past me, looking away to his left.

He flipped on the lights in the hall, completely illuminating me.

The hallway led to the living room, but he turned abruptly and went upstairs. For an instant, he faced the hallway where I was hiding behind the clock. I was obvious as hell. His upturned eyes were aimed at the second floor. I stood like a statue while he took the stairs quickly.

He stopped in midstride. I could still see his feet through the bannister. My black-clad form—an out-of-place shape in his subconscious—had reached his brain. I took two big steps, crossing the hall to a nook and tried to become invisible.

The trespasser retraced his steps. I sensed his eyes scanning the spot where I'd been standing. For two minutes he scrutinized the hall and living room from the bottom step.

"Is anyone there?" he asked.

Mercury said, *Answer him, dawg. Then shoot him.*

I said, *We can't just shoot everyone we come across.*

Mercury said, *Why not? Pia-Caesar-Sabel got you off for murdering Gottleib. When you have someone with her resources behind you, you can do anything I want.*

I said, *I didn't kill—urgh.*

I held my breath.

My adversary huffed and ran upstairs as if he were scared of the dark.

I followed him, my pistol leading the way. My heart rate soared. If the guy turned around, I was cooked. There was no way I would kill a guy to cover my crimes.

He reached the landing at the top and went into Blackson's home office. He didn't turn on the overhead light. He turned on a lamp next to a desktop computer. It was one of the funny looking ones that hardcore gamers use with a big screen. While it booted up, I moved to the door frame.

Mercury said, *If you're not going to shoot him, can we go now?*

I said, *No. He knows the house, he knows the computer, he can get me in.*

Mercury tossed up his hands in frustration. *C'mon man, he's dialing up online porn. You're not going to stand here and watch him pump his keg, are you?*

I said, *What?*

Mercury said, *He's going to tickle his pickle, wax his candle, shake his steak, whatever you horny mortals call it this century. No way I'm down for that, you perv.*

The screen came up and his first attempt at a password failed. That's when I noticed the grip of a handgun protruding from his waistband in back. The guy tried five more passwords before one worked. While the bootup process pinged, I slipped around the doorframe, into the room. Sensing my presence, he glanced right while I moved left. He returned his focus to the screen.

I checked out the bookcase next to me. A pyramid of tennis balls, a few framed photos, a few books on soccer, some history, law, and biographies. Gingerly, I lifted the top tennis ball.

My new friend leaned toward the screen and ran a search.

I pitched the ball to the staircase, where it bounced down with the right amount of thump.

He spun his chair, facing the open door, drew his weapon, and rose with theatric stealth. I stepped in behind him and tapped him on the shoulder.

When he turned around, I caught his outstretched arm and gun, put him in a headlock, cracked his elbow over my knee, pushed him forward, pounded my other knee into his kidney, and rode him to the floor, face down.

I secured his weapon and pushed the muzzle hard against his skull. The pistol looked familiar.

It took a moment before I realized whose gun it was.

Mine.

The missing Walther PP Ultra.

Mercury said, *Nice one. You've recovered the murder weapon and put your fingerprints all over it. Why not type up a confession to go with it?*

I said, *I'm wearing gloves.*

My captive gurgled some unintelligible words.

I loosened my headlock. "What was that?"

"Can't breathe." He struggled against my grip.

"That's OK," I said. "I can."

I drew an extra loud inhale to prove my point.

Rifling through his pockets, I found a business card for Brent Zola, Associate at Duncan, Hyde and Koven. I stood up.

"All right," I said. "Spread your arms and legs as wide as you can get them."

He complied.

I kicked him in the nuts as hard as I could.

He howled in pain.

I jumped on his back, pressing the Walther to his eye socket. "Quiet. I don't want you waking the neighbors. Breathe in, real deep, that's it." I paused. "Now exhale the pain. That's it. Nice and slow."

I gave him a minute to compose himself. "Sorry, I didn't bring any handcuffs. I wasn't expecting a cat burglar."

"I'm not a burglar. I'm house-sitting."

"Why six attempts to crack his password?"

"Uh…"

I smacked the back of his head. "Lying pisses me off."

"We work together."

"What kind of a coworker breaks into a guy's computer to run searches?"

"Somebody lifted files from the office. My boss wanted me to find out if Rip took them without accusing him. We're buds. That's why I have his keys. Please, get off me."

I relaxed but kept the Walther pressed to his back.

"Who the hell are you?" he asked.

"A guy with a gun aimed at the left atrium of your heart." I patted him down.

"What are you doing here?"

"Where did you get this gun?" I asked.

"My dad gave it to me when I was a kid."

I smacked the back of his head again. "What did I say about lying?"

"Why should I tell you anything?"

"Because you want to stay alive."

"You're not going to kill me. You would've done it already."

Mercury said, *Losing your alpha status pretty quick here, homeboy. Better make a run for it. You get locked up, I'm outta here. I'm looking for someone who can bring me ultra-wealthy followers, not jail-junkies. We leave them for the Christians.*

I said, *I can get cleared for the Gottleib murder. I found the gun.*

Mercury said, *How you planning to explain that? I broke into a house, found the killer—who doesn't actually live there but conveniently stopped by—and took my Walther off him? Hell, even I don't believe you.*

"You're right," I said. "I'm not the murdering type. But I'm not above blowing a hole through your thigh, calling the police, and letting you worm your way out of it with Blackson."

He squirmed under me. "You know whose house this is? Hold up. What are you doing here?"

"Looking for the guy who killed David Gottleib."

A car slowed in the street.

I stood and spread a space between the blinds.

Headlights lit up the front yard as the car pulled into the driveway.

"What is this, Grand Central Station?" I asked.

Mercury said, *Duck!*

I bent my knees and lowered my torso as Zola's fist swung over my head. He managed to yank off my balaclava.

Rising with a quick uppercut to his chin, I put him on the floor.

I pushed the muzzle between his teeth. "Get on your knees."

Struggling upright, his eyes opened wide. He tried to speak.

"Shut up," I said. "And don't twitch. I might fire by accident."

I kept the gun in his mouth while I checked the window. The car was pulling back out. They'd used the driveway as a turn-around. The car drove three houses down and parked on the far side. Two people got out and went in.

I breathed and turned back to Zola. I pulled the barrel out of his mouth and pressed it under his chin. "Tell me where you got the gun."

"You're Jacob Stearne."

I glanced at my hood lying on the floor. "Where did you get the—"

"Oh, I'm sorry, sir. I didn't know it was you. The gun? It was on my desk when I got back from France."

"When did you get back?"

"This morning. I tagged a ride with the Bennings on a charter."

"Who left the pistol on your desk?" I asked.

"I don't know."

"Do you know a guy named Shane Diabulus?"

"The head of Velox Deployment?" he asked. I nodded. "I've met him, but we're not friends."

"Is it normal in the lobbying community to find a pistol on your desk?"

"I thought it was sketchy, to be honest, Jacob."

I looked him over. "Have we met?"

"Yeah," he said as if I were kidding him. "Like. Nasiriyah, man. I was in—"

"The 3/2, Gory Platoon. What the hell, did the whole brigade muster out and settle in DC? I keep running into you guys all over the place."

"Glory, sir," he said. "Glory Platoon. Yes, David and some of his friends from Silver Spring joined up together. The lieutenant wanted to be a lobbyist and this is where it's done, so Rip and I followed him for the job. After you and Nasiriyah, some guys lost confidence in Lieutenant Koven. Not me. He promised us big things if we stuck by him. And he's made good on his—"

"That's Koven as in your firm?"

"Right. You remember him. Probably not in a nice way. But if you saw the news in the last couple days—"

"My boss was in the château. She says Koven murdered those guys in cold blood."

"No way. She's mistaken. He's a genius. He's the king of kingmakers. You know what they're saying about him? He's a brave man, a kind man, a man with plans. He took on two—"

"What are you, some kind of Koven worshipper?"

Mercury said, *Pay attention, homie. Zola's got what our relationship needs: a guy who can do what he's told and hold up his end. He's the kind who could spread a religion. Ya feel me? And what do I get from you? Nothing but disrespect and back talk.*

I said, *You want this whiny little punk? Someone set him up to take the fall for killing Gottleib and he doesn't even know it.*

Mercury said, *Any god would take a disciple over a delinquent.*

I pushed Zola away from me. "Where are Blackson's wife and kids?"

"At her parents until Rip gets back," he said. "Why are you looking for David's killer?"

"Self-preservation. The cops think I'm suffering from PTSD and soon to be the next rampage killer." I caught his gaze. "Did Blackson do it?"

"He was with me when David was killed."

"Who wanted Gottleib dead?"

Zola looked out the window and clammed up.

"Fine," I said.

I pointed at the computer. "Your search is done. Did you find what you're looking for?"

Zola hesitated, then pointed at the chair. I nodded, he sat and checked the "No items matched your search" response. He pointed at the keyboard.

"Go ahead, knock yourself out. I'd like to see what you find." I pulled up a chair and sat uncomfortably close, with my pistol uncomfortably nudging his ribs.

He ran another search that came up empty. Then another. He sat back to think before running his fourth.

"How come you weren't at David's funeral?" I asked.

"The Symposium was in progress, guests were arriving." He grimaced. Then he leaned forward and typed in another search.

"I met three guys there who seemed to know David pretty well," I said. "They're really upset that he's dead."

Zola's typing stopped then restarted. "One each, fat, skinny, and medium?"

"You know them?"

"They were in our unit." Zola finished typing in another search and let it run. "You know how you stay friends with your high school buddies, even when you should move on?"

"You, Blackson, and Gottleib went to law school while the three musketeers sweep up at the Shalom Kosher Market?"

Zola gave me a once-over. "Yeah. They weren't exactly his intellectual peers."

"Then why did he turn to them—instead of you—when he needed help?"

His face turned white when he twisted around to face me. "We had a disagreement."

"About?"

Over his shoulder the search window started compiling a long list of files. He was still staring at me when my forearm brought my full bodyweight crashing into the bridge of his nose. Zola flew out of the chair, onto the floor. I watched his feet twitch, signaling a solid Grade III concussion. I checked my watch. If he didn't come to in five minutes, I'd call an ambulance. Until then, the data was mine.

I pulled up the browser, logged into my cloud app and copied all the files from the search. While the system uploaded, I checked his search term: Gottleib liability.

Huh.

Headlights swept the window again. This time they stayed in the driveway.

The file transfer showed 83%.

A car door slammed. I risked a peek out the window. A tall, lanky African American walked up the driveway and kicked Zola's car. A few seconds later, the kitchen door opened. The file transfer read 91%.

I called our company tech support.

Bianca Dominguez answered. "Jacob, what do you need?"

"BRENT!" Blackson's voice shook the house from downstairs.

"What the fuck, man?"

Next to me, Zola stirred. Blackson's voice receded into the ground floor labyrinth.

"Jacob?" Bianca asked.

I whispered, "Can you clear a browser history from headquarters?"

"Sure. Yours or a friend?"

"Don't ask."

Blackson's voice reverberated from downstairs. "Brent, goddammit, what the hell are you doing in my house?"

From the hitch in her breathing, I could tell Bianca heard the background noise and understood the situation. "Open a browser and login to our tech support site."

I did and a second later, she took control of the computer. "Make it look like I was never here. Gotta go."

I clicked off.

"BRENT ZOLA!" Blackson's blood pressure was rising with his volume. "Come out and face me like a man."

Zola rolled over and puked. He rose to his hands and knees. From my briefing on concussions, he would be confused about what city he was in for several minutes.

Blackson bounded up the stairs.

I grabbed my balaclava, both my guns, and moved behind the door. The screen flickered as Bianca closed several search windows, cleared the 'recent' menus, and wiped the browser history.

She wasn't quite done when Blackson stormed into the room. He saw his computer being remotely shut down. He saw Zola on his hands and knees.

I slipped into the hallway.

Judging from the sound of it, Blackson's foot slammed into Zola's ribs.

"What the hell did you do?" Kick. "Who are you working for?" Kick. "What the hell is going on?" Kick.

One silent step at a time, I made my way down the stairs, trying not to creak a single tread.

Mercury said, *Homie, you're leaving them behind? You let him slide on the most important question.*

I said, *I want to get out of here before he calls the cops. Don't want to get caught with the murder weapon.*

Mercury said, *Too late. Blackson called the cops from the driveway.*

I said, *Great time to mention it. What's the most important question?*

Mercury said, *Zola admitted he had a disagreement with Gottleib. What was the argument?*

A car pulled up outside as I slipped into the kitchen. I stopped and listened. From outside came the squawk of a police radio, followed by two doors slamming. Street-side was no longer an option.

Mercury stood at the kitchen counter pointing at a newspaper. *Well lookie here, home boy. You're on the front page. Below the fold, but still.*

I glanced where he pointed. In a picture taken in front of the National Cathedral, Dr. Harrison grinned like Alice's cat. The headline read, MY PATIENT SPEAKS TO GOD.

Mercury said, *Finally! We're in! Hooboy! Hittin' the big time, bro! They'll build me a temple that'll make the Parthenon look like a doghouse. They're going to believe him, right? I mean. He went to Harvard.*

I said, *Anyone who talks to a psychiatrist is crazy.*

Mercury and I squinted at each other as we processed the implication.

A cop outside rapped a knuckle on the kitchen door. Upstairs, Blackson ran out of enthusiasm for kicking his friend. The entire neighborhood was dead quiet.

That's when my phone rang.

# CHAPTER 15

THE PASTORAL WINTER landscape of rural Germany slurred past the limo's window as Pia pressed her phone to her ear, listening to Jacob's phone ring. "Damn it. He never takes my calls."

She reached for the END button, heard his voice, and returned the phone to her ear. She heard heavy breathing and odd rhythmic pounding.

"Jacob, are you OK?" she asked. "You sound winded."

"Can I call you back?" Jacob asked. "Oof."

"What was that?"

"Had to jump a fence," he said. "Cops are chasing me."

"Did you talk to Rip Blackson?"

"He wasn't—ow—home, so I found a window and took a look around his place."

"You weren't supposed to break in! You were supposed to wait for him. We don't do things like that."

"An opportunity presented itself and I pressed it immediately," he said.

It was a quote from Pia's soccer career regarding a legendary goal she scored from the halfway line. She'd used it to energize her employees in many company emails, but Jacob had a bad habit of tossing it back at her when he was up to no good.

"Why are you whispering?" she asked.

"I'm trying to hide in some bushes. With all due respect, Ms. Sabel— I gotta go."

He clicked off.

Pia stared at her phone and repressed her rising anger with a long, deep inhale. Her father sat next to her, Carlos in front of her. Tania rode with the driver.

Alan Sabel looked up from working emails on his phone. He glanced over his reading glasses at Carlos, then Pia. "You should work with Jonelle on employee choices. Some of your—"

"Thanks, Dad."

They stared out the windows at the Dresden Heath, over twenty square miles of forest preserve on the outskirts of the city, a hundred miles south of Berlin.

After a few kilometers, Pia sighed. "Dad, I want to know why a Prince in Oman is trying to give me $20 million, how is meeting Lars Müller going to help me?"

Alan dropped his phone in his pocket and turned to her. "About a year ago, Daryl Koven came to me with three business deals. A Saudi named Suliman who I just didn't like at all. Prince Taimur from Oman, who I referred to your people. And Lars Müller who had a deal for Sabel Tech. But Müller's was a lopsided deal, so I passed on it. Like the Oman deal, Müller was prepared to pay an extra $20 million in undesignated funds. Businessmen don't give each other millions just for fun. It was a red flag for me."

"What do you mean, lopsided?"

Alan smiled. "Both sides should have something to gain in a deal. For example, I tell an Arab dictator I'm going to deploy Internet access via satellite. Free speech and Internet access is the last thing any dictator wants, so he hires Sabel Security if I promise not to deploy satellites over his country. A classic win-win."

Pia curled her nose. "I'm not comfortable with—"

"And that's what everyone is worried about, Pia. Deals like that are how you create jobs and bring new opportunities for your employees. An idealist would deploy the satellites and free the people from oppression. But that didn't work out for Tunisia, Libya, or Syria. Those countries melted down into tribal warfare. The survivors can't afford satellite access, they don't have freedom, and they're constantly killing each other. Idealism is only good on paper."

"I'm not supporting dictators, no matter what." Pia pursed her lips. "What do you think the $20 million is for?"

"I don't know." Alan lifted his chin and turned to the window. "That why we're going to see Müller. He's proposed another deal. I'm not going to listen to his new proposal until he tells us about the $20 million. Once we know that, we'll have an idea about what Oman wants."

"The Major said DHK even refused our wire refund."

"Then give it to him in cash at the symposium." Alan smirked.

Pia shook her head. "You're not going back, are you?"

Alan pulled his phone, clicked a few icons, then held it out for her to read. "Half the Fortune 100 CEOs are going to be there. If you don't go to the party, all the security deals will go to Velox."

"They rescheduled it already?" She pulled her phone and scrolled through her emails. "Looks like he invited me separately from you. And I all but accused him of murdering the Velox guards."

"Business relationships have nothing to do with being friends. You work with your worst enemies if you can make money."

She tried not to look as sick as she felt about that statement and clicked a link on her phone. "I see Senator Smith has accepted an invitation as well."

Pia turned to the window. The limo sped down Radeberger Landstrasse through the center of the forest. Trees grew in neat re-forestation rows, snow clinging to their naked branches.

The sameness of it bored her.

"Carlos, do you believe in destiny?" Pia asked.

He studied her while the car swayed through gentle curves, and held her gaze for a long time.

"You know I do, *chica*," he said. "Until I joined Sabel, I always felt like a drowning man under a sheet of ice fighting for a pocket of air. But my son, he's different. I can feel his destiny in my heart." He turned to the window. "My boy grew up in South Central, looking across the freeway at the big university. He set his mind on leaving the barrio and everything I did."

They made a left off the main road, heading for Müller's country estate in Schönborn.

"I like how you watch everyone, Carlos. But why do you keep an eye on Dad and Tania as if they might try to hurt me?" Pia asked.

"Where I come from, your brotha, cousin, mama, anyone can turn on you and—bang bang." He illustrated with two fingers.

Alan winced. Pia rolled her hand for him to keep going.

"You're like medieval royalty," Carlos said. "They never named their successor because when they did—bang bang ... from a cousin, a brotha, mama."

Alan frowned. "How do you live with that level of paranoia all the time?"

"It's what keeps you alive, mister. Watch everything. Like the car that's been following us since we entered the heath."

Pia grabbed Alan's shoulder before he turned around to look. "Carlos has it handled, Dad."

She looked at her bulldog. "Are they a threat?"

"They're looking to box us."

"Box us?" Alan asked.

"A gangbanger trick," Pia said. "One car stops in front of you, the other in back, and—bang bang."

Pia pressed the intercom and gave the driver instructions.

The driver sped through the small town, making several turns, before squeezing them between cream-colored houses and backing into a tight space. The driver cleared the privacy glass, opening Pia's view through the windshield. As soon as they stopped, Carlos jumped out and disappeared between buildings.

Tania switched places, taking the jump seat in back. "What the hell? Carlos is running away? You want me to shoot him for desertion?"

"Trust your people." Pia checked the Glock 33 in her holster.

"He's not my people," Tania said.

Alan observed the women. "For what it's worth, Tania, I think the guy is a bad idea too."

A gray Opel Astra sped by. The limo driver waited a beat, then turned into the lane and followed. It took the other car two blocks to realize they'd been tricked. The Opel sped up, taking two quick turns at the edge of town. When the car made its third turn, the driver stood on the brakes and ground to a halt.

Pia pointed over Tania's shoulder to where Carlos stood in the road, a smoking pistol in his hand. "We boxed them."

The women leaped out and ran wide from the cars, aiming at the Opel's occupants.

"You sure about these guys?" Pia asked. "I'd hate to draw on innocent locals."

"Look in the back seat—but be quick," Carlos said. "Their pals will be here in two minutes when we don't show at the ambush site."

Pia approached the passenger side while Tania took the driver. When she reached the rear axle, she peered through a layer of winter grime on the window. Two assault rifles stood upright in a ready-to-grab frame.

She tapped her muzzle against the glass.

The occupants, hands up and facing Carlos, waited for his nod before getting out. Pia and Tania pressed their Glocks to the men and forced them up against the car. Carlos patted them down, tossing knives and ankle revolvers out as he went.

Pia grabbed the passenger's head and smacked it against the car. "Who do you work for? What do you want?"

She brought his face around for an answer. He said nothing. She smashed him again.

"Take their gear," Pia said, "plasticuff their ankles. We'll leave them here."

"*Halten*," the man said with a French accent. "Ehm, stop."

"Why?" Tania asked. "So your buddies can gun us down?"

"No. I swear to you."

Pia nodded for him to keep talking.

"We were instructed to suspend your travel," he said. "An important person wants you delayed."

Pia nodded to Carlos. "You grab their weapons, we'll cuff them."

Alan came up behind her. "We've seen these men."

Pia turned the man around, the barrel of her weapon pressing his jaw high. "Where?"

"They were at the château," Alan said. "They were in uniform."

"Nice catch, Dad." Pia turned to her victim. "Where were you supposed to box us in?"

The man shrugged.

"Who's in charge of this operation?"

The man's eyes fell, his shoulders slumped.

Pia pushed him back to his car after grabbing his phone. She scrolled through the recent call lists, finding only numbers. Under contacts there was one entry, "LOCI," and a number. She took it with her.

Carlos stood at the open door.

"You ride with them," Pia said. "They'll follow us to the ambush. You make sure they flash their headlights to let us know in advance. Do you have bullets or darts?"

"Both," Carlos said. "Ever since London, *chica*."

"As soon as we stop, dart them."

Carlos pulled a magazine from his pocket, checked to make sure they were darts, and swapped it out. Moments later, their makeshift caravan was back on the road.

Pia stared out the window, her nose to the glass, her fists clenched. "Dad, could this be Müller's idea of a welcoming committee?"

"Could be," Alan said. "He does a lot of business with the Russians. But Metz is a long way to go for muscle. Seems unlikely."

"Who else knew about this meeting?"

"I called DHK in Washington to set it up. Outside of them, no one."

The driver ambled the big car through the outskirts of Langebrück. He turned on a lonely *strasse* and wound through open fields. Over the crest of a rise, a delivery truck filled the center of the road with a hazard triangle beside it. Behind them, the Opel flashed its lights and slowed.

Pia's driver nosed in close.

A man came from the front waving one hand in the air, a poorly hidden assault rifle behind his back.

Tania rolled out the left door and Pia, the right.

She rolled to the shoulder, found a man hiding behind a tree, and darted him. From the sound on the other side of the car, she guessed Tania had been equally successful. She rose to her knees to find Tania and the truck driver in a stand-off. Pia fired a dart. The driver fell.

They swept the area and found no one else. The truck's cab was empty. She checked under and around, then rolled up the door of the cargo bay.

Inside was a man tied to a chair, a gaping hole in his forehead.

Alan's footsteps approached.

She jumped when he put his hands on her shoulders.

He wrapped her in a hug. "That was Lars Müller, of the private equity firm Müller Gruppe."

# CHAPTER 16

RAIN FELL ON the snow-covered streets below Daryl Koven's office window as he inhaled the aromatic coffee wafting from his mug. Rain this late in the day would turn to black ice by rush hour, making the trip home a nightmare. A light knock at his door turned his attention to Senator Bill Hyde, who stood, like a scolded schoolboy, halfway in.

"Bill, come in," Koven said, opening his arms in welcome. "You are a rock in these tragic days. Thank you for holding down the fort."

Koven stepped around his desk and motioned for the hesitant senator to join him at the small conference table. He reached out, shook his partner's hand, and stopped, peering into the older man's eyes. "Bill, have you been drinking?"

Bill Hyde pulled his hand away and tossed a thick folder on the table. "I'm fine."

"We've discussed this too many times." Koven searched the man's watery eyes.

"You wanted to rework the arrangements Tom and I put in place only a week ago." Hyde sat and butted the papers on the table. "Let's get to it."

Koven paused before taking a chair opposite him. He stroked his chin. "There is a morality clause—"

"Which is determined solely by Tom Duncan. While the bylaws turn over his votes to you in the event of his untimely death, the directions do not distribute those particular duties. After watching you insert yourself into our clients' business dealings, we had concerns you might not value certain elements of the partnership."

"Is that right." Koven watched Hyde's bulbous nose grow redder. "Well, to the heart of the matter. I want Brent Zola and Rip Blackson to swap roles."

"Why?"

"I am relying on your sober and considered confidentiality, Bill. This is a sensitive issue. I have reason to believe one or both of them were working with the Velox men before the murder. I know Zola inside and out. I can read him like a book and would like to have him managing the day-to-day operations."

"Rip is the stronger personality and has been groomed for management." Hyde met his gaze. "What would either of them stand to gain from killing Tom?"

"I have yet to determine a motive, but you'll have to trust me for now."

"Trusting you is not in my nature." Hyde slapped the stack of papers on the table. "You stole my clients while I was out of the office. You're siphoning off millions for those odd social welfare groups you run. No, I'll trust Rip Blackson. Since there are currently only two of us, as the bylaws dictate, there will be no changes in the management of the firm."

Hyde leaned back.

"So good of you to bring the bylaws," Koven said. "If you'll be good enough to check Section VII, Article 4, you'll recall that, on a day when your thoughts were clearer, we amended the rules and appointed Brent Zola the tie breaker. Should I call him in for a vote? Or can we do this informally?"

The older man sat motionless for a moment until his hand began to tremble. "He can't vote on an issue like that. Certainly he would recuse himself."

Koven tilted his head. "You should've retired ten years ago. Now you're just a washed up alcoholic no one trusts and I'm stuck with you because some drug addict killed Tom."

"My name took Tom Duncan from a smalltime lobbyist for chewing gum companies to an internationally respected powerhouse. This is my company. You can't steal it out from under me. I built this place with my reputation—"

"Then where are all your clients?" Koven's voice boomed. "Did you bring in Sabel Industries? I had to rescue Müller Gruppe and Oman while you were on 'vacation'. What about Esson Oil or the Sulimans?"

"I'm not the first guy to self-destruct." Hyde looked at the floor. "You'll do it too, everyone does. But I've recovered. Katy Hellman and Fuchs News stayed loyal to me. The others will come back."

"*FNC, Hummingbird, the Chronicle.* Jesus, her biggest division is a newspaper. Are they even relevant anymore? They're nothing but the last thread of your generation's baby blanket. If it doesn't have a video feed, it doesn't matter." Koven lowered his volume. "Are we agreed then? Zola runs operations."

Hyde took a long, slow breath and sighed without looking up. "Can you at least wait until after the memorial service?"

"Fine. Is there anything else you need?"

Hyde shook his head, gathered his folder, and rose.

Koven watched him begin his slow trek to the door. "By the way, those bylaws are online. We could've had this discussion over the phone."

Hyde glanced halfway over his shoulder as he left.

Brent Zola waited in the hallway, observing Hyde's exit with a hint of empathy. Koven waved the young man in. Zola closed the door behind him.

"What happened to you?" Koven asked.

"Rip returned earlier than I expected. He caught me hacking his computer and got pissed."

"I'd have put money on you in a fight."

"Well," Zola hesitated. "Jacob Stearne was there before either of us and—"

"Jacob Stearne broke into Rip's house? Is he in custody?"

"The cops couldn't find him and bailed on the search."

"You failed." Koven paced his office. "I should've hired Sabel Security to check out Blackson, for Christ's sake. What was he doing there? What did he find?"

"I don't know sir."

"You mean he jumped you? Damn it." Koven slammed a fist on his desk. "What kind of questions did he ask?"

"He wants to know who smoked David and why."

"The question everyone wants to know." Koven reflected for a slow minute then jabbed a finger at a chair, ordering Zola to sit. "You were his friend; who were his enemies?"

Zola took a seat at the oversized oak desk and picked at his fingernails. "He never said anything—"

"Don't give me that. You already told me he was on about conspiracy theories. What are you holding back? Was it something about Suliman? Was it a racist remark made to Rip?"

"No. We've been friends like forever."

"Then why did he resign? C'mon, Brent, I have a right to know. I cared about him almost as much as I care about you."

He could feel Zola holding back on something big. Feel it in his bones. If Gottleib had a problem, Brent would have been the first to know about it. Why would the smug bastard hold back? Did Zola blame him for Gottleib's murder? Or did he figure something out about Duncan? Koven kept staring at his protégé.

Zola sighed and twisted toward the window. "He worried that chasing the Sabel account would lead to... well, questions about how we do business."

"Everything we do is perfectly legal."

"That's what I said." Zola's eyes wandered left and right. "But David thinks some people might characterize deals like Oman as unethical."

"That's bullshit." Koven turned his chair to the window and stared for a long time. "Perfectly legal."

"I'm just telling you what he thought."

He faced Zola. "And what do you think?"

Zola's mouth opened and shut twice before any words came out. "I think your work is epic, sir. You've worked hard and earned everyone's respect. Especially after the Three Blondes came through like they said they would."

"That won't last long." Koven planted his elbows on his desk and clasped his hands. "Have you read what Velox is saying? Velox men are drug-tested. Velox men are vetted by the highest standards. Something else must have happened." Koven chuckled. "They even made a dig at Jacob Stearne—they said their men are mentally stable."

Zola chuckled through his frayed nerves. "They're a little tripped out by you right now, after those interviews. Mr. Hyde knows Shane Diabulus pretty well. Maybe we should have him chill things with them."

Koven scratched his chin. "I'll email him, have him set up a meeting."

He saw Zola glance at his watch. "Am I keeping you?"

"Oh, no, sir. It's just that I have that flight to LA in a few. The Esson Oil meeting in the morning. I should get going. Probably."

"Esson Oil. I forgot. Be sure to mention Hyde's been drinking again." Koven nodded. "Will you see Philip while you're out there?"

"Flip, sir. Yes. I thought I'd have dinner with him tonight." Zola squirmed in his chair. "If that's OK."

"Do you worry about Sabel questioning how we do business?" Koven asked.

"No, sir. You have it handled."

"Thank you, Brent." Koven tilted back in his chair and regarded him. "Go on, have a safe flight."

As Zola reached the office door, Marthe Koven entered, gave him a hug, and exchanged pleasantries.

Koven watched his wife. She had an elegance that he could never mimic. He came across as too cold and analytical for people to trust. She smoothed over his rough places. People liked him because they liked her. She was the half of him that had always been missing.

"You'll be back for Tom's service?" she asked Zola, gripping both his arms. "We're doing a jazz funeral because he was from New Orleans and he died too young. Lots of fun and music to celebrate his life. We'll have a feast afterward at our house."

Zola gave her a grim smile and a nod and left.

Marthe swirled into the chair before her husband's desk.

"Why so glum?" she asked as he stared out the window. "I've handled all the hard work. I found the perfect castle in Germany for the Symposium. I've put together a funeral for a man who has no friends or family to do it for him. I've even ordered your secretarial staff to send out all the invitations and handle the responses. And here you are, looking morose on an already dreary day."

That was Marthe, taking care of everything again. He rose, came around the desk, and parked his butt on it, melting under her gaze.

"Where would I be without you, my dear?" He took her hands in his. "You've done so many things for us both. But I still have too many things on my mind." He threw his head back. "Oh, god, it's so hard worrying an employee might figure something out. Zola used to be the loyal one. Once he stepped in front of a mad soldier and saved my life. But now he scares me."

"Why, what has he done?"

"He's been talking to that Sabel agent, Jacob. They've put ideas in his head, I'm sure of it. He said he was going to California. And I know why. He's putting distance between us before he calls the Gendarmes and tells them everything."

"He looked perfectly happy to me."

Koven rocked from side to side. "Maybe. I don't know. I doubt everything people tell me now."

"Don't let your doubts about pawns like Brent hold you back." She stood and wrapped her arms around him. "We've reached our dream. You're the respected senior partner. If we can't be happy about that, what's the point?"

"The Three Blondes told him his son would take over the firm. Hyde has no children. We have no children. Can you imagine, leaving all this for Zola's bastard son?"

"We can still have children," she said.

"Do the math. If we have a son tomorrow, I'll be as old as Hyde when he graduates law school."

Marthe sighed.

"Don't underestimate Zola," Koven said. "He started life as a surfer, but his mind never stops working. He might back me up in gray areas, but when it comes right down to it, his survival instinct will conquer his loyalties. He'll convince himself Pia Sabel's unfounded accusations are true, then he'll choose what he thinks is the noble path. He'll turn on me the way Mark Antony turned on Augustus."

"We're past that point." She pressed her face to his chest. "No one listened to her anyway. No one cares about the rantings of some rich girl.

Put all those thoughts behind you. What's done is done."

"It should've ended in France, but we're not out of danger yet. I'm living in fear of every jerk who asks questions. I see deserters in every face. Jacob Stearne was in Blackson's house last night, looking for god knows what. Jesus, I envy Duncan now. We thought taking him out would bring us happiness, but he's the one who's resting."

"Relax." She leaned back while still holding him. "Your paranoia is the only thing that can give you away. Even if you have to fake it, put on a smile and spread happiness."

"You're right." He snickered. "You did the right thing with Brent. You were sweet to him. Keep that up even if I don't. He's dangerous to us."

He pulled out of her arms and paced away, his face turning dark. He clenched and released his fists and came back toward her.

Marthe stepped out of his path and frowned. "What's the matter?"

"Ugh." Koven turned away and grabbed his head with both hands. "My skin is crawling. I feel like an addict in withdrawal. I'm afraid we'll be discovered. Zola is the most likely to figure out what we've done. Damn it. And I promoted him today. I insisted he swap roles with Blackson to 'keep my enemies closer' and now—it was a terrible mistake."

"I'm sure it will end soon."

He shook a finger at her. "You're right, I should just end it."

Marthe stepped back. "What are you thinking?"

"Don't look so surprised, my dear. You came up with this idea. Did you think it would end in one night? One thing always leads to another. You can't just kill a man without being prepared to kill anyone who might turn against you. To keep a secret, we have to be committed."

Koven crossed to Marthe and kissed her on the forehead.

"You're right," she said. "We're committed to this—together."

He wrapped his arms around her, absorbing her shudder before she left.

Koven sat at his desk and thought through his next move. He knew very little about Jago Seyton aside from the office gossip about his past. The little guy gave Koven the creeps, that was for sure. If the rumors were halfway true, Jago was the perfect man for the job. He summoned the man by intercom.

The short man with no neck took a seat in front of the new senior partner. His face showed no emotion, neither a smile nor a frown. Exactly the emotion Koven expected of the man. He never knew where Jago stood or who he favored. He wasn't even sure who the man worked for.

"Jago, in times of transition, many employees have questions or concerns about their future."

Jago held his gaze but said nothing.

Koven leaned back. "You've been here longer than I have. I want to assure you: your position will not change. You're a key employee. I'm sure you value the firm as much as I do. Especially given your, ehm, situation."

Jago didn't move.

"When I brought my people in a few years ago, I had no idea they would make life so hard for you. It's recently come to my attention that Brent Zola was the primary instigator of all the rumors against you. Believe me, had I known, I would've put an end to it. He misled you and thwarted your promotion. Just a few minutes ago, he suggested we get rid of you."

Jago stiffened, his face still blank, his mouth still closed.

"I know that's hard to take on top of every manner of disrespect he's shown you." Koven spread his hands wide. "It's my fault, really. I've given Brent and Rip too much freedom. And you've quietly taken their abuse. I appreciate your patience. Tom explained his theories of redemption, that any man, given a good chance, would rise above the mistakes of his past. I guess Zola and Blackson never bought into that philosophy."

"What are you going to do?" Jago asked.

"I'm going to give you permission," Koven said. "Indulgence might be a better word."

Jago canted his head while holding Koven's gaze.

"Duncan's conditions for your continued employment were static, intractable. I'm opening the door for you. You've been insulted, kicked downstairs, and pushed around too long for any man to take. And yet, you've been forgiving and patient. I don't expect you to take it any longer. You've pent up that anger long enough. You have permission to unleash your rage."

Jago nodded slowly. "What did Brent do to you?"

"We're no different, you and I." Koven considered his brooding employee. "We do those things that need to be done. But there are others who think they're superior. When we were children on playgrounds, they were the ones who used words like 'fairness' and 'cheater' as if they were the anointed enforcers of some universal judicial system." Koven leaned back. "Brent has reached a position in life where he believes Daryl Koven and Jago Seyton are equals—beneath him."

Jago thought about his statement. "I do this thing, maybe a permanent thing, what happens next?"

"Freedom. You're free to take any position in the firm you desire, as long as you're qualified."

"Where is he?"

"He just caught a flight to LA."

"Out of state. Perfect." Jago stood up and extended his hand. "I'm sick of your boys kicking me around. I'll take care of this for you."

Koven leaned across the desk.

He shook Jago's hand and held it. "He has a son."

# CHAPTER 17

I TURNED UP the collar of my black leather duster and tugged down my watch cap against the frigid wind moaning its way between office buildings. Streets of ice, littered with abandoned cars, framed the snaking lines of bundled workers queuing for the Metro's Farragut West escalator. The multitudes kept their noses down and their tempers in check.

Rip Blackson pushed the edges of courtesy as he squeezed between people and made better progress for it. I stayed back far enough to avoid being recognized.

A fat lady fell and sprawled on the sidewalk like a spider. Even though I was wearing body armor, which doesn't lend itself to bending over, I did the standard Midwestern thing and helped her up, brushed her off, handed her bag back to her.

Blackson was gone.

Mercury waved from the top of a lamppost, his toga flapping in the icy breeze, and pointed down.

I wasn't sure I should believe him. I felt dumb enough after letting him badger me into wearing body armor. Sometimes you listen to a god just to make him shut up.

I pushed beyond courtesy to catch up, leaving a few heys and watchitbuddys in my wake. From the top of the elevator, I could see the tall, lanky Blackson exit at the bottom and turn for the Silver Line. The famously clean Metro system was well lit and the masses moved easily through the gates. I caught up in no time.

On the platform, I waited until the doors were about to close before pushing my way into the same car as Blackson. The crowded space smelled of wet wool and sweat and disengaged people heading home from a job they didn't love in weather they loved less.

Mercury slid in and blocked my view of a beautiful young lady.

I said, *I was going to ask her out.*

Mercury glanced over his shoulder. *Outta your league, dude. She's never going to date a guy who has his ringtone set to calliope. Tell me you turned that stupid ringer off.*

I rolled my eyes—and reached into my pocket to flip the switch to vibrate.

Done.

There was something strange about him that caught my eye: the wings on his helmet were moving.

Mercury said, *Don't be looking at my wings, dawg.*

I said, *They work? You can fly?*

Mercury said, *Do I ask you if your penis thinks? There are some things we just don't talk about.*

I said, *You mean you're horny?*

Mercury looked at me as if he'd found a nine-week-old tomato in the back of the veggie drawer. *When they flap like that, it means something bad is going down. Incoming messages from the Dii Consentes cuz I'm an important god. ...Horny? Shee-yit.*

The pretty woman behind him rolled her eyes and turned her back on me.

Bianca texted me updates on Blackson's data files. Many emails contained both the words Gottleib and liability, but not in any proximity or identifiable context. There were also documents and position papers that Gottleib co-authored that contained the word *liability*. It was too broad a search, but Zola had been looking for something. Whatever it was had yet to jump out at her.

Blackson got out at the McLean stop. I followed him down Dolley Madison Boulevard to a dogleg that led us to Chain Bridge Road. Blackson's home was another mile or so down.

The rush of workers returning home thinned the closer we got to the Dulles Toll Road underpass.

Blackson heard my footsteps echo in the winter quiet and stopped under the span of highway, where a single light illuminated a ten-foot stretch of sidewalk. He turned around.

We were alone.

He asked, "Are you following me?"

I stopped in a shadow thirty feet back. "Yes."

"Why?"

"I wanted to see if Zola got in a counter-punch."

"Do I know you?" he asked.

"Depends. Were you one of the thousand guys I met this week from the 3/2?"

Blackson didn't answer.

I continued forward into his cone of light. From the look on his face, he recognized me, but he didn't say anything.

"The cops think I'm a rampage killer who started with Gottleib. Why don't they think you and Zola did it, then alibied each other?"

"Hang on there, Stearne. We loved that guy." Blackson took a step back. "We were friends."

"Then why did Zola have the murder weapon on him?" I asked.

"He couldn't have. He would never..." Blackson frowned. "Did the cops arrest him when you turned it in?"

Since I'd stashed the Walther at Sabel Gardens, his question could only end badly for me. It was time to act like a politician and change the subject. "What other facts did Zola hide from you?"

Blackson wavered.

I liked having him off balance. I asked, "Why was Zola ripping up your place?"

"Then you really were there?"

"You don't believe your friends?" I asked.

"Not when I catch him rifling through my shit."

"Why was he searching your hard drive for 'Gottleib liability'?" I put air quotes around the term.

Blackson looked like I'd hit him with a two-by-four. I edged closer to him.

"So much crap is going down, I don't know who to believe," Blackson said. "Koven told me Brent and David were going to move to another firm, take Koven's clients with them."

"Were they?"

"No way." Blackson squinted at me. "Hey, what do you care about all this? We didn't kill him."

"My boss thinks Koven killed Duncan. She sent me to check things out. You know what I found?" I waited for Blackson to shake his head. "One strange lobbying firm. What kind of business are you in that you need a guy like Jago Seyton?"

"Creepy guy, right?" Blackson nodded. "Tom Duncan picks up strays. We have a secretary who was too old to keep hooking. An embezzler as our investigator. And we have Jago. He was one of Duncan's first employees. He's like that funny cousin everyone has, if you ask why he looks more like your dad than your uncle, you get slapped. We're not allowed to ask about Jago. He goes where he wants and doesn't say much."

"Is he the only one at the firm who carries a .45?"

Blackson shrugged.

"What did Zola and Gottleib argue about the night he was killed?" I asked.

Blackson thought it over while I stared him down. "I can only imagine."

"Imagine what?"

Blackson took a breath as he considered his answer. "If you make chewing gum, you think Tom Duncan is the greatest guy in the world. If you're a dentist with an ax to grind about gum and cavities, you think Tom Duncan is the devil incarnate. We advocate for those who hire us, but it's like walking a tightrope. Tom never flinched when someone discussed bribing a congressman, but he let the clients do their own dirty work. He would never let it touch the firm."

"What about Koven?"

"Koven's side of the business exploded after Citizens United," Blackson said.

"Why would that happen?"

"Let's say you want to privatize security for the President. Only problem is, the Secret Service is already doing that. So, you need a few legislators to push through a bill that will open the business for you. You pitch it as, 'the private sector can do it for less.' The people in Congress know it's worth a lot of money to you. But you can't just buy legislation—that's called bribery. So you hire a lobbyist to push your plan."

"No one would outsource the President's security."

"Work with me." Blackson crossed his arms. "In the old days, before 2010, a lobbyist camped on a senator's doorstep and convinced him how many jobs your plan would bring to their district. Maybe some unreported football tickets changed hands, maybe ten thousand of their books were bought by anonymous readers, maybe their kid 'won' a scholarship. But those gifts were small. The amounts involved had only one comma."

"So what did the Citizens United decision do, legalize these gifts?" I asked.

"Worse. The Supreme Court said donating money to political campaigns was free speech as long as the donors are reported. They set up the Super PAC as the funding mechanism for unlimited donations and required them to report all their donors. So far, no problem. It's all good and clean."

"Then to get my legislation through," I said, "I give $5 million to a Super PAC, and I get my contract for the President's security. If he doesn't come through, I give my $5 mil to his opponent in the next election. What's the problem?"

Blackson spent a few seconds thinking how to simplify it for me. "Let's say a guy named Senator Ratchet is having trouble financing his campaign. He wants your $5 mil, and will push your legislation, but no one in Congress will vote for it if it looks like you bribed him. And you don't want your competitors knowing what you're up to, so you need to give him the money anonymously."

"But the Supremes said I have to be named."

Blackson watched a car go by. "There have always been social welfare organizations like the NRA or Sierra Club who don't have to report their donors. So, you give your $5 mil to a social welfare group like Future Crossroads, making it tax deductible, which turns around and gives it to the Super PAC. The Super PAC reports the donation of $5 million from the Future Crossroads, not Jacob Stearne."

"Huh. I just bribed Senator Ratchet tax free. That's illegal, right?"

"No, perfectly legal. It's only a crime if someone can *prove* a connection between your donation to Future Crossroads and Senator Ratchet's legislation. Since Future Crossroads doesn't report donors, and you weren't dumb enough to put anything in writing, it's not a bribe."

I felt sick. "So Gottleib found something proving connections?"

"I don't think so." Blackson squinted. "Koven controls 112 social welfare groups and 112 Super PACs. By the way, there are 538 elected senators and representatives, meaning Koven can influence two out of ten legislators. That's a lot of power in one man's hands. So, Zola and I figured David found something on him. We went through the internal records and couldn't find anything illegal. All the money flowing into his social welfare groups comes through wealthy Americans or companies they control. Companies like Sabel Security."

"But we have money that came from Oman. That's illegal, right?"

"Maybe or maybe not. It depends on whether political favors were promised or if the Omani money can be traced to a Super PAC."

"Who does the tracing?"

"No one."

"What do you mean? Surely someone out there is watching who's bribing elected officials."

"No one can trace the money. You ask a Super PAC where their money came from and they say Future Crossroads. Then you ask Future Crossroads and they tell you to take a hike."

I leaned back against a retaining wall. "Gottleib never told either of you what he uncovered because he thought you were involved in it. That's why he turned to his high school homeboys."

Mercury said, *If you want to have a future, you need to keep your eyes and ears open.*

I said, *Give me a minute, will you? I'm finally getting somewhere.*

Mercury said, *You'll be getting somewhere in a pine box if you don't pay attention.*

"Jacob, I swear, veteran to veteran, I have not done anything illegal that David would be upset about."

"But Koven has?" I asked.

"Not that I found."

"But you suspect him?"

"After Nasiriyah, wouldn't you?"

"What the hell is with Nasiriyah?" I pushed off the wall and stepped in his space. "Everyone expects me to remember what they were wearing that day and what they had for tea. All I remember was running into a bunch of Marines, killing a few Republican Guards, and getting the hell out."

Blackson dug into his pocket and pulled out a .50 BMG cartridge. "You don't remember giving us these?"

"Oh give me a fucking break. What is with the—"

Mercury stood in the street, waving his arms and jumping up and down. *White Nissan, passenger window down, two hostiles, get your eyes open, dipshit.*

Half a block up the street, a small sedan came at us doing sixty. A small black stick came out of the window and aimed at Blackson.

I took two steps and body slammed him to the ground as three shots rang out. They hit me, center chest.

People think body armor is some kind of magic force field right out of science fiction. It's not. When you get hit in the chest by three .223 rounds traveling at 2900 feet per second, you have broken ribs at best and internal damage at worst. I fell sideways and struck my head on the retaining wall.

As my consciousness dimmed, the sedan sped away.

Rip Blackson got up and bolted down the sidewalk into the dark, his echoing footsteps fading in the distance.

I tried to breathe.

A long scary minute passed before another car screeched to a halt at the curb, three feet away from me.

I pulled my Glock and tried to aim.

"Don't shoot! It's me!" Miguel Rodriguez, fellow Sabel agent and best friend from my Ranger days, ducked behind the fender of his SUV.

Struggling to remain conscious, I waved him over.

The big Navajo knelt next to me. "What happened? Did Blackson shoot you?"

"Drive by, the car…" Talking hurt.

Sirens echoed through the city.

"Get me out of here," I said. My ribs sent shockwaves of pain that made me spasm.

Miguel, six-five and buff, picked me up and carried me to the back door of his Mercedes G63. He swept three assault rifles and several magazines from the seat to the floor, then eased me onto the bench. I lay on my back, my knees bent. He slammed the door, ran to the driver's side, and jumped in.

He put his foot on the pedal and exploded down the road with the force of a dam breaking.

"Where did … get this car?" I asked.

"Sabel Gardens, Cousin Elmer." He glanced at me in the mirror. "Pia doesn't like SUVs. She drives only two-seaters with six hundred horses, so they let me take this home once in a while."

Nice.

I saved her life twice and she gave me a Volkswagen. Miguel stands like a statue, says nothing, and gets the world's fastest—and ugliest—SUV. Maybe I should ask for a spare four-seater. Maybe the Porsche Panamera would be available from time to time.

Then I remembered: Last time I drove that car, I brought it back so shot up it looked like a colander full of green beans.

"Where are you taking me?" I asked. All I could see were the street lights flying by as we drove through neighborhoods at excessive speeds.

He flashed a grin over his shoulder. "Pia told me to take you to Sabel Gardens. Doc Günter's waiting for you."

Pain raced through my chest. I squeezed a hand under the armor. Dry. That was good. The bullet didn't penetrate.

"Wait! She's in Germany."

"She called," Miguel said. "Told me to go to some house off Chain Bridge Road." He honked and swerved and flipped somebody off. "She said you were going to be hurt and would need help. But I went there and some lady answered the door with a couple toddlers at her feet. Then I heard the shots. Had to be you."

Mercury sat in the passenger seat, staring at Miguel. *Dude, why do you hang with this guy? Have you ever seen the Navajo gods? Scary as hell.*

I said, *Am I going to die?*

Mercury leaned back and checked me out. *No such luck, homie. That body armor works better than a Roman scutum.*

I said, *How did Ms. Sabel know I was hurt and needed help?*

Mercury said, *Aw Brutha. After all these years, you still don't get it? You're working with the Messenger of the Gods, bay-bay!*

# CHAPTER 18

PIA STRODE THROUGH the guest wing at Sabel Gardens wearing yoga pants and a wine-colored pullover. One sniff had her wondering how a doctor could make such a large space smell like a hospital overnight.

Tania trotted a few steps behind.

"It's hard for me," Tania said. "Look what gangs did to my sister."

Pia glanced over her shoulder. "People who don't engage in the redemption of others are engaging hopelessness."

"You're taking his redemption too far. I know it's been a while since you've had a boyfriend—and since the last one tried to kill you, I'm not surprised you haven't jumped back into the dating pool—but this guy is not the boy-toy you deserve, girlfriend."

Pia shot her friend a withering glare.

Tania turned her gaze to the floor. "Just stating the obvious."

"For the record, my boyfriend did not try to kill me, he set me up for assassins. Don't worry about me. I never date employees." Pia stopped walking and glanced around. "Where is Carlos, anyway?"

"I gave him a day to catch up on his sleep. No one can keep your schedule. Especially the new guys."

Doc Günter stepped out of a door across the open space. "Now is not a good time, Pia."

"I thought Jacob was improving," she said.

"No serious injuries, just some cracked and bruised ribs, soreness. But…" Doc looked at the floor and rubbed his neck. "He rested last night on heavy medication and I've just given him a bit more."

"He's awake then?" Pia started for the door. "I need to speak to him."

Doc Günter put out a hand to stop her. "Have you been around patients on pain medication? Are you familiar with their inappropriate comments and romantic inclinations?"

"We're more like siblings. Jacob has no romantic feelings for me."

"Right now," Doc Günter said, "he would have feelings for Angela Merkel."

Tania said, "Jacob has the hots for anyone in a skirt—when he's *not* medicated."

Miguel's laughter roared from inside the room. "Oh yeah, I remember her. Whoo. She was fine. How'd you blow it with her, anyway?"

"I'll check back this evening." Pia squeezed Doc's arm. "Hopefully he'll be dealing with the pain on his own terms by then."

Doc nodded. "I think that would be best."

They turned and left.

Emily Lunger called from the *Post*. "*FNC*, *Hummingbird*, and the *Chronicle* have you fleeing the scene of a murder in Dresden, care to comment?"

"No."

"Aw, c'mon, Pia," Emily said. "Give me something. Or let me release the stuff you sent me. What's with those pictures, anyway?"

"When it's time, I'll explain."

Emily whined some more before clicking off.

Tania's phone chirped. "You wanted to meet Daryl Koven? He says he will clear his calendar for you anytime."

There was the opportunity for job satisfaction Pia relished. She couldn't wait to drill into Koven's twisted mind and get answers to her many questions. Just as her euphoria rose, she remembered her father's advice to keep a lid on what she knows until her adversaries played their hand. It took the fun out of it, but it made sense.

Once the arrangements were finalized, they hopped in Pia's burgundy Aston Martin Vanquish and raced downtown. Minutes later, she walked into the offices of Duncan, Hyde and Koven.

Daryl Koven greeted her in the middle of his spacious office. Tania took up a position by the door and stood at parade rest.

Koven nosed toward Pia's constant guard. "Perhaps she'd be more comfortable in the lobby."

"I'm fine right here," Tania said, and fixed her eyes on a distant horizon.

Pia waited until Koven's gaze came back to her. "You're losing employees and clients at an alarming rate. What dark crimes are you committing that lead to so many murders?"

Koven's head snapped back. "You have a lot nerve."

They glared at each other for a moment.

Then Koven said, "You were in Dresden while I was thirty thousand feet over the Atlantic. David Gottleib died at your agent's house. And you were every bit as near Tom Duncan as I. Maybe you're the one behind the 'dark crimes'."

Pia's scowl tightened. "Are you the one feeding that line to the Three Blondes?"

Koven relaxed and turned away. "You'll never make it in business with that attitude—or those outfits. They'll eat you alive. You're a prime example of why young women fail in business: too impetuous. Maybe when you're older and more mature you'll act and dress like Carly Fiorina or Christine Lagarde."

Pia's gaze shifted left for a split second. She's worn athletic outfits her whole life. Suits were for old people. Or so she used to think. Being vulnerable to fashion insults wasn't fun. Maybe it was time to reconsider.

"But that's not why you wanted to see me," Koven said. "Flinging accusations only proves how weak your investigative skills are. If you had any evidence, you'd go to the police. Now, why did you really want this meeting?"

"Your firm overpaid the Oman contract by $20 million then refused the transfer when we wired it back. Why?"

"Let's have a seat, shall we?" Koven motioned to the leather sofa. He sat near one end and stretched an arm across the back. He gestured to the other half with his free hand.

"I prefer to stand." Pia put a foot on the coffee table between them and rested her forearms across her knee.

Koven coughed and palmed his legs. "It's understandable—and reassuring—that you were alarmed by that unexplained bonus. A bonus often seems questionable if you're unaccustomed to the nuances of international business. You can rest assured, the intent is absolutely ethical and honorable. Provided you live up to Prince Taimur's expectations."

"Bonuses are spelled out in the contract. It's not a bonus."

"Is that right?" Koven gave her a tight smile. "I'll check with the team and get clarification."

After a moment's silence, Koven said, "As long as you're here, there is another matter I'd like to discuss."

Pia waited.

"There are a great number of people in Congress who would like to know you better." He rose and paced his office. "They could do great favors for Sabel Industries."

"Glad to hear it," she said. "Tell them to meet me at the shelter for homeless families, any Tuesday. Wear work clothes."

He held up his index finger as if he were going to make a point but then wagged it and decided not to provoke her. He walked around her in a circle while she stared out the window.

"Politicians have to be careful with charities. They tend to support those with a large presence in their districts. And, I think it's best to keep some relationships professional. Don't you?"

Pia didn't react.

Koven glanced up at her as he paced.

"These people are in a position to help you," he said. "For example, the Mercenary Restrictions Act is gathering steam despite Jeff Smith's feeble attempts on your behalf. We can do much more than a well-intentioned senator on his own. The point is, like you, there are others who find Congress rather troublesome. There are people who could benefit from your resources, your influence, your celebrity to help them."

Koven circled to her front side.

Pia stood up straight and folded her arms. "Tell me about these unfortunate people."

"You're being snarky." Koven smiled. "I understand your skepticism, but not everyone lives in the USA. In many countries, the powerful prey on the weak and in some they simply annihilate their rivals. Some of my clients live in constant danger."

"Like Prince Taimur of Oman?"

"He's one example." Koven smiled and rubbed his chin. "There are many others. I know a woman dangerously close to the Russian oligarchy, a man who said the wrong thing in China, a business woman in Saudi Arabia. The list is long."

"I like to help people," Pia said.

"These people need advocates in the US to help them escape repression." Koven resumed his pacing. "A couple representatives and a senator will work sometimes. A business advocate also helps. But a combination smooths the application process should the political landscape shift suddenly in their home country."

"And that's where I come in," Pia said. "How can I help?"

"Your father always stayed within the bounds of the old campaign limits. Our venerable politicians could point to his donation and say, 'See, Alan Sabel supports me!' But there is an opportunity to help on a much larger scale and without alienating your friends who may support the other candidate in any given race. At the same time, you can be seen in the international community as a supporter of dissenters. The powerless and repressed will know they can count on you."

"Why would my friends feel alienated?"

"I'm sure you have friends on both sides of various issues—abortion, deficits, tax breaks, that kind of thing—and you don't want to get drawn into arguments with them over who you support and why. With social welfare groups, you can contribute to any cause you want without anyone knowing how you stand on the issues—"

"Why?" Pia asked. "Are my beliefs so awful I should keep them secret?"

"You're quite the idealist." He frowned and wagged his finger again. "When you played soccer, your stand on any issue was your own. Now that you're in business, you can alienate customers, which can hurt revenue, which costs jobs. On the other hand, when you're known—in discreet circles—to help repressed citizens achieve their goals, your business will flourish. You'll find many powerful people in other countries lining up to hire Sabel Security and Sabel Technologies and Sabel Satellites—any division of Sabel Industries."

"You said I can contribute without anyone knowing."

"*That*," Koven smiled, "is where I come in."

"And where the bonus comes in?" Pia asked.

"Yes and no." Koven crossed his arms. "They are not connected. Let me be absolutely clear about that. Think of it this way—when you're having dinner and the waiter compliments your shoes, you tend to tip more. When the waiter mentions he gives all his tips to … what is your favorite charity?"

"Family Promise."

"If the waiter says he donates his tips to Family Promise, you'd tip more. It's natural. Bonuses often work in the same way. When a Russian billionaire worries about running afoul of Vladimir Putin, and he knows you help people immigrate to the US, then he's inclined to hire Sabel Security."

Koven gave Pia a sad look. "There are so many business people in the world, risking everything they have to improve economic conditions in their countries—and yet they find themselves tossed about in the typhoons of political whim."

"That's terrible," Pia said. "It's easy to forget how fortunate we are in America."

"And how treacherous other countries are."

"What can I do with the $20 million to help your friends?"

Koven chuckled. "North Carolina and Colorado Senate races ran over $100 million in the last election. With costs soaring, every politician is looking for generous sources. But, no matter how much you spend in a big race, you only have the ear of one senator. I recommend we look at the smaller races with the more agreeable candidates."

"They'll be more willing to help with the Prince's immigration status?"

"Let me reiterate, those two things are not linked together." Koven winked. "We want candidates who are willing to help Sabel Securities with difficult things like the Mercenary Restrictions Act. Once a candidate takes our money, it's perfectly acceptable to ask them for help on other matters."

"Like the Prince's immigration status."

Koven's face pinched, he moved between Pia and the door. "It is illegal for a foreign national to contribute to an American political campaign. You don't want foreign money influencing American political campaigns any more than I. But yours is an international corporation with many clients in many different countries. I'm sure you'll keep those funds separate. There is no connection between the bonus Oman may or may not choose to award Sabel Security and any money Sabel Security may choose to allocate to federal elections. Those two things are, and must always remain, separate in the accounting, in memos, and all communications. Are we clear?"

"Crystal," Pia smiled and squeezed his shoulder. "My father told me I'm naïve. This is good; I need to learn how things work. Thank you, Mr. Koven. I appreciate how you cleared this up for me."

Koven nodded.

"Be sure to send instructions on which candidates are the right ones to stop the Mercenary Restrictions Act." She smiled and headed for the door. "How quickly can we get that resolved?"

"These things take time," Koven said. "I'll send you a letter of engagement and we'll find the right people."

They shook hands. Tania led the way out and Koven closed the door behind them.

Winding through the maze of cubicles, a familiar and unpleasant face caught her eye. Pia stopped in her tracks. "Kasey Earl? What are you doing here?"

"They's our client." He pulled up his unshaven chin to look at her.

"Are you serious?" Pia squinted. "They didn't fire Velox after Duncan's death?"

He tilted his head. "We didn't do nothing."

"That would be the problem."

"We're expanding." Kasey tipped up on his toes to match her height.

"You're going to make more suicide vests for terrorists?"

"Them things just fell into the wrong hands is all that happened there. My design was good."

Pia shook her head. "I won't ask whose are the right hands for explosive outerwear."

"You get the Shiite radicals to blow up the Sunni radicals, and then the Sunnis will go blow up the Shiites. Win-win."

"Those kindergartners who died in the blast weren't radicals. Too bad you didn't test the vests yourself."

"Whatever." Kasey tilted his nose up higher. "We're gonna be bigger than Sabel in no time."

"How will that happen?" Pia leaned toward him. "Did Satan hire you for the apocalypse?"

Kasey backed up a step. "Shane's taking this company global. Real big time. He's doing a 'buy local' campaign." Kasey paused for effect. "Instead of bringing in mental health problems."

"Where do I apply?" Pia planted her palm on his chest and pushed him against the wall. She marched past him to the lobby.

She pushed the down button as hard as she could and waited with her arms crossed.

When the elevator doors opened, Senator Jeff Smith looked up and stared with his mouth open for an awkward, motionless second.

Pia stepped into the small space, turning him by the elbow. "Talk to me, Jeff."

"I have an appointment," he said.

"That's what worries me."

Tania joined them, blocking the elevator's exit. The senator's bodyguard backed up to give her space. The doors closed. Pia pushed the button for the parking garage.

"Who's backing the Mercenary Restrictions Act, Jeff?" Pia asked.

"There are eighteen congressmen involved."

"Koven funded them?"

"That was my first thought," Jeff said. "I sat down with seven of them and heard the same story each time. They're responding to a spike in constituent concerns in their districts. It's the strangest thing I've ever seen."

Pia scowled. "Where are these districts?"

"They're all over the country. All of them are hotly contested seats. North Dakota, Detroit suburbs, a slice of Brooklyn, a part of Nevada I've never heard of, places with demographically divergent voter rolls."

"Why the spike?" Pia asked. "What happened that ignited voter interests?"

"Grassroots bloggers and online sources." Jeff pulled out his phone. "I'll send you what my aides turned up on the districts and news outlets."

The elevator pinged and the doors open. Tania stepped out, keeping one hand on the door.

Pia squeezed his arm. "I see why my father puts so much trust in you, Jeff."

She strode into the dimly lit garage and around a corner to her car when it hit her. She stared blankly at the concrete wall.

Koven finances American campaigns with foreign money.

The biggest economy and the deadliest military in the world is governed by people who owe their offices to foreigners laundering money through social welfare groups. She had to stop it.

But where was her proof?

We don't know that our favorite politicians are taking money from foreigners in exchange for favors. We don't know that they're not. And we can't find out.

How did that happen?

Pia closed her eyes and tensed.

"You OK?" Tania asked.

Pia looked across the roof of her car at her agent. "Just trying to process all this."

She slid into the driver's seat and thought for a second. Evidence lay not far from her grasp if she played her cards right and followed her father's advice. Someone took out Müller to keep that evidence from her, but the other two, Suliman and Taimur, were only half a world away.

She hit the phone and dialed up her tech, Bianca Dominguez.

Pia asked, "In all that material Jacob picked from Blackson's hard drive, did you find any references to a woman-owned business in Saudi Arabia?"

"I saw something like that. Saudi Arabia is not known for feminism, so a woman-owned business surprised me. I think her name was Samira Suliman."

"Find her contact information and set up an appointment."

Something in Bianca's voice struck her as hesitant, uncertain. Bianca had always been upbeat and enthusiastic before coming to work for Pia. But something had changed. There could be many causes, but Pia went with her instinct.

"Megan Rapinoe was the first woman on the National Team to come out of the closet," Pia said. "She was a great player but after she came out, she had one less thing to worry about, and that allowed her to become one of the greatest. I've always respected her courage. No one has to come out if they don't want to at Sabel Security. But anyone who does, has my blessing and protection in the workplace." Pia let her words settle for a moment. "Will you set up that appointment for me?"

"I'm on it," Bianca said, her cheerful voice returned.

"Before you go, do we have the resources to do a search of news blogs in specific congressional districts?"

"Public blogs and posts, no problem. We can message or poll people if you don't mind spending some money on advertising."

Pia's brows rose, she glanced at Tania. "Could we do a poll that targets people in specific districts? For example, ask them where they heard about certain news stories?"

"It will take a day," Bianca said. "Do you want to post some news stories?"

"What do you mean, 'post news stories'? You mean, like real newspaper stories?"

"You can write your own news article and post it on dozens of websites. Facebook and Buzzfeed put a tag that says 'sponsored' on them, but there are hundreds of others that make it look like regular content. The major websites will pick it up if it gets a lot of hits."

"You mean I could pay to run a news item that says Tania Cooper saved a baby from a burning building and Congressman McCormick might be a suspected terrorist and child molester, 'vote for Cooper', then post them in his district?"

"Yes, ma'am."

"Or I could write a post about how terrible it is that Sabel Security sends American veterans to work for US enemies?"

"Yes, ma'am."

"And if a social welfare group sponsors the posts, no one will know who wrote the article?"

"Yes, ma'am. And for ten grand you can get a college professor to write a study proving a vote for Cooper expands the economy. You should read 'Dark Money' by Jane Mayer—scarier than a Stephen King story."

"Strange times we live in." Pia clicked off and sent Jeff Smith's files to Bianca.

She clicked the Aston Martin into gear and powered up the ramp.

At the street, she stopped for pedestrians. One woman on the sidewalk caught her eye. She rolled down her window and hit the horn. The woman of her interest faced her.

"Hey, Marthe, my videos uploaded to the cloud before I deleted them from my phone." Pia waited for the woman to gasp. "I'm going to figure out how you pulled it off. And then, you're going down for it."

# CHAPTER 19

DARYL KOVEN STARED down Rip Blackson, who leaned across his desk with both hands flat on the surface. Neither man blinked for what felt like an eternity.

Someone had to end it.

"Fine," Koven said. "I could've told you first. But it doesn't matter. You were Duncan's pick for managing the firm because you were his right-hand man. Zola's my pick for the same reason. We weren't going to tell you until after the funeral because it won't be effective until then."

"Last time we talked, you didn't trust him." Blackson took his hands off the desk and stood up straight.

"That hasn't changed." Koven leaned his chair back. "Do you?"

"Of course. I talked to him and—"

"Think, Rip." Koven lowered his voice. "Who tried to kill you last night?"

"Are you saying it was Zola?" Blackson asked.

Koven extended a palm as if he were giving his point as a gift. "He was rifling through your house."

"If he wanted to kill me he had plenty of opportunity that night." Blackson turned away and watched the snow fall past the window. "It has to be someone else."

"You said he was working with Jacob Stearne." Koven read every flicker in Blackson's eye. "That guy's been trying to dig his way in here for god knows what purpose. The lunatic beat up both Jago and Brent. Stearne is probably the one who turned Brent against us. Anyone who talks to Sabel Security is a traitor."

"Jacob took a bullet for me the other night. He's not—"

"Staged." Koven threw up his hands. "C'mon, who shoots from a moving vehicle and hits anything? Who jumps in front of a semi-automatic without a helmet? And who wears body armor?"

"That was unreal." Blackson folded his arms. "But it was totally Jacob. Just like what he did in—"

"Too real if you ask me." Koven stepped around his desk. "Why did you download everything about 'Gottleib liability'?"

"Me?" Blackson put his hands out. "I didn't download anything."

"The night you got back, you downloaded several gigs of data to your home computer."

Blackson clenched his fists and mouth. "That was the night I found Zola at my place. He hacked my computer."

"Tell me the truth, Rip. Were they working on something that could bring down the firm? Did Zola kill Gottleib when it went bad?"

"No way. They weren't like that." Blackson considered his friends for a moment. "Zola worships you, he'd never leave the firm. He knows he'd never get a gig this sweet anywhere else."

"He's not the same anymore. Something's gone wrong." Koven turned away.

"How do I know you didn't kill Gottleib?"

"Rip," Koven snapped a look over his shoulder, "you know that's impossible. I promoted him, and what thanks did I get? He resigned."

Koven paced away.

"Listen to us," Koven said. "We're scared and blaming each other when we should be working together. If we don't, we could end up like David or Tom."

Blackson looked out the window. "You think the killer is inside the firm?"

"Whoever he is, he's close to us. Someone knew Tom would be in France. Someone knew David went to Jacob's house. Maybe David and Brent made a deal with someone and backed out."

"What kind of a deal would get you killed?"

"They were doing something," Koven said. "They must have given you a hint. Think about what pissed them off."

"Gottleib and Zola argued about the foreign clients a couple times. It was nothing I knew about one way or the other."

"Argued enough to kill?"

"Well. Actually." Blackson paused. "Jacob told me Brent had the murder weapon on him."

"What? You didn't think to tell me?" Koven clenched his fists. "Wait, how did Jacob know it was the murder weapon?"

"I asked him that," Blackson thought for a moment. "Damn. He changed the subject on me."

"It's Brent then. He's working with Stearne."

"But Jacob wasn't in France." Blackson faced him and shrugged. "If he killed David, do you think Brent killed Tom?"

"Brent left for LA but never checked into his hotel."

"You called him? Checked his location?"

"He's off the grid."

"I'll call him." Blackson's gaze swept the carpet. "I'll check with his mom, his baby-mama."

"Thanks." Koven stuck out a hand. "You and I need to clear this up and move the company forward."

Blackson left and Koven went back to his desk and worked through his email.

Marthe staggered in with stooped shoulders. She shrugged out of her coat, letting it fall to the floor and plowed face-first into the sofa. She pulled the throw blanket over her and curled up into a tight fetal position, her back to him.

He watched her for a moment, then went back to his email.

She didn't move.

After a while, he asked, "What's bothering you, my love?"

"That girl." Marthe's voice muffled by the sofa. "She knows we killed Duncan."

"You're letting your imagination run wild, Marthe. She knows nothing."

"Have you seen how she looks at me? She can read the guilt in your eyes and see the blood on your hands."

"What on earth are you talking about? I spoke to her just hours ago. I had her eating out of the palm of my hand."

"She yelled at me when she left." Marthe rolled her face upward.

"She tried that crap with me, but I took her down a notch."

"She still has the pictures and videos."

"What pictures could she possibly have that would implicate us?" Koven asked. "It doesn't matter anyway. She came to me for help with the Mercenary Restrictions Act and left ready to work with Prince Taimur and the others."

Marthe turned her face back to the sofa. "Daryl, you're such a fool. She's a girl."

Koven turned back to his email. "Whatever that means."

"She played you. She let you think what you wanted to think. We tell you what to do and you always think it's your idea." Marthe sat up and faced him. "She's going to kill us."

"You're blowing this way out of proportion. Get hold of yourself." He stood and crossed to her. "The one we have to worry about is Brent Zola. He and Gottleib both downloaded a lot of privileged information from our servers. Information that could lead to criminal charges if they find a way to corroborate it. And now, he's gone missing."

She stood up. "What have you done?"

"Nothing. I sent Jago to find him, but he's disappeared."

"We can't have another death in the firm. It would play into Sabel's hands."

"It won't connect back to us."

Marthe crossed to him and wrapped her arms around him.

"Tell me the truth," she said. "Did you have anything to do with David Gottleib's murder?"

Koven pushed his wife back half an arm's length and looked into her eyes. "No."

She pulled herself close again. They held each other.

She said, "I feel so out of control. Everything has become too messy."

He wondered if she were blaming him. Wasn't it her idea from the beginning? She'd taken on too much. Tom's funeral, rescheduling the symposium in Germany, several trips across the Atlantic—the strain was getting to her. She was his rock, his center. He needed her back on point.

"Aren't we humans just pathetic? We want life to have meaning and be in order when it's all meaningless and chaotic." He waved his arms.

"We're born without definition or purpose. The only thing we can do is define ourselves, build something. That's what we're doing here, Marthe. We're building something big." He tightened his arms around her and whispered into her hair. "You and me. A powerful legacy. We started into this and we can't back out."

"What is that supposed to mean? You're still planning to kill Brent?" She shook her head. "I can't live with making this thing worse. No, he's gone. It's his message, he'll leave us alone."

Koven kissed her nose. "Now who's letting herself think what she wants to think?"

# CHAPTER 20

I SCANNED THE room: bookshelves, television, dresser, windows—none of which felt the least bit familiar. I threw back the covers and stood up only to drop back down with a massive head rush. Then it came back to me, where I was and who I was with. I looked around for Miguel and couldn't figure out if he'd been there earlier when I was groggy or if I'd dreamed it.

Anoshni lay on the floor next to me and looked up with big, happy-puppy eyes. Miguel brought him home from the Reservation as a peace offering after we had a territorial dispute over a woman. Naturally, we both lost in the end. Tania wasn't speaking to either of us. But I liked the dog—at least he was trustworthy.

The only thing more disorienting than waking up in the guest wing of Sabel Gardens was seeing my albatross—the homeless god—standing next to one fierce-looking brown-skinned dude at the foot of the bed.

The new guy was short and muscular, had his hair in a bun, a breastplate of polished sea shells, an illustrated loincloth, a wide black streak painted across his eyes, and lips painted white. He chanted something angry and loud and shook a stick that rattled.

Mercury said, *Don't look at me, bro. It's your fault.*

I said, *What the hell? Who is he?*

Mercury said, *Jupiter heard you say I needed cultural diversity. And Jupiter thinks you're the special sauce on the cheeseburger of human life. So here we are. This is whatcha call a cultural exchange.*

The short dude ranted more words, held up a nasty looking knife made of black glass and shook his stick. It had tiny skulls hanging from it.

I said, *I can't handle this. I'm losing my mind.*

Mercury said, *Be nice. His name is Vucub-Camé, which is Mayan for Seven-Death. He's my new traveling companion—thanks to you. Don't spook him, he comes from a long line of gods who think ripping the beating heart out of your chest with an obsidian blade is good for you. Breathe in now. Ahhh. Can you feel the cultural diversity flowing like energy from a crystal?*

I said, *I need my meds. I'm going back on my meds.*

Mercury said, *No, no, no! Don't do anything crazy. I'll take our new buddy for a walk until you calm down.*

Mercury grabbed his pal by the shoulders, turned him around, and pushed him toward the door. He looked back at me. *Jupiter and Minerva are backing you big time, homie. The least you could do is call that bat-shit crazy doctor and make us look good. Is that too much to ask?*

I said, *Will Voodoo-whatshisname go away?*

Mercury said, *I'm so disappointed in you, brutha. I thought you were all cool with expanding your horizons, but I guess that's all just empty words, huh. Should have guessed. All y'all white people are like that, ya know. 'Oh, honey, let's have our friends-of-color over for dinner and hope they don't deify Denzel Washington.'*

I said, *Don't get me wrong, I like Mayans. Some of my best friends are Mayan, or cousins of Mayans. Navajo anyway. It's just that I'm using my heart right now. If we're going to expand horizons, can we try Saint Francis of Assisi or something?*

Mercury said, *Puh-Leez. That's like Cedar Rapids having a cultural exchange with Iowa City.*

He pushed Seven-Death into the hall and closed the door behind him.

I took a deep breath.

The door opened again.

"No, not yet!" I grabbed a pillow for a shield and looked into the surprised face of Ms. Pia Sabel.

"Are you OK?" she asked.

"Sorry, nightmare." I tossed the cushion and checked my wardrobe. Boxers and a t-shirt that said, US ARMY BOMB SQUAD / if you see me running—follow.

She handed me one of the two cups of coffee she carried and moved

to the windows. She pressed a button that opened the blinds, revealing a dark sky and snow-covered garden.

She faced me with crossed arms. "I'm not happy that you brought the murder weapon here."

"Yeah. Sorry."

"I've turned it over to your attorney. He's having it checked for fingerprints before he turns it over to the police."

"Oh great. When should I turn myself in?"

"Don't be melodramatic. It wasn't loaded when it was stolen, so your fingerprints won't be on the magazine. If Zola's are, we'll know what happened."

"There won't be any. The cops found rubber gloves."

She nodded and motioned to the furniture. "Have a seat, we need to catch up."

My ribs screamed when I gingerly folded myself into the wingback in the corner.

She took the seat opposite, a pedestal table between us. She picked up the pup, put him in her lap, and baby-talked him. Anoshni licked her face.

He was mostly house-broken, but we weren't past the occasional accident stage when he got excited. I closed my eyes and prayed he would keep the proceedings dignified.

"Your idea to record Koven incriminating himself was a good one," she said, "but he was too clever to get caught. He did give me some good leads, though. I'm heading to Dubai to follow up. We ran into Kasey Earl and he gave us a good tip as well."

I sipped the coffee. Black and strong, the way God intended.

While she explained her visit to Koven, she watched me. She could see my cup shaking and knew something was bothering me. She stopped talking and patiently waited for me to explain.

"I think I'm going over the edge," I said. "I might be completely mad."

She canted her head.

"I can see the guy," I said. "Mercury. He's not what you'd expect."

"You've named him?" She sipped her coffee. "That's cute."

"You're not worried about me?"

"Why?" She set her cup down.

I gulped my coffee and considered our arrangement to help each other with our mental issues. Until now, I'd thought she was the stable one.

She could've at least acted surprised.

"Oh, I forgot," she said. "Rip Blackson wants to buy you lunch for saving his life. Lunch seems a little light, considering."

"It's a cover. He wants to talk."

"Last item," she said. "Brent Zola's mom has been calling but will only talk to you."

She handed me my phone and nodded a go-ahead.

I pressed redial on the number that had called ten times in the last two hours.

A woman's voice came on, first ring. "Is that you, Jacob?"

"Yes, ma'am. What can I do for you?" I clicked over to speaker phone and introduced Ms. Sabel.

"Brent told me you were the only person to trust. He needs your help. He's in big trouble. There was some guy hanging around outside the house just before dark and he panicked. He said the guy was there to kill him, just like he killed David. All I saw was a guy talking on his phone, but Brent was so scared he scared me. He took Flip and went to Tokyo. You have to help him. I'll give you his number—"

"Why do I have to help him? Why not call the police?"

"He said he doesn't know who to trust. The police could be in on it."

"If someone's trying to kill him, I'm not—"

"Jacob will be on the next flight," Ms. Sabel said. She gave me a scowl that made me shrink. "Ms. Zola, did he tell you who was trying to kill him?"

"No, but I saw him. Short and thin with no neck."

Ms. Sabel promised her daily updates and clicked off.

She sat back in her chair, those gray-green eyes slicing through me like a machete through a B-movie jungle set.

"OK," I said. "We help people who need help. But if Jago Seyton kills me, I'll be the one haunting you."

It was an awkward joke about her mother's ghost and way too early in our new relationship. Her mouth fell open and she paled. Then she leaned forward and her expression slowly changed from shock to amused. "Don't let Seyton get you."

We shared a tense laugh and finished our coffees.

"I'm taking my jet." She rose and headed for the door. "Dad's gone to Guatemala for something. You'll have to fly commercial."

Mercury slid into her empty seat. Seven-Death stood behind him, giving me the death-ray stare.

Mercury said, *Doood. Commercial. A fate worse than death. But All Nippon Airways has one great first class section, and it's run by sexists who still hire flight attendants based on looks, so it's not all bad. Don't forget, you have to call Dr. Harrison. Tell him all about me.*

The door opened again and Ms. Sabel stuck her head in. "Have you made any progress with Dad about my parents' murders?"

"Uh, yeah. Actually, I … um. No."

She closed the door.

The on-the-fly arrangements I had to make when assigned to a suicide mission could drive me to drinking. But my almost-girlfriend Bianca jumped at the chance to watch Anoshni. Although there was a profound note of disappointment when I mentioned Ms. Sabel would be out of town as well.

I found Miguel with his overpowered boxcar of an SUV waiting for me outside. He even had my tickets and an overnight bag. He snicked the gearshift into drive and we roared out of the gates heading for Dulles.

Blackson called on our way. "Jacob, how're you feeling today? You saved my life again. I owe you big time."

"OK, how about explaining 'Gottleib liability'?"

He choked. "Pretty vague term. It could be anything. Do you have any context?"

"Use this context: The last time I saved your sorry ass you turned whiter than the Queen of England's butt when I tossed that phrase out there. What's it mean?"

"I'm not sure."

"Could it be why Zola fled to Tokyo?" I asked.

"Brent's in Tokyo?"

"After he spotted Jago rearranging the bushes outside his mom's house, he grabbed his son and ran."

"Oh shit." Blackson took a deep breath. "You gotta save him."

"Me? Why not you? Aren't you brothers-in-arms?"

"I think Koven killed David and he's going to kill Brent. He must've hired Jago to do it."

"Call the cops," I said.

"It'll be too late by then. You gotta do it."

His eagerness sent shivers of suspicion down my spine. The scent of a trap slathered in you-can-be-a-hero tickled my senses. What did I know about Blackson? The bullet I took for him might have been meant for me. The best part: I just told him where to send his assassins for a second try. Blackson was forthcoming during our chat under the bridge, so I trusted him. But nothing he said helped me solve the murders surrounding his firm.

"OK," I said, "you come with me."

"Oh. No way. I have a wife and kids."

Mercury said, *Ain't that sweet? You're Mister Expendable. Nobody cares if you live or die because you haven't procreated yet. Better find a girl or die alone. By the way, homie, let's look for a woman who likes men this time.*

He snickered like a schoolboy.

Looking over my shoulder, I found my between-jobs god and Seven-Death sitting in the back with seatbelts on.

The Mayan had his face plastered to the glass, freaked by the speed—or Miguel's driving. Not surprising since his culture came up with the most advanced astronomical calculations known to humankind until the 1960s, but they never figured out the wheel.

Mercury said, *Hey, don't let Blackson off the hook on the liability thing. He changed the subject on you.*

Miguel glanced my way, then craned over his shoulder to look in back. "Somebody following us?"

I shook him off and refocused on the phone. "Blackson, what does 'Gottleib liability' mean?"

He sighed. "I don't know. After you downloaded all those files, Brent and I figured we were already scorched. So we searched the company servers looking for whatever David found. We came up empty."

"What did you expect to find?"

"Koven brokers deals with international companies. Let's say he helps Esson Oil get a hundred million barrels of Saudi oil for $5 less than the going rate. That's half a billion in savings. Let's say Esson turns around and gives $100 million of that to a social welfare group who gives the money to a Super PAC that gets fifty congressmen elected. Those congressmen push through a deal to help the Saudis get more anti-tank rockets."

"And David Gottleib found a memo that linked a three-way deal like that?"

"Don't think so." Blackson sighed. "But Koven thought he did, and now he thinks Zola has it."

"Then it exists," I said, thinking out loud, "otherwise he never would've killed Gottleib."

Seven-Death leaned between the seats, shaking his death stick and screaming in my ear.

Scared the crap out of me. I nearly jumped out of the car.

I said, *Make him shut up or I'm going back on my meds.*

Mercury said, *Dude, chill, will ya? He's just pointing out the obvious.*

I said, *What obvious?*

Mercury said, *Gottleib tried to give you that bullet. He said he modified it for you. I'll bet it has a little note, a confession, or something inside. Maybe Zola has it now.*

I said, *No, it's in the Montgomery County Police evidence locker.*

Mercury said, *Holy Minerva. Nice move, bro. You had it in your hands and turned it over to the cops for safe keeping? You don't need any help from the gods. No siree. You got this handled. Fuck.*

Blackson was still talking. "I'm pretending to be on Koven's side while looking for anything that ties him to David's murder or the foreign money."

"And I get to take on Jago in Japan. Nice to know you've got my six." I huffed. "I gotta go."

"Tell me the truth, Jacob." Blackson's voice dropped an octave.

"Why were you wearing body armor last night?"

I clicked off.

Mercury flicked my ear from the backseat. *I told you to wear body armor and it saved your ass, homie. Would it be that hard to say, 'I'm in tight with Mercury, a high-ranking and awesome god, and he told me to wear the armor because he knew I'd need it'? Hey. Y'know, that Noah dude didn't hold back when people asked, 'WTF's with that Ark?' Ya feel me? Hey, what's with you anyway, bro? Are you ashamed of me or something?*

I said, *I'm not sure people aren't going to react the way you think.*

Mercury said, *Yeah. I see how you are. Hey. Don't forget to call Dr. Harrison. You promised.*

"I never promised anything," I said.

"Promised who?" Miguel eyed me sideways.

"I never promised to save Zola." My fist hit the dashboard. "How did I get this deal? Why am I flying to Tokyo? I have no idea where to find this guy, who's after him, or anything. This is an exercise in futility."

I checked the plane tickets in my hand. "And the ticket's for coach! How many times do I have to save her life to get first class?"

"Chill," Miguel said. "You're in first class. That one's for Carlos."

For the next two miles I stared at the big guy with my mouth hanging open. "You're kidding, right? I'm babysitting the gangster?"

Miguel shrugged.

I dialed Dr. Harrison.

We exchanged pleasantries and he did his doctor shtick about my *feelings*. For the first time since I'd met him, he seemed genuinely concerned about my health and wellbeing and not the billable hours.

The whole time we spoke, Seven-Death was giving me the stink eye from the back seat.

"There are people working to have you committed," Harrison said. "We don't want that to happen. Tell me about your relationship with this god of yours."

"No way. You went to the press and told them all about me. That's a violation patient confidentiality."

"I never named you or gave any identifying information that could be traced back to you. It's all perfectly within the bounds of HIPAA requirements." He coughed. "Now, about God. What kinds of things does he tell you?"

"He warns me about bad things and helps me do good things."

Mercury waved his hands in front of my face to get my attention and shook his head when I turned around.

"And does he tell you to do specific things?" Harrison asked.

"Sometimes. He'll tell me which guy to shoot first and where to aim in the dark. Things like that."

"Has he ever told you to do something bad?"

"Define bad."

Mercury was having a conniption fit in the backseat. Seven-Death started shaking his stick and yelling stuff in Mayan.

Mercury said, *Don't just answer his questions. Tell him how great I am and how handsome I am—that kind of thing.*

I said, *What's wrong with his questions?*

Mercury said, *He's a weasel. He's gone bad on us.*

I said, *You're just worried he'll put me on anti-psychotics again.*

Mercury said, *Truth hurts, bro, but here it is: Tony would still be alive if you'd listened to me.*

It was a low-blow, even for Mercury. Tony was a good friend who'd fallen to his death on one of my missions. I'd been taking my meds back then and thought I was handling life without divine intervention just fine. Losing Tony drove me off medication and back into the world of gods-with-too-much-time-on-their-hands.

"Life and death," Dr. Harrison said, "right-and-wrong kind of bad. Has he ever told you to kill someone other than an identified enemy?"

Mercury's insistence that I kill Jago Seyton when he was following me came to mind. On reflection, if I'd followed his advice, I wouldn't be taking a flight to Japan and Zola would be safe at home.

"Oh yeah," I laughed. "Just the other day he told me to shoot this guy in the alley."

Seven-Death and Mercury leaned back in their seats, faced each other, and shook their heads. Their shoulders drooped and their eyes sank.

Mercury said, You're screwed, dawg. *We're getting out here. I can't watch anymore.*

With that, the two ex-gods opened the door at seventy-five miles an hour and hopped from the hood of one car to the next until they disappeared.

"Jacob," Dr. Harrison said with gravity, "I think it's time we took this thing seriously. You need to commit yourself to an institution voluntarily or someone might have you committed."

"No way," I said. "That's for the criminally insane. Look, I'm leaving for Tokyo in a few minutes. I'll call you when I get back."

I clicked off and wondered about the definition of 'criminally insane'.

Miguel kept his eyes on the road and tried to pretend he hadn't heard the conversation. I stared at him until he shrugged.

He said, "At least your gods talk to you."

# CHAPTER 21

EVEN MUFFLED BY their headsets, the constant drone of the helicopter's engines strained the conversation between Pia and Tania to the point of silence. They stared out of their respective windows, where endless waves of golden sand stretched from the turquoise sea on Dubai's coast back across empty miles to the distant mountains in the east.

Wearing an above-the-knee business skirt, Pia considered changing and wondered how formal a tone she wanted to set for her meeting. That would depend on who showed up to represent Ms. Suliman, the Saudi businesswoman. Setting the appointment had turned into a mysterious adventure without closure. None of which mattered, whoever came to the meeting might tell her how Koven operated and what his foreign clients expected in return. There had to be a paper trail of some kind.

"That thing is huge." Tania stared out at the Burj Khalifa, the world's tallest building.

"Wrong Burj," Pia said. She pointed in the opposite direction. "We're staying at the Burj al Arab."

The sail-like form of the iconic hotel blew across the waters toward them.

"Why did you change reservations? You usually stay at the nicest place in town."

"Bigger is not better. The al Arab is the nicest," Pia said. "After Herr Müller's murder, I'm concerned about surprises at planned destinations."

"And you didn't tell me. Why would your head of personal security need to know?"

"Don't take it like that. I made the change a few minutes ago."

After staring out of the window for a moment, Pia tugged Tania's sleeve. "You still haven't explained why you sent Carlos to Tokyo."

"That man was making moves on me," Tania said. "He made me uncomfortable."

"Bullshit. He's not the least bit interested in you."

"Why not? I'm mostly Latina and I'm hot." Tania drew back. "Oh, I see. You and he—"

"No."

"Well, maybe you should—then you wouldn't be so testy." Tania ducked Pia's glare. "Why did you put a big-time gangbanger in our operation anyway?"

"It's *my* operation, thank you," Pia said. "And when it concerns you, I'll let you know."

"That is *so* not you, Pia."

Pia turned back to the window. There were things she didn't have to explain, and then there were things she couldn't explain. Why did she bring a convicted felon into her personal security detail? Would Tania believe her about the dream, the demanding voice, the overwhelming impulse that drove her actions? Jacob maybe, but not Tania.

A thousand feet below them, yachts paraded up and down the coast.

The pilot swirled around the cantilevered helipad on the hotel's roof and set down. A white-gloved butler welcomed them and led them to a line of servants offering fresh hand towels, scented sanitizers, lotions, and dates while a porter took their bags to the elevator. The butler, a transplanted Englishman, showed them to the suite.

Gold-veined marble floors led to a maroon-and-gold living room and a deep blue dining room where a globe of roses rested on the polished, mahogany table. Up the sweeping staircase were two bedrooms with matching bathrooms where marble columns held gilded ceilings above round bathtubs.

"You have a freaking couch in your bathroom?" Tania stared at a woman wearing a burgundy uniform standing in the corner holding towels. "And who is she? Your lady in waiting or something?"

"This is your room," Pia said.

From downstairs the butler announced the arrival of Pia's guest.

A middle-aged woman with jet-black hair and a jeweled hijab examined Pia as she descended the stairs. There was a certain quick and cunning intellect in the lady's brown eyes.

Pia reached the bottom step and stopped, leaving a few yards of marble between them. She asked, *"Kaif halik?" How are you?*

"Al hamdu lillah, zeina." Thanks to God, I'm fine.

The woman extended a hand. She wore a dark skirt suit cut long with low pumps, a pile of pearls on each toe.

Pia stepped forward and shook her hand instinctively then remembered it was not the Arab custom for women.

"It's all right," the woman said with a light English accent. "I attended university at Oxford and have a master's from Georgetown."

Pia nodded.

"I am Samira Suliman." A hard flex of rigid determination crossed her cheek as she spoke.

"What a pleasant surprise. I understood you were sending emissaries. It is a great honor to meet you in person. Thank you for making the trip from Jeddah."

"I thought you would feel more comfortable in the Emirates."

"I've visited Saudi Arabia a few times," Pia said, "but I must admit, I was dying to drive a car."

"Just because our customs are different doesn't mean women don't enjoy life. Fifty-seven percent of Saudi women are college educated compared, to just 32% of Americans. Our women control their inheritance and dowry, and we don't take our husband's name." Samira smiled. "Why not make men do the driving?"

Pia conceded Samira's point with a small dip of her head.

Samira nodded to a man in a pristine white *thobe* and traditional red-checked *keffiyeh* who stood by the door. He bowed and exited to the hall. She then turned her gaze to Pia's butler.

Pia turned to him. "Tea in the sitting room, please. And then some privacy."

He nodded and left.

"Was it a difficult journey from Jeddah?" Pia led the way to the living room and offered her guest a seat on the U-shaped couch festooned with pillows.

"Not at all." Samira dropped her Birkin purse on the coffee table, removed several excess cushions, and sat diagonally from Pia. "But let's dispense with the Arabic custom of lengthy personal discussions before business. I prefer the American method of getting straight to the point."

Pia gave her a polite smile. "Do you work with Lars Müller or Prince Taimur?"

"Those names are vaguely familiar."

"I understand from Daryl Koven that you have some interests in the US and may need help."

"That's a dangerous statement."

It was her best, most practiced line. Pia expected the Saudi to tell her everything but now that she'd met the woman, she needed a more patient line of questioning. Again her father's advice rang true, wait until your opponent has played her hand. So, Pia waited.

"I've worked with Duncan and Hyde, DHK, for many years," Samira said. "They've buffered the dangerous territory of international politics for my late husband and now they work for me."

The butler arrived with a tea service. He set out two china cups and poured. Samira held her cup in one hand and her saucer in the other and blew across the top. The butler offered sugar and milk and was politely turned down. He bowed and left.

"I've been told my youth shows," Pia said. "Perhaps I've chosen my words poorly."

Samira sipped her tea, her intense gaze never leaving Pia. "If you were to rephrase your statement, what words would you choose?"

Pia picked up her tea cup and blew across it. "Allow me to think out loud. I implied that you needed help, which implies vulnerability. That was wrong of me. Mr. Koven let me know that several people have goals they would like to accomplish in the next election cycle and that I could give them an assist."

"Assist?" Samira said as much as asked. "Is that a soccer reference?"

"Assists are more important than goals. The player with the ball intentionally draws the defenders toward her, giving her very little chance to score. She then passes to a teammate who was left open. That's called an assist."

Samira laughed. "You fool your opponents intentionally?"

"It's an important element of the game."

"That is necessary for international business as well, is it not?" Samira asked.

Pia shrugged. The comparison to soccer techniques spiked her anger. She saw no comparison between outwitting people in sport and fooling people in business.

"We are alike in some ways." Samira clattered her cup in the saucer and leaned over to set it down, then stopped. She looked at Pia. "I hope you understand my lack of football knowledge. I could be arrested for attending a match in my country."

"You lived in England for several years. You must have seen at least one game."

"I did." Samira laughed and her eyes sparkled just a little. "I saw you play in the Olympic final. You were brilliant—or so my more knowledgeable friends told me."

"Thank you."

"DHK is brilliant in these matters." Samira's eyes narrowed. "Why don't you leave it to them?"

"Why did you come here alone?"

"You are a clever woman." Samira wagged a finger with a light laugh. "You're right. I came here because I thought you were someone I could deal with. Someone who would understand things."

They sipped their tea for a moment.

Samira leaned back on the pillows. "What kind of goals do you imagine a businesswoman in Saudi Arabia would have?"

"Now I'm the one with a lack of knowledge." Pia sipped her tea. "You know my culture far better than I know yours."

Samira pursed her lips and considered her words. "Saudi Arabia is on pace to behead 200 people this year. Everything is a capital crime, even apostasy."

"Are you going to renounce your faith?"

"Another dangerous question." Samira scowled. "Like you, I am a woman of faith. I believe in charities and spend much of my time helping the less fortunate. Because I distribute food, clothes, and medicine for victims in war-torn regions like Serbia, Yemen, Kabul, and Bosnia, I've been banned from international travel. I can go to a few sympathetic countries in the Middle East, no farther. My trip to the Olympics reduced me to using a friend's passport. Restricted travel makes an already difficult business environment all the harder."

Again the woman's words made her tense with anger. There was no comparison between Suliman's charities and Pia's. She drank some tea and counted to three to calm her voice before continuing. "That's terrible. Perhaps I could talk to someone at the State Department."

"The most efficient way to reach the State Department is through Congress."

Pia nodded. "And that's where you need my help?"

"Representatives answer to big donors, and when big donors want an old friend to come for tea..." Samira raised her cup and sipped.

Pia held her cup, inhaled the aroma and savored the taste.

"I'm not clear on how everything works," Pia said. "Do you know how much I'd need to spend in order to have the right politicians listen to me?"

Samira clicked her cup and saucer delicately on the table. "It's refreshing to work with you. Making plans with too many people involved can be expensive. DHK requires so much money it worries me."

"They provide a certain amount of expertise."

"That's true, but at a tremendous price." Samira leaned forward as if to whisper. "Twice they've charged me $10 million and only put the money in two of the races they promised." She waved a dismissive hand. "And their politicians wouldn't even talk to my emissary after the election."

"That's unreliable." Pia picked up the teapot and offered more with a gesture. When Samira nodded, she poured. "Do you have to spend more? Or can you talk to the candidates before you give them your money?"

"That is the problem." Samira winked over her teacup. "I have many friends in business who are too content with the way things are. Mostly Arab men who don't want me to travel anyway. It's terrible. I need a new partner, one who appreciates my predicament."

"What kind of business do you run?"

"Tankers, it's boring." Samira let out a little laugh. "We're about to overhaul our computer systems. Project management is the key to making money in shipping."

"One of the Sabel Industries divisions does project management, I think."

"I know." Samira sighed. "We've been talking to IBM and Hewlett Packard for ages. They're so old fashioned. My people should be talking to your people."

"Yes! They should." Pia bounced in her seat. "I'm not sure how that side of the company works. I've only been involved in Sabel Security so far. But I can make some calls and arrange whatever we need. Oh, that would be great."

"Would your father allow you to assist a friend?"

"He does anything I ask."

"What a wonderful father."

"How does it work in the end? I mean, what do I do?" Pia asked.

"You bid the project and we create an incentive paid in advance. You use the advance for the congressional races. We'll still need a lobbyist—"

The distinct pop-pop of suppressed automatic weapons fire erupted in the hallway followed by a thump. To Pia's trained ears, the thump indicated one casualty outside the suite's door.

Pia leaped across the coffee table to the archway, drew her gun, and peered into the foyer. In her peripheral vision, Samira cowered in fear at the sight of the gun. Across it, Tania descended the sweeping staircase, leaped over the banister, and backed to the wall. The butler stood in the entryway, staring at Tania with his mouth open. He slowly faced Pia, his face turning ghostly white.

"You and Samira hide behind the couch," Pia said.

He nodded, trembling, and forced himself to move.

"What is it?" Samira asked, a quiver in her voice. "Who is after you?"

Pia pressed her back to the wall and faced the woman. In a strong whisper, she said, "They're after you."

"Me? They couldn't—"

"Your bodyguard is dead. Hide now and don't make a sound."

Pia waved Samira over the couch and down. Samira complied with a yelp. The butler joined her in the narrow space between the couch and the wall.

Pia turned back and connected with Tania, who held up four fingers, indicating her estimate of hostiles outside. Then she pointed to the door handle. It jiggled partially down and came back up. A clacking sound came from the electronic lock. The handle came partway down again, then back to level. Another clack of the lock and this time the handle came all the way down.

Pia joined the telepathic grid that connected her veterans in battle, wordlessly working in unison like a choreographed and deadly dance troupe.

Two men scuttled into the room like cockroaches, one left, and the other right. Both wore black body armor and helmets.

Pia aimed for the small patch of flesh on the cheek. It would be her best shot ever if she made it, possibly her last if she didn't.

Neither man looked up to see Tania. The man on the left swept the room, leading with his rifle. Just as he found Pia in the shadow, she pulled her trigger. The dart bounced off his helmet.

He dropped to the floor in a prone firing position and fired a three-round burst. Marble splintered around her, scratching her cheek. He lowered his weapon to see if he'd hit her, giving her a crucial second chance.

She sprinted four steps toward him, hampered by her suit skirt, slid across the marble, and pounded his face with her heels. His head snapped back with so much violence he was knocked out before he dropped his firearm.

The other man, unfamiliar with the floor plan, ran forward, looking for cover from Pia's assault.

Tania darted him in the butt. She ran out, grabbed his assault rifle and magazines.

Pia tucked her pistol under her suit jacket and grabbed the other weapon.

Both women retreated to their previous positions and covered the front door with their stolen weapons.

Pia sensed someone behind her. She spun, aimed, and found Samira in her sights, peeking over the couch. Pia considered shooting the woman to get it over with, but waved her back into hiding.

Samira dropped back.

A third man ducked in the entrance and pulled back when Tania unloaded half a mag on him.

Pia aimed down her weapon's iron sights, dropped the selector to "3" for full-auto, and waited.

After a moment, a smartphone extended around the door jamb. A clever maneuver to look around corners.

She blew it out of his hand.

Feet pounded away down the short hallway to the service elevator. Pia and Tania exchanged a glance of temporary relief: the assassins were in retreat.

Tania cleared the foyer, then the open area outside the room, a small space at the top of the hotel's atrium shared by two other suites. "There's a dead Arab out here."

"Two Emiratis out cold in here," Pia said. "No ID and empty pockets. Is the phone out there?"

"All three pieces of it."

Samira's trembling voice came from the living room. "Is it OK to come out?"

"Are you ready for martyrdom?" Pia asked.

The butler poked his head up and looked around. He'd been ill. He was going to be ill again.

"What are you talking about?" Samira asked.

Pia texted the helicopter pilot as she spoke. "Why are these guys trying to kill you?"

"Kill me? They were after you!"

"Whoever killed Lars Müller is going to kill you for the same reason. Any idea what it is?"

Samira shook her head. "Lars is dead?"

On a first name basis with a man she pretended was only 'vaguely familiar'. Pia thought again about shooting the woman herself and saving the assassins the trouble.

"There have to be four more," Tania said. "We need to get out of here. Now."

Pia and Tania stripped ammo from their attackers and rounded the entryway into the hall. Pia texted the Major about their situation, requesting money, guns, and lawyers.

"You're leaving me?" Samira said.

"Yes, I am," Pia said. "Are you afraid?"

"You have to take me with you." Samira followed them to the doorway.

"Before I take a meeting with someone, I do extensive research." Pia shoved her against the wall and held her by the throat with one hand. "Who wants you dead besides me?"

Samira began to cry. "I thought we were friends."

"I hope they make it as slow and painful for you as your 'charity' made it for others." Pia saw the recognition in Samira's eyes. "I know about al-Haramain Islamic Foundation. Your husband set that up twenty years ago and funded al-Qaeda with it. The UN shut it down in 2004 so you opened another one. When your husband died, you kept it going. And now you're funding Daesh, otherwise known as ISIL. Did you really think I would help you buy elections in the United States of America?"

"Why not? Everyone else does."

Pia grabbed the woman by the back of her head, pulled her down hard, and pounded her knee into Samira's face. The Saudi slipped to the floor, unconscious. Pia propped her in the hallway where the assassins would have no trouble finding her.

"Get the others," Pia called to the butler. "We need to move them out of danger."

He nodded vigorously and called out in Arabic. Five uniformed women ran down the stairs to the foyer. They gawked at the bodies for a moment before following Pia's gestures and filed into the hall. They each gasped as they rounded the corner and found the dead Arab, his red-checkered headdress covered in dark red blood.

Pia and Tania covered each other to the stairwell. She covered the hall while Tania cleared the first flight of stairs. She then ushered the staff up a flight behind Tania. The stairwell was a typical fire escape, surrounded by thick walls of fireproof concrete, with cement stairs leading to a landing halfway between floors. The perfect place for an ambush from above. Tania crept around one more landing, daring their adversaries to appear.

Pia followed the last servant into the stairwell and watched the hall as the door closed. That's when she saw them.

Five men charged toward her, guns blazing.

# CHAPTER 22

FROM HIGH IN the castle battlement, Daryl Koven watched the luxury bus crunch across the gravel and up the Reichsburg Cochem's concentric portals with an excitement he hadn't experienced since childhood. His designer topcoat flapped as he ran through the castle's arterial gate, the shortcut used for centuries by defending knights. Finger-combing his hair, he waited at the entrance to the citadel, the inner sanctum of the thousand-year-old fortress perched 300 feet above the Moselle River in western Germany. Above him, the massive keep loomed more than eight stories high, each of its four two-story turrets perched on the corners of its black slate roof.

Koven took a moment to admire the keep. Marthe had outdone herself this time. This castle was significantly larger and more imposing that the château in France. And the river view much more breathtaking.

He took up his position near the old well, the point of the outer defensive ring where the bus would unload his guests. Castle staff lined up by the wall, ready to whisk luggage to each executive's room. Behind him, an array of heaters blasted warmth into the Rhineland winter. He patted his coat with his gloved hands and hoped his guests would be as warmly dressed.

It didn't matter—he wouldn't take long.

It was a short ride from the private airport where all the corporate jets landed in rapid succession, still, he worried that his guests might expect a line of limos. The bus was all Marthe could find in the rural towns nearby.

First off were Paul and Olga Benning. He greeted them.

"Marthe handled Tom's funeral with beauty and grace," Paul said. "That was an amazing party. I hope she'll take care of my arrangements when the time comes. And this castle is even better than the last. How does she do it?"

"With an unlimited budget, that's how!"

The two men laughed. Olga curled a lip.

Koven sent them to the inner courtyard and greeted the next guests to troop off the bus.

Fifth in line was Alan Sabel.

"Alan, so good to see you. Where is that wonderful daughter of yours?"

"She had pressing matters elsewhere."

"Is that right?" Koven leaned back with surprise. "I thought she and I would finish some business this trip."

"Don't worry." Alan walked away. "She's not finished with you."

Koven felt his face drain and his heart beat pick up. He couldn't let Sabel intimidate him like that. He had to ignore the doubters and forge ahead. He took a deep breath and continued greeting everyone, then circled around to his small stage. Overhead, a raven gave a scratchy caw and the clouds lowered the midday light to a dusky hue. A clean, cold breeze dried his skin. He sniffled and smelled baking bread.

Timing it to be pulled from the oven as the guests arrived was Marthe's genius.

Where would he be without her?

Rip Blackson gave the introductory remarks and led a moment of silence for Tom Duncan. Then he introduced Koven. "Ladies and gentlemen, our host for the next three days is a war hero who distinguished himself in Operation Iraqi Freedom..." Koven didn't hear the rest as he mentally rehearsed his speech. Then came his cue. "Allow me to introduce Daryl Koven."

He bolted up the three short steps to hearty applause, thanked Blackson, switched on his lapel mic, and turned to the group.

"Folks, it's cold, so I'll be brief." He paused and let the halogen lights catch the sparkle in his blue eyes. "Commerce is like water, it's a force of nature. Water carved the Grand Canyon and commerce carved modern civilization. Both are perpetual and relentless, constantly seeking the most effective routes. Some would dam it to harness its energy. Others would channel it for their own purposes."

He paced the stage, extending his arms. "Our investors and shareholders aren't interested in the dams and channels. They want to see commerce flow straight into our quarterly earnings. And yet, we have to deal with the reality: there are those in both parties who still toil with twentieth-century thinking focused on outdated models. The dynamic energy of free-flowing commerce no longer carves canyons; it's been channeled into stagnant backwaters and left to evaporate."

He smiled as the executives gave each other knowing nods.

"We are not alone. In other countries, from Stockholm to Johannesburg, from Tokyo to Santiago, rules and regulations prohibit tributaries from joining with our rivers. Businesses like the gold mines of Burkina Faso find themselves unable to buy American bulldozers because of outdated sanctions. The Cold War ended a generation ago and yet these ancient prohibitions persist."

He paused to look each guest in the eye.

"Future Crossroads is the place where possibility meets practicality. At Duncan, Hyde, and Koven, we specialize in opening the floodgates in both directions. Opening new markets is a simple matter of matching incentives to needs."

Koven threw his hands in the air.

"Welcome to the future, where your river will rush to global opportunity. The Future Crossroads Symposium will align your goals with someone in need of your resources."

His guests nodded and muttered affirmations.

Koven smiled. "Folks, I smell baking bread. So—who's ready for lunch?"

A hearty round of applause followed. He hopped off the stage and led the group into the Grand Treaty Room. Corinthian columns carved from solid oak held up a vaulted ceiling; knights in antique armor stood guard; priceless sixteenth-century gold and silver pieces from the castle treasury littered the ancient inlaid tables; flames danced in both fireplaces; lovely maidens in renaissance smocks served drinks.

Koven stood at one end, looking over the crowd. He smiled to himself. Everyone was talking and drinking and having a good time.

Across shoulders and between heads, he saw Rip Blackson glance at him, then quickly away. Koven's heart stopped. What was in that look? Fear? Insolence? Treachery? His blood boiled.

He cooled himself down and returned his attention to Olga Benning, who was telling him about the horrific ordeal she had endured: the limousine company sent a small Maybach for her shopping trip in Paris. Everything had gone downhill from there.

He chuckled politely before catching a glimpse of Blackson again. The traitorous son of a bitch was chatting with Alan Sabel. They were leaning their heads together, no doubt conspiring to tear down everything he and Marthe were building.

Blackson flicked a guilty glance his way and their gaze met for a split second. The younger man's eyes darted away instantly.

Sabel laughed at something and patted Blackson on the back. He turned to Bobby Jenkins of Jenkins Pharmaceuticals. That left Blackson unattached with nowhere to go. Reluctantly, the young man met his gaze.

With a flick of his nose toward the door, Koven ordered Blackson to the next room.

"Have you found Zola yet?" Koven asked when they stepped into the whitewashed Armory.

"He went to his mother's. Some kind of family problem." Blackson's eyes darted left and right.

Koven stared hard, his jaw clenched so tight his teeth ground together. Muffled laughter and music bled through the heavy oak door. Neither of them spoke for a long time.

"You've been in touch then?"

"Just a couple texts," Blackson said. "There was a lot to do getting the symposium ready."

"When did you last text him?"

"I don't know. I've been through several time zones. A while ago."

"I heard he left LA." Koven watched Blackson's eyes wander.

"Who told you that?" Blackson asked.

"Never mind. Find out where he is. I need to talk to him."

Blackson met his gaze and held it. "Why?"

Koven shook his head and waved a hand at the crowd beyond the door. "Because he has a job to do."

Blackson dropped his head. "He knows. It was a family—"

"He's not at his mother's."

Blackson shrugged, still facing the stone floor.

"Let's not kid each other, Rip. Someone inside the firm was involved in David Gottleib's murder, which means we both suspect each other." Koven waited for Blackson to look up. "I know it wasn't me. So I'm only going to ask you this once: where is Brent Zola?"

Blackson's mouth drew tight. He leaned back against the wall. "Where's Jago?"

"That's your answer?" Koven crossed his arms.

"Jago was sneaking around outside Zola's mom's house. They called the cops. What's he going to tell them? Who sent him there? For what purpose?"

"Last I heard, Jago was *your* shadow." Koven left a long gap. "Did you send him?"

"Why would I? I had a good thing going with Duncan. Now I don't know where I stand. Zola's the only one I can trust."

Koven lifted his chin and leaned forward. "You trust him?"

"I was with him when David was murdered. I know it wasn't me. And I know it wasn't him. And Jago left the office early that day. Jago never does anything without being told. In your scenario where we don't trust each other, that leaves only you."

Koven felt his rage burning his face. He raised an angry fist between them, then pulled himself under control and shoved it in his pocket. "How dare you accuse me of killing Gottleib. I let you get away with it last time, but no more. I brought all three of you up from nothing. I pulled every support-the-veteran card I could to get you into law school. Duncan made me swear the three of you would bring in enough new business to pay your salaries. I did it for you, Rip. I did it for Brent. And I did it for David. I would never kill him."

"Then who's running Jago? Where was he that night?"

The two men stared hard at each other, the threat of violence rippling between them.

"Let's ask him," Koven said.

He pulled his phone out, set it on speaker, and dialed Jago Seyton.

When Jago answered, Koven was direct. "Where were you on the evening David Gottleib was murdered?"

"Traffic school. Speeding ticket. The detectives verified my attendance. Anything else?"

Koven clicked off. The two men stared at each other.

The big oak door slammed open and bounced off the wall. Alan Sabel's bear-like frame stormed straight to Koven. His big hands grabbed the man by the lapels and threw him against the wall. Eyes blazing red, snorting like a steam engine, Alan pressed his nose up to Koven's. "What the hell did you do?"

# CHAPTER 23

PEOPLE SCURRIED AND bumped and roller bags squeaked and public announcements echoed through the cavernous terminal at Narita International Airport, Tokyo. In the middle of all that humanity, I was lonely. Lost-in-the-desert lonely. All around me people talked and called and shouted and whispered—but not to me.

I was not on my meds and there were no voices in my head.

No strange god pranced around in a toga.

The silence was chilling.

Carlos proved to be a good traveling companion; he hadn't said a word. He trotted alongside me, his short legs barely able to keep my pace.

A man bounced off me and berated me in Japanese. Carlos stood to the side, watching my passive reaction. The only word I could remember was *arigato*, thank you. I picked up the handle of his bag and put it in his hand while he continued to shout profanities at me.

I felt disconnected, as if life was an uninteresting movie.

Godless was a terrible state.

But then, so was the god state.

Which is worse: having a trigger-happy divinity whose moral compass hasn't been updated since gladiators ruled weekend entertainment, or no one at all?

Why did I miss his presence when he wasn't around? Mercury was nothing more than the god I'd grown used to. He was my comfort god. So comfortable, in fact, that if Jesus walked up to me, I'd tell him I was waiting for a different messiah. One who was easier to live with. Looser rules. Less demanding. None of this give-all-your-money-to-the-poor stuff.

*Japan. He and Seven-Death were frat brothers in god college. They're going drinking.*

I said, *God college? Don't tell me things like that. Don't even joke. I can't handle it. I'm going back on my meds.*

Mercury said, *Chill, homie. Don't do anything rash, OK? Don't worry about those two. Next time we see them, they'll be too hungover to talk. Everything's gonna be fine. Hey. Who's in need of cultural diversity now?*

I said, *Why did you leave me? What's with Dr. Harrison?*

Mercury said, *I left you because you were being a dick. But Jupiter says, that's how mortals are and I gotta suck it up. Harrison, well. Too late now. We'll figure a way out of that one later. At the moment, you're on the wrong train. Zola's at the Tokyo National Museum with no cell phone service because he went to a different country and didn't spike his plan. Since he's from California, he's not going to figure that out for another hour.*

"You OK?" Carlos asked. "Cause you look like you ate a lizard."

"We're on the wrong train." I yanked his coat and pulled Carlos through the bodies at the next stop.

After a few minutes of standing around on an empty platform, our new train slowed to a stop. The doors whooshed open, we pushed in, and grabbed new railings.

We had another half hour to kill, so I restarted our conversation. "Why were you in the prison hospital?"

"Shanked by a fucking Crips enforcer. I died. The nurse told me the doctors argued about whether I was worth it. One guy kept trying after I'd flatlined for a minute. He stuck with me and pulled me through. Like a resurrection."

He watched my eyes for a reaction. I'd witnessed many stories like his in the war. There is no end to the mystery of life and death.

We were ten minutes out when my phone buzzed.

"Jacob, it's Brent Zola," he said. "I'm at the—"

"I know where you are. What exhibit are you near?"

"How did you—"

"Never mind that. Go to the Sculpture Exhibit in the Honkan building and turn your phone off."

"OK, but—"

"Brent, shut up and do what I told you. They can track your phone." I clicked off.

Carlos stared at me. "Your angel told you where he is?"

I gave him my soldier stare until he looked away.

Pisses me off. Why don't people get it? A god is a god. An angel is a share-cropper of souls who didn't even negotiate a lease-to-own option.

People jostled and yakked while others used earbuds to tune out the steel brakes and squealing rails.

We exited the Keisei-Ueno Station and pushed our way up to the street. Breaking into frozen daylight, I checked out the foreign cityscape. Across the park in front of us, we expected to find the museum. I checked a map to get my bearings and look around.

Jago Seyton walked toward me.

From the direction of the museum.

There were several possible reasons for his presence, none of which I liked.

His eyes were focused to my left. As he came within reach, I put my hand out to stop him. "Hey Skippy, what are you doing here?"

"Visiting Japan," he said and kept walking.

I watched him and Carlos watched me.

Dark clouds gathered above the icy streets like bums around a fire. I looked around, on one side of us was a big, noisy city and on the other, a quiet park. A few moms and grandparents pushed strollers and toddlers down broad walkways. No snipers, no killers, no one out of place. I glanced at Carlos and took off running for the museum.

It was a kilometer from the subway, and I had been a track star during my one year of college. Carlos was not a runner. I got there a good minute before him. I ran inside and turned right, fully expecting to find a body in a pool of blood.

Brent Zola and a teenaged boy stared at a grouping of Buddhist sculptures. They were alive and alone in the room. And Brent was holding his phone to his ear.

Carlos skidded in behind me while I was still checking the darker corners for dangers.

We walked up to them with light footsteps.

They acted as if they were on a field trip. Zola had no idea I was there. He was a laid-back guy, born to laid-back people in the laid-back heartland. The kind destined to die first when disasters cull the population. I glanced at Carlos, who read my mind and shook his head.

I tapped Brent on the shoulder.

"Oh hey, Jacob," he said with a big smile. "Good to see you, buddy. This is my son—"

"I just saw Jago Seyton catching the subway. We're getting out of here. Where're you staying?"

Brent choked and turned white.

Carlos snapped his fingers in front of the guy. Nothing.

I looked at the boy, surfer-blond and the kind of thin you only see on teenagers who spend all day playing outdoors. "You have a hotel near here?"

He shook his head, turning as white as his dad. "Airbnb. Is Jago the guy?"

I nodded. "We need to leave."

With a tug on Brent's arm, we headed for the main door. Carlos trotted ahead a few paces and checked the main entrance and walkway.

He turned around, shook his head, and pointed behind us. "Ten or twelve coming."

"Do you have guns?" Brent asked.

"Guns are illegal in Japan." I grabbed the brochure out of Brent's hands and memorized the building map.

One other exit. After showing it to Brent and his boy, I bolted between the exhibits to the backside. They followed.

The back door opened to a tranquil, ice-covered pond surrounded by trees with an asphalt path. We slipped and slid down the icy trail around the pond. A cast-iron fence with spikes on top hemmed us in. Beyond it was a rarely traveled road and a block fence, eight feet high.

Fifty yards to our left a group of thugs appeared. We turned up the trail in the opposite direction to find another bunch of thugs.

Brent Zola vaulted the spiked fence, his son followed. Carlos and I looked at each other. I could make it, but my shorter companion needed a boost. I looped my hands, tossed him up, and followed with a fair vault of my own.

The Zola boys had disappeared behind a gate in the block fence across the maintenance road. We followed. A few strides later, we were in a graveyard. We entered through a service area and ran past a backhoe and stone-working tools. Flying onto the main drag between shrines, we realized how trapped we were. Six Japanese guys blocked our exit via the main gate, forty yards ahead.

Carlos and I glanced at each other, telepathically communicating the required dialogue between manly men who face terrible odds: *fuck it, let's take these guys down.*

We charged, head on, only to see them pull chains from their coats.

I hate chains.

The first one nailed the back of my legs as I speared the guy with my head. While I shoved him back three feet, one of his buddies landed a chain diagonally across my back. A third guy took a whack at my shins. I fell to my knees, but managed to yank the weapon from my first assailant.

Unlike fight scenes in movies, gangsters don't wait around while you beat up their friends one at a time. They come at you in numbers. While I whipped the chain around one guy's face, two more guys landed on my back. They were smaller than me by fifty pounds, but two of them cancelled my advantage.

To my right, Carlos had disarmed a guy and swung his chain around his head so fast no one could get near. I backed my two guys into Carlos's spinning chain.

It turned out to be both a good thing and a bad thing. The velocity was enough to knock both of my guys unconscious, which was good. Wrecking Carlos's defensive weapon was bad. Three guys jumped him, fists flying.

Bang. Bang. Bang. Bang.

Definitely gunfire, but I didn't feel any bullets pass through my body and the immediate threats were coming at me too fast to look around.

The guy I disarmed came back at me with a bleeding right eye. I gave him a lashing from his blind side, spinning him into a stone monument. A bamboo stick landed on the back of my head, stunning me.

For a horrible instant, I stood stock still, knowing I needed to move or the next blow would be lethal, but I my body refused to respond. I heard a *whack*.

Carlos had whipped the guy who was about to crush my skull.

There were two guys left in our immediate vicinity, but a small horde slipped between gravestones, heading our way. Brent Zola lay in a pool of blood, his son nowhere to be seen.

I landed a blow to my attacker's chin as his pal kicked me in my already-sore-as-hell ribs. Carlos brought a crowbar down on the second guy's head. He was out.

My guy was on his back but managed to kick me in the balls.

That's when the horde arrived.

With a guy like Carlos on my six, I could take down four or five guys. Carlos was good for three himself. But the unlimited reinforcements overwhelmed us.

The first of the new guys tried to nose my fist, which didn't work out so well for him, but the guy right behind him hit me in the head with a baseball bat. Things were a little hazy after that.

Dark shadows of men crowded out what little daylight made it through the clouds. Punches rained down on me from all sides. I fought and landed some kicks with no idea if they were effective. My knees went out and I fell. From then on it was all kicks to the ribs and head.

Sirens cracked through the city noise around us. Our attackers fled like cockroaches from a can of WD40 behind a lighter.

Snow began to fall. I lay on my back, assessing the damage. Pushing up to my elbows, I searched for Carlos and noticed I was using one eye because the other one was swollen shut. My new best friend lay motionless a few feet away, bleeding from a gash in his forehead. At least he was breathing.

Footsteps approached from my left, where a lone figure in a dark overcoat approached at a confident pace. He stopped a few feet away, his figure backlit by some lights on a nearby building. He looked vaguely familiar, too tall to be Jago but someone I'd known in the past. He stared at me for a moment, contempt in his posture, then tossed a revolver on my chest, and walked away.

While serving under Pershing in 1916, George S. Patton, the flashy American General and hero of WWII, carried a single Colt SSA .45 ivory-handled revolver. During a gunfight with Julio Cárdenas, Pancho Villa's second-in-command, Patton had to stop and reload three times before killing the man. He deemed the experience too close for comfort and took to carrying a pair of Smith & Wesson revolvers that became part of his legend.

The still-smoking gun that now lay on my belly was a detailed replica of Patton's first gun, the Colt SSA.

I knew all this because the revolver was mine.

The last time I'd seen it was at my house, the night David Gottleib was killed.

Scary sparkles appeared in my peripheral vision and grew together in a patchwork of gloom. I sensed myself exhale everything in my lungs. Then it was total darkness.

# CHAPTER 24

PIA OPENED THE stairwell door enough to push the barrel of her weapon into the hallway and fired a three-round burst. She withdrew and slammed the metal fire door. Bullets pinged off it, leaving indentations.

"Is there any way to lock this?" Pia looked at the expectant eyes of the staff quivering on the stairs.

The butler shook his head, his face sagging.

"Clear on this floor," Tania said in her earbud. She was one landing up, out of visual range.

Pia ushered the staff up the stairs, where Tania waved them toward the hallway. Tania covered the next flight of steps up the fire escape while Pia followed the staff into the empty corridor.

"Line up, backs against the wall," Pia said. "Put your hands out, so they can see you're not hiding anything. We're going to the helipad."

"What should we tell them?" the butler asked.

"Tell them where we are. No need for anyone else to get hurt."

A maid stepped forward and spoke in broken English. "But they kill you."

"Wish them luck," Pia smiled.

She slid back into the fire escape in time to see two men looking up from the floor below. She fired off a burst, then pushed her barrel over the railing, aiming blindly straight down, and let off another. Ricochets zinged down the structure. Twenty-one rounds left in the magazine, plus two more mags of thirty each. Her suit jacket bulged with stolen ammo.

She waited and listened. Above her, Tania opened the last door, top floor, and had a look. Below her, boots scuffled back to the landing.

She fired off blindly again, and more ricochets pinged down fifty floors.

"Clear up here," Tania whispered in her comm link.

Pia ran up the final two flights to join Tania in the plush hallway. Running to the balcony together, they considered the giant atrium below. Dubai Police were pouring in the front doors, herding guests and blowing whistles. Outside more Dubai police vehicles raced across the curved bridge leading to the hotel. Pia looked to Tania.

"Textbook police work," Tania said. "They'll have everything under control in fifteen minutes. About ten minutes too late for us."

They ran for the exit, ripped open the door, and crossed the rooftop greeting area to the helipad's stairs. The open flight would offer no protection. Pia faced the door while Tania ascended the first set. Two heads popped out and Pia brushed them back with a burst before joining Tania on the first landing.

Tania fired at the next wave of attackers while Pia made the last ascent to the round steel disc cantilevered off the front of the hotel. She looked down over 650 feet, the billowing "sail" of the building nearly obscuring the man-made island on which the hotel stood. She looked toward the airport and saw nothing in the sky.

She texted the pilot. "You are supposed to be here. Now would be a good time to pick us up."

Tania joined her at the edge of the pad and assessed their situation. Below them on the hotel side, behind the greeting area, were massive walls hiding the air conditioning, elevator mechanicals, and other machinery. At the back, two giant supports carried the structural weight of the building. The mast rocketed into the sky above them. Beyond the supports, on the far side of the hotel and twenty feet below the roofline, the Skyview Bar's wall of glass faced west over the Persian Gulf.

The pilot texted back, "Police have cordoned off the building and airspace due to a shooting. I will be there when they give the all-clear."

Tania read over her shoulder. "We're screwed."

A man stuck a gun out of the door and fired blindly. The bullets went high and several yards to their left. Tania fired back and blew off some fingers. The closing door cut off a high-pitched scream.

Pia pointed to the outer wall of the hotel, a three-foot wide rim ran above the hotel fifteen feet below the edge of the helipad. "We jump to there, run to the other side, get behind the door and fire at them as they come out."

"Are you nuts? If we don't stick the landing like a gymnast, we're splat on the sidewalk."

They peered over the edge.

Behind them, the door opened again. Two men ran out. Pia and Tania flipped over to full-auto and unloaded a magazine each.

They hit one, badly denting his body armor, but the other dragged him back inside, behind the concrete walls.

They switched magazines.

"Guess we're going to stick the landing," Tania said.

The helipad had no safety rails, relying instead on a wide net to catch anything that might leave the landing surface. Pia worked her way to the edge, flipped over, and landed like an Olympian.

Tania watched the door glancing back at Pia. "If I fall, will you tell Mama I love her?"

"You'll be fine. It's wider than it looks."

Tania stretched across the net, grabbed the side rail, and looked down. Pia looked down too. Wind whipped the Teflon-coated cloth that formed the famous sail. Cars the size of ants lay scattered about the entrance like toys.

"Don't look down." Pia pointed to the narrow strip of wall at her feet. "Look right here."

Tania huffed and jumped.

Three men flew out of the door, guns blazing at the top of the helipad.

Pia returned fire, her casings glittering like a shower of gold in the afternoon sun.

Tania landed, her arms windmilling, and continued forward over the edge.

She reached the tipping point and kept going forward.

Pia sensed the problem going on behind her. She fired off another burst with one hand, reached for Tania's collar with the other, and pulled. Her skirt stopped her from kicking out a balancing leg that would bring them upright. Tania's momentum was unabated. Pia's MP5 sprayed bullets into the air as she leaned backward. A gust of wind slammed her and tried to push her to her death.

She stole a glance over her shoulder and saw nothing between her and the ground hundreds of feet below. She tottered on her heels, straining her ankles and calves to stay upright. She bent her knees, lowering her center of gravity, giving her an extra split-second to find a way to stay alive. She refocused her efforts to bring their combined weight and momentum under control, tightened her grip, and used her core strength to pull them both back to the wall.

Tania's excitement at coming back carried over and nearly threw the two of them into the greeting area. They recovered, exposed and wobbling, before running along the top of the wall. They were outlined against the sky, like paper targets at the gun range.

The men in black found them and fired on full-auto. Their arc of lead trailed the women by a foot.

Pia and Tania scurried as fast as they could to the mechanical area, where a higher concrete wall would protect them. The bullets caught up with them, shredding the edge of the cement wall. Around the edifice, nestled among the giant, bellowing machines a level below them, they saw a door leading back inside to the service elevator. Just as they were about to jump down into the space, the door swung open and two men stepped out.

When Pia and Tania, filled with a good measure of fear but better-trained than their counterparts, saw their assailants, they turned and fired first.

Protected by helmets and body armor, the men staggered back a step, but raised their weapons.

Tania nailed one guy in the face. The other dropped back inside.

"I thought they were after Suliman," Tania said.

"Guess we became a target of opportunity."

"That means they're communicating with the head honcho."

Pia jumped down and went through the dead man's pockets until she found his phone. The last number dialed was labeled LOCI. She started to dial it when the survivor stuck his rifle barrel out of the door and fired.

Pia kicked the weapon, levering it against the door and pinning her opponent's finger inside the trigger guard. He screamed in pain.

She climbed the wall and followed Tania farther down, out of range. Across the mechanicals area, they saw three more men climbing to their level. In less than a minute, they would lose the high-ground advantage. They peppered the men with bullets. One fell back, the others ducked.

Panting hard, they ran between the two giant supports that held up the building and stopped.

Twenty feet below them was the roof of the Skyview Bar. More than six hundred feet below that, the cobalt Persian Gulf crashed into the hotel's reef.

The Burj al Arab was built on a man-made island. To secure the island and prevent erosion from the gulf's light but relentless waves, jagged boulders, each the size of a car, formed a barrier. The serrated edges broke down the water's energy and kept the hotel in place.

Tania faced Pia. "You should've let me splat on the other side. I'd make a better-looking corpse on asphalt than those spikey rocks."

Pia ran a short distance and grabbed a coil of electrical cable. "You have the wrong attitude. Focus on winning."

"Will you stop the super-athlete-positive-mental-attitude bullshit? Not everything turns out fine just because you want it to."

"If you don't focus on the goal, you'll never hit it."

"What the hell? You think we're going to rappel down the side with that?"

"Got a better idea?"

Two machine guns opened up, indiscriminately firing over their heads.

"No, that was a good one." Tania grabbed the electrical cable and looped it through a big metal ring jutting out of the cement. "If those things support window washers, they should hold us, right?"

Pia crossed her fingers.

More bullets raked the walls, coming nearer to them.

Pia aimed but found no targets.

Tania tossed the remaining cable over the roof of the Skyview Bar. She jumped down and walked backward, using the cable for support.

Pia fired a few rounds over the heads of their foes to keep them from peeking.

Tania reached the edge of the roof. Below her, a six-hundred-foot drop to the barrier rocks. She pulled her rifle off her shoulder and held it one-handed. "I'm going over. I'll shoot open the glass and try to land inside. If I make it, I'll shake the line like this." She gave the line a big shake, sending a sine wave up the line.

"Will it hold you?" Pia asked.

"Focus on winning."

Another round of gunfire sent Pia over the edge, onto the Skyview's roof.

Tania tied a slipknot in the end and slid it over her shoulders, then pulled it tight under her arms. With a last nod at Pia, she jumped off the roof.

Pia heard raking gunfire and breaking glass. Civilians in the bar beneath her feet screamed in terror.

A wave came up the line. Tania had made it.

Or.

The residual tension sent a phantom wave back up the line when Tania fell to her death.

A man appeared above her. Pia fired half a mag at him. Several rounds deflected off his armor before he fell back.

She walked down the curved roof in good-looking shoes with zero grip. The surface curved like a clamshell, growing steeper and narrower at the edge. When she reached her last step, she tried to loosen the slipknot. It was stuck.

A helmeted assailant popped up over the wall and fired. Pia fired back.

She wrapped the cable around her arm three times and held it as tight as possible.

Three more men popped up. This time, two of them took aim while the third produced wire cutters.

Pia flipped to full-auto and emptied her last mag.

Holding the cable as tight as her fingers could squeeze, she ran down the sloping roof. She picked up speed, running as fast as her world-class legs could fly, and leaped into empty space as far as she could.

For an instant, she saw only sky and the Persian Gulf's infinite horizon. She willed herself not to look at the jagged rocks below her. For an infinitely short span of time, her momentum carried her into the empty air—weightless. The remaining slack pulled out of the cable, the line drew taut, and the jerk on her arm threatened to pull it from its socket.

The cable slipped through her fingers.

# CHAPTER 25

"LET GO OF me," Koven said. "I have no idea what you're talking about."

Alan Sabel stayed an inch from his face, his fists full of Koven's suit. "She went to Dubai to meet one of your clients. An armed militia stormed the building. Latest reports are that she's on the roof, fighting for her life. I swear to god, Koven, if she gets so much as a scratch, you're a dead man."

"Are you threatening me?" Koven grabbed at Alan's grip, trying to free himself.

"Yes." Alan pushed the smaller man up the wall until his feet dangled. "This sounds like what happened to Müller."

"I don't know anyone in Dubai or any of the Emirates. I had nothing to do with Müller's murder—he was my client, for Christ's sake."

Rip Blackson shook his head. "It's true, Mr. Sabel. I've never seen any Emirates engagements on the books."

Alan snapped his glance at Blackson. "She was meeting someone there. What clients do you have in the region?"

"Suliman and Oman are clients," Blackson said. "I'm not aware of any planned meetings."

Alan dropped Koven. "If I find you had anything to do with it, anything at all—"

The big man shoved him hard into the wall and stormed down the hallway.

Koven shoved his shaking hands in his pockets. "That man's a lunatic."

Blackson's gaze fell to Koven's knees where the fabric of his pant leg vibrated. "Müller was Hyde's client. Why did you call him yours?"

Koven took a deep breath. "I met with him a couple times when Hyde was in rehab. Tom and I thought it prudent to have a transition plan in place."

A bell sounded in the guest reception. Koven shook himself like a ragdoll to purge his fears. He inhaled deeply and blew out a long stress-breath. "Showtime."

He glanced at Blackson, opened the oak door, and strode into the party. "Friends, lunch is served in the Knights' Hall. There are no seating charts, no name tags, so don't stand on ceremony."

As Koven pointed the way, his phone rang. He pulled it, glanced at the caller, and leaned in to Blackson. "Rip, escort our guests to dinner. I have to take this call."

After Blackson ushered the last guests out, Koven clicked open Skype and looked at his employee. "Jago, is that blood? Have you been hurt?"

"Must be Zola's."

"Better on you than in him. Have you taken care of that matter?"

"Zola is dead."

"Then you are the best," Koven said. "And his son, Philip?"

"Flip disappeared when the fighting started."

"That worries me. Can the boy identify you?"

"Don't worry about me. The point is, Zola's dead."

"The boy will grow up with revenge on his mind, that's my point. But a topic for another day. Good job, Jago." Koven clicked off.

He stood alone in the empty Grand Treaty Room, surveying the abandoned cocktail glasses and spilled nuts. Two workers came in and began filling trays with empties.

"My dear, why are you here?" Marthe asked from the doorway. "You should be in the Knights' Hall, making everyone feel welcome. I thought you had a toast planned, and a few good jokes. You have to set the tone for dinner, keep them from being bored. If you don't make them laugh, this whole thing is just another tourist trap."

Koven approached and put his arm around his wife. "Thank you for reminding me."

"You look like you've seen a ghost, but you're smiling. What are you up to?"

"I've just been given good news," Koven said. "Brent Zola won't bother us anymore."

"What do you mean? How was he bothering us?"

"He was digging into things. He and Blackson. And that madman, Jacob Stearne. They downloaded files from the company server."

"You said there's nothing on the server." She pressed her hand to his chest. "You always said it's the electronic record that trips people up."

"There isn't anything." He caught her gaze. "If they find paper contracts, they can piece it together. But they were looking. That's the problem. Betrayal. Mutiny. Desertion. You can't allow it for a second."

Marthe searched his eyes for a beat. "They're not the ones you need to worry about."

"You're right. Let's crank up the party, I want everyone drunk by dinner."

He took her hand and led her to the Knights' Hall. The dining room, intact from the eleventh century, sported a whitewashed barrel roof over stone walls and slate floors. Two long, rough-hewn tables filled the length with matching benches along each side. A spotlight lit up the entryway to showcase the servers as they brought in eleventh century meals of bread and meat, in baskets hanging from yokes on their shoulders.

Koven opened the door as two young maidens in period costumes approached bearing pewter pitchers and mugs filled with mead. He gestured them through and followed. The crowd erupted in applause as the young ladies introduced themselves with a microphone and announced what they were serving.

With the spotlight still shining, Koven stepped into the room to his own round of applause. One of the serving girls handed Koven the mic.

He smiled at Marthe, who smiled back. They took a bow before she darted offstage to an empty seat.

"Before you run off, ladies," Koven laughed, "could I trouble you for a cup of mead?"

One of the girls handed him a pint.

Lofting it over his head, he said, "My friends, life is a waste of our time." He waited a beat while the executives glanced at each other. "Or, is it that time is a waste of our lives?" He waited another beat. "So why not get wasted and have the time of our lives?"

To rhythmic cheers of 'chug-chug-chug', he quaffed his mead and held up his empty.

When the room quieted a little, he held the microphone to his mouth. "You know, when I started at Duncan and Hyde, I was still in college-boy mode. You remember what that's like—staying out too late, calling in sick. Well, one day, Tom Duncan called me into his office and asked, 'Daryl, do you believe in life after death?' It was a strange question in a business environment. I looked him in the eye and said, 'Yes sir.' He said, 'That's good, because while you took yesterday off to attend your grandmother's funeral, she stopped in to see your new office.'"

The group laughed politely.

"Hey, I saved you a seat!" Paul Benning motioned to a piece of bench next to him in the middle of the room.

"You know, folks," Koven said, "everyone who matters in American business today is here. If only my dear friend Brent Zola could join us. I hope he's attending his grandmother's funeral."

Nervous laughs rippled around the room.

"Did I tell you what that boy did during the Battle for Nasiriyah?" Koven asked. "We were ambushed, pinned down by a company of Sadam's Republican Guard. A crazed Army Ranger ran into our position, out of his mind on drugs or something. He grabbed my service pistol and aimed it at my head. I thought I was a dead man. Folks, Brent Zola stepped in front of me and talked the whacked-out kid off the edge. He saved my life."

A solemn silence fell over the group.

From across the room, he could feel Rip Blackson scowl at him. He spied Blackson as the young man leaned forward, the light from his phone illuminating his face. The traitorous son of a bitch was probably texting someone to check on Zola. Maybe he was texting Jacob Stearne. Maybe the police.

"I'd like to meet that man," Paul Benning said. "Too bad he couldn't be here." Benning slapped the open space on the bench next to him. "Last seat in the room."

Koven started toward him and stopped. He shouted, "Why isn't he here?"

The room fell silent.

Koven felt their eyes on him. The outburst was stupid. What did he expect, someone to answer, 'because he's dead'? Did they know? Had news alerts popped up on their phones? He glanced around. Sweat dripped down his forehead, his skin felt gray and greasy.

Marthe jumped up and ran to his side and whispered in his ear. "What the hell is wrong with you?"

She stroked his face to re-energize him, then turned to the room. "Sorry, my friends. My husband has fits of PTSD now and then. It happens when he tells a war story. Iraq brings back terrible memories for him. Go back to your meal. He'll be fine in a minute."

One at a time, conversations restarted around the tables. They went back to the topics of discussion before his outburst, politely ignoring his odd behavior.

Marthe grabbed the mic from his hands and set it on a side table.

"Look." He pointed at Blackson. She slapped his hand down. "Rip knows what's happened. That look in his eyes is Brent's look. That's how Brent looked at me at Nasiriyah. I've made a terrible mistake. I swear to god, Marthe, that boy will haunt me to my grave."

"Nice." Marthe's voice was unusually stern. "You sound like a scared little girl making up ghost stories."

"It's like the zombie apocalypse they write about in comic books." Koven focused on a point miles outside the room. "Now that Brent's been freed from his body, he can go where he pleases, appear where he wants. There's no point in burying him."

He looked at Blackson. The young man chatted nervously with a guest, his eyes flicking Koven's way from time to time. Definitely guilty of something.

Marthe followed his gaze, then moved in front of him and hissed. "Get a grip."

Alan Sabel entered behind them, blocking the doorway. He glared at Koven and showed him his phone. On the screen, a text from the Major: "Jacob & Carlos overwhelmed by thugs, fates unknown. Zola dead, son missing. UAE: Samira Suliman dead. No word on Pia or Tania."

Alan put his hand on Koven's chest and pushed him five feet back. "One scratch, Koven."

Marthe stepped between them.

Alan looked around the room, mouthed the word 'later', and left.

Marthe closed in on her husband. "Why is he pissed off?"

"I have no idea. Arabs are trying to kill his daughter and somehow he blames me."

She squinted at him, trying to gauge if he were telling her everything.

"When this castle was active," he said, "people clubbed and knifed each other to death. Buckets of blood were shed around these hills. But I can kill someone on the other side of the globe with nothing more than the powers of persuasion. I have reached a new pinnacle of power—so why do I see Zola's expression in Blackson's face?"

"Stop talking like that." Marthe shook him. "Pull yourself together and take care of the guests."

Koven glared at Blackson until Marthe pushed him out the door. Leaning into him like a worker pushing a cart, she forced him down the narrow hallway toward their room.

"Do you think the dead get revenge?" Koven stopped resisting her. He put his arm around her, his weight on her shoulder.

"You need to rest, Daryl."

"I swear Blackson knows what we did. He accused me of murder. Not even the right one. He's not loyal to me anymore. I'll monitor his calls and his emails tomorrow. I'll bet you he's up to something. Betrayal, like Zola, like Gottleib."

Marthe stopped. "Enough of this."

"I'll talk to the Three Blondes in the morning." Koven stopped walking. "They can spin Zola's murder and I'll come out smelling like a rose. Look what they did with Duncan."

He hugged her and looked skyward. "I have to protect us, keep us safe, that's the most important thing. I'll do whatever it takes. Even if it means killing another traitor. We'll survive."

He continued down the hall.

"God, that's such a strange thought: killing is easy." He looked into

Marthe's eyes. "And it's effective. Going back, pretending to be innocent is *so* boring. From now on, I'll simply trust my instincts. Act first without overthinking it." He stopped and took her by the arms. "I'm going to lean in."

# CHAPTER 26

THE PAT-PAT-PAT SOUND came closer and closer, bringing with it the mixed smell of Lysol and body odor. I struggled to open my eyes with little effect. My head banged as if a *taiko* drummer whacked on it all night and was building to a crescendo. I had to think about where I was. Tokyo maybe?

When my eye focused, I grabbed his hand.

It was Carlos. The bastard was slapping my cheek.

"We gotta go," he said.

Sitting up made the pounding in my head crank up harder and faster. While I waited for the pain to subside, Carlos was in the corner of a large room, tossing clothes from a pile. He wore a paper hospital gown with his butt hanging out. I laughed until realizing I sported the same fashion.

I touched my head and felt a helmet of gauze circling my skull.

"What happened?"

"You've been out. The *chinos* who beat on us were off-duty cops, but I worked us out of the handcuffs." He pointed to a shiny pair dangling from the bedrail.

My head pounded louder when I stood up and pulled off my pile-o-gauze. Even with it off I couldn't see out of my right eye. Touching it turned into a painful experience. I tossed the bandage in the trash just as Mercury and his two god-buddies limped in, leaning against each other.

Mercury said, *Whoo-iee, bro, you look like an extra in a zombie flick. I like your toga, though. Shows the right attitude. Minerva will be pleased.*

I said, *Where the hell were you? I needed you.*

Mercury said, *Went drinking with these guys. Man, do they know how to par-tay! Say, they got any pain killers around here? Vicodin,*

*Percocet, morphine? We're not as young as we used to be.*

Seven-Death fell in a chair and draped his arm on a gurney until he realized it held a dead guy. He jumped sky-high and nearly tossed his cookies. The monkey-god was about to follow his lead. I couldn't watch.

I grabbed my clothes, dressed, and checked out the immediate environment: an emergency room with ten drape-enclosed bays. Carlos checked on our friends while I went through the pockets of the other guys' pants. I found a crumpled business card that had "LOCI" written in English and the rest in Kanji and shoved it in my pocket. One pocket had a cop's ID card but it was all Japanese.

"What happened to your angel?" Carlos asked from one of the bays.

"He's a god. Sometimes they're unreliable." I pulled back the curtain on bay four.

A half-dead Japanese guy, mid-forties, pudgy, past his fighting prime, and looking like a solid middle-class citizen who'd been in a car accident, was pinned with two IVs. From the look of him, he had been forced into this job by medical bills or college loans, some kind of financial disaster, because he didn't have that criminal edge to him.

"Definitely not *yakuza*," Carlos said, looking over my shoulder.

"What's the last thing you remember?" I asked.

"An American walking up and shooting Zola in the heart."

"Dark overcoat?"

"*Si.* And Zola's boy wrapped up by two Japanese. Right at the end, your pal 'Skippy' showed up and checked out Zola's corpse."

A nurse came in, took one look at me and gasped.

"Do you speak English?" I asked.

The tray in her hand clattered to the floor as she ran away.

"So it's true," Carlos said. "You are good with the ladies."

I gingerly limped over to the entrance to see who was out there.

A Japanese woman, young and serious-looking, with shoulder-length hair, a somber suit, and a grim look in her big, brown eyes headed straight for me.

Time slowed down and Demi Lovato marched behind her singing, "Confident". She had it in spades. It was the kind of authority that comes from beating out your peers for promotions at every opportunity. I sensed

a well-defined clarity of thought as she examined the scene before her in a single sweep.

She smelled of lotus blossoms with a hint of vanilla.

"You are released by doctor?" she said, tilting her head a little. She spoke slowly, searching for each word, working hard to be perfect. No doubt she took top honors in high school English but never spoke it again until now.

"Are you the doctor?" I asked.

"No." She stared at my swollen eye.

"Then, yes," I said, "the doctor released me. Where can we catch a cab?"

She cocked her head and crossed her arms. "I present National Police Agency."

The NPA is a big-league outfit that outranks the Tokyo Metro Police, based on my last brush with them. But that was a long time ago and I beat the charges. All I wanted was to distract her long enough to sneak out of there.

"I like your shoes," I said.

It was a safe bet. I may not know jack about shoes but I know most women are more intentional about shoes than husbands.

She blushed and checked the linoleum. "Inspector Yoshida release you too?"

"Yes." My headache pounded so hard I could barely hear her. "Do you know who attacked us?"

"You not true. You no leave yet." She crossed her arms and gave me a serious look—an adorable expression on her. "Murder very big deal in Japan. Fire-arm make very, very big deal."

"Big deal for me too," I said. "Brent Zola asked me to keep him alive, but these guys killed him and kidnapped his son."

I thumbed over my shoulder at the emergency bay where Carlos tried to interrogate the middle-aged guy with his limited Japanese.

She looked impatient and a little superior. "They say, you attack them."

"You think Carlos and I came through customs with chains and crowbars? The weight alone—"

Her face exploded in crimson when she realized I was right; we were victims not perpetrators. Every part of her face clenched as if she were about to detonate. She stormed over to a bay and started tearing apart the guy on the gurney in Japanese. Carlos and I watched over her shoulder. She gestured and stuck a finger in his face, clamped her handcuffs on his wrist and the bed.

I'd have to make sure I never pissed her off. She could deliver an epic rant.

I nodded to Carlos and we started backing out for a quick getaway. Somewhere in Tokyo there was a boy who needed rescue.

We made it halfway across the room before she screamed at us in Japanese. We froze.

She scurried to us, bowing as she came near, her head down. "So sorry. Off-duty patrolmen. We believe them first but some bother me about crime scene: you have no GSR. You right, you not bring chains. We see airport video and museum video. Mistake my fault, not Inspector Yoshida."

She looked up at me with an apologetic expression that changed. She had something in her eye. A spark?

I felt one of those inexplicable connections that transcend race and culture and roles. She was the woman I'd been looking for all my life.

Definitely.

Maybe.

"Who were they working for?" I asked.

"He not say. Sticks to lies."

I pulled the business card I'd found. "What does this say?"

She glanced at it then at me. "Low-see Deployment. First word not translate."

I rolled her phonetic translation around in my aching head. It meant something to me. It was related to the guy in the overcoat who had my gun. And related to something back in the States. Whatever it meant was stuck in the back of my brain-damaged skull.

Shouting erupted outside the emergency room.

"Where's the back door?" I asked.

She shook her head. "You not leave."

Carlos was running through the space, opening doors, looking for a way out.

I pointed at the guy on the gurney as I ran to join my new best friend. "His pals are coming to make sure he doesn't talk. I'll call you."

Carlos found something and waved me over before disappearing into a small door. I piled in after him.

It was an operating room with a whole lot of people in scrubs and masks. They looked up, surprised and angry.

The surgeon started bellowing in Japanese, waving his scalpel at us.

Gunshots popped loud and sharp outside the emergency room.

Every head swiveled in unison to face the wall that separated us from the noise. No one spoke for a full second, then a woman screamed in horror.

Carlos asked something in Japanese and they pointed to double doors beyond racks of equipment. I followed him into a short hall that ended at a T-intersection. We checked left and right.

He checked one end of the hall and I checked the other. My end was clear. I turned to summon my partner.

Carlos was running back, which I took as a bad sign.

We rounded my corner. I instinctively reached for a weapon that wasn't there. Japan may have the lowest murder rate in the world and only eight gun-homicides in 2013 compared to the USA's 14,196, but when someone is shooting at you—with a gun they stole from your house—being defenseless sucks.

Screams echoed from two directions and two guys ran from one side hall to another.

We rounded another corner and found a crowd of nurses huddled together.

Mercury stood in the hall, shaking his head. His god-squad leaned against each other, heads lolling side to side.

Mercury said, *Go that way, second left, then left again. There's an Uber driver just dropping someone off.*

I said, *Low-see, why is that word familiar to me?*

Mercury said, *Bro, you don't have time for a Latin lesson. Move your ass.*

"C'mon, this way." I pulled Carlos and tried to get the Uber app while running.

We skidded to a side door as the detective rounded a corner and ran into me.

I caught her, arresting her momentum, and tried to keep us both upright. She was a perfect fit in my arms, as if we had been made for each other. She looked at me with love in her eyes.

Or fear. It could've been either.

Tears filled her eyes like any new recruit in her first battle. All those promotions had been for her intelligence, not bravery under fire. It was her first encounter with deadly weapons and all she brought to the gunfight was a business card.

I ushered her outside and opened the car door. She yelled at the driver and flashed her badge. He put his foot to the floor and pulled away while Carlos and I were still getting in.

When we reached the end of the parking lot, she buzzed down the window, leaned out, and puked her guts out.

I stroked her back.

The Major called me from headquarters and started talking the instant I clicked in. "We have a ransom demand for Flip Zola."

"Already?" I asked. "Why did he call you?"

"You're the ransom." She paused. "I told him no."

I looked out the back window to see if we were being followed but couldn't see anything because Seven-Death and the monkey-god were sitting on the trunk, arms wrapped around each other, heads together. Mercury leaned in the window from outside, squeezing in over my detective's shoulders.

Mercury said, *Homie, do these losers think you're going to give yourself up for some kid you've never even met? Kidnapping 101: ransom demands should be realistic.*

"He killed Gottleib and Zola," I told the Major. "I have an idea about who he is, but I don't know why. Where and when is the exchange?"

"Haven't gotten that far. He's on the line."

"Put him on."

The detective, whose name I'd yet to learn, pulled back from the window, turned to me and wiped her face with her sleeve. "He shot all the men. He walk up, put gun on head. Bang. Six mens." She leaned out for a dry heave, pulled back in, and ran her fingers through her hair. "Why he do that?"

I put the phone back to my ear and heard an electronically altered voice on the line saying something I didn't care about.

"You kidnapped a teenager," I said, my voice terse and bitter. "Get on your knees and pray to whatever god listens to scum like you—tell him you're coming home."

# CHAPTER 27

PIA TIGHTENED THE muscles in her shoulder, willing them to hold her arm in place and keep it attached as her momentum threatened to rip her apart. For the first few slow-motion milliseconds, Pia fell straight down. Then the cable hit the fulcrum of the Skyview's roofline and swung her back toward the building. But she was facing out to sea, flying blindly backward with no idea how to find the window Tania had shot out.

As gravity took over her fate, Pia's mind reached warp speed. From her many skydiving lessons, she had learned her terminal velocity was roughly 120 mph or 200 feet per second. Falling twenty feet would take a tenth of a second. Not enough time to turn around and control her landing. Despite a lifetime of athletic achievement based on her constant, diligent, and disciplined control of her regimen, she would either live or die based on physics that a chaos theoretician could not calculate in time to make a difference.

There wasn't even enough time to pray.

Pia's weight carried her inwards, toward the hotel. She sensed a bit of structure in her peripheral vision. Then, without warning, a large piece of cloth flew up, blocking her view of the sea. Her momentum reached the end of the swing and reversed direction. She heard someone yell something and the cloth smashed into her body firmly at the very moment she began to exit the broken window.

She let go of the wire and the cloth shot her into the hotel like a slingshot.

She crashed into a cocktail table, sending drinks and hors d'oeuvres flying in every direction. She crabbed around on the carpet until her feet were under her. She popped up and looked around quickly, slightly embarrassed about her awkward landing and half-hoping no one noticed.

Three pistols pressed to her face.

The good news: the pistols were in the hands of uniformed police officers. The bad news: they were unimpressed with her party crashing.

Then the pain kicked in. Her arm hurt from her socket to her fingertips. Her hip and butt where she hit the tables. Several other places were swelling fast.

Near the window were two men in the act of dropping the tablecloth that had arrested her outward momentum. Next to them stood Tania, blood dripping from lacerations to her face and left shoulder where the glass had been unforgiving. An officer held a pistol to her forehead.

"Drop your weapon, please," said a man beyond the immediate ring of officers. "You are under arrest."


LATE IN THE evening, after the statements were taken, and the security videos checked, and Tania's lacerations bandaged, Dubai's Director General of Criminal Investigation escorted Pia and Tania past workers patching bullet holes in the halls.

He stopped at her suite. "This is not house arrest. It is for your protection. Walid will remain at your door at all times. There are ten officers in the lobby, and one more on each floor. I assure you, this hotel is safe. You may receive visitors if you wish, but the government respectfully requests that you do not leave until the official inquiry concludes."

Pia faced Walid, a uniformed officer, and pointed to the bloodstained carpet. She said, "L-O-C-I."

Walid choked and looked at the Director General, who looked oblivious.

"Do we get our guns back?" Tania held out her hand.

"Regretfully, your permits have been temporarily revoked."

"I'll bet they have." Tania gave him a once-over. "How many of those guys worked for you?"

Pia slid her card in the lock. When it clacked open, she dragged Tania inside.

The butler greeted them with pomegranate juice. He took stock of their bruises and cuts, bandaged roughly by a police medic, and brought ice packs and summoned a proper doctor.

Bianca buzzed her Skype app. Pia took the call and discovered Bianca had the feed displayed on several screens in the office. Grim congratulations were offered by her employees. They knew she survived an ordeal that was far from over. When all the prayers and wishes were offered, Bianca narrowed the session to the two of them.

"I traced 147 blog posts about the Mercenary Restrictions Act," Bianca said. "The sites involved won't divulge who wrote them but they all source content through *Hummingbird Online*."

"*Hummingbird* is owned by Fuchs News?"

"Yes, ma'am. The posts on MRA were high-concentration posts that targeted only the congressional districts where a representative was fighting for his office and needed a new issue to champion."

"Any idea who paid for them?" Pia asked.

"A social welfare group called Future Diversions 732. The group was approved a few weeks ago and opened with $6 million in cash. They don't disclose funding, but I found their only named officer, Jago Seyton."

"Jacob's favorite lobbyist."

"I found an odd list of nineteen names that included Müller, Suliman, and Taimur. Next to each name was a number, Taimur's was 20. It looked like a key to a hidden ledger of donations."

There was a brief lull as Pia thought through all the connections.

Bianca said, "I appreciate what you said the other day about coming out. Since you already figured out my sexuality, I'll spare you my speech. I just wanted to say thank-you. It means a lot to me."

"You're welcome," Pia said. "New topic. Can you track down a company called L-O-C-I? I don't know if that's a word or an abbreviation, so it won't be easy."

They clicked off.

The *Post's* Emily Lunger texted. "*FNC* and *Chronicle* claim Jacob led a massacre in Tokyo. You guys are getting lots of bad press. Can I release those videos from France now?"

Pia texted back. "No."

She exchanged texts with Jacob regarding LOCI. They had similar experiences but learned nothing conclusive.

Pia and Tania went to their rooms and spent a fitful night with ice packs and new bandages. The next morning was not a good deal different. Crashing through tempered glass takes a toll on a body.

In the afternoon, Tania came to Pia's room and laid out the spare-parts kit. From it, they assembled two Glocks each.

"The killers carried MP5 rifles like ours," Pia said. "Were they trying to frame Sabel Security?"

"Pakistan Ordinance Factories—POF—licenses the MP5 from Heckler & Koch and calls them SMG-PKs. It's the standard-issue weapon for police in the Emirates. The US Army also sources them from time to time as part of the campaign to bolster commerce in the region."

"You still think they were cops?" Pia looked at the phone she'd won during the fight. "Then who or what is LOCI?"

Pia clicked a magazine of Sabel Darts into one of her Glocks, and armor-piercing rounds in the other.

The butler stood at the door. "Prince Taimur of Oman to see you, ma'am." He tried not to look at the contraband weapons a second time. "I've put him in the lounge as the living room is not yet finished."

Pia and Tania exchanged glances.

"Did I schedule this?" Pia asked.

"He said you were not expecting him," the butler said. "But in light of yesterday's tragedy, he thought it best to accelerate an inevitable meeting."

"Is anyone with him?"

"A bodyguard and his advisor, ma'am."

"Tell his people to wait outside in the hall."

The butler drew back in shock. "Begging your pardon ma'am, but he is a prince."

"I jumped off the roof of this hotel yesterday. I'm not in the mood for unscheduled visitors, princes or paupers."

"Yes, ma'am." He turned to leave, paused, turned back. "May I offer a bit of cultural etiquette appropriate for this region?"

"Snub the monarchy at your peril?"

He tightened his lips, closed his eyes, and gave a slow nod. "A succinct synopsis, ma'am."

"His people wait outside anyway. You can take them tea and cookies" Pia faced Tania. "Thank God for democracy."

The butler bowed and left.

She waited out of sight at the top of the stairs, counting the number and direction of footsteps until the prince's entourage had been escorted out. Then Pia descended.

Tania followed to the edge of the lounge where she paced out wide to the right.

Pia observed the man in the gold-trimmed black robe, black leather sandals, topped with a blue-and-red turban. With his neatly trimmed beard and piercing eyes, he had the handsome, polished look of a movie star. Behind the attractive face was an inquisitive look that appreciated her height and athleticism without objectifying her. She felt a strong warmth and re-heard the butler's words: *but he is a prince.*

She took a deep breath, flipped her switch to professional mode, and stepped forward.

She said, "As-Salam-u-Alaikum wa rahmatullahi wa barakatuh." Peace be unto you and so may the mercy of Allah and his blessings. "How is your uncle, His Majesty, Sultan Qaboos bin Said?"

"I am concerned about the disturbance yesterday." Prince Taimur's accent was thick. He turned and walked to the window.

"I asked you a question."

The prince spun back to her with angry eyes.

Pia crossed her arms.

"Ah, yes." He wagged his index finger at her and closed the distance between them. "You have a reputation for being direct, but I was not prepared for impertinence. I am willing to overlook this—"

Pia pulled out her phone. "If you lecture me, I'll cancel our contract and have my people return home tomorrow."

The prince's mouth dropped. "You can't do that."

"You hired my company to save your ass from an inevitable coup d'état led by your difficult cousin Haytham. No one can keep you safe like Sabel Security. You know it. I know it. So, don't mess with me."

The prince bowed to concede her point, though his gaze never left her. "His Majesty is in fine spirits and good health; praise be to Allah."

"Why are you here?"

He opened his mouth, then backed up a step and glanced at Tania. "Why does she stand so far from us?"

Pia said nothing.

Prince Taimur paced back to the window. "I've been told you have not yet donated my thirty million to the chosen campaigns. It was a source of embarrassment in recent conversations."

Pia nodded at Tania. "She stands over there to make it more difficult for you to pull a gun and shoot us both."

"Ah." He smiled. "But I could get one of you."

Pia shrugged. "You gave Koven thirty million? He gave me twenty." She frowned. "No wonder he can afford all these castles and bodyguards. Anyway, I wired it back and he refused it. If I'd known you were coming, I would've brought it to you in cash."

"Why?" The prince's eyes opened wide. "That was the deal. That's why we awarded the contract to Sabel Security."

"No one has yet told me where the money came from or what it's for."

"To fund campaigns for three representatives and two senators." He shrugged as if it were old news. "They were pre-selected and have already agreed to help."

"Help what?" Pia motioned to a chair.

"I'm not at liberty to say." He flourished his robe and took a seat.

She sat in a chair across from him. "Do you work with Samira Suliman or Lars Müller?"

"I've met them." He shook his head. "We worked on the same politicians through DHK, but we have different interests." He paused and looked away. "Very different."

A muffled sound, like shuffling feet came from outside.

"Who knows you're here now?" Pia asked.

"My staff," he shrugged. "And DHK."

Pia stood and gestured for him to follow. "How did you get here? Did you take the hotel's Rolls service?"

Tania drew her Glock and tiptoed to the door. She waited for Pia's signal with one hand on the knob.

"I have my bird on the roof," he said. "Why are you acting so strangely?"

"Because someone has been dispatched to kill you."

Pia waved off the butler, pointing him back to the kitchen. She drew her pistol, aimed at the door, gave Tania a nod.

Tania ripped open the door and Pia pressed her Glock to Walid's head. The uniformed cop held a pistol in his hand, aimed at the Prince's bodyguard and advisor. Pia removed the cop's gun and ordered him to the foyer floor, where she darted him.

The bodyguard exhaled.

Pia faced the butler. "Get the other employees into a bathroom. The marble and tub should keep you safe from stray bullets."

"Bullets?" the prince asked. "Surely you're overreacting."

"The local cops staged the attack earlier. I'm not sure if the Director General is in on it or not, but we're going to the roof. Tell your pilot to spin up those blades."

Prince Taimur's advisor gasped and shook his head.

The bodyguard watched everyone speaking English, but clearly didn't grasp the rapidly evolving situation. Pia spun him to face her, reached in, and pulled his pistol. She checked it, chambered a round, and handed it back to him, then pointed to her eyes.

He nodded.

Tania checked the hall, and ran to the emergency stairs. The very same path they'd taken only hours earlier.

Pia took the hallway and glanced over the rail to the lobby below.

No one in sight.

Not good.

She motioned for the prince and his men to follow Tania.

When they hesitated, she pushed them. "They're coming. We have to get—"

The elevator doors dinged softly. Pia faced it and waited.

The doors opened painfully slowly, revealing only an empty space at first. But the mirrored walls showed four men pressed to the sides. She fired three darts that hit only metal but held her attackers at bay.

She bolted to join the prince and his entourage as they followed Tania into the stairwell.

This time the assassins were already in the stairwell.

Pia manned the door to the hall, firing a blind shot that actually hit one of the pursuers.

Tania emptied her pistol and swapped magazines.

The prince's bodyguard tensed and bunched his muscles and rocked on his feet. When he wound up his courage, he ran past Tania, firing upward, and took the next floor's landing.

Tania and the others ran past him to the last level, where the fighting intensified.

"Didn't we just do this?" Tania screamed over the heads of the prince and his advisor.

"We don't have enough rounds," Pia answered.

"I heard that." Tania fired two more up a floor. "I told you that Director General was running this operation."

"Once 'LOCI' hired a dozen dirty cops, paying the top guy would be an unnecessary expense." Pia fired down. "Now he has to go along with it to cover it up."

Two men in black came up from the floors below, firing on full-auto. Pia waited, listening to their footsteps. When she figured they would be crouching before rounding the next corner, she vaulted the railing, aiming her body as a projectile. She landed on the legs of the second soldier, throwing him face-first into the hard steps and fell on top of him, spread-eagled. Her dart popped in his butt, below the body armor. He slumped.

While her right hand holstered her pistol, her left hand grabbed the darted-guy's SMG-PK. Inside the trigger guard, her finger slid overtop his, forcing his finger down. Bullets stitched through the front man's foot, then calf, knee, lower thigh, and buttock before the body armor protected him.

In excruciating pain, the injured man turned to face her, hatred blazing in his eyes. He attempted to bring his muzzle around but was hampered by his bullet-shredded leg. He fell on his elbow, pinning his weapon at an awkward angle.

Pia scrambled and grabbed it by the barrel and pushed it to the floor. The leveraged trigger guard snapped his finger like a twig. The rifle emptied its magazine into the wall. She reached for her pistol and darted him.

Pulling spare magazines and weapons off the failed assassins, she ran up the stairs two at a time.

She handed Tania one of the SMG-PKs.

Tania said, "About time! I had three darts left."

"Can we get to the helipad?"

Sensing the situation, the prince's bodyguard boldly took the next landing. He drove forward like the hero in a war movie, firing as he went—and paid the price. His body rolled back to them and blocked the corner.

Prince Taimur stared in mute shock.

His advisor, an older man with resolute eyes, held out a hand. "I was once a soldier."

Pia handed him a pistol, then pointed to Tania. "We work together. You take the rear. Wait for my signal."

She leaned out and fired upward. Tania ran underneath her and took the next landing. The advisor kept the area below them secure.

Pia ran up, repeating the stair-clearing procedure until they burst out onto the greeting area's deck.

The four of them ran for the chopper on the helipad. They fired pings at the door at every opportunity to dissuade anyone from taking a look outside.

The pilot lifted off before they were belted in. He flew an evasive path across the city, using the larger skyscrapers as shields.

Settled in with headsets and safety harnesses, Pia grabbed the Prince. "How are you connected to Samira Suliman?"

# CHAPTER 28

STANDING IN CASTLE Reichsburg Cochem's parking lot, the reporter found shelter from the freezing gusts behind the *FNC* network van. She tilted her face to the sky, shook out her blonde hair, and unbuttoned her Burberry coat. A makeup girl, her jet-black hair brightened with a green stripe, placed an apron around the reporter's neck, tied it, and dragged an applicator across her left eyebrow. As the girl switched to the right eye, the reporter's video link beeped.

A severe looking assistant appeared on her phone. "Ms. Hellman will speak to you now."

The reporter held a finger between her face and the makeup artist. "I have to take this."

"You don't have time," the makeup girl said.

"Work around me."

Katy Hellman sat in her London office and tugged her burgundy Escada suit. A diminutive frame housed a giant personality accustomed to the unquestioned obedience of everyone around her. She pointed at the screen and turned to her assistant. "What's this? She's in makeup. Give me her undivided attention."

"I go live in three minutes, it's all I could do," the reporter said. "Say, you look angry."

"Bloody right I'm angry. Who owns your network?"

"You do, but—" The makeup girl pulled the reporter's chin from the camera and tweezed her eyebrow.

"My back is turned for a minute and you've turned this insignificant tosser into a household name." Hellman's voice rose. "You made a hero out of a dodgy lobbyist."

"We thought you wanted us to work him," the reporter said. "He appeared to be the right material. We thought he'd be in line by now."

"You let him get away from you. He shows no respect for my authority. Have him speak to me right away. A few minutes with me and he'll feel invincible."

The reporter jerked from the makeup artist's hand and faced the camera with a twitching grin. "Invincible?"

"What do the invincible always deliver?"

"Ratings." The blonde smiled until the makeup girl tugged her chin again and applied lipstick.

"Are you there now?" Hellman asked. "Germany?"

"All three of us," she answered without closing her lips. "Bitter cold."

"Why is it so dark?"

"Storm coming." Again without moving her lips.

"Who is the interview?"

"Bobby Jenkins, Jenkins Pharmaceutical. Rumor has it he got mad about campaign donations last night."

"Nothing gets on the air about that. Do you hear me? NOTHING."

Noise in the background distracted the reporter.

She ripped the apron from her neck and handed her phone to the makeup girl. "Bring this, hold it so she can hear the interview."

The frightened girl stared dumbfounded into the camera for a moment, then followed the reporter to a place near the castle's first portal.

Dark stone walls formed a canyon, eighteen feet wide, with an imposing archway above where boiling oil once rained down. The reporter stood poised at the public entrance, her cameraman rolled out to her left, positioning her, and checking the light. He motioned for her to take a few steps back.

Two well-dressed men approached, luggage bouncing over the cobblestones behind them.

"Bobby Jenkins!" the reporter said. "A word, Mr. Jenkins?"

The short, wiry man stopped. His son stopped two feet back.

"Why are you leaving the symposium early?" She stuck the mic in his face.

"Pretty strange things going on around DHK these days." He took a few steps forward.

She sprinted in front of him, her cameraman scurried ahead for the angle and light. "What do you mean?"

"We've talked about this before, off the record, so you can interpret what you will. But it's odd how quickly Koven mourned Duncan after he was dead. Wasn't it brave of him to kill the killers while they were still high on drugs? He saved us all the pain and anguish we would've felt to hear those guards defend themselves against the accusations."

"That was several days ago, yet you came here to the rescheduled symposium. Why leave now?"

"It keeps getting worse. Haven't you heard? Another junior partner was murdered. Killed by his estranged son, if you care to believe it."

"Are you saying Daryl Koven committed a murder in Japan while he was in Germany?"

"It's a global economy." He pushed forward.

She stuck her mic in the face of the surprised young man following. "You're Jasper Jenkins, right?"

He held up a finger and checked out the camera. "Uh, I go by 'Jaz'."

"Will your father go to the police with his theories?"

"I dunno." Jaz looked into the camera. "He's pissed about more than just murder."

He kept moving. She put a hand out to stop him. "What do you mean?"

He pointed back at the castle. "They just asked us to bribe US senato—"

"And there you have it, ladies and gentlemen." She twisted to fill the video frame. "The founder and CEO of Jenkins Pharmaceuticals boldly accusing Daryl Koven of international assassination. You heard it here first, on *FNC*."


DARYL KOVEN WRUNG his hands as he paced the castle's kitchen again. "He's spilling everything to that damned witch of a reporter. I just know it."

Marthe, her robe and nightgown twisted sideways, her hair a mess, stared at her coffee. "They're not the ones you need to worry about."

"The hell they aren't." Koven glanced at his wife. "Darling, get dressed. We have a lot going on today."

He watched her dig at something under her fingernails. Moving cautiously toward her, he touched her sleeve. "You've spilled half a gallon of wine on your sleeve and stained it."

"I didn't sleep last night." She wrapped her fingers around the coffee mug and sank to the table. "I haven't slept for days."

Koven looked out the small window again.

He cursed and ripped the kitchen door open. Barreling outside, he slammed the door behind him and crunched through the thin sheets of ice hugging the cobblestones. Through the first portal and on to the next, he marched like a Marine on parade. As he rounded the bend, he could see Jenkins and his boy, climbing into a waiting limo.

He charged up to the blonde reporter, rough and angry.

The reporter started talking with a big smile. "Could I get an interview with you—the king of kingmakers—Mr. Koven?"

"What did Jenkins say to you?"

"He babbled mostly." The reporter brushed her blonde locks from her face. "No usable footage. But he did have what sounded like accusations forming in his head. You'll want to get on record before he finds a reporter stateside and has his conspiracy accusations firmed up."

"You're playing me." Koven recoiled. "What are you up to? Why are you here so early? Why interview my guests?"

"Never ask questions unless you want to know the answer."

"I don't know how you go about your job, but I demand a straight answer."

He watched her think up another flippant response and cut her off.

"I'm not afraid of you," he said. "Yes, I know you can blow over any fool who makes a statement and you can swamp mayors or congressmen. And you can cause an earthquake for presidents. I don't care about that. Tell me what you're doing here."

"Why not ask Ms. Hellman?" The reporter pointed at the makeup girl holding her phone.

The shocked girl still held the phone with what looked like a framed picture of Margaret Thatcher. The picture flickered.

Koven approached her. "Who are you? You look familiar—"

"What eats you up at night is the thought of betrayal," Katy Hellman said. "Who has his own agenda to which he's never invited you?"

"Are you talking about Rip Blackson?"

"Ask yourself, who benefitted from all the death? Who seems so sincere at every turn? But enough of this idle banter. My next meeting already started."

"Wait! We've met before, haven't we? Where was it? At the firm?"

The screen froze Hellman's face in mid-word, her image covered by an endlessly rotating circle.

Koven snapped his fingers at the makeup girl. "Bring her back. I'm not finished."

The makeup girl shrugged her shoulders to her ears and turned her wide eyes to the reporter.

"It's the Wi-Fi." The reporter waved her arm at the town three hundred feet below them. "Bad connection out here."

Katy Hellman's face reappeared on the screen with a flicker. "If we met, you didn't leave an impression. What firm?"

"DHK, Duncan, Hyde and Koven."

"Bloody bold, aren't you?" She frowned. "Bill Hyde would never promote you. You've stolen your position from him—like everything else."

"Tom promoted me just days before his murder."

"You have nothing to worry about then. Be brave and proud, don't worry about little schemes and conspiracies. No one on Earth can attack you."

Koven smiled and breathed the cold air deep into his lungs. "Then I can rest as soon as I've taken care of that Blackson business. But whom should I worry about? My wife thinks this Sabel girl will be a problem."

"Pia Sabel a problem?" Hellman laughed and scowled. "I've arranged to have the local police take care of her. And they'll look after you too. You have nothing to fear until the *Oberstdrogen* rises from the grave."

Koven laughed. "Then I'm good until the second coming of Christ."

Katy Hellman nodded at the reporter, who reached for the button to end the call.

"One more question." He held a hand out to stop the blonde. "I must know. What about Zola's son?"

"Don't you know?" Hellman raised an eyebrow. "Berkeley has their eye on him for their rugby team. The coach is holding a place for him. Here, watch this little clip the video crew put together for you."

She laughed and clicked off, but the video feed switched to a picture of Brent Zola's face, cold and gray and blood-spattered, lying in the morgue. His face morphed, feature by feature, into the face of a pimpled young man.

"Horrible!" Koven spun to the laughing reporter. "What is this? How could you do such a thing?"

"Shocking, isn't it?" the reporter called as he trudged away. "Don't act so surprised, this is *your* work after all."

Koven stormed back up the incline, through the portals, to the kitchen.

His wife was gone.

He pushed through the heavy doors to the room where the servants waited. Two men, one in uniform, stood eating a brötchen, a German roll.

Koven pointed at the man he knew, Kasey Earl. "What the hell are you doing here? I had you banned after Tom was murdered on your watch."

Kasey grinned from missing-ear to missing-ear. "Sometimes things don't work out like you want. I'm here with Franz to protect you."

The uniformed man put out a hand and bowed. "Herr Koven."

Ignoring the officer, Koven faced Kasey. "Did you speak to the Three Blondes on your way in?"

"Didn't see no one when I came in."

"One drop of alcohol on your breath and you're both dead men." Koven shook a finger in Kasey's face. "Why are you here?"

"We're the reinforcements Ms. Hellman ordered. Me and Franz. He's with LOCI. They got the town covered and I brung some of our guys to man the walls."

"Where the hell is Blackson?"

"He went home." Kasey fidgeted his roll. "USA."

"Damn it." Koven spun away and paced. "You waste even one precious second, opportunities disappear just like that." He snapped his fingers. "From now on, I'll act as soon as I think of it. I won't allow one hint of insubordination. Not one whiff of betrayal. Do you hear me?"

"Dunno what you're talking about." Kasey thumbed at Franz who shrugged. "And his English ain't so good."

Koven crossed the room, his hands locked behind his back. "These bastards think they can plot behind my back and take these deals away from me. I'll show them. No more waiting around. No more talking. No more pathetic excuses. I'll destroy them. Their happy little homes, their wives, their children. I'll crush them all."

# CHAPTER 29

THE NOISE OF Washington's Dulles Airport crashed into my ears despite having eaten ibuprofen like popcorn through the whole flight. The icepack the flight attendant gave me reduced the swelling around my eye. I could see a little. But judging from the way strangers gagged when they saw me, I didn't look so hot. Maybe that's why my new love interest, the Japanese detective whose name I had yet to learn, refused to accompany me to the US to find the killers.

The Major hadn't heard from the kidnapper about exchanging me for the Zola boy. No surprise. Spiriting a kidnap victim out of the country probably took longer than just leaving, so I had a head start. If he was half a day behind me, my plan could work.

All I needed was a plan.

We made our way out of the airport's labyrinth customs area when someone called my name. I looked up to see three Virginia state troopers, along with detectives Czajkowski and Lovett, waiting for me with Dr. Harrison on the sidelines.

Carlos trotted on one side of me.

On the other, Mercury dragged a comatose Seven-Death by the collar as if he were roller luggage.

Mercury said, *Dude, don't talk to those guys. Back to the terminal. Quick, follow me.*

I said, *I don't have any outstanding tickets. Let's see what they want.*

Mercury said, *Remember when I told you not to talk to that cray-cray doctor? This is why.*

I walked up to the group. "What's up guys? Find the Gottleib killer yet?"

One of the Virginians had me on the ground and cuffed quicker than a calf-roper in a rodeo. I waited for someone to call out his time in seconds.

"What the fuck are you doing?" I asked nicely.

"This is a 10-622, I'm having you committed," Dr. Harrison said. "You're a danger to the community."

Carlos, standing behind the cops, pulled a knife that should never have gotten to Tokyo, much less there and back. I shook my head at him. "Call the Major, have her get my lawyer."

Carlos gritted his teeth and hid the knife behind his leg when the cops faced him. He walked away.

They dragged me to the airport police station and discussed extradition options. I opted for going to Maryland as soon as possible in the hopes of getting this over with. Half an hour later, Czajkowski and Lovett processed me into the county detention center.

Lovett, taking personal pride in my arrest, smirked when he closed the holding cell. "Told you I'd get you. Now we have you linked to two weapons used in two murders in two countries and a doctor who says you talk to God. You know what the best part is? I'm going to get your Army records out of this. You're as looney as they come, Stearne."

My head ached so hard I could barely think. After he left and slammed the outer door, I managed to shout a snappy comeback. "If you won't leave me alone, I'll find someone who will."

Mercury sat in the corner, his head in his hands. *This is so lame, homie. We don't belong in here, ya feel me? We're used to being gods to the rich and powerful. This sucks.*

He rose and paced the wide, empty cell with a hard scowl.

Seven-Death curled up like a snail in the corner under a metal bench and groaned in pain.

Mercury said, *This is why Jesus is going bald, dude. Elijah and Muhammad too. 'Cause you damn mortals never listen to us. I mean really, when a god speaks to you, why not just listen to—*

I said, *Leave me alone. I've got to figure a way out of this. Flip Zola's life hangs in the balance.*

Mercury said, *I told you everything you need to know about this shrink, fool. I walked you through everything. There's a solution to this problem in there, all ya gotta do is think. If you can manage that anymore.*

Since my case wouldn't come up until morning, I settled in for a long night. From time to time, drunks were tossed in, puked their guts out, and bellowed about the injustices they'd suffered. My favorite Mayan patted them on the back, empathizing with their pain.

In the morning, my fat, expensive lawyer managed to get my arraignment moved up to number one on the docket and, after a breakfast of cardboard pancakes, I stood in front of the judge. My pre-court consultation with my attorney consisted of me listening to his side of a phone call to someone higher up the socioeconomic food chain than I. At least he brought the week-old newspaper I requested. I could handle the rest without him.

The process began with a prosecutor who knew little about my case other than what was on a sheet of paper in front of him. He rattled off a request to commit me to an insane asylum with all the enthusiasm of a ninth grade boy reciting Elizabeth Barrett Browning in class. *How do I love thee? Let me count...*

I waved at the judge. "Your honor, if you'll allow me to play a ten-second recording of Dr. Harrison, I guarantee you'll throw out the charges."

My attorney tugged my arm to scold me. I shook him off and stared down the judge. He nodded at the bailiff. I borrowed my counselor's phone to pull up my cloud drive. I accessed the recording—the one Mercury insisted I make during my last session—and plugged it into the court's sound system:

"What's the career path for a psychiatrist?" I asked.

Dr. Harrison responded, "Doing good is my reward. Maybe a published book about an extraordinary patient would cap off a career nicely."

"How about a patient who talks to a god? Would that help you write a book?"

"That would be perfect!" Harrison laughed.

I clicked off and held up the newspaper with Dr. Harrison's picture beneath the headline, MY PATIENT SPEAKS TO GOD. I faced the prosecutor, held the paper high and underlined the article with my hand.

Everyone in the room was dumbstruck.

"Draw your own conclusions, your honor." I sat.

The judge was trying hard not to laugh.

My attorney turned to Dr. Harrison. "We're suing for breach of confidentiality!"

The judge pulled the attorneys in for a chat at the bench. After some shrugs, they came back to their respective tables.

"Mr. Stearne," the judge said in a classic courtroom voice, "do you speak to God?"

I stood. "Yes, sir. Every day. His name is Mercury, son of Jupiter and Maia, husband of Venus, cuckolded by Mars. He's the winged messenger of the Roman gods and an eternal member of the *Dii Consentes.*"

I tilted my head and gave him a shit-eating grin.

The judge slapped his desk and roared with laughter. "I don't know why you're antagonizing this naïve doctor, but you sure have your shtick down. Go on, get out of here."

When my attorney pointed the way, I all but ran out of the building.

Mercury caught up with me, Seven-Death stumbling in front of him on the slow mend.

Mercury said, *Hey, great job in there! You came right out and said it all. We still have a long way to go on your presentation. But—did you have to bring up that crap about my cheating wife and that son of a bitch Mars?*

I said, *Who put him up to it?*

Mercury said, *Depends on who you ask. She said Mars seduced her but he claims—*

I said, *No, who put Harrison up to this crap?*

Mercury said, *Oh yeah, it's all about you, I forgot. Hey, bro, you know I'd tell you if I could, but that's like giving out lottery numbers. No can do.*

CARLOS CAUGHT UP with me at Sabel Gardens. We spent the day with Bianca and the Major working out where the exchange might take place and how they would try to double-cross us. We kept the news blocked on our phones to avoid even looking at the headlines. According to some news sources, I executed several off-duty cops in Japan while Ms. Sabel did the same in Dubai. Ours were coordinated attacks reminiscent of al Qaeda, they said. No mention of LOCI or cops gone bad.

We worked until night fell and everyone headed home.

I walked out to the car barn on the south side and sensed Carlos loping after me.

"Go home," I said. "Get some sleep. I've got a couple errands to run."

"You and I have something in common, *ese*." He patted my shoulder. "We don't watch TV for excitement, we go out and find it. You're about to do something, I don't know what, but I want in."

I stopped and looked him over. "Back in the 'hood, did you have a nickname?"

"They called me the Colonel."

"I was expecting something in Spanish like, *combate loco*." Crazy fighter.

"So were the cops." He smiled in the dark. "Let's go."

It was hard to turn down his brand of cold enthusiasm.

At the barn, I asked Cousin Elmer for something fast and quiet. He handed me the keys to a dark blue Tesla P90D with the Ludicrous Speed mode. Seats four, just short of seven hundred horsepower, faster than a Lamborghini, and doesn't roar, it hums.

We parked four houses down in a nice, tree-lined neighborhood in Chevy Chase. A casual stroll up the street and a duck between shrubberies took us into the backyard of our target. No cameras, only a wired entry alarm. My magnetic circuit-killer kept it from blowing the klaxon while Carlos slipped the lock open with his blade. We stepped into the ground-floor office.

We proceeded to the next room, where a middle-aged woman cleaned the kitchen.

Carlos hung back, watching me.

I crossed to the woman. "Mrs. Harrison, why would you serve red meat to a man of his age?"

She spun around, too scared to scream. She grabbed a knife from the block behind her and held it between us.

I faked a left jab. When she slashed at it, I grabbed the back of her wrist, twisted, and dropped the knife into my hand. "If I wanted to hurt you, you'd be crying. So chill with the knives. I have to speak to you and your husband about some urgent business. Call him, please."

Her eyes, big as the dinner plates in her sink, began to narrow to near-normal. After a couple soundless attempts, she managed to shriek out his name in a voice she borrowed from *Dawn of the Dead*.

We heard him fumble around upstairs, then tramp down, loud and clumsy. He staggered into the kitchen with a revolver in his shaking hands. The barrel wobbled in my direction.

"Did you join the Taliban?" I asked.

He shook his head and squinted down the sights with one eye.

"No wonder you don't scare me." I held up my palms. "Who's the one menacing society, doc? I came here to ask you a couple questions. What kind of reception do I get? Your wife tries to stab me and you wave a gun at me. It's a good thing Carlos isn't the jumpy type or he'd have split your head open."

Dr. Harrison saw Carlos for the first time.

I said, "Here's a statistic for you, Doc: twenty-two to one. For every intentional gunshot victim brought into emergency rooms in this country, there are twenty-two accidental victims. Put the revolver down before you turn your wife into a statistic."

"What do you want?" His voice trembled like a tenor at the opera.

Carlos took two steps, grabbed his wrist, squeezed the weapon loose, lowered the hammer, laid it on the cooking island, and returned to his spot by the refrigerator.

Harrison stared at him the whole time.

"What do I want? You tried to have me committed when you know I'm fine." I snapped my fingers in front of his nose to bring his attention back to me. "You told someone about my Army psych evaluations. I want to know who and why."

His head moved side to side but no words came out of his flapping mouth.

"You sold me out, Doc. I have it on good authority that someone held a knife to your throat the first time. You told that person things that should've remained confidential. But then he or she came back and threatened you again. Who was it?"

"How do you know that?" he squeaked. His face flattened. "It was God, wasn't it? It's true, you really *do* talk to God."

"Doc, get a grip." I closed in on him. "Who was it?"

"We don't know." His wife grabbed my shoulder. "Like you said, it was a guy with a knife the first time. There were three of them the second. They said—"

"Julie!" Harrison shouted. "They said they'd kill us."

Carlos did a quick glance at the street-facing windows, then around the room, and stepped between the glass and us. He waved his arms as if shooing cattle into the hall. It was a good call on his part; if someone was watching from the street, the shooting could start any second.

I followed the doctor. He stuck his head into the TV room and pointed to a lipstick camera resting above a portrait of some old guy.

I clicked my link to Sabel Security HQ, "Get me five agents over here right now."

The front door caved in and three black-clad hostiles charged through the opening. Carlos popped one of them in the head before he crossed the mini-foyer. I pushed the Harrisons into the windowless TV room and dropped to the floor. The second guy came around the corner, firing high—like a noob. I popped two rounds in his thigh. He went down cursing. I grabbed the assault rifle out of his hands and slammed the butt into his face. He was out.

"Where'd the other guy go?" Carlos asked from around the corner.

"Not in here." I tiptoed to the edge of the hall and on to the kitchen archway.

Three shots rang out from the kitchen. I listened but didn't hear anything. Not Carlos in pain, which was good; nor the bad guy, which was not good. Nor did I hear any footsteps to give me a position.

I rolled onto the kitchen floor and found no one at the sink.

No one stood at the fridge, or at the cutting board, or in the pantry.

Looking up, I aimed just as the guy standing on the cooking island swirled around on his heel and brought his barrel up.

I've played this game too many times: First guy to the trigger lives.

My opponent did not understand how the game worked and took the time to aim. My finger was halfway through the trigger's travel when he realized this was pass/fail. The only way to improve your skill is to win every round.

I'd won every round from Mosul to Kabul.

He crashed to the floor with a heavy thud.

I ran back to where the Harrisons cowered in the TV room. "Call the cops. Get them to send Lovett and CJ. Tell them what happened here. I gotta run—"

Dr. Harrison looked up with tear-filled eyes from the floor where his wife lay bleeding. She was breathing and conscious, but white and clammy. Her eyes darted left to right, like a speed reader.

Carlos knelt next to her and pulled a shoulder up while I looked under. The entry wound was typical of a small caliber, but her exit wound was the size of a fist. I grabbed the rifle off the floor and ejected a bullet. Definitely a 5.56 NATO round. Originally developed by the USA for the M16, NATO adopted it for automatic weapons because you could pack a lot of them into a smaller space and, despite their small diameter, they traveled at high velocity and tumbled in soft tissue, causing maximum damage.

The casing had a thirteen-digit NATO Stock Number. I didn't have the tables for reference, but the 01 designation for the USA was in the right place and the 74 designation meant it had been shipped to Pakistan. I'd fired many rounds with those identifiers in Afghanistan, which is where this bullet was meant to be. The third identifier made me sick. They weren't sold as Army surplus. They were built with extra care and precision to ensure fewer gun jams and misfires. They were made for American Special Forces, specifically the Rangers.

A couple million rounds had been stolen from an armory at the end of the Afghan entanglement. Stinger missiles, rocket propelled grenades, and plenty of SMG-PKs had been taken in the heist as well.

I took a quick look at the identifiers on the MP5. It was a POF SMG-PK.

The Pentagon had always blamed corrupt officials for the missing ordnance. I suspected the mastermind behind the robbery was the founder of Velox Deployment, Shane Diabulus.

What the hell did he want with my psycho?

Carlos called 911 while I squeezed the doc's shoulder. "I've seen worse on the battlefield, Harrison. She's going to make it. Now listen to me. When Lovett and CJ get here, tell them the truth. Tell them the whole story about being threatened."

"Where're you going?"

"They're about to kill an innocent boy."

"But they'll kill me." He turned his gaze to his wife.

Her eyes fluttered.

"They threatened to kill you to keep a secret," I said. "If you put the secret out there, killing you only increases their chances of getting caught. Be brave, stand up to the criminals and talk to the detectives."

"You did this!" Harrison turned red and scrunched his face. "It's your fault."

"Who breached confidentiality, Doc?"

"They threatened me."

My blood boiled. The stress of the last few days snapped me. I shoved a finger in his chest. "I've seen soldiers fight and die for twenty grand a year to protect your freedom and you cave at the first guy who shows up with knife? Grow some balls, Doc."

Harrison cradled his wife in his arms and cried.

A car screeched to a halt in the street. Five doors slammed: four passengers and a tailgate.

Carlos poked his head around the corner and nodded at the backdoor. "Not our guys. Not cops."

I nodded and turned back to Harrison. "Gotta go, doc. Tell the cops the truth."

He looked at me like a sad puppy.

I handed him the assault rifle, set it to full-auto, and flipped the safety off. "Try not to be a statistic."

Carlos had the back yard cleared when I caught up with him.

Sirens filled the frozen night.

We leaped a hedge, crossed a neighbor's yard and ran down an alley that would come out near the Tesla.

Seven-Death, his health restored and back in furious-god mode, popped out of the bushes and knocked me down. He stood over me, waving his obsidian blade, shaking his death stick, and ranting in Mayan with his trademark bug-eyed scowl.

Mercury stepped out of the bushes behind him. *You're not leaving the good doctor behind, are you? That's not your style, dawg.*

I said, *Why should I care about that coward?*

Mercury said, *Cuz he's a convert and we're a little short right now. Besides, he went to Harvard.*

I said, "If he's so smart, let him talk his way out of it."

Carlos said, "You mean Harrison?"

Muffled gunfire raked Harrison's house from inside.

# CHAPTER 30

PIA LEANED AS the chopper swerved around the Burj Khalifa, her conversation insulated from the thundering engines by the thick headset. After one more evasive maneuver tossing them left, the pilot flew toward the overflow parking lot for private jets at Dubai's airport.

"These people already killed Samira Suliman." Pia tapped Prince Taimur. "My people can only protect you if we know what's going on."

"Suliman was nothing to me." He slapped his knees. "I met her when Daryl Koven introduced us a few weeks ago at the al Arab. I disliked her intensely. She was a radical, the kind who're ruining Islam and the world."

"Did Koven promise American politicians would push legislation for you?"

"Do you even know what you're talking about?" He faced her and threw up his hands. "Do you know what I want?"

"It doesn't matter. As a foreign national, you're not allowed to put money in American elections."

"More than half of General Electric's revenue comes from outside the USA." His voice rose. "They can donate as much as they want. Chevron, Teamsters, Apple, Ford, do you question where their money comes from? All large American companies and unions are international. They can pour money into elections—why do you refuse?"

Pia looked out the window. Below them, flashing lights on police cruisers sped through traffic, racing them to the airport. She pulled her phone and texted her pilot to be ready for wheels-up the moment she came aboard.

"OK," Pia said. "I'll consider it. Tell me what I'm considering."

"The politicians have already agreed, there is nothing for you to consider. You are simply the delivery girl."

"If you want me to be your 'girl', I have to know why."

Prince Taimur clenched his fists and zipped his mouth. After a long time without blinking, he shook his head. "We had a deal. We worked on this for months. Long before Koven took over and recommended Sabel. He said your father would do what we asked. I do not have to tell you anything."

He faced forward and shut down the conversation.

The helicopter turned slightly and began its descent. On the other side of the terminal, a fleet of police cars slammed to a stop and disgorged a small army. Pia found the landing zone and gauged the distance. If she ran, she might be airborne before the cops got through the airport buildings and onto the tarmac.

"If you're not going to tell me," Pia said, "I will cancel the contract."

Prince Taimur pulled off his headset, unbuckled his harness, and glared at her. "The original plan called for Velox Deployment. I should never have listened to Koven. Fine. Have your people out by morning." He tensed every fiber in his body. "You're an impudent girl. I simply cannot abide by fools."

Pia glared back at him. "Apparently your mother could."

She jumped to the tarmac before he could throttle her.

Tania and Pia ran for the jet. The copilot was standing by with the airstair ready to close. They bounded up the steps and felt the jet rolling before the door locked.

Pia marched into the cockpit. "We might be a little tight on this one."

The pilot looked over his shoulder as he pushed the throttle forward. "Like Minsk?"

"Yeah, like Minsk—only worse."

The copilot chuckled. "Are they going to shoot us down this time?"

"If they do," Pia sighed, "it would be the better alternative."

The pilot held a hand up. "They're telling me to get off the runaway."

"You can understand these guys with their thick accents?"

"Copy that, tower," the pilot said. "Taking off now."

The pilot pushed the throttle and powered into takeoff position at the same time a jet with an Omani flag on the tail tried to get in front of him.

He swerved to the front as both gained speed, the jet next to them slightly behind but keeping pace.

They were wingtip-to-wingtip, inches from each other as they reached seventy knots. A combined hundred thousand pounds of explosive aviation fuel roared down the asphalt in a game of runway chicken.

Three police cars sped across the taxiway, heading for them, their lights flashing bright colors into the dark sky.

"What was that, tower? Repeat." The pilot, pale and sweating, checked his right window.

Pia leaned over his shoulder and saw the Omani pilot flip them off while refusing to give in.

They gained speed. The copilot checked numbers and ran through checklists, paging through screen after screen with his cursor. He closed his eyes and crossed himself.

Both jets rolled side-by-side as they reached ninety knots.

"His jet is the next size down," the pilot said. "And he's probably carrying less fuel, which means he'll gain a little more speed before takeoff. If he doesn't back off, we could end up—"

The police were on the runway ahead, coming straight at them with no sign of letting up.

"Tower, could you please repeat that?" the copilot said. "I'm having trouble understanding your accent."

The line of vehicles coming at them were going flat-out, closing the distance at a combined 200 mph. Pia could see the faces of the officers, shocked and scared, but unrelenting, coming straight at her. The car on the left couldn't take the drama and slammed on his brakes. He slid sideways.

The pilot prayed and pulled back on the controls. The front wheel lifted off. The angle felt right to Pia, but the lift didn't follow the way it should. He was attempting to take off in too short a distance.

The fuselage shuddered, and groaned, and finally climbed into the air.

Flashing police lights disappeared underneath them with only inches to spare.

"Oman Seven, where are you?" Both pilots looked out their windows. "I'm rolling left; you roll right in five… four…"

Pia relaxed and walked back to her seat.

Tania pointed out the window. "There was another jet—"

The pilot called back to her. "They're scrambling an F16 to escort us back."

"Are we over international waters yet?" Pia asked.

"We might make it before they get to us, but then we need permission to cross other countries. So far, Iran, Iraq, Qatar, and Saudi Arabia have denied us airspace. We have to go back."

"There has to be another country we can fly through."

"Oman. But we just outran their prince and his pilot is still cursing me over the airwaves. You'll need to smooth it over with him."

Pia shuddered and closed her eyes.

Tania waved a hand. "Hey, do you want to know what's on *FNC* or *Hummingbird* right now?"

"Give me the short version."

"They're calling it 'Pia's War on the Emirates'. They're putting up clips of the gunfight at the Burj al Arab and in between, they're streaming videos of legislators lining up to endorse the MRA."

"Perfect."

"It gets worse," Tania said. "I kept my earbud on inside my headset, so my recording was crystal clear. I sent it to Emily and she said we need something to back it up. A transcript, sworn testimony, an email, anything to verify what he said from Koven's side. We need to keep the conversation going. So suck it up, girlfriend. Call your Prince Charming."

Pia inhaled the panic that accompanies every human on the cusp of eating crow. Her mind raced through a hundred scenarios in the hopes of finding an alternate way to both confirm the story and find safe passage. Nothing workable came to mind.

Tania handed her a phone.

Pia dialed. "Prince Taimur, I'm calling to apologize. My father tells me I'm far too hot-headed for business negotiations. Guess he's right. I hope you will forgive me for my disrespectful language." She waited but he said nothing. "I had no right to ask about the terms of the deal. If you're willing, I'd like to apologize face-to-face."

"That would be acceptable," he said. "Meet me in Khasab. There is only one road in, one landing strip, and a narrow harbor. Our Emirati friends would not think to interrupt us there."

Pia clicked off and relayed the destination to the pilot. He showed her where it was: an isolated cove at the end of a rocky peninsula jutting into the Strait of Hormuz. The lone road from the United Arab Emirates followed the coast around 130 miles of craggy inlets and desolate mountains resembling the desert version of Norway's fjords.

Jacob texted his theories on the source of the SMG-PKs and ammo. He believed Shane Diabulus either supplied LOCI as an arms dealer or had some connection to them. But how that fit with Jago, DHK, and the MRA legislation was unclear.

Bianca supplied Shane's financial profile, complete with details of his personal bankruptcy and new address. The boss at Velox was staying at Kasey Earl's house. Leaving Pia with the question, who's funding Velox and LOCI?

When they landed, an official leaning on a cane, wearing a white thobe and silver-beaded masarh, a Bedouin turban, greeted them. In broken English, he offered them a tour of the town while they waited for the prince, who was halfway to Muscat and would have to turn around.

Pia turned to her pilots. "Stay close to the jet and plot a course to India or somewhere else, anywhere else."

"Faiz my name." The graying official introduced himself and bowed deeply. "Great honor to host friend of prince. You ride with me."

He gestured to an open Toyota SUV and held the door for them, talking fast as he limped around the truck. He was a pocket-sized man, rail-thin and sun-darkened; the prince's orders had made this the most important day of his long career as a forgotten official in an isolated corner of the world.

With great alacrity, Faiz explained how the Portuguese built a stone castle in the early 17th century to control trade in the region. He pushed his cane in and took the wheel. The city was nestled in a narrow valley, dramatic cliffs loomed over it, ready to pounce on it at any moment.

They passed white and beige plastered buildings while driving through the quiet town of mostly new construction. Faiz continued his monologue. Accessible only by sea for centuries, the town was now a weekend retreat for the people of Dubai. They passed a mosque with dual minarets and another with a tiled dome.

He explained how dozens of Iranian smugglers crossed the strait every day at dawn and left before sunset to avoid Oman's visa requirements.

Toward the center of town, a cruise ship hummed with late night activity. They rounded a bend where the ancient crenelated walls of the Portuguese castle rose from the dusty street, thirty to forty feet high, its weathered stone illuminated for tourists. He stopped in front of an ornate wooden door, hopped out, and hobbled to the entrance, fumbling through a ring of keys until he found the right one.

"Come, come." Faiz waved them over with a big smile. "I give special tour. Many tourists come see fortress, but none be friend of Prince. Much great honor. Come."

"Friend of prince, mmm." Tania elbowed Pia. "I did see that look in your eye. And he's a hottie."

Pia scowled.

"It's been a long time, hasn't it?" Tania nudged her again. "A better option than Carlos."

"Carlos is not an option."

Pia picked up her pace and followed Faiz through the low door to the inner courtyard where several antique dhows were arrayed in the dark.

"One minute. Faiz find lights." His cane tapped off into the dark. A few seconds later, floodlights lit up the courtyard. He returned and waved at the boats. "These, masterpiece of Oman! We make bigger today."

"Thank you, Faiz," Pia said. "I'm honored, but tired. Could we find a hotel for the night?"

"Yes, yes. First. One more thing." He waved at the round tower. "You see rooms. Magical place for people those days many century ago."

Tania shrugged and Pia shrugged back. They followed him through a stone arch into a dark hallway. Tapping like a blind man, Faiz disappeared down a curved stone staircase. They followed, one hand on the wall for reference and another in front for obstacles. They reached a

flat floor where Faiz took Pia's hand and guided her a few more feet.

"Oh. Oh." He snapped his fingers. "Faiz forget lights. One minute."

He tapped away in the dark.

An iron clang rang out and reverberated for a full second.

"Hey, wait a second," Tania said.

The cane tapped away, followed by the sounds of a door slamming and a bolt engaging some distance up and away.

Pia and Tania hit the flashlights on their phones at exactly the same time. They faced a windowless stone wall. They turned toward each other. Tania had her phone in one hand and her Glock in the other. They turned again and found another stone wall, then a third. The fourth was an ancient iron grating with openings no larger than a hand. In the center was a massive iron door—locked.

# CHAPTER 31

KOVEN WATCHED PAUL Benning closely as the CEO of Esson Oil looked over his proposal in the Grand Treaty Room. The silence between them had grown to the point where he could hear the light snow falling outside the castle's thick walls. He dared not interrupt Benning's train of thought at this delicate juncture. This was the moment of truth. Some people understood how the world worked, while others left their future to fate. Koven was betting that Benning knew how to work it.

"The British are OK with this?" Benning asked.

"They're not fans of the Muslim Aid Foundation, which is why the directors are looking for a new home in the US. Since most of your oil comes from Muslim countries, I thought you'd be sympathetic to their cause."

"It's tempting as hell." Benning scratched his chin. "And in exchange, they can deliver oil below market? I'm skeptical there."

"Other oil companies are in this. That's why their returns are beating Esson's. Of course they can deliver."

"Alan Sabel told me these guys were banned in the UK for 'fueling hatred, division and violence'."

"Fuck Alan Sabel." Koven struggled to keep his voice at a polite volume. "Your company is ten times bigger than his. Do what's best for your shareholders, not him. He doesn't deliver the quarterly earnings report to your shareholders with recurring excuses about the falling price of oil."

"True enough." Benning nodded. "My last concern is where the MAF gets the oil they'll deliver."

Koven glanced around the room at the other deals in progress. Twenty other people talked in hushed tones.

"Eastern Syria and Western Iraq," he said. "But don't worry about that end. All you're going to do is help a charity relocate."

Kasey Earl approached and pulled his hand across his throat. "Need a word with you, Mr. Koven."

Koven excused himself and pushed the young man back into the corner. "You better have something damned important, Kasey. Or you're the next Velox employee I shoot."

What was left of Kasey's ears wiggled. He frowned and pushed past Koven, back to the table where Paul Benning checked his notes. Kasey grabbed the man's suit coat, ripped it open, and pulled a thumb-sized Bluetooth microphone from inside the lapel.

Over Benning's protests, he held it up for Koven to see. "Everything you done said's been uploaded to the Sabel cloud."

Koven shook with rage. He glanced around the room to see how many were watching them.

He pushed Benning and Kasey through the side door into the kitchen, where four Velox guards and three local police waited. "Put them in chains. Sabel and everyone with him."

Kasey cuffed Benning.

Koven faced the CEO. "I brought you a deal that could pad your bottom line by billions and this is your answer? Blackmail?"

"It's not blackmail." Benning spat his words. "We know damn well MAF sells Daesh's stolen oil to fund the terrorist state."

Koven turned to his Velox men. "Take him out and shoot him. Chop up his pieces and throw them in the river. I'm done playing games with these bastards."

Benning struggled but the guards beat and gagged him before he could start yelling. They tied his ankles and wrists, and carried him out.

Kasey stayed behind. "There's an extra charge for termination services."

"Fine! Fine. Just make him go away. And where's his whore, Olga? Do the same for her."

"She up and went to Paris. Shopping, I think." Kasey tilted his head. "What cover story do you want?"

"What do you mean? He left this morning, right after Jenkins. You remember. Now leave me alone, I'm getting a headache."

"One last thing: why not dispose of Sabel too?"

Koven pushed his face into Kasey's ugly mug and spoke through his clenched teeth. "Because he has the cloud data, you idiot. We need to get that deleted first."

Koven pushed Kasey into the wall and stormed out.

He took the stone steps two at a time. Throwing open the heavy door to his bedroom, he walked straight through, into the bathroom, barely glancing at his wife. He grabbed four aspirin and a bottle of water and went back to the room.

Marthe lay on the bed, her face buried in the pillow.

He stared at her. The tablets crunched under his molars and slushed down his throat riding on a gulp of water.

He shook her. "Marthe, get up. It's afternoon for god's sake."

She pulled her tear-streaked face from the padding long enough to shake her head, then sobbed back into the tangled sheets and pillows.

He sat on the edge and stroked the back of her legs. "My dear Marthe, what's the matter with you?"

She answered with muffled sobs.

"The guests, darling. You've conjured up this marvelous venue and threw an incomparable party. Now is the time to take your bow."

Her head lifted momentarily and she craned over her shoulder. Her red, puffy eyes engaged him before more tears spilled from them. "We killed them, didn't we?"

"You know what we did."

She sat up and dug viciously at her fingernails with a file.

"But why Gottleib?" she asked. "That's what started it all. You had to go and kill that poor, innocent boy."

"I swear, I had nothing to do with killing David Gottleib." Koven clasped his hands, rested his elbows on his knees, and drooped. "You never said anything about that when you wanted Duncan out of the way."

"I should never have cleaned up after you. I saw him. He was a kind old man, Tom Duncan. And there he was with his head opened like a smashed melon, blood and brains spilled out all over the place. It's like you said, there's no reason to bury the dead. He comes back to me when

I close my eyes."

She went back to her pillow, muffling her moans.

"You really should get up." Koven rubbed her back. "Some fresh air would be good for you."

She continued to sob. Her right hand reached out and grabbed his.

He patted her hand. "I have to go."

"Stay with me."

"Sabel is causing trouble." He pried her hand from his and stood. "I have to end it."

She sat up. "I told you that girl is a witch!"

"Not the girl. I don't know why, but Arab countries are lining up to kill her." He sighed. "It's her father. He's been recording things."

Marthe threw her arms around him. "We're one of them now, the ultra-rich. We don't have to be afraid of the police anymore. Go kill them. Kill them all. We can get away with anything."

She picked up her file again and plowed into her fingernails.

"What are you doing?" Koven asked.

"There's blood stuck under them and I can't get it out."

He grabbed her hand. "The blood is coming from your fingers because of the excessive picking. Stop that."

"It doesn't matter." She breathed hard and sank into the covers, muffling her voice. "I still can't close my eyes without seeing his blood everywhere."

He rose, crossed to the bathroom and returned with water and a bottle of pills. "Here, these will help you sleep."

Her buried head refused to rise.

As much as he relied on her help, she wasn't in the mood. What's the use in trying to drag her to her feet if she's going to wallow in self-pity? There's no helping some people. He would let her find her own way out.

He left the medicine.

Outside his room, Velox guards waited and ushered him downstairs. Kasey pointed the way to the basement down a stone spiral and through two heavy steel doors to a long storeroom. At the back, under a bare lightbulb, was a stainless steel cage.

Inside stood Alan Sabel and his bodyguard, Agent Dhanpal, bound with hand and ankle cuffs.

"Goddamn it, Koven," Alan yelled. "Let me out of here this minute."

Koven approached the bars and examined them. "Amazing how fate works, isn't it? This ancient dungeon was remodeled to keep the treasures of the castle safe from thieves. And now it serves to keep the thieves in. I doubt we're in danger of you stealing any of these relics. You don't see the value in small objects. You can only see values in companies and technology and intellectual property. So why would you stoop so low as to steal my trade secrets?"

Alan stepped close to the bars, snorting with anger. "You let Dhanpal go and we can talk."

"Let your minions loose?" Koven laughed. "I was told he took out five Velox men before they subdued him. Do you think I'm dumb enough to let him wander the castle? No. You talk or I take him out and shoot him."

"What's your endgame? You think the police will just look the other way? You're finished, Koven."

"How could a man of your position so grossly underestimate the power of money?" Koven backed up and waved his hands around him. "The police have already murdered your friend Benning."

Kasey stepped out of the shadows. "Hey, they didn't do nothing. That was my guys."

Alan scoffed. "You hire only the brightest."

"It doesn't matter. It doesn't matter." Koven waved his arms to quiet everyone. "I spoke to Katy Hellman this morning. Her reporters, notorious for hacking crime victim voice mails, are working to hack your recordings. She said no one on Earth could stop me except some dead guy."

"What dead guy?" A new voice came from the dark.

"Who's there?" Koven spun around, looking down the gloomy hall.

Senator Bill Hyde stepped into the dim light, his watery eyes lowered. "What dead guy did she say could stop you?"

"Someone called *Oberstdrogen*."

"Never heard of him." Hyde came closer. "I was worried she meant Jesus Christ."

Koven scowled at him. "What are you doing here? You're supposed to be at the office."

"We ran out of gin."

# CHAPTER 32

CARLOS HELD THE dim blue light over my shoulder while I opened the electrical box and flipped the breaker marked "kitchen". Nothing will get a family man outside quicker than turning off his wife's kitchen at dinner time. Carlos backed into the bushes.

My phone vibrated. The Major was calling at a terrible time, but I answered it anyway.

"The kidnapper is on the line," she said. "Says he's ready for the exchange."

"Patch him in."

A second later I heard an electronically altered voice. "Jacob, go to the Joyce Kilmer Service Area on the New Jersey Turnpike and wait for further instructions."

"No."

"What?"

"If you want to meet someone in New Jersey, try OKCupid.com," I said. "Where did you get that stupid voice scrambler? It sounds like a prop from an '80s movie."

"If you don't do what I say, the boy dies."

"So what? You already killed his dad, which tells me you plan to kill him too. I don't know—or care—about either of them."

"But you agreed to the ransom." His mechanical voice rose in pitch. "You have to do what I say."

"Or you'll kill some unfortunate teenager? You think that's going to motivate me? I got news for you—thirty-nine people were murdered in this country yesterday. That many will die today and tomorrow. You're threatening me with a statistic."

"You don't fool me, Jacob Stearne. You went to Tokyo to save Zola.

You want the boy safe."

"Listen up, stupid: You want me. And you want me bad. You've proven it. You tried to kill me outside Rip Blackson's house and failed. You tried and failed at Harrison's. You tried and failed to frame me for two murders, and now you have some dumb idea that you can trap me in a murder-suicide scenario and make it look like I killed all those people because I was having an affair with a fifteen-year-old boy. So, no."

"That's not our plan."

"I'm busy right now and can't talk. Text me your number and I'll call you back later. You can make up a new plan and tell me all about it."

I clicked off while he struggled to reply.

Six seconds later, Captain Cates of the Montgomery County Police Department, Criminal Investigations Division, rounded the side of his house with a flashlight and a jacket tossed over his casual slacks and shirt. He hadn't bothered with a hat for his gray crewcut.

"Holy mother of God," he said.

"Of all the accusations against me, that's a first." I flipped the breaker back on for him.

"What do you want?"

"The bullet David Gottleib gave me that's now sitting in evidence." I closed the breaker box with a slam.

"I can't give you that," he said. "It's not my case, and besides—"

"I can deliver the killer."

"You know who it is?"

"I can deliver. Do you want him? Or should I try working with Lovett's captain?"

He chewed the inside of his cheek while he figured out how I knew his departmental rival and how badly he would love to show up the prick.

He said, "Let's go inside."

"I'm not exactly presentable." I pulled his flashlight to my face, showing off my blue, black, and yellow swollen eye and severely damaged cheek, complete with butterfly stitches.

Despite his revulsion, we went in the house, leaving poor Carlos hidden in the cold. Cates walked me into his study before his wife and teenaged daughters saw me. We sat in leather chairs in a small home office crammed with cardboard boxes overflowing with case notes. A small, cheap desk stood next to us and a packed bookshelf filled the wall behind it.

"Lovett put out an APB on you." He rubbed his face and sighed. "Something about a murder in Tokyo involving one of your guns. It's my duty to turn you in."

"You're going to hang with me as the situation develops throughout the night. If I don't deliver the killer by sunrise, you can bring me in."

"Yeah," he said and scratched his jaw. "The NPA detective argued with him. She says you didn't do it."

"She's here?" My voice was unintentionally high and loud. "The lady from Tokyo?"

His eyes snapped up to mine. "Before you get a hard-on, let's keep focused on why I shouldn't call a squad car."

"Yeah. OK." I reined in my breathing and took a long, slow look around the room to relax.

Elbows on my knees, I rubbed my palms together. "First, you have to tell me what happened in Nasiriyah."

"You really don't remember?"

I shrugged.

"It was the early days of the invasion." He crossed his ankle over his knee and leaned back. "Saddam's Republican Guard platoons were abandoning their posts quicker than we could engage with them, which was fine with us. We didn't want casualties. Lieutenant Koven was itching to be a hero, so he took his platoon off the map. Later, in the debrief, his sergeants said he was hunting for Iraqis. He found them all right. He ran into a company of them. The center of their formation fell back."

I put my hand over my eyes. "And he fell for it? Drove into the middle?"

"Exactly. Classic ambush maneuver that predates Alexander the Great. He was surrounded—they had him in a crossfire. Three Iraqi snipers began picking them off. Koven and his men hunkered down and called for assistance, but they were way outside our contained area. The Iraqis started shooting anyone who manned the BMG mounted on a

Humvee. Koven's men said he freaked. He crumpled up in a ball and covered himself with body armor."

Cates grabbed two bottles of water from a mini fridge next to his desk and tossed me one.

"That's when you showed up," Cates said. "You jumped a wall, running scared, and thought you were saved. When the men explained the situation, you volunteered to take the .50 BMG and wipe out the Iraqis. That's when Koven came out of his shell, ordered you not to take the gunner's turret because there wasn't enough ammo. They were down to forty-nine bullets and there were more Iraqis than bullets. You argued that his men were still heavily armed. He said you were a spy and tried to shoot you with his service weapon."

The memory came flooding back to me in a hot rush. Mercury had been talking to me, guiding me over walls and telling me where to turn. He'd been right on the mark every time. When Koven tried to kill me, Mercury told me when to duck left and right and then when to grab Koven's weapon. I wrenched it out of his hands and turned it on him. The rest of the platoon nodded as if to say, "Please do it. Get rid of the lieutenant for us so we can get out of here." Zola stepped in front of Koven and told me to think about it.

I gave the pistol to Zola and jumped up in the Humvee. A bullet pinged off the sheet metal and I ducked.

Mercury told me to quit worrying, stand up, and let him guide me. With Mercury telling me where to shoot, I knocked off twenty-nine Iraqis, starting with the snipers and ending with the commanding officer. When their commanding officer went down, the rest of them disappeared like mobile homes in a tornado.

The surviving Marines were pretty happy about being liberated from certain death. They carried me around on their shoulders, gave me a Hershey's bar, and crowned me with an ammo belt. I awarded them the remaining .50 BMG cartridges like a king handing out knighthoods.

Koven exploded in a jealous rage and tried to kill me again. But Mercury was a step ahead of him. With his sketchy but divine guidance, I stole a Humvee and drove back to my company.

"And the Army never gave us back the Humvee," Captain Cates said.

"Koven's version was different?" I asked.

"His version omitted you altogether. Zola, Gottleib, and Blackson recanted their original stories and resubmitted versions that sounded like Koven had coached them. But your story became legend in the battalion. I was determined to dig out the truth when the brass decided to make the run to Baghdad the next day. We had Koven reassigned stateside at the first opportunity."

Mercury, at the small desk next to us, wiped a tear from his eye. Seven-Death stood behind him, giving me his bug-eyed glare.

After you've seen a god so hungover he can't stand up, it takes extreme will power not to laugh in his face, especially when he's doing his fire-and-brimstone shtick.

Mercury said, *Oh, those were good times, dawg. You listened to me back then, none of this juvenile backtalk.*

I said, *Tell me something useful. How am I going to get the Zola kid back?*

Mercury said, *Beats me. Your little chat with the kidnapper took me by surprise. I'm out.*

Mercury stood up as if to leave when the wings on his helmet wiggled. *Oh, dude, they're going to kill Blackson. You might want to warn him—unless you still don't care about anyone but yourself.*

I said, *What's that supposed to mean?*

Mercury said, *Harrison was our best chance, man. You let him twist in the wind—he was the psycho to all the rich and famous people in DC. We coulda gone big with him, ya know what I'm saying?*

I said, *He's alive and well.*

Mercury said, *What? How do you know?*

I said, *Because I challenged him to be as much a man as any eighteen-year-old private and he rose to the occasion. I've given that challenge a hundred times—just before the shooting starts—and you can see it in their eyes. I saw it in Harrison's eyes. He's a fat, lazy, self-absorbed intellectual, but he sure as hell wasn't going to let his wife die.*

"So, who killed Gottleib?" Captain Cates asked.

"I'm about to find out." I told him my plan for catching the killer and asked him for logistical support.

He refused to let any officers risk their careers on such a dumb idea, but he was willing to watch.

And bring me in if I failed.

That left me short on manpower.

TEN MINUTES LATER, I was knocking on the door of a guy named Avi Damari. He was the quiet guy at David Gottleib's funeral. He kept up the silence when he answered the door, just held it open a foot and stared at me.

He looked over my shoulder at Carlos, weighed our intentions, then opened the door and gestured for us to come in. He dropped into a chair at a small dining table and waited until we were seated.

"Where did you work after you left the Marines?" I asked.

"Bullshit question."

"OK, answer the question I should've asked."

"My last job was at Velox Deployment."

"Jesus," I said. "You were assigned to Koven's firm."

He nodded.

Either he'd been hit in the head real hard or he was wicked smart; it was hard to tell. "Why is Koven *harah*? And what does that mean exactly?"

"Hebrew for s*hit*. You already know why."

"Because he tried to kill me?"

Avi shook his head.

I could feel his hatred like radiator heat and began to understand him better. "Because he was a coward at Nasiriyah."

Avi gave me a single nod.

"Why did you quit Velox?" I asked.

"Shane assigned me to open an office in Tel Aviv. I was excited about going home until I found out what they did."

"What makes you think Koven killed Gottleib?" I asked.

"Professional."

Laconic guys can be hard to understand. I glanced at Carlos to see if he followed the logic.

Carlos said, "Only a coward contracts a hit."

Avi nodded at him. The two were wired into some kind of assassins' code of ethics. Real men do their own killing.

Several pieces fell into place and a few questions in my head clicked closed while several others opened up. Jago walked away in Tokyo, which made him a coward in the assassin's worldview. And a suspect in mine. But a suspect for which of the hundreds of crimes around him? And why?

"Do you know who pulled the trigger?" I asked.

Avi shook his head.

"Do you and your pals want a part in cornering the guy?"

"When and where?"

Mercury slid into the fourth chair at the table, looking a bit rushed. *Dude, you need to make some arrangements right now. The kidnappers are talking about sending the kid's body parts to you every hour. Oh, and there are people hunting Blackson. But I don't think you get why you need to save him. You need someone inside Koven's camp. He's your last hope.*

I said, But can I trust him?

CARLOS LOOKED LIKE a kid in a candy store when we traded the Tesla for something with longer range. I chose the Audi R8. The ice-cold gangster almost giggled when I handed him the keys and told him to drive. We crossed the river into Virginia on I-495.

Our last stop for the evening was Rip Blackson's house. A fine-looking woman with a child clinging to her dress answered the door. We exchanged pleasantries.

"He came home but left again." She put a hand on her child's head. "He says Koven's lost his mind."

"Where did he go?"

"Why do you want to know?" She squinted at me.

"Either he's smart and running to hide somewhere, or he's dumb and doing Koven's bidding."

"Don't matter," she said. "Koven sees him as a deserter anyway."

"Go somewhere, like your mother's or something." I tried to sound cheerful, but a line like that sounds ominous no matter how you say it.

"Why should I hide? I'm no threat to anybody." She closed the door. "Leave us alone. We're not part of this."

When I got back in the car, Carlos stared at me a long time. "What makes you think the guy's in danger?"

Ignoring his question, I pointed at the road.

We headed out I-66, making for West Virginia.

I called the kidnapper. "One measure of how desperate you are: you gave up your cell number. I turned it over to the FBI and they're searching for you right now. Best thing you can do—leave the kid wherever you are and meet me. But you're in this too deep to think straight, so you probably won't do that. Here's the alternative: we'll do the exchange at Memorial Tunnel, outside of Standard, West Virginia. Be there in five hours or I'm gone for good."

"Wait." His voice-changer couldn't mask his frustration. "I can't be there in five hours. I need…" I sensed he was fumbling through his mapping app. "I need seven."

"Fine."

I clicked off. "He's bringing more firepower."

Carlos put the hammer down and we flew into the dark. We drove the first hour in silence.

"You ever have dreams about your destiny?" Carlos asked. "Like where you're going to die?"

"No," I said. "But if I did, driving to an abandoned tunnel in the middle of the night to meet a kidnapper would be likely scenario."

# CHAPTER 33

THE CLATTER AND clanks of a nearby wharf coming to life in the morning began to filter through the dungeon's thick stone. Pia had been through worse situations than a cold dungeon, yet this time a sense of desperation tried to pull her into that dark place where things spiraled downhill. Growing up, her friends were always jealous of her wealthy, single dad. She was jealous of the hugs their mothers gave them. She would never know, but she liked to dream that a mother's hug could lift you from the pit of despair. But there were more pressing problems than hugs or despair.

Prince Taimur held the keys to unraveling Koven's funnel for foreign money pouring into American elections. That was her focal point, nothing else mattered.

Tania paced their dark cell and smacked the wall again. "Why can't we get a signal in here?"

"Like I said last time," Pia answered, "it's the stone ceiling. Satellite phones can't get a signal and cell towers can't penetrate the walls. Besides, no one covers this tiny corner of the globe."

"Well, the Major better have a rescue operation going before I get hungry." Tania paced some more. "And I'm hungry. How long have we been in here?"

Before Pia could answer, a banging of doors and a tapping cane came from one floor up. She said, "Faiz, tell me you brought coffee."

"And a porta potty," Tania said.

"Yes, yes," Faiz said. Dim lights snapped on in a stone room beyond the iron grate. "Coffee and potty."

"You want to explain why you locked us up?" Pia asked.

"No, no. Prince say. Faiz do. No explain."

Their host appeared in the hall, twisting around his cane while carrying two awkward bundles in his free hand. He stopped at the iron door and shooed them back. He canted his head and smiled. "Be good to Faiz. Outside door locked, guard watches."

Pia and Tania backed up to the far end of the cell. Faiz opened a pass-through and pushed in a small plastic porta potty followed by a basket. They tumbled to the floor. Faiz clanked the portal closed. "Faiz back soon. Eat and fresh. Prince to see you."

He tapped away, mercifully leaving the lights on.

Tania ran to the goods and looked them over. She grabbed the porta potty, gave Pia a look, and carried it to the darkest corner. She said, "Faiz will be the first to die. Motherfucker didn't bring any toilet paper."

Pia dug in her thin pocket, produced two clean, crumpled tissues and offered one to her friend.

"You carry tissues?" Tania asked. "My grandmother carries tissues."

Pia started to stuff them back in her pocket.

Tania snatched one out of her hand. "My grandmother's a smart woman."

The basket held a thermos, two cups, and two omelet-stuffed *chapatis*, the local variation on pitas.

They ate, finished their coffee and waited. An hour later they heard clangs upstairs.

Faiz appeared and opened the giant iron door. He carried in two large pillows and one chair. He placed them in the center of the cell, then smiled at the ladies.

Behind him, Prince Taimur stepped out of the shadows carrying a briefcase.

Tania drew her Glock and aimed at his striking face.

"No need for violence." The prince sat in the chair as if he owned it. "I left you armed because we are not enemies."

Pia put her hand on Tania's wrist and pushed it down.

The prince gestured to the pillows at his feet.

Tania gave the prince a nasty look, gave Faiz a nastier one, and took up a defensive position against the far wall.

"Do you need new bandages?" the prince asked.

"I'm fine." Tania crossed her arms with a sneer.

Pia stepped into his line of sight. "Why are you holding us in a dungeon?"

"To me, you are both good and bad." He gazed at her with no emotion. "Yesterday I was very angry, but overnight I gave it some thought. When I was a guest in your house in Dubai, you protected me with your life, like a good Muslim. But later, you badgered me for what you wanted, like a disrespectful teenager. On the one hand, I admire your heroic efforts. On the other, I should have you flogged."

"You'd be dead before—"

"I've come to understand your insolence and your reluctance to work with me." The prince smiled with perfect, shiny teeth. "This deal was made with your father. My sources tell me you've taken over. Perhaps it would be best if we reviewed our goals."

"Your sources are wrong." Pia squinted. "I've not taken over. My father is still the CEO."

The prince smiled knowingly and nodded. "You honor his position, regardless of who makes the rules. I respect that. It shows some form of humility exists inside that difficult exterior."

Pia clenched her fists behind her back.

From upstairs, a woman's voice called out in Arabic. Faiz looked up with a pale face and tottered down the hall.

Prince Taimur opened his briefcase and extracted a stack of papers. "DHK insisted that our contract consist of two copies only, never to be photocopied and to be kept secure at all times. There are no electronic versions of this. These details are stipulated in the terms."

He handed her the papers.

With some reluctance, she took it and glanced at the cover page and contents. It was all typed on a typewriter that left the paper with indentations. "This is your contract with them?"

"Look it over. I think you will see how certain people are willing to help me." He looked at her with sad eyes. "I love my country. I love my family and our traditions. I am loath to leave my homeland. But I do not live in a civilized democracy."

Pia flipped through a few pages of legalese. "What did he promise you? That these American legislators could influence immigration or something?"

He leaned back in his chair and rested his hands on his knees. "In short, they would push through a bill that allows a certain company to register in the US as an American company while retaining the proven reserves it holds now."

Pia read several pages, then peered at him. "You would be transferring oil reserves belonging to the Kingdom of Oman into an American company, putting it under American protection. If someone hostile to American interests were to take over Oman, the USA would be obliged to protect the company, its officers, and its assets."

"The USA already protects Kuwait, Saudi Arabia, and several other countries."

A level above them, a door slammed and Faiz began tapping his way back downstairs.

"The politicians who agreed to this are aware of these terms?" When he nodded, she gave it some more thought. "Then why involve Sabel Security? Why not have Koven distribute your 'donations' to the appropriate politicians?"

"We already donate huge sums to think tanks, the ones you see giving opinions on the news and cited in major newspapers. We also pay for university studies that prove whatever we want. That is all perfectly legal because it's not an election. But we need someone to sponsor the bill, and that's where the randomness of my birth place prevents me from giving money to those campaigns. I can't donate, but unions and corporations can." He pointed his finger at her. "You can."

Faiz tapped his way to them and stopped. "My wife say—this."

He held out a roll of toilet paper.

Prince Taimur glanced at the roll, then saw the porta potty for the first time. He jumped to his feet. "How careless of me. I most humbly apologize for my manners. I had given instructions for your internment. I failed to realize how unseemly—"

Pop-pop-pop.

The unmistakable sound of automatic weapons echoed through the stone building.

"Get behind me." Pia pulled her pistol and crossed the hall to the stairs.

Tania joined her. They proceed up the curved stairway. The prince and Faiz reluctantly followed.

"Your friends from the Emirates?" Pia asked.

"How do you know they're not after you?" the prince asked.

Tania hissed. "They would've sent more men."

Pia opened a heavy wooden door, took a peek outside, and retreated. "Two in black on the left shooting at three in beige on the right."

"My men wear beige," the prince said. "They will win this."

"They're pinned in a corner and it's not looking good."

The prince shrank.

"Is there another exit?" Pia asked Faiz.

"Cheap Portuguese, door of one."

Pia turned to Tania. "The only cover is behind the old dhows."

Tania shrugged. "Open a second front, hope the prince's boys figure out we're the good guys."

Pia gestured the prince and Faiz back down the stairs. When they were a safe distance away, she counted down from three.

Tania shoved the door open from floor level while Pia fired. Their darts bounced off the heavily armored men in black. Tania landed her last round in one man's cheek. He dropped.

Three new men in black ran through the outer gate. They mowed down the prince's guard detail and turned their attention to Pia at the very instant she caught the nearest man in the small amount of exposed neck.

Before she could celebrate, a storm of bullets flew at her. She retreated down four steps. Tania secured the door, skipped the stairs, and jumped to the dungeon floor below.

"For the record," Tania said, "Jacob's right about darts versus bullets. We should carry more armor-piercing rounds."

Pia's stairs followed the base of a round tower, bending away from the door. It was that curve that saved her from the onslaught of lead that blasted through the wood.

The rounds kept coming. The men outside fired and reloaded and fired and reloaded until the door hung in tattered shreds of kindling. Blinding daylight poured in from outside.

One head stuck through the gap, nothing more than a featureless silhouette. Pia fired at it anyway.

He pushed through the door with his shoulder, raised the barrel of his weapon and aimed.

Before he pulled the trigger, he fell, face first, to Tania's feet on the stone floor.

"Clear!" Miguel's booming voice echoed in the courtyard outside.

Tania ran up the stairs and squeezed through the remaining slivers of door. Pia grabbed the prince's briefcase and waved for the prince and Faiz to follow.

In the yard, Miguel surveyed the scene, unmoved by the carnage. "We gotta go. There's ten more coming with heavier weaponry, missiles and grenade launchers."

Pia shuddered.

Three Omani guards ran in and put their hands up when Miguel turned his AR15 their way.

He turned to Pia and shrugged. "I already told them I'm after the Emiratis, not them, but I guess there's a language barrier. Where's Jacob when you need his Arabic?"

Pia gave him a big hug. "I thought you were in Germany guarding my dad."

"It's below freaking zero in Germany. I heard there's a beach and sunshine here. But we gotta run." He turned and sprinted for the gate.

Everyone followed him.

"Thank you for saving me—again. I owe you," the prince called out as his men herded him into a Land Cruiser. He leaned out his window and shouted to Pia. "We should race jets again. But this time, I go first."

"Don't take your jet!" Pia watched the prince speed down the road. Hearing her warning would've been impossible. She texted her message to him and watched the send bar proceed halfway before stopping.

Faiz turned to her. "Faiz go with Pia, more safe."

"I'll bet you'd like that," Tania snarled and faced Pia. "You still have the Prince's briefcase."

"We need to copy the contract and upload it to Emily at the *Post*. But I can't even get a text message going." Pia turned to Faiz. "Where can I find those smugglers you told me about?"

"Faiz take you." He pointed to his open Toyota.

They piled in and took off in the opposite direction from the airport. He drove past a cruise ship and several docks of dhows and small outboards until he passed the last few ships.

At the end of the harbor, a sambuk, the ancient boat design of deep-water ships in the Persian Gulf, took on cargo. The bow rose from the water with a curved swoop; the stern ended in an abrupt transom carved with elegant designs.

Faiz gestured to the aging wooden craft. "Smuggler take any places."

"Does it have an engine?" Pia asked.

"Sails and engines."

"Is it fast?"

He shrugged with his arms out, palms up. "You say smuggler—I bring you smuggler."

"Will it outrun other boats?"

"Maybe." Faiz turned and shouted to men onboard.

Across the harbor, two trucks pulled away from the fortress. One drove up the road toward the airport; the other crossed the bridge, bringing them to Pia's side of the harbor.

Faiz and a bearded man haggled over prices. Pia took a wad of hundred-Euro notes from her waistpack and handed it to the Captain. She said, "Now."

They climbed aboard and cast off.

Within minutes, they were out in the open bay. Miguel perched high on the stern while Pia and Tania sat on a bench on the aft deck. Despite Tania's repeated pleas to toss him overboard, Faiz wandered among the crew.

The air was cool, the sea was calm, the sun was bright, and the breeze gentle. Without communications, it was a beautiful day. Yet that nagging sense of desperation tugged at Pia. She couldn't shake it.

The sound of a jet roared overhead. They looked up to see the red, green, and white stripes of the Omani flag on the tail. The wing dipped a salute. Everyone waved except Pia.

"You're going to help the prince, right?" Tania asked. "He seemed so nice. And he's handsome. And he's a prince. And you like him. And he's a much better choice than Carlos."

From the shore, a missile whooshed over their heads.

Two thousand feet above them, Prince Taimur's jet exploded.

# CHAPTER 34

KOVEN USED BOTH hands to grab the heavy curtains and throw them open with a violent burst, but it added no light to the castle's dark bedroom. Instead, the vast countryside sucked the room's warmth out through the glass, chilling his black mood. He turned to the lump of sheets and pillows. "Marthe, for god's sake, get up. Enough of this moping."

A single hand emerged from inside the layers of blankets and comforters and shot straight up.

"What is this?" he asked.

Her voice came muffled from the pillows. "You don't see it? My hand is stained."

"It's as pale as snow." He ripped back the covers. "You're still wearing that filthy nightgown with the wine stain."

He stared at her unmoving form.

"I need you now," he said. "I had to put Alan Sabel in the dungeon and those idiots from Velox took me literally when I joked about cutting up Benning. It's all going to hell around here. I need your help."

She met his gaze with trembling lips.

"What in god's name is wrong with you?" He grabbed her shoulders. "Your eyes are black and swollen, you look terrible."

"All I see is blood." She curled up to a kneeling position, held her hand out, and pulled up the sleeve of her nightgown. "I washed all night. It's no good. I'm no good. I'm lost."

He looked at the back of her sagging head. They were strangers from different lands with no common language between them. He shared her desperation, but they were heading in different directions. He wanted a solution. She welcomed defeat.

Her voice came down to a soft whisper. "What makes you so afraid that you need me, my big, strong war hero?"

"That bastard Hyde showed up drunk." He patted her back. "I think Jago is fond of that old goat."

She nuzzled him. "Don't be so hard on the old man. He came to see me earlier. We have nothing to fear."

"Hyde came up here? Why?"

"Looking for you. He tried to cheer me up." Scratching at her arms, she wobbled like a drunk. "He said you have $100 million stashed away. We don't have to worry about anything anymore because we're rich. That's what he told me. So why should I care that my arms are stained?"

"Your arms are not … you need rest, my dear." Koven gazed around the room. Clothing lay in clumps as if she'd tried to dress several times and saw nothing but futility in it.

She sat still and sniffed. "Hyde said you're invincible. We don't need to be afraid."

"You didn't take the sleeping pills?" Koven reached to the nightstand and retrieved the bottle. "You should take one of these. I don't know anything about medicine but take something, whatever you need to get a good nap. Then get dressed and join me, there's work to be done."

"If you didn't kill Gottleib, who did?"

"Where did that question come from?"

"I don't know. I'm tired and my mind wanders. But who killed him?"

"I told you, I don't know." He rose and headed for the door. "I thought it was Zola, then for a time, Blackson, but I don't know anymore."

"Hyde said you're the only one who stood to gain."

"Whatever he knows." Koven stopped mid-step. "What would I have to gain?"

"Did you kill Zola's boy too?" she asked.

He continued to the door. "No."

Downstairs he found Hyde and Jago in the Grand Treaty Room, shaking hands with the Russian oil baron, Mikhail Yeschenko. A short, stocky man with a scar across his eye, he rested an arm on a cart full of suitcases.

"Mikhail, you're not leaving, are you?" Koven asked.

"Your firm is unlucky," the Russian said with his thick, guttural accent. "Putin and I want the sanctions lifted but not so much that I can afford to get involved with you. There are too many other Super PACs."

He grabbed his supermodel wife's hand and left.

Koven turned to the aging alcoholic. "What did you say to him, Hyde?"

The old man shrugged, lifting his hands. "Well. Maybe they're worried about what you've been doing."

"Why?" Koven peered at his partner. "What have I been doing?"

Hyde looked around the room and rubbed his balding head. "There have been a lot of deaths around—"

"Why would they blame me? People die all the time. Day after day, the dead stack up like cordwood all over the country. How is that my fault?"

Koven stared at Hyde until the old man turned to Jago.

Koven turned beet red and shook with rage. "You *told* him?"

Hyde grabbed Koven's arm. "He never said a word to me. He didn't need to. I just watched the Velox men cutting up Paul Benning's body in the kitchen while that off-duty cop ate an apple. You and I both know Velox wouldn't do anything without an authorization for the extra charges."

"You sound awfully calm about it."

Hyde let go and grabbed a chair for support. "It took me a minute to understand what drove you to such extremes. I've been around long enough to know this is not the time for insubordination or betrayal, Daryl. Jago and I discussed it. We're with you. We don't want to end up like Benning."

Koven stared long and hard and ground his teeth. Finally, he took a breath. "Good. I appreciate your support. There's much to be done." He turned to Jago. "First, I want to hear what happened to Zola."

"I told you." Jago faced him. "He was shot to death."

"Since we talked, I saw a report on a Japanese news site. It said Stearne was with him."

"He was shot with Stearne's gun."

"It also said several off-duty police were involved and five went to the hospital where they were later executed."

"I don't know anything about the *yakuza*," Jago said.

Koven stepped closer to Jago, nearly face to face. "The news reports said the executioner was American. But the eyewitness accounts described a man much taller than you."

Jago didn't blink.

"I didn't want anyone else involved in this."

Jago shrugged.

Koven thought through some options for handling Jago but none of them changed things. A third party was involved now, like it or not. Another betrayal, this time a betrayal of common sense. No, Jago couldn't be that stupid. Maybe he was in league with Blackson and Zola. Maybe he was talking to Stearne already. The only way to find out would be to test Jago's loyalty. Sure, a test. He scratched his chin.

After a few seconds, the tension in Koven's face subsided, and he turned away.

"What does that have to do with us?" Hyde said.

"There's something going on around here." Koven turned to the former senator. "Something I don't like."

"What?"

"Those Velox men killed Benning without a second thought. They wanted authorization, but they didn't care about the moral question."

"Aren't they CIA contractors?" Hyde asked.

Koven snorted and paced.

"It was a risky thing." Hyde put his hands out. "People will come looking for the CEO of a major corporation. And locking up Sabel was—"

"He was recording our conversations." Koven crossed to Hyde and grabbed his lapels. He yanked his jacket open and searched. When he saw nothing, he squeezed the material between his fingers. "Is that what you're doing, Bill? Are you in with Sabel too? Is that why you're asking all these questions?"

Hyde stood still.

Koven spun to Jago and pushed the coat off the man's shoulders. "What about you, Jago? Are you worried about your future? Maybe willing to take a deal in exchange for a reduced sentence?"

"Who isn't guilty?" Jago hunched his coat back on his shoulders. "You could turn me in too—but I'm not losing my temper."

Koven raised a hand to strike Jago across the face. The younger man caught his wrist and held it. Jago's strength surprised Koven, but he refused to ease off.

Their arms shook with tension.

"There's no sense arguing about things we don't control." Hyde separated them.

Koven pulled away and straightened his jacket. "It doesn't matter. The Three Blondes will cover me. I spoke to Katy Hellman and she said no one on Earth can touch us. Let the Bennings and Yeshenkos and Sabels flee in fear. Let them join the self-righteous fools who think life should be rational. We don't need them."

"Then everything is fine," Hyde said.

"No, everything is *not* fine." Koven's voice shook the room. "Blackson's been in contact with that crazy soldier, Jacob Stearne. Now he's gone. I meant to have Blackson chopped into pieces, not Benning— but that's how it goes sometimes."

"Who is Jacob Stearne to you?"

"One of those soldier wannabes who concocted some crazy story about the war in Iraq. Made himself out to be a hero. For some odd reason, everyone believes him. My own platoon believed his bullshit. They forgot about him until that stupid Gottleib went to talk to him. Is that why everyone thinks I killed David?" Koven looked to the ceiling. "Doesn't matter. Blackson's been working with Stearne, so now it's time to deal with him."

Half of Jago's mouth smiled. "Put him in the river with Benning?"

"He ran home to hide. Get back there and burn him out." Koven faced Jago with rage in his face, his eyes bulging. "Burn down everything so there's nothing left."

Jago glanced at Hyde. The old man gave a gentle bow of his head and the younger man left.

"How are we going to explain the deaths of our clients?" Hyde asked. "Müller, Suliman, Taimur?"

"I don't know anything about them." Koven crossed to the fireplace and stared at it for a long time. "I thought that was Pia Sabel's doing."

"Not her style."

Koven put his hands on the mantle and leaned to the fire. "What is her style? What do you know of her?"

"Tom knew her better than I." Hyde stood next to him. "I only met her a couple times. I got the distinct impression she's a destroyer."

"You sound like my wife." Koven cracked a short-lived smile. "For thousands of years, people have tried to destroy what they think is evil, but their destructive power becomes the very evil they seek to destroy. From the Salem witch trials to the atom bomb, what good has it done? None. We're still killing each other and justifying it any way we like. What I want to know is, how do we attack her?"

"You have her father. She'll attack you soon enough."

"Let her try, it's a fortress." He stood back and crossed his arms. "You're saying I should wait for her to attack? Let our destruction descend on us? Ha."

"Ha, indeed." Hyde closed his swollen eyes and shrugged. "She'll descend on you like a Valkyrie and take you to Odin."

"You sound happy about that outcome. I have every confidence in my fate, I'm not going to wait around. Let's do this."

Pulling his phone, Koven dialed her number. He went straight to her voice mail. "Pia, this is Daryl Koven calling. You have something I need, and I have something you need—presuming you care about your father's life."

# CHAPTER 35

IT WAS A long, lonesome valley, the kind a country singer would bring to life in terms of county jails, broken down cars, and cheating hearts. Black, leafless trees covered the steep, rolling hills and weak moonlight sparkled in the snow.

Carlos tossed a tarp over the razor wire and held the ladder. I climbed over and jumped to the ground. Carlos replaced the equipment in the shed where we'd found it and took up his position on the hill. I made sure there were no tracks left to give away my presence and went in the tunnel.

Memorial Tunnel was built in the 1950s to carry traffic, but the interstate took a different path thirty years later. The enterprising West Virginia National Guard turned it into the Center for National Response to train fire and rescue personnel as well as prepare military units for terrorism responses. In different sections over the half-mile, they keep two subway cars parked in a mock station; a careful replication of a fifty-car pileup; simulated terrorist caves; and even a collapsed building. Several times a year, Sabel Security rents the place for training sessions.

A hundred yards in, I staked out a spot in a subway car that had easy access and good places to hide nearby. Carlos did a sound check on our earbud system. Then we settled in for a long wait.

After an hour, Carlos came over the comm link. "Three guys got out of a car. One is working his way to you."

Mercury and Seven-Death came up from deep in the tunnel.

The Mayan god stared at me as if I'd been stringing up cats. Then he turned to the entrance and shook his stick and chanted and stomped and chanted some more. He pulled his knife out, stabbed it into his chest, pulled out his beating heart and held it high over his head. He shouted and rattled his stick.

Mercury yawned and waved a dismissive hand at his friend. *Save me, bro. He's been doing that trick for three days now.*

Mercury took a seat on a pile of rubble, elbow on his knee, chin in his palm.

Seven-Death turned around and waved his heart in front of us. Blood squirted from the arteries. The thing still pulsed. Mercury pushed him away. The Mayan turned to me with his fiercest glare. I thought his eyes would pop out.

I said, *You've seen one god, you've seen 'em all.*

Mercury said, *He's blessing you for battle, bro. The least you could do is look interested.*

Too late.

The Mayan looked at me as if I'd killed his puppy. He stuck his heart back in his chest and plopped down next to Mercury.

The faint sound of bolt cutters snapped down the tunnel.

I texted Carlos: "They have arrived" and slid my thermal imaging visor down. One lone figure with NVGs scanned the tunnel without a thermal option. Approaching with the caution of a bomb squad tech, he inched past me. I resisted the urge to shoot him and unmask him but I was sure the boss would've sent a grunt to walk point. After reaching the far end, he came back and eyed my subway car for a hiding place. He reconsidered and tried calling someone but couldn't get a signal.

He moved closer to the entrance and made his connection. "All clear, commander."

A few seconds later, Carlos's phone rang. Bianca had set us up so his phone mimicked mine; I could take calls from his location to prevent the tunnel's echo chamber from giving away my position. I listened via my earbud and answered by sending a text which the system would send as a synthesized voice.

The caller came through. "Jacob Stearne, we're here as agreed. Show yourself and the boy will be released."

I texted back. "Do you realize why Shane Diabulus sent you instead of coming himself?"

The delayed response told me he was either easily confused or communicating with Shane; probably both.

Finally, he responded, "Why the voice box?"

My response: "Because I'm chewing gum and walking. Duh. The reason Shane sent you in is because he knows it's a suicide mission. I have a bead on you, just below your body armor. If you were someone else we'd call that target 'the family jewels,' but on you, we'll call it Darwinian debris."

In the dark, he checked his crotch—which told me all I needed to know about both his IQ and his experience. He was not a soldier.

I sent another text. "Send me proof the boy's been released and we'll negotiate whether you die where you stand or wait til you're outside the tunnel."

Again he looked around, somewhat spooked. He moved in deeper, watching his signal meter.

His new position allowed me to see more of him. He had two phones and spoke into the other one. I couldn't make out that part.

"OK," he said to me, "the boy's been released."

I rolled my eyes. "Pinky swear?"

Mercury said, *Dude, You got any of those stupid Sabel Darts? Now would be a good time for them. Drop this clown and wait for his boss to come looking.*

I said, *You told me to never touch Darts again.*

Mercury said, *That's what you heard? You're just like a teenager, man; you hear what you shouldn't and ignore everything else. Fucking mortals.*

Seven-Death nodded and put his fist out. Mercury bumped it.

The guy made his call. He was close enough to hear this time. "I don't think he believes me."

I snuck out of my subway car, making my way behind him while he listened to his instructions. I pulled my knife and pistol and waited until he finished his call. When he lowered the outbound phone, I pressed my knife to his neck and the barrel to the bottom of his skull.

I said, "First, we're going to walk backward to where your friends won't see us. Then, you're going to toss your weapons six feet in front of you."

We did our little dance and his assault rifle clattered to the ground. He held his hands up.

I pounded my knee in his butt. "Pistol? Knife? Anything else that will get you killed when I search you?"

Gingerly, he reached into several pockets and pulled weapons: two knives, two pairs of cuffs, brass knuckles. Last to fall to the ground, a Glock 22 in a .40 caliber. I knocked his Kevlar helmet off to make sure he understood how vulnerable he was.

"Where is Shane?" I asked.

"I don't know who you're talking about."

I smacked him in the head.

He changed his answer. "He's not here."

Another smack.

His voice trembled this time. "He's in Rockaway."

"Where is the boy?"

"I just said what the commander said. That was the first I heard of a boy."

"You're a cop and you didn't think to ask what this was about?" I asked.

Shocked I knew him so well, he twitched and started to turn. I smacked his head.

I sighed. "You looked at your legs when I claimed to have a bead on you. Only TV snipers use red laser dots. Anyone with basic military training would know we use an infrared targeting laser in real life. You need special glasses to see them—that way the enemy doesn't know you're targeting him." I paused. "Plus, you're carrying a standard issue Montgomery County Police pistol. Even has the MCP property stamp on the grip."

He swallowed so hard it echoed.

One of his phones rang.

End of game time.

I smacked the cop over the head so hard he was out before he hit the ground.

I picked up the guy's other phone and accepted the call. "Let's cut out the middleman, shall we, Shane?"

The inhale on the other end was satisfying. But the bastard made me wait for an answer.

"You're a dead man, Stearne." No voice box this time.

The voice sounded familiar. I hadn't spoken to Shane in a long time, so I couldn't be sure it was him.

I said, "All the wit of a third grader. Is the boy safe?"

"So you do care about him after all. I'll put him at the mouth of the tunnel. You come out and he goes in."

"No dice. You come in, then put the boy in the tunnel. Anyone shoots him, you die. If he gets to my backup guy, I'll come out."

"What? No. Then I'll be a hostage. That won't work."

The Shane-guy wasn't as dumb as I'd hoped. I needed a new plan.

Carlos's voice came into my earbud. "Six guys heading for the tunnel. Want me to take them out?"

I texted him back. "If one of them is on the phone, yes. Otherwise no."

"No one is on the phone. Standing by."

They were moving in faster than I wanted. Paranoia crept through me as I slapped plasticuffs on my first captive and shoved a rag in his mouth. I made it back to my train car as the advancing troops peered around the corner, into the tunnel.

The Shane-guy on the phone said, "Tell you what. I'll have the boy out front. You come out close enough to see him, but not close enough to get shot. Then the boy can take off. When that's done, you walk out. Deal?"

"If you stand next to him. Wear body armor if you want, but keep your hands open and out wide."

"Done." He clicked off.

His voice rang in my ear. It was familiar, too familiar. I couldn't pinpoint why. Maybe I was expecting Shane to do more trash talk. This guy knew how to have a negotiation without losing his cool. I was leaning toward it being someone other than Shane.

He might not be on the phone, but he'd masterminded Tokyo. Of that, I had no doubts. Not even the creepy-as-hell Jago dude would execute people in an emergency room. That meant Shane was somewhere near the operation.

All six intruders snuck in the entrance. Four were using commando tactics like the well-trained soldiers Velox employed. Two hung back, looking a bit awkward, as if they were playing follow-the-leader. They took up positions behind concrete barriers on either side and waited. Several long seconds ticked by.

I calculated my chances. Bad and getting worse.

Sweat trickled down my temple. I could not let the kid die in this. Maybe I didn't know him and didn't have any allegiance to his mom, but Shane had beaten me in Tokyo and I couldn't let that happen again.

This time, the good guys win.

Carlos said, "Two more coming. One is big, the other smaller. Might be the kid."

After a few long seconds, two figures stood in the moonlight out front. The boy with his hands behind his back, the other, a fat guy, holding the boy's arm.

I resisted moving a muscle. The riflemen at the entrance were there to take me out and they were pros. Breathing would tip them off to my hiding place.

Adrenaline poured into my veins, icing my thinking. I set my rifle on full-auto, switched the infrared targeting laser to a frequency they would not expect, and turned it on.

After enough time had passed, and they decided I wasn't coming out, the fat guy out front untied the boy and pointed to one side. The boy ran.

On my earbud, Carlos said, "Boy is running back down the road. He's clear of the cars and heading for the houses in that village over the creek."

I texted my containment element, Carlos. "Fire at will."

Carlos instructed the others over the comm link. "Going hot."

Four guns opened up on the riflemen from Carlos' position. Two went down. One clutched his leg and screamed for a medic. The other was dead still. The fat guy took a couple rounds in the body armor and staggered for safety behind a forklift.

The only ones left were too deep in the tunnel for Carlos to reach.

It was me against four trained, deadly soldiers working together.

No problem.

I moved up to a stack of pre-stressed concrete beams and aimed.

One of the killers tapped the shoulders of three guys, who then peeled off to attack me. Classic military moves. I aimed for the guy giving orders but couldn't get a shot off before his minions started firing. I ducked and waited for them to empty their magazines, but they were disciplined soldiers.

Keeping focused on the highest-value target first, just like the Rangers taught me, I moved, aimed, and nailed the leader.

Three against one.

I rolled to a new hiding place. One of them shot at my old spot and I took him out based on the flash from his muzzle. I rolled again.

I played deadly tennis with the last two. They fired and ducked and moved. I fired and ducked and moved. But they had the advantage of moving in different directions. Within a couple volleys, I had to shoot twice, exposing myself to one of them. After hearing a round of lead buzz my ear, I started tossing chunks of cement around. The tension was too much for the guy on the right. He fell for one of my rocks and rolled out from behind a sand pile. But my mag was empty.

I pulled my pistol and aimed.

Seven-Death reached over my shoulder and pushed the barrel a millimeter up.

I made the shot and nailed the assassin in the face.

What most people don't understand about gunfights is that people don't die when the bullet strikes them. Even men who've been shot in the head can live for ten or fifteen minutes and are able to talk. The man I shot stared at me, his mouth moving as if he wanted to say something. This was the perfect time to take out his compatriot, while he was in shock over the loss of his friend. But the not-yet-dead can still pull a trigger.

I put another round through his eye. Cold but necessary.

I popped up to find my last adversary folded in half, breathing his last.

Avi Damari and his two buddies—David Gottleib's friends—strode into the entrance as if they were filming another remake of *Gunfight at the OK Corral.*

Mercury kicked my latest kill and said, *Dude, that was the coldest thing I've seen since Domitian sentenced Epaproditus to a poena cullei.*

I said, *I don't want to hear about it.*

Mercury said, *That's when they sew you in a large leather sack with a bunch of wild animals. Like, badgers and wildcats and snakes and shit.*

I said, *Ah, the good old days.*

Mercury said, *Damn straight. None of this namby-pamby lethal injection crap. Hey, don't let the fat guy get away.*

Carlos was checking the dead and wounded. Behind him, on hands and knees, the fat shadow—the one who had accompanied the boy— tried to crawl away.

I ran over, grabbed him by the body armor and stuffed my Glock in his mouth.

My instincts were on target; it wasn't Shane Diabulus. So where the hell was Diabulus?

Captain Cates walked up. "Tell me you have the evidence, Stearne."

"Only more questions." I caught his gaze and nosed down at the guy at my knee: Detective Lovett.

# CHAPTER 36

ASHES AND BURNING wreckage fell from the infinite blue above to the deep blue below near the sambuk that carried Pia, Tania, and Miguel. They leaned over the edge of the deck, silent and shocked, as each piece splashed in the sea. The boat's crew was equally stunned when Faiz explained who owned the jet.

The captain said a heartfelt prayer for the prince, translated by Faiz, and then they all stared in silence for a long time.

Pia felt her stomach wrench and twist and boil. Her entire body felt suddenly hollow. Seeing someone shot out of the air took a toll on her perception of security. Lives had ended with no chance for survival, no hope of rescue, no miracles.

There was nothing she could do. The things that needed to be done were beyond her reach. She felt disconnected, out of control, alone. There were others in as much danger as the Prince. She had to get moving before LOCI chalked up more dead. But first, she had to find a way out of the region.

They sailed north, rounding the point at Kuzmar, then east into the Strait of Hormuz on their way to rendezvous with the Sabel Industries' 360-foot yacht, *Asteria*. They would be out of the ship's helicopter range for several more hours. Pia's jet had been searched by the LOCI Emiratis in Khasab and released. Her pilot flew to Karachi to wait for her. For now, she was hours away with nothing to do but sit on the sambuk's deck and watch the coastline recede.

Miguel and Tania soaked up the warm sun while Pia paced the decks.

A smaller boat trailed them, slowly narrowing the distance. The captain changed course twice only to have their shadow follow.

Eventually, the smaller boat came within hailing range. Arabic and

Persian bounced over the waves on megaphones.

Faiz and the captain approached Pia.

"Emirati gain on you." Faiz leaned on his cane and shrugged. "Also, offer money for captain. He give you them. So sorry."

"Told you we should've tossed him." Tania stared daggers at the old man.

Two crewmen raised ancient rifles aimed at Pia.

Miguel stifled a laugh. "Want me to take them out?"

Pia put her hand up to stop her people and faced the captain. "Faiz, translate for me. Tell him you saw me arrive on my own jet. And tell him who saved you at the fortress. Tell him to make a decision about whose side he's on."

The two men argued in Arabic for a long time.

Faiz broke it off. "Captain like cash. Jet nice but jet not cash, not boat. Faiz argue but Faiz like cash too. Difficult argument."

"Tell him I'll give him that boat," She nodded to the approaching craft, "and all the cash on it."

The Emirati ship narrowed the distance.

The captain scratched his beard and stared at Pia as if measuring her for a coffin.

Faiz shrugged.

The captain looked back and forth, then grabbed the gun from her holster, spun her around and held both her hands behind her back. He held her weapon high above his head, showing it to the approaching vessel, then shoved it back inside the elastic of her yoga pants. He continued to restrain Pia's hands.

Over his shoulder, he nodded at his men who did the same thing to Tania and Miguel.

The smaller ship pulled alongside and lashed to the sambuk amidships.

Pia's captain gestured and shouted and made the approaching captain identify himself and his crew. Then he insisted they line up to make sure there were no tricks involved. Three Omani crew and four Emirati assassins showed themselves.

When the crew finished lashing the boats together, and the four body-armored assassins stood in a line, the captain let Pia go.

She whipped her Glock out from behind her back. Her first dart hit the other captain in the neck. The black-clad attackers turned, startled by the unexpected sound, and in that instant of curiosity, Tania and Miguel leaped over the railings and onto them. At six-four, 220 pounds, Miguel took down two, one under each foot. A more efficient method than shooting.

Pia followed, but lost her pistol when she hit the deck. She planted a right hook on the jaw of a man trying to raise his rifle. He staggered left and lost the grip on his weapon. She pulled a knife from her legging, slashed at him, and slit his bicep. His attention left the fight as he attempted to staunch the arterial flow.

She scrabbled around, found her Glock, and darted a man struggling to free himself from Tania's grip.

Miguel threw one man into the sea while the last man jumped on him from behind. Tania turned and put a dart in the attacker's leg. Miguel bent at the waist, tossing his drugged opponent overboard.

"Get him out of the water," Pia shouted. "He'll drown."

On the sambuk's deck, Faiz and the crew watched, chins resting on palms as if it were a soccer match.

The two remaining crew ducked into the wheelhouse before returning to the fight. One carried a shotgun, the other an iron rod.

Pia launched herself at the man with the gun, wrapping her arms around his shoulders. Due to her momentum and angle, the barrel dipped when he pulled the trigger, sending the buckshot into his foot. Pia plowed him into the deck. She jumped up and landed her bodyweight on his stomach, making his eyes bulge out. She rested for just a second before darting him.

The last crewman made the ill-advised decision to hit Tania with his iron. Her left foot landed in his groin while the rod was still over his head and coming forward. The man lost his grip, in effect handing the weapon to her. She began probing the location of his kidneys with rapid strokes of the rod as he cried out in pain.

Pia grabbed Tania's hand. "We don't need to kill him."

Behind her, Miguel splashed into the sea and rescued the darted assassin. Faiz threw him a rope and, with the help of the crew, pulled them aboard.

Pia strode over to the man with the sliced arm and darted him, then knelt and made a tourniquet to reduce the bleeding.

One Emirati remained in the water, struggling to keep his body and fifty pounds of armor above the surf. She called to Faiz and had the man rescued and disarmed. They pulled him aboard the Emirati's ship and darted him. The captain's men secured the pirate ship and crew.

Five minutes, start to finish.

Pia called out to Faiz. "Tell him this is legal compensation for disarming pirates at sea."

The captain smiled and bowed to her. He sent a man to pilot the smaller boat.

They sailed into the Indian Ocean until late afternoon before the *Asteria's* chopper came into view. It hovered over the sambuk's stern and one by one, they climbed in.


TWO HOURS LATER, Captain Chamberlain welcomed them aboard the *Asteria*.

Pia and her team had dinner on the upper deck before going to her stateroom on the owner's deck.

They were too far from Sabel Satellite coverage for their phones to work, so Tania checked in via the ship's systems.

She reported back. "Rip Blackson showed up in our Paris office asking for help and protection. Jacob went to exchange himself for the Zola kid. No word on the outcome yet. The guests have been leaving the rebooted Future Crossroads Symposium early. A reporter fished Paul Benning's dismembered body from the Moselle River just below the castle. Your father has not been in contact for a few hours and his phone is offline. And the worst part is, just to piss each other off, every now and then the Iranians and the Americans jam each other's radio and satellite signals in this part of the world, so we've lost ship communications. Captain Chamberlain says we'll be clear of their problems by morning."

Tania held out several sheets of paper. "We don't have Internet, but Bianca figured out a way to get a report printed onboard."

Tania had been up, popping Provigil—stay-awake pills—for several days. Pia sent her to get some sleep.

Bianca's report described LOCI, a security firm working overseas. The founder was a soldier who died in combat three years before the company was formed. A company so bad even the founder was a straw man. Like the social welfare group Jago headed, it opened a bank account with $6 million. LOCI offered security services tailored to meet local laws and customs. Very little else about the company was available.

Everything in the report bothered Pia.

She texted Jacob: "I know Koven killed Duncan—but not Gottleib or the clients. I think you already figured out who did it, so tell me."

She pressed send and watched the screen respond, "No signal."

# CHAPTER 37

THICK CLOUDS HUNKERED down for the night, obscuring the last sliver of moon as Jago Seyton drove north on I-270 to Frederick, Maryland where he bought a movie ticket beneath a security camera, marched in, stuffed the stub in his pocket, and walked out the theater's side door. He pulled his fedora down tight, turned up his collar, and wove a path to his car, avoiding the lighted areas.

After putting tape on his license plate to change the number, and covering part of the taillights to change the profile, he drove on back roads to Boonsboro and crossed into West Virginia at Shepherdstown. There he paid cash for a chemical sprayer at an old hardware store that didn't have video surveillance. Staying on the back roads, he made his way to Lucketts, Virginia where he put four gallons of diesel fuel in the sprayer. From there he went back to the movie theater in Frederick, snuck in, and complained to the manager about the movie.

Then he drove to McLean, where he rented a car using Rip Blackson's credit card. He drove through Blackson's neighborhood once, noting there were two cars in Blackson's open garage. He drove to the mall, switched hats and coats, then returned to Blackson's street where he rolled slowly by, noting how many windows were lit up.

He switched to his own car, the plates still taped, and came back an hour later. The garage was closed and the pattern of light in the windows had changed; the occupants had moved upstairs.

He drove to Maryland and had a late dinner at Sandy's where the waitress knew him because he never tipped. He asked the waitress for her phone number. She turned on a self-righteous heel and walked away. He tossed cash on his half-finished meal and left in a huff, throwing the door open.

Switching back to the rental, he put on a ski mask and drove slowly down Blackson's street. All the lights were out. He parked at a darkened house a block away. He retrieved his chemical sprayer from the trunk and made his way through bushes and hedges to Blackson's house.

He found the water main and shut off the supply that fed the fire suppression system. Then he pumped up the sprayer and coated the sideboards and shrubs and foundation with a fine mist of diesel fuel.

Most people think gasoline is the best fire accelerant, but diesel burns hotter and soaks deeper into wood. He paid special attention to the windows and doors to make sure there would be no escape. He found the cellar door locked and gave it a good soaking. He did his best to cover every inch of the ground floor's exterior walls and as far up the second floor as he could reach.

When Jago emptied the last of the four gallons, he stood back for a moment to admire his work.

He lit a trail of fuel at the back stoop with a butane lighter and tossed the chemical sprayer near the garage. As the flames began to lick up the walls on the backside, he retreated into the hedge at the back of the property near a gate to the neighbor's yard. He slid between the branches and crouched.

Modern suburban homes have evolved to become sound-proof and insulated cocoons, as if we would rather not know what's going on next door. Had he torched the house fifty years ago, at least one neighbor would have smelled the fumes before Jago could've finished his work.

But several minutes had gone by and not a single alarm had been raised. No one shouted, and no one came out. Part of that was due to his professional choice of accelerants. By choosing diesel, there would be no loud *whoosh* nor giant towering flames.

At least not yet.

The first scream of terror came from inside the house.

Every exterior wall of the home blazed in blue flame with bright yellow tips that reached the gutters. The best part was what he could see through the windows: lots of smoke on the ceilings of the lower floors. That meant the heat was building up to the flash point.

More and more yellow flames appeared in the flame, telling him the wood was burning more than the fuel. There would be no stopping it now.

The screams inside grew, everyone was awake and shrieking in horror.

Jago rubbed his palms together.

A woman came out of the house next door, her face lit yellow by the bright flames. She turned and shouted to her husband inside. Another house across the street awakened and a thirtyish man came forward brandishing a garden hose.

Perfect.

A jet of water hit the side of the house where it immediately turned to steam and carried unburned droplets of diesel into the air, raining fire in all directions.

The neighbors who lived behind the Blackson's marched through the gate, an arm's length from Jago.

He froze.

The man was older and wiser than the others because he carried a kitchen fire extinguisher. It was exactly the kind needed for this type of fire, a chemical retardant. The old man looked at his equipment, and looked at Blackson's house, and instantly knew he would need a bigger extinguisher. But the valiant old man gave it a shot anyway.

When the old couple ran toward the flames, Jago slipped into their backyard.

Halfway across the space, he hesitated, wanting one last look, and snuck back to the gate.

He took a peek.

A window on the top floor opened. The blackened arms of an adult raised the sash. But the heat inside the house fought for that exit and won. It blasted out the window, shooting long ribbons of yellow flame into the sky, cooking every ounce of flesh on its way.

The Blacksons were dead.

All of them.

There could be no escape.

The flames spread to the garage, where the remaining fuel in the sprayer exploded like a bomb. The do-gooders scattered and watched in horror, except for the old man plying his kitchen extinguisher like a hopeless wretch trying to dry up the ocean with a sponge.

Jago closed the gate and slinked away through the dark.


DARYL KOVEN SLAPPED a piece of bread on top of the sliced turkey and cut the sandwich in half, diagonally the way his mother taught him. He placed it on a small plate and cursed the chill. For all the romantic lure of a castle, they turned out to be useless things, dark, dank, cold, and full of drafts. He felt one of those errant cold winds ice his neck as he turned to the prep table.

He drew a sharp breath. "Marthe, you startled me. I didn't hear you come in."

She sat at the table, staring at the surface.

It was butcher block, thick for commercial use, and hosted four chairs.

He crossed to the table. "I'm glad to see you up, my dear. Are you feeling better?"

"It's quiet," she said.

"Everyone left, I'm afraid." He put his plate down and pulled the chair out. He paused to look her over. "I could've used your counsel earlier."

He sat and put his napkin in his lap.

She groaned. "It doesn't matter."

"Of course it matters. I can fix this, but I need your help." He took a bite and chewed. "Katy Hellman is working on it for me. She made promises and her reporters are making good on those."

She made no remark.

"Now it's time to separate the sheep from the goats." Koven smiled at his disheveled wife. "I'm done playing games with these fools. We're a team. You've made me everything I am today. And together, we're invincible."

Marthe reached across the table and grabbed his hand. "We're finished."

"My dear, you underestimate the power of the press. *Fuchs News Channel, Hummingbird, Chronicle*, they control the flow of information in the industrialized world."

"The media isn't one big machine." She let go. "The left cries about *FNC* brainwashing people and the right cries about 'liberal media bias'. Everyone complains when the news contradicts their worldview. But it's supposed to be that way. Reporters are part of the entropy of civilization. Like ants in the forest, they break down the powerful and chew them up. No tree is too big for the millions of pincers they bring to bear. It doesn't matter who you are, they exist to take you apart."

Koven took another bite and stared at his wife and considered her words while he chewed. "That's a rather dark way of looking at it. They would argue their function is to take apart the unworthy."

Her eyes lolled, her head drooped.

Koven tried to catch her eye. "What's gotten into you?"

"I figured out what she did."

"Who?"

Marthe glanced around the room, her body swaying in the chair.

"Marthe, you need to snap out of it. What are you talking about?"

"Pia Sabel. She's going to ruin us." Marthe dropped her elbows on the table and put her head in her hands. Her hair fell between her fingers in front of her face. "It's been churning in my head ever since she showed up in France. It's why I can't sleep." She lifted her head and met his gaze. "She took videos of the remote triggers and uploaded them to the cloud."

"Damn it." He slapped the table. "Wait, if she found those, why hasn't she told anyone?"

Marthe nodded and leaned over as if she were about to throw up. "Because she's waiting for the right moment."

He took another bite. "I don't understand."

"She's going to release the videos of the firing mechanisms." She grabbed both his wrists. "She videoed how the remote inflates the rubber bulbs to the right diameter to squeeze the trigger in a dead man's hand. She videoed the crime scene, took pictures of the bullet holes high up on walls, the blood stains on the seat cushion. Even a child could see the men were dead when you staged the gunfight."

He pulled away from her.

"You're imagining things." He finished his sandwich and wiped his mouth. "What 'right moment' is she waiting for?"

"She's stalking us like a tiger, Daryl. Waiting for us to weaken so she can move in for the kill. She's waiting for my cousin's report. His inquest will clear us of any responsibility. When his report is published tomorrow, she'll release the pictures and videos. It will prove his investigation was a sham. The government will send an independent investigator. They'll know."

Koven turned in his chair, spread his knees, and palmed his face. "But the Three Blondes have tied Pia Sabel to the crime and they've tied her to a string of gangland murders from Munich to Dubai. No one will believe her."

"We will. We've sinned."

Koven looked up at his wife. She had never used the word *sin* before.

"You said, 'to keep a secret, we must be truly committed.'" Marthe rocked back and forth in her chair. Her right hand lay on the table in front of her. "You know what the Bible says?"

He shook his head. "About what?"

"If thy right hand offends thee, cut it off."

With a forceful overhand swing, a steely resolve driving every ounce of strength she possessed, she brought a butcher's knife over her head and slammed it down on the table, cleaving her right arm in half.

They stared at the blood spurting from her severed limb. Their eyes rose to meet each other.

She said, "I took all the pills."

Koven stood and picked up his small plate and carried it to the sink.

He sensed a presence at the other end of the kitchen. "Ah, there you are, Hyde."

Hyde asked, "Don't you think she needs a doctor?"

# CHAPTER 38

THE MOON SQUEEZED a shaft of light between clouds to light up Captain Cates's stunned face framed by his sheepskin coat collar. I tugged Detective Lovett to a standing position after Carlos plasticuffed his wrists.

"What the hell are you doing here?" the captain asked.

Lovett didn't look talkative.

"Aren't you going to arrest him?" I gave the captain my soldier stare.

The former Marine captain was immune. He poked Lovett in the chest. "I asked you a question."

"I want a lawyer." Lovett shut his mouth and lifted his chin.

I said, "How did Shane talk you into taking the fall for kidnapping?"

"I'm not saying anything until I get a lawyer."

Avi Damari and his pals came from the tunnel to report three dead, one pretty close, and two who might make it.

Cates turned to me. "Why does Lovett hate you so much?"

"That's a good question." I turned to Avi.

Working with him was like working with a wall. I stared down the quiet man.

Avi stared back. Not a single part of his body moved, not even his pupils.

I said, "Back at David's funeral, you told me you could help."

Nothing.

I glanced at Lovett. The cop had some kind of mean, hard scowl going at Avi. It was the kind you give a guy when you find out he's been sleeping with your wife but you're still in polite company and can't beat the shit out of him yet.

Avi waited until I brought my gaze back to him. He nosed in Lovett's direction. "LOCI."

And right then and there, it all clicked for me.

Off-duty cops went after Ms. Sabel in Dubai. Off-duty cops went after me in Tokyo. One local cop in the USA wanted me behind bars or in a nut house.

I looked at Avi. "LOCI is Shane's international company? His 'buy local' schtick?"

Avi nodded. "Cowards and criminals. That's why I quit."

The only born-again-asshole I ever met in uniform was Captain Shane Smith. In a remote Forward Operating Base, ten klicks north of nowhere, he destroyed a rape kit to keep Military Police Captain Tania Cooper from making a case against a corporal named Kasey Earl. When she discovered his crime, she ignored procedure and beat the crap out of Shane with a baseball bat. She was demoted. He was discharged. He changed his name to Diabulus because he was a Latin nerd in high school. He went on to become second-in-command at a CIA contractor that was so bad, even the spooks banned them. The spooks still needed a contractor so Shane started up Velox Deployment, hired every dishonorably discharged vet he could find, and took over the old contract with the CIA.

His fingerprints were all over LOCI. He had to be somewhere nearby.

Captain Cates tilted his head, curious. "What's LOCI?"

Bullets buzzed our heads and pinged off nearby metal.

Detective Lovett dropped like a rag doll. Blood poured out of his skull and formed a black puddle around his head.

We ran for the tunnel, grabbing rifles and ammo off the dead and wounded Velox guys in the entrance.

The six of us waited for the shooters to come in with whatever firepower they had. But nothing happened. Everything was silent.

Mercury and his Mayan buddy stood in the entrance, silhouettes in the moonlight. They gestured wildly for me to run outside.

Mercury said, *WTF dude? He's getting away.*

I said, *If I come out now, he'll mow me down like alfalfa under the baler.*

Mercury said, *Are you a soldier or a farmer? C'mon, homie, get out here. It's hero time!*

Seven-Death shook his rattle-stick and bellowed something that probably rallied the Mayan boys back in the day.

Mercury said, *He's running for the barn, up I-79. Move it, brutha!*

I took off running.

Carlos got up and ran two steps behind me, never questioning why.

Cates and Avi and the others questioned me big time. "There's an active shooter out there. Get back here."

"He's making a break for it." I shouted over my shoulder as I ran. "Call the cops and clean up this mess."

I stopped at the entrance. "Cates, I need that .50 cal out of evidence."

"Consider it done." His voice echoed down the tunnel.

The engine roared to life. Carlos dove for the passenger seat. All four wheels burned rubber up the short road to the freeway as we blasted north just after 3 a.m. We hit 100 mph before catching the first whiff of traffic, four cars passing a tractor-trailer on an uphill slope.

After waiting my turn to get by the slower truck, I tore through the knot of cars and ran it up to 130 mph.

"Where're we going?" Carlos wound his fingers into the grab handle.

"Rockaway, New Jersey if we don't catch him on the freeway."

"Wouldn't he go up the 81?"

"A little birdie told me he was going this way."

Carlos did a slow, serious turn toward me, his brow furrowed. "Your angel?"

"He's a god."

There were patches of ice in places and the Audi's all-wheel drive was doing fine so far, but we were living on the edge, just a hair away from losing it and turning into a news item on local TV.

"Who are we looking for?" he asked.

"The guy behind all this crap. The guy who killed David Gottleib and set all this in motion."

"What's he drive?"

"Probably a Corvette, recent model."

We came up behind a small convoy of cars. I slowed to make sure none of them were cops or 'Vettes. We wove through, looking at each driver. When we found the lead, I punched it. Despite the late hour, traffic thickened as we reached Charleston and crossed the river. We screeched onto the Jennings Randolph Highway and found it empty.

A long slog uphill, the Audi ate it up and reached 150 when we crested the hilltop. On the other side, across a narrow valley, a lone pair of headlights wound up the next hill.

I hit another patch of ice.

Nothing makes your heart beat faster than a split-second loss of control at high speed. The car fishtailed. I kept my wheels pointed straight ahead and hoped the machine would come around. The sound and smell of burning rubber filled the compartment. The tires gripped and we barreled down the slope's gentle curves.

Gotta love German automotive engineering, the manual listed the top speed of this little go-cart at 168 mph. At the bottom of the hill, on a flat stretch, we leaned into a long right-hander and hit 168 for a full minute before the incline slowed us to 164.

Another patch of ice claimed my heart quicker than a Mayan god. This time the fishtail went sideways, the back coming around on the right. I tried to handle the drift while the car went up on two wheels.

Speed scrubbed off fast under shrieking tires.

We crashed back to the surface with a bone-rattling *bang* and slid to the left, reaching the shoulder. Our bumper skimmed the rail, clicking down the rivets, before I brought it back under control at 95 mph.

I glanced at Carlos. His face was fixed, ready for the fight ahead, not an ounce of concern about our near-death experience.

I took a deep breath and put my foot down.

Over the next rise, I managed to pass a car in the right lane.

Seven-Death sat cross-legged on the hood.

I said, Not now, guys. Not NOW!

The Mayan shook his stick and leveled it at the car beside me.

I saw him plain as day.

Shane Diabulus in a brand new Z06 Corvette.

Still rattled from my ice-skating adventures, I nearly missed him.

His car had less-refined handling, poorer braking, but a higher theoretical top-end and more horsepower than mine. On this open, hilly highway, we were about even.

When he realized it was me, he opened the throttle and managed to inch ahead with his extra ponies.

We stayed with him.

In the valley, slower traffic closed his short lead.

Carlos lowered his window and drew his pistol. At the top end of the engine's capabilities, the aerodynamic drag of the open window had a noticeable effect. We lost a couple miles per hour.

Shane made the first gap between cars and sliced through to the other side. The Audi's superior handling pulled us through like a space ship on a gravitational slingshot around a planet. We were on him again, doing 150 through a farm valley.

Shane hit the ice patch first.

His car swung around in a giant arc.

I hit it an instant later and swung around in a giant arc.

We ended up nose to nose, out of control, sliding and spinning sideways, staring at each other's faces.

I was scared as hell.

Shane was scared as hell.

Carlos couldn't care less. The only thing the gangster wanted was a clear shot at a guy he had never met.

"Aren't you scared?" I shouted. "Just a little?"

"Nah. I don't die here, *ese*." Cool as an autumn morning.

Shane hit dry ground first and nearly flipped. He left a chunk of bodywork hanging on the milepost and burned rubber up the next hill.

When the Audi stopped sliding, I tried to breathe but nothing happened. Strange, unearthly noises came out of my throat.

We were pointed the wrong way. I downshifted, spun it around and headed up the hill.

Shane was stuck behind two tractor-trailers trying to pass each other on a steep slope. He checked the shoulders on both sides but decided not to risk it due to the frequency of broken beer bottles.

He was doing 50 when I caught up.

We slowed by 118 mph. Carlos looked at me and I looked at him. We both shrugged. After flying at 168, slowing that much feels like you're walking.

I pulled into the left lane next to Shane.

Carlos gave him a toothy smile.

Shane lowered his window and pointed a pistol at my front tire.

Carlos put a bullet through Shane's right rear.

I felt my front tire go. I never heard his pistol over the sickening screech of eight tires on asphalt.

The Audi had run-flat tires. They allowed me to limp along at 55 until I could get it fixed. Shane had the same thing. Our high speed chase turned into a low-speed chase, which, given the ice, wasn't such a bad thing.

But it was weird.

Before Carlos could get off another shot at Shane, we topped the hill and found the roadway blocked by ten police cruisers parked sideways, multi-colored lights flashing a psychedelic beat across a field of pristine snow.

# CHAPTER 39

PIA RAN A cool-down 10K on the treadmill in the master stateroom's exercise room, facing the endless deep blue sea, thinking about how deep the conspiracy ran and how to expose it. Miguel rowed on a machine next to her.

"Were Müller and Taimur targeted before I reached out to them, or because?" Pia dropped the treadmill speed to 14 mph.

"Why do I have a feeling you already know the answer?" Miguel asked.

"How were they connected?" Pia asked. "Why kill them if they were shelling out tens of millions?"

"Koven's nuts?"

"Koven didn't kill them. That much I know. What I don't know is who did."

Tania knocked and opened the door at the same time. She carried a coffee carafe and cups. "Captain Chamberlain says we're almost within chopper range of Karachi."

She glanced over her shoulder. "Are the phones working yet?"

Tania set the tray on a nearby table. "Not as of five minutes ago, but any minute now."

Pia shut off the treadmill and wiped her face. Who killed Müller, Suliman, and Taimur? Somewhere inside her head was the answer, but she couldn't shake it loose.

She strode into the bathroom's marble showers and whirlpool tubs. She turned on the shower and put her hand in the stream. She peeled off her workout spandex and tossed them in the hamper and stepped into the shower and closed the door.

She turned her face to the warm water and let it slide down her body.

She soaped up and rinsed off and shampooed and conditioned and rinsed and stepped out. She toweled off and blow-dried her hair and brushed her teeth and darkened her eyebrows and dragged out a thin line of eyeliner and applied a light lipstick. She pulled out a new Lululemon outfit, donned it, and did a once-over. She put the cap back on her lipstick.

She looked down at her makeup on the counter—and then it hit her.

She knew who it was. Jacob told her days ago but neither of them knew what it meant.

It all came down to lipstick.

She went back to the gym to tell Tania and Miguel but they were in a deep conversation about something. Since they had been an item at one point, she decided to leave well enough alone for the moment. She picked up her phone to call Jacob, saw she had messages, and decided to listen to them.

The first was from Captain Cates, who had discovered the information David Gottlieb tried to give Jacob in a .50 caliber bullet. Cates explained the contents in great detail. Pia's next message was from the Major, updating her on Cates, Jacob, and the status of operations.

The third message stopped her heart.

"Goddamn it!" She grabbed Tania by the shoulder. "Koven's holding Dad hostage."

Tania and Miguel shook their heads in disbelief.

"What do we know about his defenses?" Pia asked. "Who are the authorities in that region?"

"Rip Blackson walked into our Paris office yesterday," Miguel said. "He'll have those answers."

Pia called Emily Lunger at the *Post*. "It's time to release your scoop, and it's bigger than you can imagine."

She explained how the pattern of shots fired in the château, first one, then a second, followed by two more in rapid succession, a three second pause, and two more fit the profile of the remote triggers. The first two shots were Koven killing the Velox men, the two quick shots were the remote triggers, and the final two were execution shots. The patterns of ricochets and blood splatter would prove the Velox guns were fired from the floor, not standing positions.

She explained the foreign contributions to American political campaigns and referred her to Captain Cates for the Gottleib recordings. She sent photos of the prince's contract, the corroborating evidence, and her recordings of Koven, Suliman, and Taimur. She shared her cloud drive with Emily and clicked off.

"Koven can't be that big a threat," Tania said.

"He's the fall guy," Pia said. "There's something bigger driving LOCI and something sparked the murder of Gottleib. That's where the threat lies."

She took a deep breath and called Koven back. The instant he picked up the phone, she ranted. "Say your prayers, Koven. You'll be in hell in thirty-six hours."


NARROW STRIPS OF white snow glinted on the edges of Paris's gray-black slushy streets when her jet broke through the overcast skies.

Jacob finally answered his phone.

"They let him go." Jacob shouted. "Un-fucking-believable. Apparently, if you're a black-budget contractor, you don't have to answer for murder and kidnapping. The CIA pulled a get-out-of-jail card and he's—"

"Do you think he's behind LOCI?" Pia asked.

"No question. He's wired into every dirty cop on every continent."

"Then who funded him?"

"Good question."

"You already know. When you rob tens of millions from the world's rich and powerful, you need a security team like LOCI, not Sabel Security. Koven thinks he's building an empire, so it wasn't him. Who just lost everything?"

Jacob inhaled. "You're right. I can't believe it. All this over a daddy-likes-you-better thing."

"A what?"

"If you had siblings, you'd understand."

Pia emailed Bianca while she talked. "We have Blackson."

Jacob asked, "Will he know who's calling the shots on the ground?"

"Would you trust his answer?"

"I have a good feeling about him—even if he was a Marine. Why? You don't trust him?"

"Why did Blackson come to us now, after Paul Benning's body was found?"

"Yeah. He opened up to me about Koven's dealings, but he never shed light on Suliman or anything else." Jacob thought for a moment. "I feel you. Tell him I'll kick his ass if he lies to you. Hey, they're calling our flight. By the way, Carlos is stoked about you buying him a first-class seat. He's never ridden up front before."

Pia clicked off.

They made their way to the Sabel Security offices overlooking *Esplanade de La Défense*, in the business district of Paris. Blackson looked like a man who'd spent the last two days hiding in a business office, sponging his baths and sleeping on a couch—because he had. He sat at a large conference table, leaning on it to keep from falling over.

Pia put the briefcase on the table, turned her phone off, and sat a couple seats away. "This is a quiet enough place where we can discuss the horrible things your firm has done."

"My firm?" Blackson looked up quickly. His mouth hung open, his hands spread wide in protest. "You have to help us. You can put a stop to this madness. I spoke to Brent's baby-mama a few days ago. It sickened me to make that call."

"I hate murder as much as you." She fixed an angry gaze on him and leaned back. "I've discovered evidence of Koven's heinous crimes. I will be sure he faces justice." She pulled Prince Taimur's contract out and slapped it on the table. "But your actions tell me you considered Koven an honest man for years. You served under him in the Marines, you joined his firm, and you made a lot of money. Why should I trust you now?"

"I'm here. I'm offering my help."

"How do I know you're not offering me up as a sacrifice?"

"I'm no criminal."

"And Koven is." She tapped her finger on the table and let the awkward silence stretch. "How do I know you're not here under duress?"

Speechless, he sat still. The building's central heat kicked in and warmer air poured over them, taking the edge off the chill. He exhaled and glanced around. He put his hands on the table and slumped.

"You were my best hope." Blackson dropped his gaze. "If you don't trust me, I'll have to find someone else."

Pia watched him.

He pushed back from the table and gathered his thoughts. "It's a sad day if I've failed to convince the only woman above bribery to save our country. I guess Koven wins. He can influence the election, bend the rules, line his pockets with donations from foreigners."

"Don't pull that passive-aggressive crap on me." She pushed the contract across the table. "Only a fool would trust you without checking you out first. So tell me, why did you come here now? Why not earlier, when David Gottleib reached out to Jacob?"

Blackson leafed through the contract. "Until Tom's death, Koven never confided in me. I wasn't on his team. Then he didn't trust me. When he rescheduled the symposium, he had to rely on my help. I was the only one left."

He scanned several more pages, then stopped and held his place with a finger.

"When I figured out what he was doing," he said, "I was disgusted. I couldn't hide it any longer. It was the same stuff that pissed off David. I worked with your father and Benning to record Koven incriminating himself, but he discovered the microphone."

Blackson's lips trembled. He buried his face in his hands. "I ran."

"What makes you think I'm not out to take over these contracts?"

Blackson looked up and shook his head. "Jacob wouldn't work for someone like that."

"You think Jacob is honest?"

Blackson told her the story of Nasiriyah.

"Some of the guys said he was guided by God," Blackson said. "I'm not religious. But there was something beyond the human experience in what he did."

"There's more to Jacob than most people realize."

"Koven promised me a job after the war," Blackson said. "We changed our stories to make Koven look good. I know for a fact that

Jacob is willing to fight and die for people he never met, and that Koven is willing to lie and cheat to get what he wants."

"I'm sure you've heard the news imply that I killed Müller, Suliman, and Taimur. Why would you trust me?"

"Because you don't have the motive. I don't know who's responsible for those murders, but I know why."

Pia gestured for him to go on.

"Our firm had over $100 million in several funds destined for the Future Crossroads Super PAC. You know about Müller, Suliman, and Taimur. There were sixteen more foreign players trying to lobby Congress. I looked up a few of them. One was a businessman out of Mumbai who died in a boating accident three days ago. Another was a Serb who was shot by cops at a traffic stop last week. Two days ago, someone sent the money to a numbered account in Switzerland and then transferred it to a brand-new company in Luxembourg. In a week, that money will be in Singapore or the Bahamas."

Pia sat back. "You think Koven is stealing from his own bribery funds?"

"Everyone else is dead." Blackson rubbed his face. "But it doesn't make any sense. Some of those guys are bad dudes, like the Russian, Yeshenko. They'd kill him and he knows it."

"It's not Koven. There's another person who had access—"

A young man from the Paris office rushed in, out of breath, his cheeks red. "Sorry for the interruption, *mademoiselle*. There has been a fire. Terrible, terrible fire."

He showed her a news item on his smartphone and glanced at Blackson.

Pia read the screen and followed his gaze. Blackson returned their looks with a growing understanding of the implication.

"You're not talking about my house." Blackson stared down the Frenchman.

"I am most sorry sir." The Frenchman hesitated. "They said all lives were lost."

"My wife? Oh my god. Not my children. My innocent children?"

"They said everyone, I am sorry..." The young man glanced back at

Pia. She excused him with a nod.

"I should've been there." Blackson stood, pounding a fist to his forehead. "Coming here because I hate Koven so much cost them their lives. I should've gone home. I could've protected them."

Pia rose and put a gentle hand on his shoulder. Memories of violent men crashing into her parents' home flooded her mind. Blackson's grief was her grief, but she pushed her memories from her head and focused on his loss. She knew what hit him, the emptiness of losing everyone in your life at once. Visions of the lively spirits you knew so well, gone. No goodbyes, no parting words, no miracles.

Blackson sobbed for a minute then sniffled and flinched as anger wrenched his heart. "That son of a bitch, I'll kill him."

Pia said, "I'll take care of that part."

"Take me with you." He faced her, anger and grief contorting his face. "I know the castle."

In a soft voice, she said, "It won't bring them back."

He turned away and broke down. Tears leaked between the fingers covering his face. His sobs echoed in the room. He staggered to a chair and collapsed in it, his elbows hit the table, his face in his hands.

Pia stepped behind him. In her experience, there were no words that could soothe the flayed soul.

In the hall outside the glass wall, the staff of the Paris office commiserated in muted support. Like bystanders at a train wreck, they felt the pain and sorrow yet felt helpless to help. Nothing could be offered beyond sympathy.

Pia pulled her last tissue from her pocket and offered it to Rip Blackson.

Blackson blew his nose and took a few deep breaths that he held in a desperate attempt to pull himself together.

"It's OK," Pia said. "Grief is what forms us."

"I can't believe they're gone. Maybe there was a mistake."

She shook her head and handed him her phone, opened to the *Post*'s coverage of the blaze in McLean.

He read it and broke down again.

After a long time, Pia asked, "What can you tell me about the castle?"

"He thinks he's unbeatable. He says that no one on Earth can touch him."

"He's wrong."

# CHAPTER 40

THE LAST RAYS of sunlight stabbed between the horizon and the low-hanging clouds, lighting up the underside in a glorious yellow that quickly gave way to orange, then turned blood red before darkening out. Koven stood at the tower window, watching the brief sunset and listening to the Velox men as they joked with each other across the castle walls.

Someone knocked on his door. He told them to come in.

Kasey Earl entered. "It appears the Sabel agent, Dhanpal, done escaped somehow."

"Somehow?" Koven stayed at the window, his gaze fixed across the river. "As if you weren't in charge of his captivity? Do you think I'm that stupid? Why not just admit it—Alan Sabel bribed one of your men."

"Well, that's the thing. Alan's still here. If he done the bribe, he'd be gone and Dhanpal would—"

"Oh god, you're an idiot. Men like Sabel don't run, they let their servants go. It seems like an honorable thing, but in reality, he wants to see if you'll shoot Dhanpal in the back."

"We didn't shoot him in the back."

"Then take ten men, track him down, shoot him in the back."

Kasey said nothing.

Koven turned to face the earless man. "You lost him, go get him back."

"Yeah, um, we only got thirty-two men left. And, well, he run off this morning."

"You're just telling me now?" Koven's face flushed crimson and shook with rage. "What the hell happened to all the men we've been feeding these last few days?"

"Oh, the cops is with LOCI." Kasey shuffled his feet. "They kinda freaked about the Benning thing."

"And they deserted at the last minute?" Koven took a deep breath and tugged his jacket. "Let them run. Damned cowards. I had enough courage to face down a hundred Iraqi Republican Guard in Nasiriyah, I've never been afraid of anything."

Kasey stood at sloppy attention the way lazy men will. His eyes rolled listless and unfocused.

Koven said, "You look pale, Kasey. Are you scared of something?"

"Them three blonde ladies are out there, interviewing everybody, and we've been thinking—"

"You fool! Those reporters are on my side." Koven stepped closer and lowered his voice. "But you're not worried about the press. What is it? Out with it."

"Word is Pia Sabel's on her way, gonna rescue her dad."

"So?"

Kasey said nothing.

"You have plenty of men." Koven's volume increased. "You own the high ground, you're in a stone fortress that's lasted a thousand years, and you're afraid of a girl with a few washed-up veterans?"

"Cooper and Stearne ain't exactly washed—"

"Everyone knows what's coming. These walls will keep them out. Let them try climbing up or throwing a line over. They'll end up sitting outside waiting until they get hungry and go home with their tails between their legs. If we hadn't lost half of your people, we could've taken the fight to them. Grow some balls. Your CO told me you're unbeaten."

"Uh. Usually. Except for the times we tangled with Sabel—"

"Get out of here." Koven turned back to the window. "And put some makeup on that lily-white face of yours before you scare your own troops."

Kasey dashed, leaving the door open behind him.

Another knock made Koven furious. He turned, face flushed, ready to scream at Kasey. Instead, he found a man leaning against the door jamb.

"Jago Seyton," Koven said through clenched teeth. "You've returned."

Jago patted his thighs and made a small smile.

"I'm sure you've read the news," Koven said. "Blackson got away but you managed to burn his wife and children alive."

Jago shrugged.

"That's all you have to say about your spectacular failure?" Koven peered at the man. "Why in god's name did Tom hire you?"

"He didn't." Jago pushed off the jamb and strode into the center of the room. "Hyde insisted he bring me on. You see, Hyde and I go way back. All the way to the beginning of time."

Koven laughed once and turned back to stare at the valley. "This is what I get? Failures and deserters. No one who can do a simple job properly."

Jago frowned. "You talking about me?"

"I'm talking about everyone." Koven swept his arm over the countryside. "I'm at the pinnacle of my career, Jago. I hold the future of our country in my hands. The power that everyone seeks through their endless intrigues is mine—all mine. I'm the guy they write books about!"

He strode across the room, hands clasped behind his back. "I should have thousands of followers on Facebook. I should have blog posts dissecting my path to success. I should have people tripping over each other to carry my laptop. Instead, I have you, an incompetent killer, his aging alcoholic mentor, and a platoon of scared Velox men manning the ramparts."

"Against what enemy are they defending me?" Koven tossed a tablet at Jago, open to a defamatory website. "Even if bullets stop my problems I still get nothing but allegations from unnamed sources. They write backstabbing innuendos about the evils befalling our august firm. They claim it's some form of instant karma. Well, damn them all to hell."

Jago shrugged, his eyes narrowed to slits. "People like you talk a lot when they're scared."

Another knuckle rapped the door.

Koven turned to Senator Hyde, who stood in the doorway, his swollen eyes downcast.

"She didn't make it." Hyde's voice was soft. "They did everything they could."

Jago and Hyde stood still.

Koven crossed to them and stared. "Hell, who even cares? She ran out on me when I needed her strength the most."

Jago and Hyde looked at each other with arched brows.

"She should've waited until after the fight," Koven said. "She would've been proud of me. I would've had time to give her a proper funeral."

He turned back to the window.

"Our days slog by in a miserable parade until something kills us. A heart attack, a bullet, what difference does it make? Marthe chose to cut her engagement short, not that I blame her." Koven threw his hands in the air. "Why do I struggle against the inevitable when everything that's happened is one less thing that will? Quantum physics tells us everything is already done; we live in the reverberation of time. Our lives are nothing but shadows of the past. We're nothing more than a video, made by MFA students, full of earth-shattering emotional revelations, posted on YouTube only to collect six likes—and those from family members."

# CHAPTER 41

VOICES ECHOED IN the hangar and sleet pinged off the thin metal roof as I considered how nice and safe and warm it was inside. A smart man would stay put, work up a better plan, enlist a few reinforcements, wait for the local cops to take our calls seriously. Instead, I listened as Dhanpal walked us through the castle's layout on maps downloaded to our smartphones.

An outer wall encased a hilltop, allowing access via a spiral pathway that led through a series of gates. Our objective was the Eifel House, one of the inner-most buildings and therefore one of the most heavily defended. Towering above it was the Keep, from which enemies could rain lead on anyone trying to reach Eifel House.

Coming up the road from the town would take us through a series of portals designed by the medieval boys for tossing rocks and boiling oil on passersby. We would have to pass several buildings that also served as stone bunkers for the modern version of pikemen: Velox agents with assault rifles. Rather than deal with a pitched battle where Velox had a huge advantage, we would parachute in.

Between several buildings were small courtyards. Dhanpal asked us to zoom in on the largest courtyard, between the "gambling house" and one of the "ancient squire's houses". This tiny patch of real estate had been chosen as our drop zone. The DZ was about 2,500 square feet, less than one percent of the recommended minimum.

A night jump is the most dangerous of all jumps. A confined castle courtyard where the battlements above the DZ are guarded by heavily armed soldiers was the worst site in the history of jumping.

I would've complained bitterly, but it was Ms. Sabel's idea.

'Nuff said.

Dhanpal continued on. We would secure the DZ, proceed past the gambling house to another courtyard, sneak past the "stronghold"—hoping Velox reinforcements wouldn't pour out of the other two ancient squire's houses, or the witches tower, or the primary dwelling, or the chapel, not to mention several other places—and takeover Eifel House, rescue Alan Sabel, and get the hell out before dawn.

I picked up my assault rifle and followed Ms. Sabel across the dark tarmac to what would probably be my death.

Just another night at the office.

Tania, Miguel, and Dhanpal formed a line to climb aboard the de Havilland DHC-6 jump plane ahead of us. While we waited for our turn, I noticed Carlos fiddling with his gear.

"You good there?" I asked.

Carlos looked up and tapped his altimeter. "I'm not sure it's working right. But it doesn't matter, I'll follow your lead."

Over my friend's shoulder, I saw my second-hand god sitting on the wing behind the starboard engine.

Mercury said, *Your gaucho looks like he's in line for a movie, homeboy. He must not have any idea where you're going. Did you bother to teach him how the parachute works?*

I said, *He had three jumps at Camp Sabel. We even use the same plane. He'll be fine.*

Mercury said, *Did you tell him he's jumping into a live-fire battle this time?*

I said, *Where's your buddy?*

Mercury said, *He's not good with the altitude thing. The highest point in the Yucatan is K'awiil's Temple in Tikal. Said he'd meet us there.*

We climbed in and took our places. The pilot went over the procedures. We checked each other's equipment one more time. And then we were airborne.

Jump planes have an empty area in back. When it's time, you stand up, walk to the end, jump out the door. We sat in two rows along either side of the fuselage.

On the way to battle, your mind wanders in search of any topic other than your immediate future. You wonder if you left the stove on, what to get Mom for her birthday, the name of that guy in that movie. Any topic that did not involve dealing with the present.

Unless you're a reformed drug dealer from LA.

"Does your god help out at times like this?" Carlos asked.

I bit the inside of my cheek and wondered if he was making fun of Mercury or genuinely interested.

"How hard is it to shoot a guy in the eye at sixty yards, when he's wearing a helmet and body armor?" I asked.

"While he's shooting at you? Pure luck."

"In the tunnel, I took a guy out, one shot with a Glock. Did I get some kind of cosmic help?"

He nodded as if I'd said something profound.

"Why'd you quit the gangs?" I asked.

"Lousy retirement plan." He turned to me and decided to share his story. "You know why you don't hear about gangs anymore?"

I shook my head.

"Drivebys, *esé*. Gangs were huge in the '90s, but went quiet in the '00s. Nobody liked the drivebys. So, we took the business off the streets, enforced territories, tightened up relationships and supply lines— we professionalized crime. But when a dude messes you up, you still have to retaliate."

He rubbed his hands together and stared at the floor.

"I never told anybody this, so you're hearing my confession." He twisted around to give me a hard look. This was serious to him, so I nodded. "After five years of peace between the Norteños and Sureños, Frederico moved on my guys. He failed, but I had to send him a message. We did a driveby at his safe house. We put thirty-two bullets through the living room window. Frederico died. So did a nine-year-old girl. She was sleeping on the sofa."

He put his head in his hands.

"Nobody talks to you when you do something like that," he said. "Not even your mom. No matter how tough you are, you need the respect of your peers and the love of your family. So, when nobody else talks to you, you turn to God. I prayed, but I never heard anything. Even He was mad at me."

He sniffled and sat up, rubbed his palms on his pants. "The cops knew I did it, but they couldn't prove anything. I spent two years in jail on a weapons charge. I deserved the death penalty, *esé.*

"I rotted in prison. But my son came to see me every week. He was the only one. He was in those special years, when he could choose the family business or find a new way. He chose to focus on college. He asked me to leave the life, to do something good."

He stopped talking and looked away as if he regretted letting out that much.

"So your son told you to straighten up and you did it. And here you are with a new career."

He bit his lip hard before turning to me. "It's not that simple, amigo. After the Crips shanked me, I knew I'd been resurrected from the dead for a reason. But I didn't know what reason. Then I had that dream, the one I told you about."

How do you tell a guy who's spilling his guts that you didn't commit his dream-story to memory? We had a lot going down at the time. So I covered up the way everyone does. I said something profound enough to confuse the issue.

"Death is inevitable, yet we taunt it every day. No matter what we do, we'll be forgotten after the next viral video. All we can do is make the world a better place while we're here."

It worked. Carlos gave me a somber look and nodded slowly. "That's where I'm going with this, *ése.*"

Mercury said, *Where's he going with this?*

I said, *Beats me. I'm only talking to him to beat the boredom.*

Mercury said, *For what it's worth, Mother Mary was talking to him before, during, and after the driveby. But like all y'all earthlings, he wasn't listening.*

Miguel rose and rolled up the big door. He and Dhanpal took a quick look at the ground below and gave everyone the thumbs up. We lined up and waited. Carlos stood in front of me.

I tapped his shoulder. "Nervous?"

"Nah, I know when I'm going to die."

Before I could ask what the hell he meant, Miguel jumped. Each of us stepped up and leaped into the dark. I braced myself for the hard slap-in-the-face we would feel when we reached the gray-and-white clouds. They look nice and soft, but try hitting higher density air at 120 mph.

The moonlight above didn't shine far into the depths. We sank into them and were enveloped in absolute dark with nothing but air screaming past our ears. I switched on my thermal visor and found the group forming up. We gave each other hand signals. Dhanpal pointed down to the left. Miguel would lead the way.

Mercury glided into the formation next to me, his toga flapping in the icy air. *I love this shit, brutha! We gotta do this more often. Hang on to your drogue chute, we're going to cut this one close.*

I said, *What're you talking about? We have a deployment plan. I'm sticking to it.*

Mercury said, *Do the math, dawg. They won't hear you coming, but your plan says Miguel lands first and when a two-hundred-twenty-pound animal lands on the ground at eighteen miles an hour, there's going to be a big ol' thud. Even if they don't get him, the rest of you will be floating right to them like a carnival shooting gallery. Someone has to land first and shoot the guards off the walls.*

I said, *Why me?*

Mercury said, *Dude! You're the only one who has a god on his side.*

One by one, they tossed their drogue chutes and their canopies opened. I went screaming past them, my head down, my shoulders tucked in, flying like a javelin straight for the DZ.

Ms. Sabel was the first voice on the comm link urging me to deploy my drogue. Then they all chimed in with rapidly increasing anxiety.

Mercury said, *Don't listen to them, dawg. I got this. Hang on tight.*

It occurred to me that my last shred of sanity had checked out and I was going to die because the Romans were wrong, there is no messenger god. But once you've committed to a plan, why not live or die by it?

I hurtled to Earth, watching with rising panic as the odd shapes on the ground became identifiable. First the quilted land became defined farm fields with fallow rows. Trees turned from dark blobs to scratchy lines. The castle loomed larger and larger.

I was in a hurry to land well before them so I could take out as many defenders as possible before dying a horrible and painful death—because the voice in my head told me to.

I screamed at Mercury. *Now?*

My team screamed back in unison, "Yes!"

Mercury said, *Not yet, bro. Hang in there!*

Panic redlined near the mental-shutdown stage as I determined the weather vane on top of the castle Keep was a bronze rooster. The slate roof tiles were close enough to count. Freezing cold air numbed my ears and nose. My whole body was cooling rapidly. Hypothermia could kill me, sparing me the pain of impact.

"Jacob, pull the drogue!"

I had no idea whose voice was screaming into my comm link due to the rushing wind.

Terminal velocity is calculated for a jumper with his arms and legs spread out, creating as much drag as possible. Sane people keep their speed around 120 mph. Sky diving champion Marco Wiederkehr set the world record for speed sky diving at 330 mph. I was closing in on his numbers.

I couldn't breathe.

Mercury lined up next to me. *I can't remember if I carried the six when I worked out my calculations. Guess we'll find out. Hey, dude, are we having crazy fun or what?*

I said, *Now?*

My team screamed, "Yes!"

Mercury said, *Don't listen to them. But do get into the box man position. Slow it down a little. We're getting close.*

With great difficulty, my arms and legs formed the X-shape of standard sky divers. My speed scrubbed a little. But the Keep's towers were far too close, the DZ, far too small. I was close enough to read the artist's signature on the gargoyles. I closed my eyes.

Mercury said, *OK, drop the drogue and land in the corner.*

I deployed the chute and started breathing again when the chute opened. I brushed against the Keep's bricks, which should have collapsed my canopy, but Mercury held the whole thing together. My feet touched down six inches from a stone wall.

I gasped for air repeatedly.

Mercury said, *Hey, get that rifle off your shoulder, you've got some work to do.*

I said, *They're behind stone walls, I can't see them with my thermal imaging.*

Mercury said, *Make you a deal. You aim and I'll take it from there.*

I said, *What's the deal?*

Mercury said, *You take your religion public. Make a statement.*

That was a tough one. Crooning about a mythological god was less appealing than letting my friends float through a hail of gunfire. I could only imagine how popular I'd be with the ladies after advocating for a return to the pagan pantheon. Maybe there was a circus somewhere that needed a sideshow.

Of course, I could do what every other desperate guy does when he's praying for salvation: promise anything then ignore my end of the bargain later.

I pulled my rifle around and aimed at a window. My body was still shaking from the ride down and the barrel shook like a leaf in a storm.

Mercury said, *Chill, dude. You're golden.*

He aimed my barrel at an empty window and I squeezed one off.

Mercury said, *One down, thirty-one to go. High five me, bro!*

The castle had inner and outer walls. We targeted the inner courtyard for our DZ, not because it was smallest and most likely to kill us, but because it would be where they least expected anyone to initiate an attack. The theory was holding true. I could only find three more thermal signatures anywhere near the courtyard.

Mercury held the muzzle while I squeezed off six shots. *You nailed 'em, bro. The DZ is all clear.*

I crossed my fingers and hoped he wasn't lying.

As the others dropped closer to the courtyard, Mercury pushed each of them off the wall of the Keep, grabbed their lines when they were about to tangle up on the gargoyles, and basically kept them from the most likely fate: shredding a chute on a sharp spire sixty feet up and falling the rest of the way. Miguel hit the ground, with the predicted *thud*, and cleared the space just in time for Dhanpal. Tania and Ms. Sabel landed in relative silence. Carlos arrived last. We set aside our weapons to shrug out of our rigs.

An alarm blasted our eardrums.

# CHAPTER 42

WITH THE KLAXON shaking her insides, Pia stepped out of her harness and tossed her gear aside. Everyone formed up near the old well and slapped their helmets back on. A soft snow began to fall. She looked around, surprised at the lack of gunfire.

To her right, the giant central tower loomed above them, backlit by the soft glow of light from the city of Cochem. She raised her arm and charged toward the gambling house. The castle's fourth concentric gate was a small arch stretched between two stone buildings. She pressed her back to the wall, followed by her agents. They waited and listened.

"Damn." Tania stared up at the roof line. "We could've been impaled on those spires."

"Where are the guards?" Pia whispered.

Dhanpal and Miguel shrugged.

Tania pointed. "I'll take point."

"I'll take the narrow by the squire's house," Miguel said.

He turned to take up his position when Pia grabbed his collar. "Carlos will take that."

"I know the plan, but he can barely carry the SAW." Miguel referred to the squad machine gun.

Heavy as it was, Carlos cradled it in his arm and headed to his assignment.

"Carlos takes it." She yanked on the big man. "That's an order."

"I can take that post." Jacob leaned in next to Miguel. "It's a suicide mission. He's got a better chance at sainthood than surviving the night. Besides, the guy has a son. I don't."

"Stick to the plan." She shoved them both forward.

The alarm stopped as suddenly as it had started, leaving her ears aching in an eerie silence. Heading for the arch, they crunched over ice on the cobblestones.

"They're dead." Tania stood with her back against gambling house, pointing to a body hanging out a window.

Pia looked at Jacob, shaded an eerie orange in her thermal visor. "How the hell did you do that?"

"They're wearing a lot of body armor," Jacob said. "Don't assume they're all dead."

Pia went left with Dhanpal and took up covering positions. Miguel and Jacob scurried into the narrow archway and knelt in firing positions.

Nothing moved. Nothing showed on their thermal imaging.

Miguel gave the signal. Tania ran through the space.

An unsilenced weapon opened up from above.

Tania rolled up to the wall beneath the shooter.

Miguel and Jacob fired at a gunman they couldn't see. Jacob moved right a few paces to get a better angle but still couldn't find a target.

Everyone waited and listened. They could hear boots clomping toward them.

Around the corner, a hundred yards behind them, Carlos opened up with the SAW. He reported over the comm link. "Twelve coming my way."

Pia ran through the archway as bullets raked the ground behind her. She squatted behind a planter with Miguel. Jacob opened up from ten yards away.

Jacob updated everyone. "Shooter's using an arrow slit."

"No wonder we can't see him on thermal," Pia said. "Tania's pinned."

Miguel ran to the next cover, a short stone wall, and rolled in behind it. He popped up and fired. His bullets ricocheted off the stone, sending sparks into the night.

Dhanpal ran through the archway, firing at the arrow slit as he came. No one returned fire.

Pia caught her breath. Her heart pounded harder than ever before as the reality of the battlefield sank in. She'd led her people into a stone kill zone. They were the best in the business, but this might have been beyond anyone's capabilities.

Flashes from another muzzle caught her eye before the noise reached her ears.

Miguel groaned and fell.

She started to move to him but felt strong hands grab her body armor and yank her backward. She fell against Jacob behind a stone planter.

He scrambled to his knees, aiming his rifle left and right.

She joined him and saw a shadow at the next building. She squeezed off a three-round burst and heard a shout of pain. The shadow fell to the ground writhing, and rolled over. He pulled his weapon around and aimed at Pia. Even in the dark, with nothing but the strange colors of thermal imaging, she knew she was looking directly into the barrel of his rifle.

A strange sense of calm came over her. She thought it through logically in an instant. She could try to flee, but in the hundredth of a second she had left, she could only hope to take a bullet in the shoulder when she turned to run. Or she could fight, but retargeting and firing would take longer for her than him. Her third option was the quickest but the scariest. It required blind faith in the newer MICH helmets she authorized for the company. They contained slow-memory foam and more flexible shell compounds that could absorb a bullet's energy, while the older, standard-issue helmets suffered catastrophic failure from a direct shot.

She went for the third option and dipped her face downward, tilting her helmet toward the shooter.

The bullet hit hard near the back of her skull at the top of her tipped head. The projectile caromed off. Her head rang like a bell, but the helmet saved her.

She raised back up, reacquired her target and squeezed off another three round burst.

The shadow fell.

He must've been wearing the older helmet.

Jacob had been firing over her head. He moved his rifle across her back and fired. He stood and grabbed her hand, pulling her up. Together they ran to a massive wall, slammed their backs to it and raised their rifles to the roof line and the upper-story windows behind them.

Clear.

For a moment at least, they could breathe and think.

In the cleared courtyard, Tania and Dhanpal pulled Miguel to his feet. They ran to a nook in a retaining wall.

"I'm good," Miguel said. "Knocked the wind out of me."

More gunfire erupted in the night. She couldn't see anything and guessed it was coming from the other side of the wall. She and Jacob were exposed to the south and could only move north, where the bullets were coming from. Across the cobblestones, Miguel opened up on a target beyond her wall. For the moment, she was helpless.

She'd heard her veterans talking about the abject fear of patrolling a hostile area where snipers or bombers could strike from any direction at any time, and how that dug into the fabric of your life, raising your blood pressure to the breaking point, and making you hyper-vigilant. Many of them spent so much time in sheer terror that it left them changed for life: fully aware of their mortality and equally aware of an undefined spirit-world just out of reach. The ghosts of war.

For the first time, she felt that terror. She felt close to that vague world beyond life. It called to her.

A shadow on the roofline caught her eye. She aimed at it but held her finger off the trigger. A gargoyle.

The snow came down thicker and swirled, giving life to shadows. She jerked left and right, her eye lined up with the iron sights on the barrel. Fear made her twitch with each object in her peripheral vision. A bird, a window, a flag pole. Her heart beat out a rhythm like a timpanist pounding the kettledrums hard and fast.

Jacob fired at a window. A body slumped in the frame.

Dhanpal ran ahead; Jacob followed. Then Tania, then Pia followed her people. Miguel watched the back.

Three guns opened up straight in front of them.

Pia dropped, rolled, and returned fire. Tania and Jacob fell back until they were behind her, then turned and fired.

Dhanpal grabbed her elbow as she pushed off the ground. Together they staggered back to a retaining wall and fired around it. Dhanpal knelt and Pia stood to give the others cover.

But they weren't there. The cobblestones were empty.

Pia gasped for air as if she'd sprinted an entire marathon. The adrenaline surge of being in a kill zone with nowhere to run and a third of her squad missing overwhelmed her.

Dhanpal touched her and pointed left and up. A window was opening.

Pia took aim and waited.

"Had to retreat." Miguel's voice on the comm link. "Making my way back."

Shots came from the window and pinged off the stones next to her face. Her attention snapped back to the shooter. She adjusted and fired a triple. The man in the window recoiled. She'd hit him, but not fatally.

"We're in the Eifel House," Tania said. "Three more Velox boys are waiting for the undertaker."

"We're on our way." Pia waved Miguel forward.

Dhanpal touched her leg again and pointed up to the same window. She understood her assignment. While they moved forward, she was to make sure anyone wanting fresh air would die for a breath.

Dhanpal followed Miguel across the next stretch of open cobblestones.

Pia was ready to follow when something appeared in the window. She fired before she understood what it was: an arm lobbing a grenade.

She sprinted around the wall and ran for the next safe zone, Eifel House. She flew to the open doorway where Dhanpal waited for her.

The grenade went off with a deafening roar. Brilliant orange exploded behind her. Shrapnel splintered the air. Her ears rang. She could see Dhanpal shouting but couldn't make out his words.

She looked at him and, for the first time since meeting the former Navy SEAL, she saw fear in his eyes.

He raised his barrel level with her head. She figured he was shouting "duck" and dove to the ground like a runner stealing second base. She slid between his legs. She still couldn't hear anything but she could see brass cartridges raining on the floor around her.

He was firing on full-auto.

Desperation mode.

She scrambled to her feet in the cramped kitchenette behind him and caught a glimpse of Jacob and Tania firing into the next room. She sensed Miguel doing the same thing in another direction.

Eifel House was a trap.

# CHAPTER 43

"JAGO!" KOVEN SHOUTED. "Jago Seyton! Goddamn it, where is my body armor? Bring me something. I hear their suppressors popping already. Seyton!"

Former Senator Bill Hyde pushed the door open and held up a bottle of vodka. "How about some moral armor?"

Koven stared at the man. "You really are a wreck. The living embodiment of Seneca's warning."

"Seneca? I didn't know you read books longer than a Tweet."

"Seneca said, drunkenness is voluntary insanity."

Hyde moved to the window and looked down. "What do you call this, then? Rational life?"

"Get away from the window, you idiot!" Koven grabbed the man's shoulder and pushed him to the middle of the room. "Can't you hear the gunfire?"

Hyde dropped onto a couch by the fireplace, reflected flames dancing across his bald crown.

Koven paced the room, shifting his Beretta from one hand to the other.

Hyde poured himself a shot of vodka.

Koven gave him a hard look before storming to the door and shouting down the hall. "Where the hell is Seyton now that I need him?"

"You don't know who you need." Hyde held up his glass and downed it.

Koven spun away from the door and lapped the room. He glared at Hyde. "Why are you even here?"

"Because I'm the one who had Gottleib killed and I thought it only fitting to see it through to the end."

Koven stopped pacing while he processed the man's words. He went slack. He laid the pistol down on the center table and crossed to Hyde. "Why? What did that boy ever do to you?"

Hyde picked up the vodka and poured out two shots. "It's not what he did to me that matters. It's what he did to you."

Gunfire barked outside their window. Bullets cracked off the stones beneath the window.

Koven flinched. Hyde didn't.

Red-and-yellow reflected flames danced in the shot glasses. Hyde picked up his and waved it at Koven, then slid the liquid down his throat. He slapped the glass on the table, exhaled a contented breath, and nodded at Koven's drink.

Koven didn't move.

"He bugged your office and tapped your phones," Hyde said.

Koven dropped onto the couch opposite and kept staring at Hyde.

"Oh yes, my bright-eyed young genius." Hyde chortled. "You've been working on your project in secret for a long time. But I found out. David and a friend of his bought me drinks and asked funny questions. It was obvious he was on to you."

Koven couldn't hide his shock. David had been a loyal worker for years. He would never have trusted an alcoholic like Hyde.

Hyde continued. "I audited our books. Our banker told me we had a hundred million more than we knew. What a wonderful surprise."

Koven reached for the shot glass.

More rounds skittered off the walls.

"Then you convinced Alan Sabel I'd been drinking too much." Hyde poured himself another. "He went to Tom and insisted I go back to rehab."

"Your drinking problem was obvious. I never told Alan anything about it."

"Don't lie to me." Hyde's dulled eyes flashed. He pulled a gun from his pocket and looked pleased when Koven take a quick breath. "Alan and I were just reminiscing about that in the new guest quarters. By the way, he's not happy with the accommodations."

Koven stared at the Smith and Wesson .45 aimed at his chest. His eyes flicked to the table where he'd left his weapon. "If Sabel got that impression from anything I said—"

"Smart people know when to play dumb. You're so good at it, I forget when you're playing."

Koven twirled the shot glass without breaking eye contact. "OK, I'm sorry."

"You wrecked my firm, Koven."

"If you're going to pull that trigger, do it."

"If you're not man enough to kill yourself, don't think I'm going to do it for you." Hyde pulled the trigger.

The bullet tore through Koven's bicep. His vodka flew skyward.

"You shot me." Koven screamed. "What the fuck is wrong with you?"

Jago Seyton came in, carrying a heavy vest with Velcro straps.

"Get the man some bandages, Jago." Hyde watched him writhe in agony with dispassionate interest.

Koven slapped a hand over the bullet hole and rocked back and forth, gritting his teeth.

Hyde stood, stepped around the low table between them, and stared down at Koven. "Katy Hellman and I used to be an item back in the day. Did you know that?" Hyde waited, but Koven was preoccupied trying to breathe away his pain like a woman giving birth. "No reason you would, I guess."

Jago ran back into the room with a medical kit. He cut off Koven's shirt and cleaned the wound. Despite its large diameter, the bullet went straight through without hitting any major veins. He used butterfly sutures to close both ends, then applied antiseptic, followed by copious amounts of gauze bandages. Finally, he wound medical tape all the way around it.

Koven looked up. "I'll kill you."

"Good luck with that. You're a dead man already."

"Katy Hellman might've put up with you in your dreams, but she told me no one on Earth could touch me."

"And she was right. Pia Sabel and her people parachuted in." Hyde smiled. "She also promised you'd be safe until the *Oberstdrogen* rose from the dead. Here's a newsflash you didn't pay attention to: that machine gun you hear in the courtyard is manned by a former drug dealer known as 'the Colonel'. In the German army, a colonel is called an *oberst*, and *drogen* means drugs. He died of stab wounds in prison but the gods decided to spare him for one more mission. This one."

Koven kicked the coffee table. "You've been working with her all along?"

"We thought you might pull off this Future Crossroads symposium, so we let it play out. Her reporters started following you as soon as we found out what Gottleib was doing. They were there to build your story either way, hero or villain. But after the *Post* ran their story on you this morning, we decided to move on. Did you know Pia Sabel gave them a photocopy of the prince's contract with your signature on it?"

"She killed Taimur. No one will believe her."

"Oh no, my dear boy. Don't give that muscle-headed athlete credit for my hard work. I thought we had them both in Dubai, but she got in the way, so we had to shoot him down in Khasab. Shame, really. Waste of a perfectly good Gulfstream. It doesn't matter, the Three Blondes are posting reports that pin all those murders on you."

"My god, Hellman asked me who stood to gain. She was talking about you." After the realization came to him, Koven opened and closed his mouth but only managed simple grunts of confusion. After a few tries, he managed some real words. "Müller? Suliman? Why? Those were profitable business relationships."

"You make me feel so smart—by comparison." Hyde aimed his revolver at Koven's thigh. "Do you know how easy it was to get Shane Diabulus on board after you gave the Oman deal to Sabel? Not only are they competitors, but it seems Pia and Jacob made him look bad on a couple high-profile missions. Turns out he was dying to get rid of Jacob Stearne and took to his tasks with glee. I was surprised how quickly he dispatched your clients. And not just Suliman and Taimur, but all of them. Now all your social welfare cash accounts are mine. Katy was screwed out of her inheritance by her misogynistic father and I was screwed out of my retirement by you. So we took your $100 million as our retirement plan. Isn't that nice?"

"Don't shoot. Please. I'll do anything." Koven doubled over on the couch, trying to make himself smaller. "Just tell me what you want."

"I want my business back, working the way it was before you came along." Hyde fired into the couch and laughed when Koven jumped. "But it's too late for that. So, you'll suit up and take the fight to Sabel."

"Kasey and his guys are working on that now. Please, don't shoot."

"Kasey is just another boy with a rifle, but you are the war hero. Go out there and show the boys how it's done—the way you did it in Nasiriyah." Hyde fired another round next to his thigh. "May the best man win."

Hyde rose, crossed to the fireplace and watched the flames. He downed another shot. "My money's on the Sabel girl, though."

Jago stepped forward with the vest in his outstretched arms.

Koven looked back and forth at the two men, fear in his eyes. He rose and put his good arm through one side, then gingerly arranged the other. Jago pulled the Velcro tight and smoothed it flat.

"This is so much heavier than I remember." Koven tried to chuckle. He shifted his weight under the vest. "And so thick."

Jago handed him the Beretta.

Koven turned and aimed it at Hyde and pulled the trigger.

Nothing happened.

He pulled the slide back to find an empty chamber. Turning the pistol over, he discovered an empty slot for the magazine. He turned to Jago.

Seyton held two magazines, one in each hand. He turned to the door, tossed them out, then turned back to Koven and nodded at the hallway. "Fetch."

Koven faced Hyde. "Why are you doing this?"

"When you tried to take over the Fuchs News account, Katy called me. I began checking around. You were careful and left very little trail. But it's the money that tripped you up. As soon as I talked to the bankers, I found your off-books accounts. At that point, I could've saved the company. Then I discovered Gottleib finishing up his recordings. We killed him, but he'd already turned them over to Jacob Stearne. It was only a matter of time before Stearne and Sabel went public."

"Why didn't you just help me?"

"Ah, so young and stupid." Hyde laughed. "Everything you did? I've been doing it for years. And I'll keep doing it for many years to come. Hell, thousands of people are pouring enticements, foreign and domestic, into elections every day. Although I do it with a lot more discretion and a lot less greed."

Hyde poured himself another shot. "But don't worry, I'll keep funneling money until the voters stand up and do something about it."

Koven swiveled to the door and back. "You expect me to go out there and die?"

"Yes," Hyde said. "We would've been fine if we stuck with Velox. But you had to bring Sabel Security into this deal. Your wife was right—the Sabel girl's been prowling your perimeter, waiting for the right moment since the day you met her. Kidnapping her father certainly accelerated her timetable, didn't it? Marthe took the noble way out. But then, she always was the one with balls."

They stared at each other as the chill sank deeper into their bones.

"Although cutting her arm off was a bit dramatic." Hyde smiled a sick smile. "Ah, but you have to admire her dedication."

# CHAPTER 44

TANIA PRESSED AGAINST my shoulder, blasting a table in the hallway while I fired through an open door into a gift shop. Behind me, I sensed Ms. Sabel slide into the kitchen and join the fight. I faced two hostiles huddled behind a book rack, and a third who squatted behind the cash register. Next to me was a light switch. I flipped it on because incandescent lights won't mess up thermal visors, but they blind night vision. And the last time I dealt with the yoyos from Velox, they were wearing NVGs. Their boss is cheap.

The clowns stood up, blind and defeated, hands in the air.

I ordered them to come forward and waited until they were in a tight line right in front of me. I pulled my sidearm, filled with Sabel Darts for just such an occasion, and put down all three.

My mental countdown had a maximum of twenty-three Velox men still capable of shooting at us, minus those Carlos neutralized.

I moved through the room and found a back door to Tania's hall. She'd just put down the poor dog by ripping the table to shreds with lead. I could only hope she had a whole lot of spare magazines.

Tania covered the rear while I joined Dhanpal in the entry. Miguel and Ms. Sabel worked on some guys on a staircase.

Seven-Death, no stranger to all-out war, reached across her body and nudged Ms. Sabel's muzzle. She fired and a body tumbled down the stairs. Mercury leaned against an oak bookcase, staring at me, and shrugged.

I have to admit, sometimes gods come in handy.

Over the comm link, I heard Carlos check in. "They're getting past me." The SAW kept a gut-wrenching beat in the background. "Can't hold them much longer."

"Hang in there, we're coming," Ms. Sabel said.

I looked over Dhanpal's shoulder to the route we would have to take. At least four guns fired at us from that direction.

"Did you get your dad?" Carlos called as he fired his SAW.

"Not yet," she said.

Something in her eyes caught my attention, some kind of conflicted decision making. She was torn between saving a gangbanger and saving the man who adopted her as an orphan.

"You go get him first, *chica*," Carlos said.

"I'll go." I patted her shoulder. "He saved my ass in Tokyo, McLean, and the tunnel. I owe him big time."

Mercury leaned against the wall and shook his head. *He's a dead man, and you will be too if you try any hero shit.*

I said, *Aren't you always trying to get me to die in glory?*

Mercury said, *That's not where this will lead, bro.*

"Don't come down, *ése*. A bunch of them peeled off and went through the citadel." Carlos clicked off in the middle of an explosion.

I leaned over Dhanpal and aimed outside. He aimed right and I aimed left. A heat signature lurked beneath an overhang. I fired and nailed the guy.

Dhanpal backed up and I pushed through. He covered my run to the next safe spot behind a wall.

Mercury stepped in nose-to-nose with me, blocking my path. *Where do you think you're going? He's a goner, dude. Let it go.*

I said, *Are you saying the Moirai have already decided his fate? I'm going to help—*

Mercury said, *Moirai? Fuck. You throw Greeks at me? Greeks are nothing. Nobody listens to them anymore. Hermes is in Paris, designing women's fashions. Did you even read that book on Roman religion I gave you?*

I said, *Yeah, I read, you know, some. A little. I skimmed it.*

Mercury said, *You're talking about the Parcae. Nona spins the thread of your life, Decima measures it, and Morta cuts it. Don't worry about Carlos, dawg. His thread's been spun, measured, and cut. He knows how his life ends. Remember that little dream of his? He's living it now. Pia-*

*Caesar-Sabel knows it too. Now get back in there, she needs you.*

Staring at death from any angle was never easy. I had a great deal of unwanted expertise on the topic. Once someone fought alongside you, it was hard to let him go, even if he was a murderous gangbanger who claimed he deserved the death penalty. Through the ether or the Force or whatever, I could feel him taking bullets to the chest and head, getting knocked around. Carlos was dying two hundred yards away and there was nothing I could do.

It didn't take long. His earbud was still transmitting a few seconds later when we heard him choke down his agony, breathing hard. Then we heard a lone execution shot followed by nothing.

Hate and anger filled my chest. I wanted to scream. I wanted to kill every murdering Velox man in the castle.

Bullets pinged the stones next to me. The flash came from my right.

I rolled left and fired as I landed on Mercury's feet. I fired from a prone position while Mercury stuck his foot under my barrel, raising it significantly. My next shot hit the Velox man in the neck.

Running back into the Eifel House, I passed Dhanpal and burst into the hall where Miguel and Ms. Sabel fired up the staircase. I charged up it like a madman and took out a man on the landing. At the top of the stairs three men ran at me. I turned and fled. They gave chase.

The three guys clomped down the stairs at a full run. They ran straight into the bullets Miguel and Ms. Sabel fired. A classic ambush.

We called out "clear" from our various positions and joined up near the stairway.

Dhanpal led us to the dungeon's door and opened it. Inside was stone, dark, and cold. I took the lead as we inched down the steps.

We maintained separation to prevent any enemy fire from taking us all out at once. I crept into the dark, switching my visor from thermal to night vision and back. There was nothing to see. The stone was too cold to register on thermals, there was no light for night vision to amplify, and there was nothing for the naked eye either.

I felt the wall with one hand and tested the way forward with my foot. We descended a curved stairway with a cold wall on one side and empty space on the other.

"Lights go on together," Ms. Sabel whispered in our earbuds. "On three."

She counted off and our five lights snapped on. A long shaft stretched below us with the steps built into the wall, curving downward into the dark. Leaning over a good stretch, I could make out the bottom. No soldiers between here and there.

I looked up.

There was only one way in or out of this hole. One grenade and we were cooked. Miguel followed my gaze and ran up, taking two steps at a time. He would keep us covered from above.

We made the landing and opened a thick ancient door. I found a light switch and turned it on. Inside was a store room filled with boxes.

At the far end was a cage.

Empty.

Dhanpal stepped around me and stared at the empty frame. "Damn. They've moved him."

Forty feet above us, bullets ricocheted in the round chamber. Miguel returned fire.

# CHAPTER 45

PIA CHARGED UP the stone spiral and knelt at the doorway opposite Miguel, observing the scene across her iron sights. She fired blindly into the hall while Miguel fired the other direction. Incoming bullets shrieked past her ear.

Miguel waved to her: hold up. She stopped and watched smoke sift through the bullet-riddled gathering room.

Lead splintered the door jamb next to her. She'd always been a fatalist, unconcerned about her life in this world, but the splinters she brushed off her cheek reminded her of the danger facing her agents.

She gave orders and her people readied for the counterattack.

Pia counted off and opened fire with Miguel, unloading half a magazine each, brushing back the Velox men. They paused while her people ran through the kill zone to the back hall, then unloaded the second half of their magazines. She swapped mags and switched to three-round bursts with more precision in her aim.

Jacob, Tania, and Dhanpal did the same from the rear.

The surviving Velox soldiers ran out a side door. Pia picked off one, Tania nailed another one.

They checked the building before working their way outside. The castle was quiet, the snow falling faster. They sprinted into positions to cover each other, advancing one at a time.

With the courtyard cleared, they had a tense moment to collect their thoughts.

From across the courtyard, Dhanpal and Jacob laid down covering fire.

Miguel ran under the bullets to find cover behind a planter. Tania followed a moment later.

Pia took her turn running through the crossfire.

Dhanpal noticed it first and brought it to Pia's attention: the sound of muffled boots in the courtyard beyond the gambling house. They stopped advancing when they reached the archway between courtyards. Tania tossed a flare ahead, blinding anyone wearing NVGs. Dhanpal and Miguel ran through while Jacob and Pia covered them. Tania ran through next.

The gunfire began, but something behind her caught Pia's attention.

She turned in time to see a man strangely dressed in a business suit with a heavy vest over it. He had no helmet and no NVGs, but he carried a Beretta pointed at the ground. He staggered toward them, unable to see Pia and Jacob in the dark.

Jacob kept his rifle trained on the man. Pia waved him off.

Tania reported over the comm link. "Cornered the last of the Velox guys behind a kiosk. Are you coming for the mop-up?"

The strange man walked like a zombie past them and through the arch, still blind to their huddled forms.

Pia texted the others to let the man pass. "It's Koven. He can join his men and surrender or die."

The snow fell. A tense, eerie quiet enveloped them as Koven plodded his way to the lower courtyard.

He called out in the darkness. "Kasey! Kasey, where are you?"

Hushed answers guided him to the stone planter where his men hid.

Pia rose and slinked to the archway, found a spot, and aimed.

When Koven reached the edge of the planter, one soldier ran from the group in the opposite direction from Koven.

Pia began to squeeze her trigger, but before it reached the sear point, Koven's vest exploded.

A brilliant yellow-orange fireball rose into the sky, lobbing body parts across the cobblestones.

Pia and her agents approached the wreckage with caution. One man lay on the ground ten yards away. The rest were killed by the blast.

"What the hell?" Tania asked.

"The Velox suicide vest." Pia stared at the gore. "They're made to look like body armor."

"He was going to blow us up?"

From a few yards away, Miguel called out. "Guess who's the lone survivor?"

Jacob answered him. "My money's on Kasey Earl."

"How'd you know?"

A tentative voice called from inside the citadel. "Pia Sabel, thank god it's you. Is it safe to come out?"

Dhanpal and Jacob slid into positions to cover the door, then nodded to her.

"Identify yourselves and come out with your hands up."

Two figures stepped into the dark, hands in the air. "I'm Senator Hyde, and this is—"

"Jago Seyton," Jacob pressed his rifle in one man's back. "How've you been, Skippy?"

Miguel searched them and gave the cleared sign.

Pia pushed the men inside the nearest building. A large fireplace dominated a stone foyer big enough to park trucks in.

"Where's my father?" she asked.

"I don't know." Hyde held his hands out, palms up. "Daryl lost his mind. He kidnapped us and has been holding us against our will."

"You look pretty liquored up for a hostage," Tania said.

"He was civil about it." Firelight flickered on the side of his face.

"Tania, go check on Carlos." Pia turned to the others. "The rest of you men, clear the house and find Dad."

When the room emptied, Jago moved to her left, away from Hyde.

"Do you think I'm dumb enough to let you get behind me, Seyton?" Pia fired a round that creased his ear.

Both men blanched.

She spoke softly. "Stand still. I want to have a look at you."

She walked around them, checking out Hyde first. Then came around Jago's back. She said, "I'm betting it wasn't Hyde who burned down the Blackson home."

Jago's eyes followed her.

She had a five-inch height advantage over him and used it to intimidate him, but he showed no concern. As she came around his right side, she stretched her right arm out in front of him. His eyes followed her hand as she placed her middle finger on her thumb. She snapped her fingers.

At the same time, she twisted off her back foot and crashed her left elbow to his temple.

He never saw it coming.

Jago fell to the floor, stunned and concussed but not out. He rose to his hands and knees and shook his head.

She pulled her Glock and pushed it into Hyde's groin. "I'm twitchy as hell, Senator. Try not to spook me."

She squatted to Jago's level. She grabbed his chin and tried to catch his wandering gaze. "Can you hear me? Are you in there?"

His eyes found her and, after a moment, focused.

Pia stuffed the barrel of her assault rifle in his open mouth. "Men like you killed my parents right in front of me, Skippy. When I look at a man who burned an entire family alive, I wonder if I should turn you over to the police or find a more satisfying form of justice for you."

Jago looked up with pleading eyes.

She rose and faced Hyde, a weapon holding each man in place. "Did you know Kasey designed the suicide vests for Velox?"

"Is that so?" Hyde's swollen eyes lolled.

"He knew what Koven was wearing. That's why he ran away." Pia tilted her head. "Since he didn't get very far before Koven blew up, we can assume he didn't pull the trigger on that vest. Which leaves us with the question: who did?"

Hyde shrugged. "We're victims here, Pia. Koven held us prisoner. Just like your father."

"Sounds like you're not going to confess," Pia said. "Jacob knew early on that Shane was the guy who tried to pin Gottlieb's murder on him. What we couldn't figure out was how he got Detective Lovett involved. I missed my first clue when Kasey Earl told me they were building a global outfit. But when we found out LOCI was founded by a long-dead soldier, we knew Shane was fronting a worldwide crooked-cop network. Only Shane Diabulus would do something that low. But where would he get the start-up capital?"

"Katy Hellman of the Fuchs News empire," Hyde said as reflected flames danced on his soft skin, "is waiting for me down the hill. She'll vouch for me."

"Jacob noticed the lipstick she left on your collar when he first met you. It took me a few days to piece it together but that's how I knew it was you and not Koven."

She adjusted both barrels. Each man twitched and held his breath.

"Prince Taimur showed up in Dubai and said DHK told him where to find me." Pia held Hyde's gaze. "You were the only guy left in the DHK offices."

Hyde blubbered a couple false starts before finding some coherent words. "Why would I kill Taimur or any of our clients? It was Koven. He went mad."

"What will we do for love?" Pia watched the old man's eyes wander in search of a new way out. "Of all your heinous crimes, the Blackson murders sickened us the most."

Hyde cringed.

"Why burn the Blacksons alive?" she asked. "Why the innocent children?"

"It was Koven. He ordered Jago to do that one. I had nothing to do with it."

Jago growled.

"Squealing on your partner already?" Pia looked down at Jago. "Is that right, Skippy? Did you murder a mother and two children because Koven told you to?"

Jago stared daggers at Hyde.

"Did Koven know you stole his money?" Pia turned back to Hyde. "My people traced over a hundred million winging its way around the world."

"It's my money." Hyde watched the flames.

"Want the bad news, Senator?" Pia smiled. "I have a brilliant analyst from the NSA. She figured out your password and transferred the money to *Médecins Sans Frontières*—Doctors Without Borders—on behalf of Gottlieb, Zola, and Blackson."

Hyde's fire-flecked face turned red and began to swell with rage.

"You can't do that. The transactions will be reversed right—"

"Who's going to report it?" She reached in his coat pocket and pulled out the remote trigger for Koven's suicide vest. She held it between them.

"Carlos didn't make it." Tania walked in carrying two heavy vests. "He did damn fine job of holding our six. A dozen bodies are scattered around his."

Pia nodded and bit her lip. She took a deep breath through her nose.

Tania draped one vest around Jago, the other around Hyde and sealed them in with Velcro.

"Sorry, guys," Tania said. "We ran out of plasticuffs. All I could find are these suicide vests. From the look on your faces, I'm guessing you know how the remote triggers work. Nothing happens if I press down, but when I let go—boom. That was in case someone shot the terrorist before he worked up the nerve."

Tania put the detonator for Hyde in Jago's hand and Jago's in Hyde's. She pressed their thumbs down on the triggers. "Now you're his bitch. If he dies, you die a nanosecond later. You can't win, you can't break even, and you can't get out of the game."

"Pia, I was duped." Hyde's voice shook and his jowls trembled. "Surely you can see that."

"That's 'Ms. Sabel' to you." Pia kept her voice low and soft. "Someone gave Shane Diabulus enough money to start LOCI. If you know your etymology, the Latin for 'local' is *locus*, and the plural is *loci*. Your investment allowed him to expand into foreign countries with a 'buy local' marketing campaign. He started a service that competes with me in fifty international cities."

"So what?" Hyde's forehead poured sweat. "Take these vests off of us."

"We followed the money. Guess where it led?" Pia gave him a few seconds, but he didn't speak. "It led back to your girlfriend, Katy Hellman. The two of you engineered a way to get the Mercenary Restrictions Act through Congress so Shane could corner the market. Then Koven blew up your business by hiring us for the Oman deal. What I don't understand is why you blame Koven when your mistake was investing in Shane."

She lifted the pistol from his crotch and smiled.

"Even though he went to a fancy private school and an Ivy League college, he's never been as smart as he thinks. When a grown man changes his name to Diabulus—Latin for 'the devil'—then opens Velox—Latin for 'rapid'—and then starts up LOCI, he should expect people to connect the dots."

Jacob buzzed her comm link. "We found your dad, but we have a problem—there's a bomb."

Pia looked at the pair in deadly vests. "Hope your thumbs can take the strain."

She took off, taking the stairs two at a time.

At the top of the stairs, in a small room, under a bare bulb hanging from the ceiling, Pia's father sat on a wooden box. Jacob, Dhanpal, and Miguel stood around him.

Jacob was in the middle of speaking to Alan. "Don't take this the wrong way, but I'm going to stick my foot under your ass."

# CHAPTER 46

BROKEN SHARDS OF moonlight knifed through the clouds, illuminating the new snow and fresh bloodstains. From the arrow slit in the Witch Tower, Shane Diabulus considered his next move. He knew what he had to do and knew it would not be easy. He cursed and kicked the wall and lifted the plywood off the floor, reopening the unfinished ceiling below. He quietly retrieved the workman's ladder and dropped it down to the second floor where it knocked over a paint can with a crash.

Diabulus's heart stopped. He froze and listened.

A cold breeze rounded the towers with a soft moan. A mouse scurried somewhere on the lower floor. The paint dripped. Everything outside was still.

He calculated his danger. The Sabel agents had checked the tower and considered the construction equipment unmolested, so a noise coming from there would alert them. But the castle's grounds were huge and the walls thick, the sound might not travel far. If it did, he could only hope they were too preoccupied and too distant to notice.

After a few seconds, he moved again. He swung his legs over the edge and tested his weight. It held. He climbed down. He checked out the lower window on two sides: all clear. He slid down the scaffolding to the ground floor and slipped outside into the snow.

He found Kasey Earl unconscious where the Sabel agents left him, bound and propped against the wall.

He hefted the man over his shoulder and retreated to the squire's house. Once inside, he dropped Kasey in a chair and cut the plasticuffs from his ankles and wrists. Kasey's eyes lacked focus and his head wobbled.

He slapped the earless man. "What country are you in?"

Kasey smiled. "Toledo."

"Shit." Shane paced the small room. "I should've killed Jacob in Tokyo. Why did I listen to that old drunk?"

"You have anger management issues."

Shane stopped midstride. "Kasey, are you with me?"

"Sure, buddy." Kasey smiled.

"What city are you in?"

"Harrogate?"

Shane shook his head. "You've got to pull yourself together. You were in a blast zone, but you can clear your head."

Kasey nodded. "It wasn't cuz Tania whupped me upside the head when the others wasn't looking?"

"You remember that?" Shane ran to him and shook him by the arms. "How many men do you have left?"

"Hey, when did you get here?"

"After they landed. Where are your other men?"

"You didn't help much." Kasey looked ill. He swayed, then put his head between his knees and barfed.

Shane backpedaled fast. He turned to a window and surveyed the snowy courtyard. "You've lost them all, haven't you?"

Kasey spit and coughed up something and spit again.

Shane faced him. "Thirty-two men against six. You let one Mexican take out twelve men."

Kasey looked up, his eyes focused for the first time. "You seen that? You was here when they landed. Why didn't you take that guy out? He had a SAW."

"Where'd they take Hyde? Hellman sent me to get Hyde."

Kasey rose, stepped into Shane's personal space and stared. "You musta been behind him to know it was one guy. You shoulda taken him out."

Shane pushed Kasey back. "Officers have to stay out of the fray."

"Our major used to march with us. He even gone on patrol with me once." Kasey stepped up to Shane. "You're a coward. You let us die out there."

"You ruined my company, you son of a bitch." Shane pounded him with a right hook. "You've wrecked everything. Why am I surrounded by idiots?"

Shane stormed outside into the cold winter air before remembering he was outnumbered. Keeping to the shadows, he slinked across the courtyard to the gambling house and searched it. He checked the destroyed Eifel House and decided no one in there was alive. Next, he made his way across the citadel to the main tower.

He snuck in and saw Jago and Hyde wearing suicide vests. He backpedaled before they saw him.

Small, distant sounds came from the upper floors. Sabel and her squad.

Shane slipped back outside and returned to the squire's house.

Kasey was gone.

He opened his comm link. "Kasey, where are you? You have to help me get Hyde out of here."

No answer.

Noises came from the chapel. He ran down the steps across the corner of the courtyard and stood in front of a large open door.

Kasey pushed a Ducati Scrambler out of the dark.

"Where do you think you're going?" Shane asked.

Kasey glared at him. "Getting the hell outta here."

"I need that bike. I need to get Hyde to safety."

"Not my problem. I quit." Kasey hopped on the Scrambler and tried to kick-start it.

In his still-wobbly state, he lost his balance and fell over, leaving one leg pinned under the bike.

Shane pulled his SIG-Sauer and aimed at Kasey.

The young man stopped struggling. "You wouldn't bother taking out one Mexican with a SAW, but all a'sudden you grow the balls to shoot me in cold blood? Figures."

"You're going to help me get Hyde out of here."

"Why? Who cares about that old goat?" Kasey extricated his leg and stood up.

"Katy Hellman cares about him. She's paying for his extraction. And I care about him. He owns LOCI and most of Velox."

"Tough shit." Kasey raised the motorcycle and swung a leg over.

Shane lifted his SIG.

"How do you expect me to help you if you shoot me?" Kasey looked disgusted.

"If you think you'll be alive ten yards from here, think again."

"All right. Here, hold the bike, I'll get my rifle." Kasey dismounted and shoved the Ducati toward Shane.

Instinctively, Shane grabbed the four-hundred-pound bike with both hands as it knocked him off-balance. He looked up in time to see Kasey pull his pistol and shoot him in the eye.

Shane fell over, the Ducati on top, crushing him.

"I am *so* sick of you and your bullshit." Kasey's voice was strange and distant. "You people think you're smarter'n me. You cut my ears off and order me around like I was stupid or something. Well, I got news for all you morons: I ain't taking shit from nobody, no more."

Shane Diabulus felt Kasey's pistol press against his forehead, he heard the second shot, but he didn't feel the bullet enter his brain. He felt his heart beat once, twice—and that was it. He fell down a dark hole for a long time. Then he was dead.

# CHAPTER 47

I TOOK OFF one boot while everyone in the room stared at me. "They told him he's sitting on a trigger. If he moves, the bomb goes off. So—I'm going to stick my foot under him and see if I can locate it."

No one spoke.

Alan Sabel, whose billion-dollar butt was about to be prodded, won the prize for most stunned look.

"Why not use your hand?" Dhanpal asked. "Your fingers have more nerve endings so you could tell what's going on."

"Cause I'd rather lose a foot than a hand."

That statement sobered everyone up fast. Especially Ms. Sabel. When she joined the party, she had the same look on her face that everyone else had: *Oh sure, Jacob will get us out of this.*

Back in the war zones, I'd known more than one bombsquid who miscalculated something and—BANG. Lives and limbs can disappear in a split second. This was a game with no second chances.

In the corner, Seven-Death rested his elbow on Mercury's shoulder. They looked on with the usual fascination the immortals have when witnessing earthlings risking their lives. I wondered if they were betting on the outcome the way God and Satan bet on Job.

I said, Got any great ideas?

Mercury said, *Not my millennium, bro. Spears, arrows, shields, burning oil I understand, but this shit's over my head. Last's year's keynote speaker at the gods convention made a logical argument for letting y'all torch the nuclear stockpiles so we could deal with you on the back side.*

I said, *What god would say a thing like that?*

*Buddha.*

I checked out the box. I'd seen two pounds of C4 destroy a Humvee. The box we were dealing with could hold fifty.

It was the most awkward of social situations. No one wanted to be there. No one wanted to watch. Yet no one could look away.

It didn't escape my notice that none of them offered to take my place, either.

From as far away as I could stand and still reach, I took a deep breath and wiggled my toes under Alan Sabel's rear end. He leaned away. I couldn't blame him.

"Don't do that," I said. "Keep your weight even. Please."

"Yeah. Sorry." He stared at his daughter. "Pia, you should leave. Just in case."

Everyone in the room turned to her. It was a big decision: Should you watch your father die? Is being in the next room somehow better?

She stepped right in front of him, picked up his hand, and held it to her cheek. "If anything happens to you, it better finish us both."

I choked.

My foot found the switch.

Maybe.

A patch about three inches square felt spring-loaded. The box was made of old, thin plywood, which could flex a good deal. I wasn't sure if I was feeling a soft spot, or the detonator.

Ms. Sabel turned away. "Miguel, go get Kasey."

Dhanpal went with him, the two clunking down the stairs, glad for a distraction from the tension.

Sweat formed on Alan's brow. I felt a rivulet run down my cheek.

I took a deep breath. "So here's the procedural question: if I find it, how sensitive is it? If I press down too hard, will that set it off?"

Alan and Pia stared at each other.

Pia said, "Hold it steady. Neither up, nor down."

"Depending on how strong the spring is, I'm not sure my foot is at the right angle to hold it down."

"Let's wait for Kasey." Pia stroked her father's hand.

"You think he's going to tell us?" Alan asked.

"He might have some good ideas if he's in the blast zone."

A distant gunshot echoed outside. Our ears perked up.

"I'm on it." Tania was out the door and down five steps when she spoke.

I was alone in the room with Alan and Pia Sabel, and neither of them was going anywhere.

"While we wait," I said. "I think it's time you two talked about something."

For the first time since I'd met her, Pia Sabel's face turned white as cream cheese.

"What?" Alan asked with the clueless tone of voice reserved for fathers.

"Clear the air about things from long ago. You know, talk like you do in family therapy, only without the therapist."

Alan looked at Pia. She shrugged.

"For a while now, your daughter has been asking me to pry information out of you about her parents' murders. She thinks you know something you're not telling her."

"We've been over this with shrinks a hundred times." Alan's head sagged and shook back and forth.

"The trouble with that scenario is that therapists aren't professional killers. They don't understand the logistical problem."

He turned to me. "What does that mean?"

"The police investigation shows two guys broke into her house while she was cutting up veggies with her mom. One guy killed her dad and stole a hard drive. The other guy strangled her mom while she watched. She grabbed the vegetable knife and stabbed the guy several times. One of those stab wounds sliced his femoral artery and he bled out. That's when you, the neighbor, came in."

Ms. Sabel said, "That's how I remember it."

"Kids remember stories funny," I said. "Memories can feel real if the story is repeated often enough. That's why siblings argue about childhood events. They've heard the story about a sibling so many times they think it happened to them."

Alan said, "Well, that's what happened."

"See, that's where I come in." I took a moment to look at each of them. "I've stabbed a guy to death. It's not easy. The femoral artery is under a lot of muscle. She's strong, but she was four. I doubt even a strong, motivated four-year-old could reach the artery."

Alan's face grew red, his gaze swept back and forth between us. He fixed his angriest look on me.

See, this is why I never liked therapy. Emotions go haywire and I get the blame every time. Last time an ex-girlfriend dragged me in for therapy, I swore off it for life.

Mercury said, *You did promise to marry her, bro. And you promised her sister the same. That was wrong.*

I said, *How was I supposed to know they took me seriously?*

Mercury said, *Even Romans, who had a divorce rate slightly lower than you guys, took their vows seriously.*

I said, *What about the Roman orgies?*

Mercury and Seven-Death gave each other knowing, nostalgic looks and bumped fists.

Mercury said, *Yeah, those were good times, homie.*

I faced Alan. "Even I can tell you're holding something back. Just tell her what you're hiding. It feels good to get things off your chest. It lightens your soul."

Alan's rage exploded. "Who the hell do you think you are?"

I would never make it as a Buddhist or a real Christian. They react to adversity with calmness. When someone yells at me, my anger takes off and I shovel it right back.

My voice jumped up a hundred decibels. "I'm the guy who's risking his life to save yours."

"You think that gives you the right to 'lighten' my soul?"

"Yeah. I think she deserves a straight answer." I caught a glimpse of Ms. Sabel with an embarrassed look on her face.

"I made her a billionaire. I didn't do that out of guilt or hate or shame. I did it because she deserved it." He leaped to his feet and poked a finger in my chest. "You don't deserve shit. You hear me? You think you're important enough to go digging around in people's souls? You think you can handle that?"

"Yes I do." Our voices were ringing the stonework.

"Then why don't you ask her why she quit the National Team?" He was in my face, nose to nose. "She was at the height of her career. She was the best in the world. She set more records than anyone her age. And she walked out hours before a game. Never looked back. Did you ever ask her why?"

My mouth opened but no words came out.

Ms. Sabel's face was down, staring at the ground, her arms wrapped around her father, her head on his shoulder.

I looked at his feet.

Then I looked up at him.

I spoke softly. "Um, you're off the box."

He spun around as if I'd shouted "snake".

We turned in unison to the box where my outstretched foot held down a metal plate. The trigger was secured for now.

But my sock was dirty.

At times like this, when your foot is all that stands between life and death, you regret blowing off that last load of laundry before you left town. I prayed to the real God: *Please don't let me die with dirty socks.*

"You did it!" He grabbed me by the shoulders, ready to jump for joy.

"NO-No-no! Don't jiggle my foot."

"Oh, right." He turned and swept up Ms. Sabel. They shouted and bounced with happiness.

Sometimes family therapy ends with hugs. Even if nothing was resolved.

Miguel came bounding up the stairs with Kasey Earl draped over his shoulder. "Guess who Kasey just killed?"

Dhanpal came in behind him and told the story of finding Shane's body beneath Kasey's smoking gun. We shook his hand and patted him on the back.

Tania came in and reported Jago and Hyde missing, but we weren't too worried about how far they could get in explosive vests before a thumb would slip off the detonator.

Ms. Sabel swept Kasey's feet out from under him. She grabbed a handful of hair and pushed his nose to my foot. She said, "Kasey, Jacob is going to pull his foot off the trigger. You're going to hold it down with your nose. Understand?"

Kasey gasped something resembling an affirmative.

I pulled my foot out.

She let go of his head.

Kasey did his best to hold his nose on the trigger. "Hey guys. Whoa. Where you going? Wait a second here. Hey. You're not leaving are you? Hold on. Hey! Jacob! Tania. C'mon guys, this ain't funny…"

# CHAPTER 48

COOL, PREDAWN LIGHT spread across the tranquil landscape, glowing blue in the snow as Pia and her team began their search of the grounds. Before they reached the outer courtyard, Dhanpal reported several emergency vehicles trapped behind an overturned Velox van at the bottom of the hill. One of Kasey's ultimately unnecessary defenses.

Miguel called in a sighting of Seyton and Hyde trying to unlock the massive gates. From their various corners of the castle, the team headed there. Pia came around a corner and fell in step with Tania.

The pair wound their way across the body-strewn courtyard and past the gambling house.

"I've been thinking," Tania said. "Instead of waiting until you get too hard up for a boyfriend, we should do something proactive. Like set up a grotto back at Sabel Gardens and make the guys wear g-strings. Parade them around for some entertainment. You know what I'm saying?"

Pia gave her a sideways glance. "You did not just say that."

"Oh, yes I did. It's high time we turn the tables on the men in this world. The patriarchy has objectified us for centuries. I say we objectify their asses right back. You ever read about women in business back in the Fifties? Talk about harassment. They owe us for the Fifties alone."

"Fine. Write up a plan and submit it to HR."

"They're useless." Tania shoved her hands in her pockets. "They throw out all my ideas. Want me to take a class on sensitivity."

Pia slowed to a stop and surveyed the carnage outside the squire's house. "Is that Carlos?"

Jacob strolled up and stood with them. "He kept the apocalypse from coming up our backside."

"I'll get something to cover his body." Tania took off.

Pia faced Jacob and watched his clouds of breath in the cold. "Thanks for that intervention with Dad."

"Didn't get anywhere, but it's a start." He appraised her. "I don't suppose you're ready to tell me why you left the National Team."

"No." She looked back at Carlos.

"How about Carlos?" he asked. "He told me you two had a deal of some kind. Want to explain that one?"

She took a moment to toe the snow with her boot. "You know that voice you listen to? My voice told me Carlos was going to sacrifice his life to save mine. The next day he sent me a letter. He dreamed he would die in Germany and that somehow I was involved. We made a deal. He came to work here, and if his premonition came true, I promised to put his son through college."

"I don't know who he was in the rest of his life," Jacob said. "But he was a damn good man in the end."

They watched the sun claw to the horizon, piercing their world with cold yellow.

"What do you think of what my father *didn't* say?" Pia asked.

"To be honest, every time you asked me to dig into the story, I was annoyed. Who am I to get involved? He adopted you the day your parents were murdered—which damn few single grad students would've done—and you wanted me to dig into *his* story? That was awkward and uncomfortable to say the least. But after today, I understand where you're coming from. I'll keep working on him."

She put her arm around him and gave him a squeeze.

"One thing I should clear up for you," she said. "The day my parents were murdered was the first time I heard the voice in my head. She told me exactly where to stab the killer. Said she was a hunter and knew about those things. She kept saying, 'harder next time, to the right, again.' She's been driving me like that ever since."

Miguel's voice crackled over her earbud. "Seyton and Hyde made it through the main gates. Want me to shoot them?"

Pia stayed their execution and raced to join him.

A twenty-foot wooden gate stood open at a slight angle, leaving enough room for a person to walk between wood and wall. Pia was the first through the opening. She stopped just outside.

A hundred yards downhill, two men walked toward a news van parked on the side of the road.

Tania pulled up next to her and raised field glasses. She said, "It's Katy Hellman and the Three Blondes. Hyde's asking for help with the vests."

With a good deal of caution, Pia headed their way and hailed them from a distance.

"Those are very dangerous," she said. "I have a demolitions expert on my team."

A reporter and a cameraman cut her off halfway. The blonde stuck a microphone in Pia's face. "We're live from Germany where Sabel Security agents just slaughtered more than thirty competitors. Ms. Sabel, why did you kill all those men?"

"They kidnapped my dad." Pia pushed the woman aside and pointed to Seyton and Hyde. "Let my people disarm those bombs."

The reporter turned to follow her gesture. The cameraman looked over his shoulder-cam.

Down the hill, next to the two men in suicide vests, Katy Hellman fisted her hips and stuck out her jaw. "Stay away from us, you bloody bitch. You've ruined everything."

The reporter ran back to her boss. The cameraman turned to follow.

Pia grabbed his elbow. "Are you a contract worker or full-time with them?"

He frowned at her. "Contracted this morning."

She pulled him. "Quick, follow me."

She ran up the incline to the thick wooden gate. The cameraman hesitated, then followed her.

The blast threw him and his camera through the narrow opening. His lenses shattered on the cobblestones and skittered five yards from his outstretched fingers.

Miguel and Jacob helped him to his feet. His backside singed, he rose with his arms around her agents' shoulders.

He looked up at Pia and asked, "What was that?"

She peered past him at the burning wreckage. "Justice."

# CHAPTER 49

I STOOD AMONG the folding chairs and looked around at twenty or so people gathered in the church basement. "Uh, my name is Jacob and I'm *not* an alcoholic. Um. That might not be entirely true. Maybe I am ... but that's not why I came here."

The middle-aged guy in the two-thousand-dollar suit looked up from his phone. A pretty girl with flowers in her hair, way at the back, sat up and smiled at me with a big grin. The front-row group, the regulars who sit together, waited with the patience of Job.

"See, I have a problem. Oh, not a problem—that's not the right thing to call it. Um. I have a voice."

Mercury leaned against a pillar at the back, his toga soaking wet from another misguided ritual bath. He smiled and waved me on.

I would rather pick up a rifle and charge into an al-Qaeda training camp than be here.

But a deal is a deal.

"I wasn't sure who to turn to, but I figured you folks would hear me out and maybe not get pissed off." I fidgeted with my jacket's zipper until I felt all those eyes on me and realized I'd been silent for several seconds.

I looked up. "I talk to god."

Everyone nodded as if this is a normal state of affairs. The housewife in the too-tight-for-common-sense spandex, the guy with the yellow BestBuy nametag on a bright blue pullover, the older woman in the tennis outfit all give me a sympathetic look. Maybe it was one of the twelve steps or something, I didn't know.

After a second, the guy in the suit looked around. He looked skeptical. "Does He talk to you?"

"Oh, yeah. All the time. Too much. But, um, that's not the problem."

Everyone leaned forward. My response had been too quiet.

The woman in the tennis outfit rolled her hand. "If God talks to you, you're one of the lucky ones. What does He say?"

I raised my voice. "Mostly he tells me who to kill."

Wow.

Some sentences just don't sound the same outside your head.

They all leaned back—way back—as if I might explode. A certain amount of shock colored their expressions and fear widened their eyes.

"No, no." I waved my hands. "That's not what I mean. I…"

The big construction worker, halfway down the aisle, planted his feet, ready to jump up and rip my head off if I pulled a gun on them.

"I'm a veteran, y'know? Five tours in Afghanistan and three in Iraq. Anyway, he started talking to me in the wars. He watched over me, and made sure I had everything I needed. He pointed out the soft places where I could lie down. And helped me find water in the desert. He led me on all the right paths—"

The suit-guy raised a hand. "Are you going to paraphrase the whole 23$^{rd}$ Psalm?"

Damn, I knew it sounded familiar.

Several of the others glanced at each other with knowing nods. They were going to tell me to sit down and shut up.

"You've been chosen by God." The girl in back, with the flowers in her hair, stood up. She wasn't hard to look at. A nice, clingy gray dress showed off her curves better than Saran Wrap. She spread her bright red lips into a wide smile.

Everyone else in the room ignored her as if she wasn't there.

"Yeah, well, the God part of it is, um…" I had no idea what to say next. I wanted to run. The construction worker and the suit-guy were off the charts on the not-happy scale. The tennis lady soured. The regulars up front were the only ones still interested. "I have a different god."

"Jews are welcome here too." The voice came from behind me. "I'm Jewish."

"Oh. Thanks. But. No, I'm not—"

"Muslim, Hindu, anything that keeps you sober is fine with us."

The people muttered among themselves. Their voices grew louder. I was losing them.

"His name is Mercury. He's the winged messenger of the Roman gods." My voice echoed in the dead silence that followed. "He was the god of commerce and messages, and a member of the *Dii Concentes*, the twelve big-time deities. He calls it the 'Board of Directors for gods.' Heh. Well. He thinks it's funny. Anyway. His first temple was built in 495 BCE in the Circus Maximus. He was the most popular of the Roman gods. The English and French revered him too—after they were conquered but before the spread of Christianity. Oh, and his festival day is the ides of May."

No one moved. No one closed an open mouth.

Finally, the construction guy crossed his arms. "You need professional help."

Suit-guy nodded and jumped a thousand socio-economic barriers to mimic his working-class friend's crossed arms. "Yeah, you're fucking nuts."

"I think it's wonderful." The woman in back threw her hands in the air.

The guy who led the opening prayer stood up and motioned for me to sit down, which I did. Quickly.

He closed the session with a prayer, wisely leaving Mercury out of it. We began shuffling out.

The lady in the tennis outfit came up to me. She wore half a pound of diamonds around her neck and wrists. She reached in her purse, retrieved a card, and extended it in her fingers. "You should give this man a call. He's the best with problems like yours. He committed my husband when I couldn't get anyone else to do it."

I gave her a polite nod. She turned up her nose and strode out.

I looked at the card. Dr. Harrison.

Lovely.

I shoved it in my pocket.

The suit-guy came next. "If you need any help getting into a permanent institution, please, let me know. I'll do anything to keep you off the streets."

With a quiet thank-you, I pocketed his card and made my way to the last row where the curvy girl with flowers in her hair waited for me. She grabbed me and gave me a big hug.

I've had worse things pressed against my chest.

She pulled back, found her balance on the stiletto heels, and grabbed my shoulders. "Oooh. I just love a good prophet. I'm part of a fun group you'd like. It's a Bacchus group. You know what I mean?"

I dragged my eyes off the floor, up her thigh, around her hips twice, over her boobs, and all the way up to her face. She appreciated the way I appreciated her with a giggle. She was a platinum blond with green eyes and the flowers were fresh.

I couldn't think, much less speak. "Uh, group?"

"Olivia, Aletta, Terry, Nannette, Sandrine, Tony, oh, they'll just love you to death." She gave me an inch of space. "Tony's a fun old goat, you'd like him."

Her eyes drilled mine for clues to my reaction.

Mercury stood behind her beaming a Cheshire-cat smile. *Dawg, you are in! High five me bro! You've hit the jackpot here. Whoo-ee!*

I said, *I don't get it. What's a Bacchus group?*

Mercury's expression changed as if I'd just shot Vesta. *Bacchus was the god of—?*

I said, *Wine?*

Mercury rolled his eyes. *Yes, and since you're in an AA meeting, that's probably not the part of the Bacchus ministry she's focused on. So, he was also into—?*

I said, *Music and blissful dance?*

Mercury said, *Yeah. OK bro, and liberated spirits and nymphs and satyrs. Now for the extra-credit question: blissful dance is a euphemism for—?"*

I said, *Orgies?*

Mercury said, *Thank Jupiter, you're not as dumb as you look. We are in, bay-bay! I told you proselytizing would pay off, didn't I? See what happens when you listen to your favorite god?*

She saw the light bulb go off over my head. She bumped her forehead against mine. "Let's go back to my place and call a meeting of the Bacchus group. You can channel your god—and make us do whatever you want."

My mind spun in circles. A hundred questions poured into my head.

Were her friends as gorgeous as she? Did I care? Should I ruin the moment by asking her name? How fast could we get to her place? Would I have time to stop for protection?

"Great job, Jacob." Ms. Sabel's voice splashed in my ear like a bucket of ice water.

I turned slightly to face the sound of her voice, my vision still cloudy. "You came?"

"Hope you don't mind." She glanced in the direction of curvy-girl, then back. "You were quite brave. Maybe not as prepared as you could've been, but you were brave. I've never told anyone about my, um, voice. Not completely."

She waited for me to say something.

The only thing on my mind was getting to my first Bacchus group meeting. There's no such thing as fashionably late where orgies are concerned. Not that I had any expertise in that area.

"We all make choices in life," Ms. Sabel said. "We can choose to allow our delusions to cloud our vision or we can take a hard look at reality. You chose to get real about your, ehm, condition. I'm here to support your decision."

I looked at my blonde. She was already swiveling her hips around the wrong way, turning her back to me.

Mercury slipped his arm around her waist. They leaned into each other and they walked away.

Ms. Sabel put her hand into the crook of my elbow and tugged. "There's a woman who showed up at the Gardens just before I left. I forgot her name. She's a detective. Said she met you in Tokyo."

"Really?"

"Yes, really. Do you think I make things up?"

I felt my feet walking with Ms. Sabel while my heart and several other organs tried to follow the blonde. "Oh, she must have questions about the Zola case."

Ms. Sabel laughed. "Trust me, Jacob, when a beautiful woman flies all the way from Tokyo, it isn't to talk about the Zola case."

**The End**

# TO YOU FROM SEELEY JAMES

I hope you enjoyed the story and will join my VIP Readers by signing up at SeeleyJames.com/VIP. I hold a drawing every month for things like gift certificates or naming characters in upcoming books. I also give VIPs the inside scoop on things like how certain characters were named; which Shakespeare soliloquies I ~~plagiarized~~ drew from; what I'm working on next, etc.

Please remember to leave a review! Indie authors live and die by reviews. If you didn't enjoy it, that's OK, sometimes the magic works and sometimes it doesn't.

If you want to chat, please email me at seeley@seeleyjames.com or join me on Facebook: SeeleyJamesAuth. I love hearing from readers.

# EXCERPTS FROM SABEL SECURITY SERIES:

### ELEMENT 42, SABEL SECURITY #1

The voice in my head returned when I stopped taking my meds. My caseworker said the voice was part of my condition—PTSD-induced schizophrenia—but I call him Mercury, the winged messenger of the gods, and a damn good friend. For years, he was my biggest ally in combat and helped me predict the future. I'm not talking about very far into the future. Sometimes minutes, sometimes seconds, and sometimes just enough to see it coming.

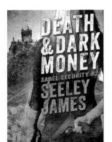

## DEATH AND DARK MONEY, SABEL SECURITY #2

Sixteen minutes before David Gottleib died, I was alarmed that a nearly-naked black man leaned against my refrigerator with a casual grin. It wasn't because he was tall with supernaturally chiseled muscles. Nor was it the lone fig leaf he sported over his substantial manhood. It wasn't the leather sandals or the bronze helmet with small bronze wings either. What alarmed me was that I could see him at all.

No one can see a god.

At least, no one with a shred of sanity left.

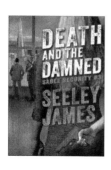

### DEATH AND THE DAMNED, SABEL SECURITY #3

Who to trust is the scariest decision we make in life. I grabbed him by the hair, pulled his head back, and, cheek-to-cheek, we contemplated the sparkling stars dotting the moonless Syrian sky. I sensed his eyeballs strain all the way to the right to look at me. His fingernails dug into my forearm. Anxiety caused him to miss the grandeur of the moment. Too bad. It was stunningly beautiful. You don't see that many stars from over-lit American cities. But I tired of our two-second relationship and drew my blade across his throat, severing his carotid artery and larynx before he could scream a warning to the others. I dropped his carcass on the other jihadi at my feet. He trusted me because I speak Arabic. Bad idea.

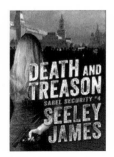

### DEATH AND TREASON, SABEL SECURITY #4

The president, a billionaire, and a disgraced FBI agent were talking about disrupting democracy with the casual air you and I might use to pick a movie. It made my blood boil. Back when I was an overconfident, pimply-faced teenager, I joined the Rangers and swore to protect the Constitution from all enemies, foreign and domestic. That commitment still anchors my soul. My outrage nearly caused me to miss the conspirators' after-thought scheme to kill my boss, Pia Sabel.

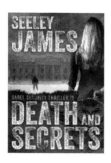

## DEATH AND SECRETS, SABEL SECURITY #5

A voice in a dream said, "Do you remember who shot you?"

Someone tugged me through a murky world. When the gray globs in my vision thinned, I recognized my sister. She kneaded my right hand and said something underwater. I blinked. Tubes hung down around me, metal rails on either side. A rack of machines with flashing lights towered over my shoulder. On my left stood a man in a white lab coat with the educated gaze of a doctor.

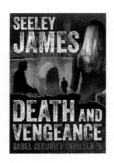

## DEATH AND VENGEANCE, SABEL SECURITY #6

Annie Wilkes had been expecting to spend the rest of the day in emergency calls about the bombing. That changed when she stepped out of the ladies' room. A pistol peeked from under an overcoat draped over a stranger's arm. She scanned the Mumbai Hilton's lobby for her security detail. Five yards away, her lieutenant lay face down on the floor. Farther away, her chief of staff struggled against restraints and a gag, his arms held in check by two men in business suits.

# About the Author

His near-death experiences range from talking a jealous husband into putting the gun down to spinning out on an icy freeway in heavy traffic without touching anything. His resume ranges from washing dishes to global technology management. His personal life stretches from homeless at 17, adopting a 3-year-old at 19, getting married at 37, fathering his last child at 43, hiking the Grand Canyon Rim-to-Rim several times a year, and taking the occasional nap.

His writing career ranges from humble beginnings with short stories in The Battered Suitcase, to being awarded a Medallion from the Book Readers Appreciation Group. Seeley is best known for his Sabel Security series of thrillers featuring athlete and heiress Pia Sabel and her bodyguard, unhinged veteran Jacob Stearne. One of them kicks ass and the other talks to the wrong god.

His love of creativity began at an early age, growing up at Frank Lloyd Wright's School of Architecture in Arizona and Wisconsin. He carried his imagination first into a successful career in sales and marketing, and then to his real love: fiction.

For more books featuring Pia Sabel and Jacob Stearne, visit SeeleyJames.com

Contact Seeley James:

mailto:Seeley@seeleyjames.com
Website: SeeleyJames.com
Facebook: SeeleyJamesAuth
BookBub: Seeley James